*Daphne Wright*

Daphne Wright is a historical novelist with a special interest in the way wars have liberated women. Born in London, she worked in publishing for ten years before becoming a writer. After six historical novels, she turned to crime under the pseudonym of Natasha Cooper. She now divides her time between the city and the Somerset Levels.

*Daphne Wright*

# NEVER SUCH
# INNOCENCE

B E L L

First published in 1991 by Little, Brown and Co.

This edition published 2012 by Bello
an imprint of Pan Macmillan, a division of Macmillan Publishers Limited
Pan Macmillan, 20 New Wharf Road, London N1 9RR
Basingstoke and Oxford
Associated companies throughout the world

www.panmacmillan.com/imprints/bello

ISBN 978-1-4472-3910-9 EPUB
ISBN 978-1-4472-3909-3 POD

A CIP catalogue record for this book is available from the British Library.

Printed and bound by CPI Group (UK) Ltd, Croydon, CR0 4YY

*For Mary Carter*

# Author's Note

Apart from the facts of the Kesselring case (which are clearly set out in *The Kesselring Case* by A. P. Scotland, Bonn, 1952, *The London Cage* by A. P. Scotland, London, 1957, and in contemporary newspaper reports), everything that happens in this novel is a product of the author's imagination, as are all the characters, who bear no relation to any real people, living or dead.

# Chapter One

'Isn't it wonderful?' yelled Mark over the heads of the crowd between them. In all the din, Julia could not hear what he said, but she could see his face and read his lips. Pushing her way towards him through the packed, sweating, embracing bodies of her fellow-Londoners, she shouted back:

'At least it's over. We did it. Thank God.'

Someone's Union Jack slapped her face in a sudden breeze and someone else trod heavily on her right foot as a new sound began to float across the great circle in front of the palace.

'What's that tune?' asked Mark more quietly as she reached him at last.

'I don't know,' said Julia, listening to the sound of a jazz band thumping up from the Mall. 'It's familiar, though.'

'It's *High Society*, you poor, middle-aged miseries,' said Mark's son, Richard, leaning on his stick and laughing at them. He looked younger by years than he had since he had been repatriated from France the previous year. 'I've just been told the trumpeter's Humphrey Lyttelton.'

Not wanting to add to his picture of a 'middle-aged misery', neither Julia nor Mark asked any more questions. Another heavy foot mashed down on Julia's as an excited group of hatless girls and half-drunk men in uniform danced past and her patience gave out.

'Let's get on,' she said to the others. 'It's all very wonderful, but it's damned uncomfortable. Oh, good, here's George. I thought we'd lost you in all this. I'm heading off. Are you coming?'

'Rather. It's all a bit much, isn't it? I can't think what they're all hanging around here for. The royals aren't likely to appear again,' said George Wilson, gesturing to the red-draped balcony in the centre of the palace's smooth, grey-stone façade. 'I'll push a way, Julia, if you stick close behind. Mark and Richard can look after each other.'

George Wilson, tall, thin and asthmatic, headed off into the dense, shifting crowd and Julia followed, wishing that she could share the ecstasy she saw on the faces all around her. She felt detached from the crowd and rather unreal, as though an important part of herself had been mislaid somewhere early in the war and she had only just noticed the lack.

'Come on darling, give us a kiss.'

A large navvy pushed his red face towards her as she fought her way through towards Green Park. When she gave him her famous cold stare, he made a rude face and yelled after her:

'Nothing to be sour about any more, ducks. Haven't they told you? We won the war. Hitler's dead!'

'I know,' said Julia under her breath. 'And thank God for it.'

A space opened up in front of her and she saw a vast mass of flames crackling and spitting on the grass. Above them, through the new leaves that were shrivelling and turning brown in the heat, she could see searchlights sweeping and meeting across the darkening blue of the twilit sky. Fireworks exploded somewhere close by, splattering the sky with coloured fragments that looked like the hundreds-and-thousands she had sprinkled on her bread and butter as a child.

For a moment Julia forgot her troubles and her dislike of crowds and let herself share the triumph. A pair of golden fountains shot upwards, spread and began to fall, their sparks fading and dying. In the light of the fire she saw faces that looked happy as well as mindlessly excited; a young woman with a toddler in her arms watched the fireworks with an expression of such abandoned relief that Julia could feel it too. A major in uniform who was standing close behind the woman put a hand on her shoulder and she dropped her head slightly to stroke his hand with her cheek. They were happy; the war was truly over for them; they were beginning again.

The stick of a rocket plunged back to earth with the kind of whining whistle all Londoners had come to dread, and Julia tried to cling to the faith that had kept her going for so long.

'Think of the good things,' she apostrophised herself. 'Look for the good things.'

That was an exercise that she had practised increasingly often as the war dragged on and on, and it had helped her to keep up the appearance of stoic calm for which she was well known among her colleagues. There were plenty of good things to look at in the crowds around the leaping, dazzling fire and Julia gradually fought down the memories of the Blitz and the Vis, which the fire and the lights and the explosions had brought so vividly to mind.

She felt an arm across her shoulders and looked round expecting another Bacchanalian reveller. All she saw was Mark's familiar worn face, full of concern.

'All right, Julia?' he asked. 'You look pale.'

She nodded and then explained about the fire and the bangs and the searchlights, and the avid excitement on some of the faces in the crowd. There had always been some who had looked like that at any 'incident' in the Blitz, people who had loved the drama of watching bodies being carried up out of the rubble and apparently found it easy to ignore the agony.

*Think of the good things.*

'Don't they look happy?' she said to Mark, gesturing towards a couple embracing under a tree as completely abandoned to each other as though they were in their own bedroom.

'Perhaps, but I think it's a bit much, carrying on like that in public,' he said severely. Julia managed to laugh at his dry voice.

'Well at least they don't look as though they're trying to remember the bombs,' she said.

'I don't suppose any of us who were here will ever forget, do you?' said Mark, remembering the night the Temple was bombed. He and Julia had arrived for work the following morning to find half their chambers blown apart, their carefully hoarded library burned and the remains of confidential trial documents blowing in the street.

'Quicker than those poor devils in Cologne and Dresden, I expect,' answered Julia, thinking of the horrific newsreel films she had seen. Then she remembered those other newsreel films of what had been revealed when the Nazis' concentration camps were opened and she shuddered. She sometimes thought that the sick horror she had felt then would never leave her. Mark squeezed her shoulder and then removed his arm.

'Don't think about any of it,' he said firmly. 'Tonight it's over. Tonight it's reasonable to forget and to celebrate. The courts are closed. The bells have rung; the lights are up. Tonight we ought just to let rip like the rest of them. What did the old man say in Whitehall? Someone told me . . . Richard, wasn't it you?'

'Something about giving ourselves a short period of celebration. I can't remember exactly. Father, we're going to be late if we don't get a move on, and you know what Mother's like,' he said.

Mark looked at Julia in the dusk and gave her a small, unhappy smile that seemed to hold an apology for his wife and a plea for Julia to understand her, and perhaps a hint of nostalgia too. Then he turned back to his only-surviving son.

'Yes, I know. You go on ahead. George and Julia and I will follow on in our middle-aged way,' he said.

'Speak for yourself,' said Julia, falling into a teasing voice as though determined to join in the celebration. 'I don't admit to middle age, myself.'

Mark laughed and they walked up the hill towards Piccadilly in deliberate cheerfulness.

Sylvia Heathwood was indeed waiting for them in the restaurant Mark had chosen for their celebration. They found her tapping her foot in irritation as she sipped a cocktail. They had agreed not to dress, but Sylvia was wearing a beautifully draped silk frock in her favourite lavender colour with an immense diamond brooch on the left shoulder. As always, Julia was amazed by the other woman's immaculate clothes and hair, and by her apparently inexhaustible supply of silk stockings and cosmetics. It was as though for Sylvia the war with all its terrors and readjustments and shortages had never happened.

Julia herself eked out her own miserable supply of stockings and lipstick for as long as she could by going unpainted to court every day and wearing thick, ugly lisle stockings for all but the very best occasions. Her own dark-grey utility suit and well-washed pre-war blouse looked decidedly shabby beside Sylvia's elegance.

'How sweet you look, Julia dear,' said Sylvia, holding out a scented, creamed hand for Julia to shake. 'But Mark must be working you far too hard,' she went on. 'You look exhausted – and far too thin. And he really ought to give you time off to get your hair properly done. It's too bad of you, darling,' she said, turning to her husband and displaying her ownership of him with a minatory pat.

'It isn't Mark, Mrs Heathwood,' said Julia, wrily noticing Sylvia's need to place her as an unalluring, ill-dressed bluestocking, 'but my clerk who insists on giving me too many cases and works me far too hard. As for being too thin, thank God for it! At least the war's meant that there's been no need for banting. I always tended to put on weight in the old days.' She laughed, but Sylvia ignored her, turning her impeccably dressed silvery-blonde head towards her son and waiting to be kissed.

Richard obliged and then called a waitress over to order drinks for them all. In the confusion Mark whispered to Julia:

'Sorry about all that.'

'It couldn't matter less, Mark,' she said. 'She feels at a disadvantage – understandably – and is trying to turn the tables. It's not important.'

'A son is such a comfort, Julia,' Sylvia called across the little group as she noticed Julia and Mark talking quietly with their heads close together. Julia felt Mark flinch beside her.

'Richard's a dear,' she said with as much sincerity as tact. 'You're very lucky.' Richard grinned at her and raised his glass in a silent toast.

'Well, here's to peace,' said Mark suddenly, raising his own glass. They all echoed his toast and then George made one of his own:

'And to absent friends,' he said quietly, looking at Julia. She saw his expression and smiled shakily in gratitude for his remembering. To control her sudden childish urge to cry, she took a large gulp of her cocktail and almost choked as the spirit burned her throat. She hoped passionately that somewhere, anywhere, Anthony might benefit from the toast.

'Shall we go in?' said Sylvia, getting up to lead the way into the high, pink-and-gold dining room. Julia followed obediently. She was only twelve years younger than Sylvia Heathwood, but whenever they were together Sylvia behaved as though she were a great lady and Julia a cross between a poor relation and a skivvy. Having had plenty of practice in dealing with her mother's disdain for her appearance, Julia usually managed to ignore both the patronage and the sneers, and almost always allowed Sylvia her petty triumphs. The only things she had that Julia envied in the least were the presence of her husband, safe and well in London, and her son.

'Won't it be wonderful to have new clothes again?' Sylvia said as she was shaking out her napkin and laying it on her silken lap. 'And proper shoes and hats.'

'And hot baths,' said George Wilson, entering gamely into the spirit of her conversation. 'What about you, Julia? What things – material things – have you missed most?'

'Since 1939?' she said to give herself time to think of anything other than Anthony. 'Um, fresh butter, I think. Lots and lots of melting butter on crisp, hot crumpets for tea after a long, cold, winter's walk.' In fact, almost more than any food she longed for inexhaustible supplies of sanitary towels and lavatory paper, which had at various times during the past five years been almost impossible to buy in adequate quantities. She turned to Mark Heathwood. 'What about you, Mark?'

'Petrol – the freedom to get in a car and go anywhere that takes my fancy,' said Mark with a grin that transformed his thin, serious face into an almost boyish mask. Most of the time it looked much older than his forty-eight years.

'But darling,' protested his wife in her most irritating drawl, 'you never – ever – went anywhere of your own free will. Don't you remember, Richard? I always used to have to drag Daddy off to

Cassis in the summer or Scotland for the shooting. All he ever wanted to do was work and sweat out the summers in chambers even out of term time.' She directed a venomous look at Julia as she spoke, although before the war Julia had been far too junior a member of chambers to have had much influence on Mark Heathwood KC.

'Holidays!' she exclaimed to deflect Sylvia's attention. 'Just think: we'll be able to go abroad again. . . .'

'Yes, and swim in the sea without risking bumping up against a mine,' said Richard cheerfully. He had been horrified by the change in his mother when he had been invalided home the year before, but he had become accustomed to her new character by then and was quite used to jollying her along and ignoring her attempts to provoke arguments. 'No more barbed wire on the cliffs either – or mines on the beaches.'

'Back to innocence, perhaps,' said George more seriously. 'Ah, food. Thank you.'

He looked down at the plate a waitress had put in front of him and then raised his eyes again.

'What I look forward to most is proper meals again. None of this. "If you have bread with your soup, you can't have pudding" nonsense. Game and burgundy on a winter's evening after Julia's crumpets . . .'

'Caviare and vodka,' said Richard with a beatific expression on his face. Julia rather doubted whether he had eaten much caviare before the war, which had, after all, broken out when he was seventeen.

'Vulgar!' said his mother, lifting up her knife and fork.

Through all the lighthearted discussion that followed of what they planned to do in the new world of peace and plenty, Julia thought of her husband. Until she knew where he was she could not bring herself to make any plans at all, even the most trivial. It was only when the conversation turned to what each of them most dreaded about life after the war that she came to life again and joined in their frivolity.

'That all the things I've missed so far because of it, and longed for, will turn out to be dull after all,' was Richard's contribution, which raised a laugh from his elders.

George, who had been exempted from conscription because of his weak heart and his asthma, said seriously:

'That we'll mess things up. There's such a chance now to put right everything that was wrong before the war, let alone during it, but can we do it?'

'I doubt it,' said Mark. 'Not everything.'

'Here or internationally?' asked Julia, interested.

'Both, I suppose,' answered George, having drunk a spoonful of his depressing-looking soup, 'but I really meant here: employment, housing, education and so forth. But what about you, Mark? What do you most dread?'

'Much the same as you, I suppose,' he said, carefully not looking at his wife, 'finding that nothing has really changed despite the horror and the sacrifices. Julia?'

Knowing that what she most dreaded was not a suitable matter for conversation on such a night, she buried it again and smiled disarmingly at her two colleagues.

'All the men coming back from the war and competing for briefs. I can see it now: that wretchedly misogynist clerk of mine will give me nothing but contracts and arbitrations and written opinions; I'll never see the inside of a court again; my wig will fall to pieces through lack of use; and my sharply honed advocacy skills will be blunted by time and boredom; and I'll be forced into premature retirement and have to learn to cook.'

Everyone except Sylvia laughed at Julia's mock-tragic tone. Mark looked as though he was about to speak, but George started first.

'Even Bill Tomkins is too sensible to let his well-known views on girl barristers make him waste the talents of one of the best juniors of either sex,' he said.

Julia was touched and her face took on a gentleness it rarely wore in the company of any of her fellow-barristers.

'Thank you for that, George,' she said seriously.

Two weeks later Mark walked into her room in chambers and

asked her if she had a minute to spare. Laying aside the brief on which she was working and closing her copy of Archbold, Julia leaned back in her revolving chair and waited for what he had to say. When it came it surprised her.

'I've been asked to go to Nuremberg for the UN trials,' he said abruptly, 'and I'll need an assistant. Would you come if I asked you? We'd probably have to leave in July or August.'

'I can't, Mark,' she said, without even thinking about the pros and cons of his proposition.

'Why not?' he asked, his head on one side as he examined her face. 'Surely you're not one of these people who don't believe that the Nazi leaders must be tried?'

'Good Lord no!' she said, 'and I should think it would be a fascinating job . . . if rather horrible. It's good of you to think of taking me with you. I'm flattered.'

'But you won't come,' said Mark, ignoring her politeness and answering the tone of her voice. 'You're not really worried about your career at the bar when the men come back, are you? George was right on VE night: you of all people have no need to worry.'

Julia smiled at that and shook her head, although it was a real concern to her.

'Then what?' asked Mark.

'Mark, how could I leave London?' she said. 'Now at last there's a real possibility of getting news of Anthony. If I were to go away and he came back home, what would he feel? What would you feel if you were in his position?'

Mark sat straighter in his chair and grasped the lapels of his jacket as though they were the edges of his gown. His face settled into the familiar persuasive seriousness with which he always addressed juries on difficult points in a case. Julia looked out of the window at the plane trees in the middle of the square. Their leaves were heavy with dust. She did not want to hear what she knew he was about to say, but she could not stop him. All she could do was detach herself by looking away from him as he said it.

'Julia, you mustn't pin your hopes on his coming back. If there were any chance that he was still alive I'd urge you to stay; you know that. It's not for my own selfishness that I want you to come away – although it would make life there much … Never mind that now – but because I just don't want you to be living here on your own, waiting for news that's never going to come.'

At that piece of pessimistic common sense Julia's normally well-controlled temper snapped. She stopped looking patiently at the plane trees and faced him across her desk.

'There is no more reason to suppose him dead than there is to believe that he is alive,' she said as coldly as she had ever spoken to Mark. He winced and so she tried to moderate her voice as she went on: 'You should know that. It's our job to weigh up evidence. Anthony is missing. There is nothing to prove any more or less. He escaped from the camp when Italy surrendered to us in 1943. He's probably been in hiding somewhere, unable even to get to Switzerland ever since. You know what it's been like in Italy since they changed sides. … Remember that piece I showed you from *The Times* last year about the British, American and Australian ex-prisoners who have been running partisan groups in the mountains?'

'I don't know what it's been like in Italy and nor do you,' said Mark. 'Julia, God forbid that I should make you unhappier than you already must be: I just cannot bear the thought of your being strung out on unrealistic hope for years to come. You have to get on with your life. It's two years since Anthony escaped from that camp. Don't you think that if he had either been recaptured or successfully evaded capture for so long you would have heard by now?'

'Not necessarily,' answered Julia stubbornly. She got out of her chair and walked across the room to the long mahogany bookshelves that lined the wall opposite her desk. Squinting sideways at the dull gilt titles of the books, she went on:

'You and I have meant a lot to each other in the last couple of years, and I'll never forget what you've done for me or cease to thank you for it. I'll always care about you more than anyone except … but I can't let you take my last hopes away.' She looked away from the books and addressed the back of Mark's greying head. 'They're all I have now.'

'Oh my dear,' he said, sighing. He turned in his chair so that he could look at her and balanced himself with his hands on the chair back. Julia stood with her back against the bookshelves and watched his face. The misery in it dispelled some of her residual anger.

'Mark, you seem to think that I'm clinging to a forlorn hope. It isn't like that. Now that the war is over, there is a real chance of news. Until now there have been all sorts of reasons why I might not have heard anything. I'm not mad enough to spend the rest of my life waiting for him,' she said. 'Don't forget that it's been only two years – the law doesn't allow a presumption of death after so short a time. Why should I?'

Something about the way she lifted her chin as she made her declaration touched Mark Heathwood and he could not protest any more. He had admired Julia Gillingham ever since she had come to his chambers as a shy but determined pupil ten years earlier, and he had watched her coming to terms with the intensely masculine and competitive world she had entered and gradually beating back its prejudices against her.

Somewhere on her journey to her present security in that world Mark had fallen in love with her: not with her face, which was no more than pleasantly attractive with its good bones and warm brown eyes, nor with her charm, which she rarely exercised. At times he had asked himself almost despairingly what he could possibly see in her to arouse such depths of feeling in himself. In the end he had decided that it was her gallantry, the courage with which she met difficulty and tedium and the horrible moral choices that their job threw up from time to time.

But there was more to it than that. Despite Julia's determined avoidance of sentimentality, there was a tremendous fund of warmth in her, and it was on that he had drawn so heavily during the excruciating misery he had suffered when his elder son had been killed in Crete. Without Julia's unfailing if rarely expressed sympathy, he sometimes thought he would not have been able to go on. Sylvia had dealt with their tragedy by pretending that it had never happened and that she had never had another son but Richard.

There had been times in the months after the telegram when Mark had watched his wife endlessly prinking before her looking glass and wanted to throttle her. He could not even remember what it had been about her that made him believe himself in love with her twenty-five years earlier. His hands clenched on the back of his chair.

'Mark?' Julia's cool voice broke into his thoughts. His eyes focused and he relaxed his grip on the back of the chair, untwisted his back and stood up.

'Sorry,' he said abruptly. 'I was dreaming.'

Julia's pale face broke into a smile of such affectionate sympathy that he almost lost control of himself and told her again that he loved her, that if her husband could be proved to have died, he would divorce Sylvia and beg Julia to marry him. But they had fought that battle long ago and had agreed to ignore the temptation that each represented for the other.

'What were we talking about?' he said, feeling exhausted almost beyond bearing by the struggle to keep going, to forget his anguish for his dead son and his anxiety for Richard, crippled at twenty-one; to ignore his frustrated love for the sensible, rational, kind, intelligent woman in front of him, and his growing loathing for the beautiful, unintelligent one that he had married so long ago.

'You were trying to persuade me again that Anthony is dead,' Julia said drily. 'Please don't.'

He shook his head.

'No, it was Nuremberg. Are you really sure, Julia? It would do your career no harm at all. It's the most important trial I can imagine happening in my lifetime or yours . . .'

'I can't leave London,' she said again, walking back towards her laden desk. 'Not until I know what has happened and . . .' Her voice almost broke and she took a deep breath before ending the sentence: 'whether he is alive or dead.'

# Chapter Two

Two weeks later, Julia was in Bristol, defending a man who had been discovered to have two wives, one living in Bristol and one in Southampton. It had appeared at first sight to be a case of the utmost simplicity. The man had two wives, and he was therefore guilty of bigamy, either deliberate or accidental. Julia's intention was to prove that it had been accidental. Her client had told his solicitor that he believed the first Mrs Smith had died in one of the bombing raids on Southampton and neither the solicitor nor Julia had any evidence to prove that he was lying. But he had not waited the necessary seven years to have her death presumed and his apparent ignorance of that part of the law was no defence.

The house the Smiths had rented in Southampton had been bombed to smithereens, and when Mr Smith was able to go back there on leave from the aircraft factory where he worked as a skilled mechanic, he had not been able to find any trace of his wife. None of the neighbours had seen her since the bomb, but he alleged that none of them had told him that they had not seen her for months before it either.

The prosecution alleged that Smith knew perfectly well that his wife had been staying with her parents in a farmhouse well inland in the middle of Hampshire at the time of the raids on Southampton, and that he had not even bothered to write to his parents-in-law to ask if they had any news of her. What complicated the case was that both of Mrs Smith's parents had since died and could neither confirm nor deny the defendant's story that he had in fact written to them.

The prosecution's evidence took most of the first day to present, and Julia began her cross-examination of the first Mrs Smith in the late afternoon. She looked scared, which was not particularly surprising, but she looked malevolent, too, and that aroused Julia's suspicions. She had a reputation at the Bar for being able to find the weak links in any chain of evidence quicker than most, but her greatest skill was probably her talent for seeing past the improved character a witness presented in the box to the hidden reality with all its inadequacies and petty lies. She was known around the Temple as Boadicea, because she cut such a swathe through her opponent's witnesses.

'Now, Mrs Smith,' said Julia in a voice that betrayed no emotion other than a mild sympathy, 'please don't be alarmed. Could you tell the jury in your own words just how you and your husband communicated during the war?'

'He didn't do no communicating,' answered Mrs Smith with a satisfied glance at the prosecuting counsel.

Julia smiled kindly.

'And you, Mrs Smith? Where did you address your letters to him?' she asked.

'I didn't know where he was, Miss,' answered Mrs Smith, looking less satisfied. 'It's his fault. He knew where I was but he never did no communicating.'

'Do you mean, Mrs Smith, that from 1942 until January 1945 you never even tried to get in touch with your husband? How did you live? Did you not expect him to send you any of his pay?'

'Not him,' answered the woman, clutching her scuffed black handbag. 'He wasn't never a good provider. When he disappeared I thought Good riddance! That's what I thought.'

Julia cast a sideways glance at the prosecuting barrister and saw his thick black eyebrows twitch together in an unusually frank expression of irritation with his witness.

'And you never tried to write to him at the factory?'

'I didn't know he was at any factory,' she said. 'One day I came home to get his tea ready and all I found was this note saying he was leaving me. I've never had a word from him since.'

'And have you got the note?' asked Julia in a voice of the utmost reasonableness.

'I burnt it.'

'Now, Mrs Smith,' said Julia. 'Are you really asking the jury to believe this story? And to accept that you never asked for information at your husband's place of work? After all, they knew perfectly well that he had been sent to Bristol.'

When Mrs Smith had eventually been persuaded to admit that she had never tried to track down her husband, the judge leaned forward from his high, red-leather chair to adjourn the court for the day. Julia had a word with her instructing solicitor and their client, packed up her papers and retired to the hotel where her clerk had booked her a room. She shared a depressing dinner of thin soup and horse-meat stew with the solicitor and went early to bed to console herself with a new book she had bought at the railway station.

The next day she set about demolishing the prosecution's case. Gradually, with the skill she had developed over the years, Julia cast doubt on each piece of evidence they had tried to establish, showed the first Mrs Smith's actions to have been eccentric at least, and built up a picture of her client as a patriotic man genuinely believing his wife to be dead, who had buried his grief in hard work producing aircraft for the RAF and in the innocent affection of a young woman who worked for him at the factory.

With her own long wait for news of her husband at the back of her mind, Julia did not find it at all difficult to produce a moving plea on her client's behalf and towards the end of the second day the jury acceded to her plea for clemency and refused to convict him.

Later, when she had removed her wig and gown in the room that had been set aside for her when it was discovered that Mr Smith's barrister was to be a woman, Julia went to get herself a cup of tea before leaving for London again. On her way to the tea room she ran into the barrister who had been acting for the prosecution.

'Nice work, Mrs Gillingham,' he said with a wry smile. Julia had not appeared in a case with him before and hardly knew him; it was pleasant to be complimented when she had inflicted a galling defeat on him.

'Thank you, Mr Hands,' she said and asked him whether he was on his way to the tea room. He looked quickly down at his watch.

'No, I'm afraid I must run if I'm to catch the four-forty back to London. My wife worries if I'm late. Aren't you . . .?' Julia shook her head.

'It's too much of a rush,' she said. 'I'm going to take the later train. Goodbye.' They shook hands and parted.

Three minutes later, Julia was sitting in front of a cup of milkless tea in the almost empty canteen, envying her late adversary his desire to get home. Hers was almost the last place she wanted to be. She sipped the scalding, bitter tea and tried to remember her home as it had been when they had all been happy there.

It was a big house in one of the shabby Georgian squares that made up so much of Bloomsbury, and Julia had bought it with her husband and his sister in the autumn of 1936 soon after she had completed her pupillage.

She and Comfort had become such close friends at Oxford that they had decided to share rooms in London when they had finished their last exams, protecting each other from the pains and difficulties of emerging from the chrysalis of university life. They had shared their fears, their early failures and their slowly increasing successes, and when Julia and Anthony fell in love the three of them formed such a close alliance that after the wedding it would have seemed unthinkable to any of them that Comfort should be excluded.

They had spent months searching for a house close enough to the hospital where Anthony worked and big enough to contain a studio for Comfort as well as rooms for them all to live and entertain in and yet not so vast that they would need armies of servants to run it.

Eventually Comfort had found a house in Brunswick Square and shown it to the others with a tentativeness that was rare in her. Julia saw its possibilities at once and joined her sister-in-law in trying to persuade Anthony that he would like it as soon as the horrible decorations had been changed and the grime scoured from the windows and the paintwork. He had stood in the dusty drawing room and put one arm around each of them, she remembered, and told them that if they liked it so much, he would do his best to learn to appreciate it, too.

Julia had then watched in admiration as Comfort had transformed the house, ignoring both the conventional rules of interior decoration and the cold excesses of the modernists. When she had finished, it was light and elegant, but comfortable, too, with room for them all to live and work without getting in each other's way.

They had moved in soon after the New Year and been happy. Trouble was brewing in Europe and the possibility of war loomed, but it did not seem to affect any of them then. They had behaved as though they had time for everything they wanted to do and the means with which to do it. Comfort had painted better than ever, Julia had battled to persuade her clerk to give her briefs, and Anthony had pursued his dangerous, brilliant, experimental surgery at the children's hospital. Then the war had come, he had volunteered at once and been sent straight out to the Middle East.

Julia had kept her doubts about his action to herself, believing that she had no right to interfere in a decision of such importance, but Comfort had shown no reticence at all. There had been terrible scenes in which she had demanded that he think of his patients if not of her and Julia. There was no need for him to go to war, she had told him over and over again. The work he was doing in London was essential. He would be wasting himself, possibly throwing his life away for nothing. At thirty-five he was years older than the other volunteers or conscripts.

Julia had tried to keep them from hurting each other, but she had failed. They had parted in furious anger and it was clear that Comfort blamed her for it. Rationality had never been Comfort's strongest suit, and whenever she was unhappy she tended to look for someone to blame. Julia had always known that and accepted it as part of Comfort's character. It put a high price on their friendship, but it had been a price that Julia had been prepared to pay, because she cared for Comfort and because their friendship gave her so much that she had lacked throughout her lonely childhood.

Comfort was the first person Julia had ever met who had seen through her gaucheries and naïvety to the person that she really was, or might become. Comfort's encouragement and freely expressed affection had given Julia the confidence to believe in her own abilities and to aspire to far greater achievements than she had thought possible.

She would never be able to forget the debt that she owed to Comfort for that invaluable gift, whatever Comfort did. But Comfort had begun to change once Anthony had left England and she became progressively antagonistic as the months of the war dragged out into years. By the time the last of the maids had left, the two sisters-in-law no longer even ate together. They had drifted apart in the big house until they hardly ever saw each other. Comfort had a double gas ring in her studio and she cooked for herself up there; and she moved her clothes and possessions up into one of the spare bedrooms on the floor above Julia's. They communicated mainly by notes left beside the telephone in the hall. Only during the Blitz and the doodlebug attacks had they come at all close, huddling in the basement working or reading immensely long nineteenth-century novels until the all-clear rang out. At times they had managed to discuss the books they were reading and talk with as little constraint as they had in the heady weeks they had spent at Oxford, before Julia had even met Anthony, let alone fallen in love with him. But all too often they kept their thoughts to themselves.

At one time life in Brunswick Square had become so difficult that Julia had bought the lease of a much smaller house in Kensington so that she would have a refuge if she ever had to leave Bloomsbury. It was a mad thing to do when so much of London had been bombed and she would probably never be able to sell the house if she decided she did not need it, but its presence was a comfort and knowing that she owned it made it possible to carry on.

A shadow fell across the table in front of her. Julia looked up, so startled that she almost dropped her cup and splashed cooling tea over her hand.

'Hello, Michael,' she said as she recognised an old friend. She put the cup down in the slopped saucer and carefully dried her hand on her handkerchief. 'I didn't know you were here.'

'Or I you, Julia. I've been prosecuting a grimy black-market spiv for stealing petrol and nylons from the local Yanks, and I need to take the taste of it out of my mouth. Can I get you another cup of tea? That looks horrible.'

'It does, doesn't it?' she said, looking down at the grey-brown scum that lined the thick white pottery cup. 'Yes, I'd love another. Thank you.'

'What have you been doing?' he asked when he came back with two fresh cups of tea.

'A bigamist. Defending,' said Julia, putting out a hand for her cup.

'Get him off?'

Julia just nodded with a small, pleased smile. Whatever life was like in Bloomsbury, however desperate she felt about her missing husband, at least she had huge satisfaction in her work; and in her friends, she reminded herself, smiling across the table at Michael Hendrick. He had been called to the bar a year after she had, and unlike some of the older barristers had always taken her presence for granted. They had met often and he had occasionally asked her advice. Over the years they had become friends. Like George Wilson, he had not been fit to go to war, and there had been many times when Julia had blessed the ailments or weakness that had kept both of them at home.

They discussed their cases and crowed over their particular triumphs for a while, but eventually Julia's enthusiasm dwindled as she thought more and more about the big house that seemed full only of solitude and anger.

'Are you all right?' asked Michael, stirring the last dregs of his tea round and round. 'You look a bit down in the mouth.'

'As one of my grandmother's American friends used to say, "I feel so low I'd need a ladder to look into a snake's eye",' Julia confessed.

'Why? You should be rejoicing. The war's nearly over. We'll get ... Oh God, I'm sorry,' he said, remembering at last. 'Is there still no news?'

Julia shook her head.

'But it's not just that. In a way, I've learned to live with that. Provided I don't let myself think of all the awful things that might be happening to him, I can contain my feelings about it. After all, there's nothing I can do except wait to hear, and so I wait ...'

'Except, presumably to write to the Red Cross, the prisoner-of-war department at the War Office,' said Michael, 'and –'

'I've done all that,' said Julia. 'Long ago, and I badger them at intervals. No, what's been making me gloomy is the thought of Comfort.'

'A most inappropriately named female, I've always thought,' said Michael bravely. Julia's brown eyes narrowed and the first signs of the celebrated cold stare began to harden her pale face.

'Don't do it to me,' said Michael as he recognised the phenomenon. 'I'm not a hostile witness or a misogynist judge. I'm on your side.'

'So you are,' said Julia, deliberately letting her face relax. She put both elbows on the table and rubbed her forehead with both hands as though she could rub away the nagging headache that seemed to have settled over her left eyebrow. She looked up. 'Things have just been very difficult with Comfort recently, and yet ...'

'I know: she's your best friend,' said Michael, swallowing the last of his well-stirred tea. 'That's better. I can't decide which is worse: rationing or the black marketeers it spawns. And there's no sign of an end to it.'

'It's a bit more than just being friends,' said Julia, ignoring his attempt to cover his gaffe. Working as she did almost entirely with men, she had hardly any women friends except for Comfort. Until the war had destroyed their utterly satisfying affection, she had never needed any others.

'I know. I'm sorry. I should never have said it. I know how fond you are of her. But look, we'd better drink up or we'll miss the train. You are coming back tonight, I take it?'

'Yes, I suppose so.'

'Wake up, Julia,' said Michael, wondering what it was that was really the matter with her. He had never seen her so *distraite* or so vulnerable before. Throughout the war she had kept going apparently undaunted by the enormous amount of work they all had to do, the miserable food, the lack of heat or reliable transport, the endless news of the death of friends and the fears they all tried to ignore. 'Where's your bag? This it? Come on.'

She got up obediently and followed him out of the room as he carried the red bag containing her wig and gown and the clothes she had worn to travel down to Bristol.

They caught the train easily and sat opposite each other in chilly discomfort as it rattled its way across the south of England. Their carriage was full until Swindon, where all the other passengers except for one very old man got out. As the train pulled slowly out of the station, Julia noticed the well-lit sign and commented on how pleasant it was to be able to read the names of stations again.

'Yes,' said Michael judiciously, 'but I'll be happier when they manage to have restaurant cars again. Eating real food on trains is one of the things I miss the most.'

Julia laughed.

'After the dinner I had in the hotel last night,' she said, 'I'd say that eating real food at all is what I miss.' The old man in the corner coughed and Julia thought she heard him mutter some kind of agreement.

'Hasn't Comfort any relations who can send you delicacies from America?' asked Michael, ignoring the third passenger.

'There is her mother, and she has been sending us parcels whenever she could. It's ungrateful of me to have moaned, because they have always been splendid: tinned ham, chocolate, tinned butter –'

'I hope you had your fair share of it all,' Michael said, interrupting briskly.

Julia frowned.

'I know that you've never liked Comfort much, but that was

unjust,' she said severely. 'We have our difficulties, but she'd never hog something like that to herself.'

'Glad to hear it. What are you reading?'

Julia held out her book, *Time Must Have a Stop* by Aldous Huxley.

'Have you read it?' she asked. 'It came out in February, but I haven't had time until now.'

Michael shook his head.

'I've never got on with his books. I like something with fewer ideas and more grip. What's this one like?'

'Odd,' said Julia shortly. 'But interesting. It's less funny than the old ones, but . . . oh, I can't make my mind up about it yet. I'm only halfway through.'

'I'd better stop distracting you from it then,' said Michael cheerfully, pulling out his own book. Julia, squinting at the cover, saw that it was the new Margery Allingham and smiled. She had a weakness for detective stories herself.

They got into London just over an hour later and parted on the platform, knowing that they would run into each other pretty soon in one or other of the courts. Michael set off for his rooms on foot while Julia took the tube to Tottenham Court Road and walked the rest of the way back to Brunswick Square.

There were no lights in the house when she put her key in the front-door lock and she thought with a mixture of sadness and relief that Comfort must be out to dinner. As she walked into the hall, she sniffed and noticed that the house smelled musty and a little damp despite the warmth of the June day. The long cracks in the Wedgwood-blue walls seemed wider than they had the last time she had looked at them and the black-and-white floor dustier. She dumped her bag on the floor and pushed open the double doors into the drawing room that neither she nor Comfort had used since the earliest days of the war.

All the furniture was covered in the old, pre-war dustsheets and cobwebs were festooned along the cornice. Just as the evergreen swags that Comfort had tied with red ribbon and hung in the rooms each Christmas had celebrated hospitality and warmth and generosity, so these grey, sticky-looking garlands pointed up the emptiness and coldness of the house.

They had used the room chiefly when they were entertaining and its silver-grey walls had proved an ideal background to a room full of people. Now, empty, cold and dusty, it seemed horribly depressing. Julia thought of her small, dark-green study upstairs and retreated. Once there was news of Anthony she would be able to do something to make the grand downstairs rooms habitable once more. Until then, there seemed to be no point.

She collected her bag and carried it upstairs to unpack. That done, she changed out of her suit into an old but comfortable pair of flannel trousers and a jersey and went down to see whether there was anything edible in the larder. Neither she nor Comfort had much time to queue for food and so they depended on the basic rations and what Comfort's American mother could send across the Atlantic.

A crock of eggs sent by one of Comfort's admirers and carefully preserved in waterglass looked tempting, but Julia did not feel justified in raiding it. There was, however, plenty of bread and the end of one of the American tins of ham and so she made herself a thick, butterless sandwich and ate it at the kitchen table with a cup of ersatz coffee. Her depressing meal over, she felt restored enough to go and see whether Comfort had left any of her curt messages by the telephone.

They both used old envelopes on which to write their notes instead of squandering untouched sheets of paper and from the top of the basement stairs Julia could see a small stack of them beside the telephone. Half reluctantly she went to pick them up.

As usual Comfort had timed and dated them and Julia ran through them from the top. Her clerk had telephoned apparently, hoping that she would be back from Bristol in time to talk to him that afternoon; a man from whom Comfort bought her paints and canvasses had told her that he could lay his hands on some paint for the house and she wondered whether Julia was interested; the plumber Julia had been hoping to persuade to repair the leaking cistern in her bathroom had telephoned to say that there was no chance 'this side of Christmas'. Julia shrugged – she had not really expected anything else – and turned to the last note.

> The War Office telephoned to say that Anthony is alive and well in the Italian Alps. We should be hearing from him presently.

At first Julia could do nothing but stare down at Comfort's elegant black italic handwriting, reading and rereading the words in case they did not mean what she thought they meant.

She had waited for two years for the news, never allowing herself to fantasise about what she would feel when it came, and yet always believing that one day it would come. Now that it had, she was surprised that she felt no terrific euphoria. Instead she felt slightly sick and rather unsafe, a little as she felt in lifts that plunged downwards too fast. She sat down on the stool beside the telephone and waited for the odd sensations to pass.

While she was waiting, she looked again at the note and saw that the message had been written the previous afternoon at five-thirty. Furious anger displaced the sickness in her mind. That Comfort could have left her to read such news more than twenty-four hours after it had come seemed worse than anything else she had done. It would have been so easy for her to get a message to Bristol and she had not bothered. Julia suddenly felt as though the battle to remember the magical days of Comfort's affection was the hardest she had ever fought.

# Chapter Three

Anthony Gillingham was sitting at the table that served as both desk and dining table in the rooms he had taken in Venice, struggling to write a letter to his wife. The warm July evening was muggy and the canal that moved so sluggishly outside his windows stank of corruption. He was hot, desperately tired and unable to make his mind work properly.

What he had to tell Julia was simple, but he had to find a way of making her understand it, and that was not simple at all. If he could only remember her properly, he thought, it might be easier to find the words he needed. Put baldly, his message was: 'Dear Julia, I am not coming home. After six years of war, I am going to stay on in Italy, working in an orphanage. I do not know when the job will end or when I shall see you again.'

Unless she had ceased to care for him, that announcement would hurt her intolerably, and he had never wanted that. Somehow he had to find a way to explain to her what he did not fully understand himself: that the thought of returning to the life he had lived with her and his sister before the war made him feel as though he were suffocating. He was aware of some of the reasons for his reluctance to go back, but was not prepared to look below the obvious ones to the others that might be revealed beneath them.

The door opened and his housekeeper came into the room, carrying a tray with his meagre dinner on it.

'*Dottore*,' she said, scolding him as she so often did, 'you must not sit by an open window in this weather. It's so bad for you.'

'It won't do me any harm, Annunziata,' he said, looking up and trying to smile at her. She gave him a look from beneath her half-closed eyelids that told him just what she thought of his views on medicine and health and put the tray down on the table in front of him.

'How were the *poverini* today?' she asked, not having seen him since he came in from his long day's work at the orphanage.

'The same,' he said sadly. 'Hungry, damaged, afraid, full of infections, needing food and drugs and clothes and homes and hope – all the things that Europe won't see for months yet ... years perhaps.' He looked at her and saw that she was not even listening to him. He knew what she was going to say next and he braced himself to give her the horribly familiar answer.

'*Dottore*, is there any news?'

'No, Annunziata,' he said as kindly and patiently as possible, 'there is no news yet, but you mustn't give up hope. There are hundreds of thousands of people trying to get home, waiting in camps, trying to get news of their families. It will take time.'

'I understand. Thank you,' she said with great dignity and left him to eat his cooling pasta without appetite.

Before the war Annunziata had been the wife of a modestly successful Roman craftsman. They had had three children: one son who had escaped from Italy to England after getting into trouble with the Fascists even before the war broke out, and two daughters. One of the girls had married a German Catholic in the days when Italy and Germany were still allies and had gone back to Germany when he was posted away from the Italian front. At first she had written to her mother as often as she could, but there had been no letters for some time. The other daughter had run away to join the partisans in 1944 at the age of sixteen and had disappeared.

Annunziata's husband had died three months before the end of the war and she had had no news of her children since then. Anthony had come across her when he was in Rome at the end of the war and had persuaded her to become his housekeeper when he took the job in Venice. Since then he had been doing what little he could to find out what had happened to her children and nearly every day Annunziata asked him for news. It was the pain he could see in her black eyes that made him so wary of hurting his own wife.

Julia was in a happier position than Annunziata, for she had known by then for nearly a month that he had survived the war. He had written to her and she to him. He had tried to tell her a little of what had happened to him and had read her accounts of her own war with disquiet. They, and his sister's version of the same story, had aggravated the anxiety in his mind that they would never be able to understand what had happened to him and what he felt about the people who had sheltered him and the others with whom he had fought for two dangerous, uncomfortable years.

He sometimes wondered whether it would be easier if he could get back to London and tell Julia what he had decided face to face. But that was not possible. Roads and railways all over Europe had been bombed and mined and sabotaged. The only practical form of transport was by air, and it would be a long time before anyone could hop on an aeroplane for private reasons. Besides, talking directly to Julia might not have helped at all. He was afraid that despite their marriage they would be virtual strangers to each other again.

When he had left England, they had been married for four years. Now they had been apart for six. He had left her when she was a barrister not long out of pupillage struggling to make her mark in a demanding profession. Now, as he knew from Comfort's first letters, his wife was an established and successful common law junior. For six years they had lived lives that could hardly have been more different. How could he expect her to understand and not be hurt?

Opening his wallet he picked out the small, creased photograph of Julia that he had carried throughout the war. It was a picture he had always liked, because it showed her at her most relaxed. The two-by-one-inch rectangle of grey and black card could give no idea of the depth of her brown eyes or the rare warmth of her dear creamy skin, but it showed the alert carriage of her head, the strength of her square-jawed face and the generosity of her smile as she tossed her thick long hair back with one hand. It had been a hot summer's day when Comfort had taken the photograph, and Julia had been wearing a short-sleeved linen shirt with an open neck, which showed off the fine lines of her throat and shoulders.

Looking down at her photograph, Anthony found himself smiling involuntarily. They had been friends in those days. Whatever might have happened to the passion that had briefly flowered between them, that friendship might have survived even the war. He pushed aside the supper tray and picked up his pen again to write to the girl in the photograph; the girl whose common sense and straightforwardness he had always trusted, whose intelligence had never been tainted with arrogance; the girl he had learned to love.

My dearest Julia [he wrote carefully],

Your letter filled me with delight. After so long without news, it is wonderful to know that you and Comfort are well and safely through all the things about which we have only dimly heard here. It seems strange that the three of us, who once did everything together, should have lived such completely different lives for so long. I can hardly imagine yours and I don't see how you could possibly imagine mine.

I could write you pages and pages of descriptions of fighting in North Africa, of life in prison camp, of the exhilaration and utter terror of the escape ... of the misery of being on the run, the desperate cold and hunger we all lived with in the partisans, the thrilling moments of a successful raid, the bitter battles with disease and wounds that I had to treat without drugs or equipment, the amputations I had to carry out without anaesthetics, the terrible choices we all had to make all the time, and you would still not be able to imagine any of it. One day, perhaps, we'll be able to talk about it all together.

But that can't be for some time. You were right when you wrote in your letter that we oughtn't to be too optimistic about an early demobilisation, although I think this time they'll do better than after the last war. Whatever happens I won't be coming home just yet.

I have accepted a job running a hospital and orphanage here in Venice. Julia, try to understand if you can: there are 10,000 orphans of partisans in Venezia Giulia alone. They are malnourished and ill and many of them have terribly neglected wounds, too, from shells and bullets and mines. Life here has been completely disrupted first by the Fascists and then by the war. They haven't enough doctors. I have to stay.

Much as I want to come home to you and Comfort, I cannot leave this country until I've done my small bit to help it on its feet again. I am sure you would understand if you could only see the children . . .

He broke off then, wondering how to end the letter. He had already begged her to understand. To tell her that he knew she would be disappointed would be presumptuous: she might well be relieved to have more time to herself. To tell her that he was disappointed would be a lie: he had, after all, chosen to stay.

Will you tell Comfort? I'll write to her in a few days' time [he wrote]. 'I long to see you. Is London very battered? You say the house has had its windows blown out once or twice. If that's all, it sounds as though you were lucky.

Anthony.

Having read the letter through, he thought that it would just do, put it in an envelope and addressed it to Julia at her chambers. He knew that Comfort did not subscribe to conventional ideas about the privacy of other people's letters and it was possible that if she saw a letter addressed in his handwriting she would open it, irrespective of the name on the envelope. He wanted Julia to have the news of his delayed homecoming first. That seemed to be the least he could do for her.

The letter reached Julia two weeks later when she went back to her desk in chambers after losing a case. Her client had been convicted of grievous bodily harm and sentenced to three years' imprisonment. She had been feeling as depressed and inadequate as she always did when she had failed to prevent a client being sent down, but the sight of the letter lying in the middle of her blotter brought a smile to her wide mouth. She had recognised her husband's writing from the door.

Pulling off her wig with one hand as she ran to her desk, she seized the envelope and ripped it open. The delighted smile on her face stiffened as she read, and slowly died. When she reached the end of the letter she let her hands fall into her lap, still holding it, and swivelled in her chair to look out of the dusty window over the square. She closed her eyes and tried to deal with the unacceptable emotions that were bombinating in her mind.

When the buzzing in her head had stopped and every last trace of resentment had been scoured away, Julia stood up and went to hang up her gown. She then combed her hair, brushed a few stray hairs from the shoulders of her black suit, pulled the seams of her stockings straight and went to see whether Mark Heathwood was in his room.

He looked up from his papers when she walked in and the quick, intimate smile that flooded his face gave her a moment of intense pleasure, which dismayed her.

'Hello,' he said, gesturing to the chair on the opposite side of his desk. 'What can I do for you?'

Julia sat down, keeping her long back very straight.

'I just wondered,' she said, 'whether you have found anyone to go to Nuremberg yet?'

Mark took off his spectacles and rubbed his eyes with his right hand, ending up gripping the bridge of his nose between finger and thumb.

'Yes,' he said, taking away his hand and looking back at her. 'The appointment was approved last week. Have you changed your mind? Why?'

'Anthony,' she started to say with a faint smile and then found that she could not go on.

Mark got out of his chair and came to stand very close to her. He put one hand on her shoulder.

'Have you had bad news after all?' he asked quietly. 'I thought he was all right.'

'No, nothing like that,' said Julia, finding that she could speak calmly so long as she kept her mind detached from her rebellious feelings. 'But he has decided that he cannot desert the Italians. He has accepted a job running an orphanage in Venice and has no plans . . .' Her voice cracked again. She took a deep breath: 'And he has no plans to come back at all.'

'Oh my dear,' said Mark, still holding her shoulder.

'Yes,' she said, answering his tone rather than his few words. 'I find that it is absorbing all my energies to take it philosophically. Perhaps it's just as well that I can't come to Nuremberg with you.'

Mark removed his hand then and went to the corner cupboard where he kept a bottle of sherry for emergencies or very important clients. There was just enough left to give them each a small glassful and he poured it out.

'Here, Julia,' he said, handing her a glass. When she accepted it, he said: 'It probably is. I'm not sure that I could spend much time with you and go on ignoring it all as we've done these last two years.'

'I know,' she said. 'And yet it would be a waste of that whole battle if we succumbed now.'

'Shall you tell Anthony about any of it?'

'I don't know,' said Julia. 'It so much depends on what happens, why he has really decided to stay away. But I might. He'd understand, I think. You never really knew him, but he is kind and very . . . very sensible . . . not possessive at all. Did you ever tell Sylvia?'

Mark shook his head.

'I didn't have to. . . . By the time I realised what had happened to me I'd talked far too much about you at home for her to be under much illusion, and when I suddenly stopped doing that and no doubt exhibited all kinds of peculiar reactions to her she understood at once.'

'No wonder she dislikes me so much,' said Julia with a small regretful smile. 'I never wanted . . . One of the reasons . . . Oh, never mind that now.'

'And yet,' said Mark looking down at his sherry, 'it's not as though she has any feelings for me or wants . . .' He, too, broke off. They had never had to put everything into words, even at the time when she was trying to explain to him why she would not become his mistress.

'It's all such a waste,' said Julia with an unusual hopelessness in her voice. 'All the affection one's capable of giving: and the people one's allowed to give it to don't want it, and the ones who do aren't allowed it.'

'I'm sure Anthony does want it,' said Mark, trying with some difficulty to be fair to her husband. 'He probably realises that he's unlikely to be demobbed for ages and decided to do something useful while he's stuck in Italy.'

Julia smiled and the self-knowledge in her eyes reminded him that she was no sentimental adolescent demanding to be comforted, but a woman of independent mind who could take care of herself perfectly well.

'What will you do?' he asked.

'Carry on, I suppose, and "keep smiling through",' she quoted with a derisive note in her usually smooth voice. 'And first do as he asks and tell his sister. That won't be easy. If she blamed me for his going to war, she's not going to be able to forgive me for this. I suppose I'd better go and tackle it now.'

'Well, don't forget to vote, will you?' said Mark, as she pulled her long body out of the chair. She looked at him over her shoulder.

'Surely it's hardly necessary?' she said. 'Churchill could carry the whole party back into Parliament, let alone enough members to keep a majority.'

Mark considered for a moment and then, with his head slightly tilted to the left, he smiled his familiar smile.

'Don't you think after everything women went through to get the vote you ought to exercise the right?' he asked.

Julia laughed.

'You're right, of course, dear Mark. I'll go on my way home. So long.'

He was laughing when she left his room and she was grateful

for the small respite he had given her. She called in at her local polling station on the way back to Brunswick Square and cast her vote for the Conservative candidate. Folding the paper and sliding it into the splintered ballot box she said a silent word of thanks that she had been born in 1914 and not thirty years earlier. At least she had been spared the dilemma of whether to join the marches and the smashing of windows, and the hunger strikes in prison that had led to all the horrors of forcible feeding.

Walking back to Brunswick Square, she tried to plan the best way of telling Comfort that Anthony would not be coming home. It crossed her mind that simply leaving a note by the telephone would be fair retribution for Comfort's having left her to discover the news of his survival like that, but she dismissed the impulse as petty and unnecessarily cruel.

She let herself into the house and, without waiting to change or even take off her hat, she climbed up the increasingly steep stairs to the attic, where the maids had once slept. Comfort had transformed a series of warren-like rooms into one vast studio with skylights in the roof and windows at either end. She had filled it with some of the best and most comfortable furniture from the rest of the house. There were paintings on the walls, her own and other people's, and a fine Persian carpet lay under the model's couch. A handsome screen covered in blue-and-green tapestry hid the gas ring and sink at the opposite end of the huge room from the dais where her easel stood.

When Julia opened the door, she saw that the canvas on which Comfort was working had been covered with a dustsheet and had a moment's impulse to retreat. Only when Comfort was working satisfactorily could she be relied on to see difficulties in any but the most melodramatic light.

'Is that you, Julia?' Comfort's voice came from behind the screen and sounded a little warmer than usual.

'Yes,' she said, keeping up her courage. 'I've heard from Anthony.'

Comfort emerged from her screen with a cup in one hand and a drying-up cloth in the other. Her eyes were alight with happiness and her lips were curled upwards in pleasure. She had obviously been working on a drawing, for there were charcoal smudges on her fine-boned cheeks and between her eyebrows.

'Tea?' she said with an easier voice than Julia had heard for a long time.

The first thing anyone ever noticed about Comfort's face was that it was beautiful. It was only later, after they had taken in the brilliance of her slate-grey eyes, the exciting curve of her lips and the delicacy of her pink-and-white complexion that people wondered about her nose. Like her brother's it was both large and bony. On him it looked exactly right, austere and slightly noble; on Comfort it looked extraordinary, but it saved her face from being merely pretty, which she would have hated. Her hair was as fair as his, but it was rarely disciplined into the tidiness that was one of his most characteristic features. On that evening the tangled blonde mass hung in wild curls about Comfort's dusty face: not for her the patriotic dullness of the 'liberty cut' or the severity of the chignon Julia always wore.

Julia was tempted to ask Comfort how her work had gone, but she knew what a dangerous question that could be. If it had gone well, Comfort would probably tell her in any case; if it had not the effort of having to say so and perhaps produce an explanation or excuse could cause her acute distress. It had taken Julia some time to understand the mixture of bad temper and moroseness with which Comfort had greeted her well-meant questions, but she had done so, and in those first post-war days rarely said anything unprompted about the paintings.

'May I see the letter?' asked Comfort, draping the cloth over her arm and holding out a hand. Afraid that she might be hurt by Anthony's casual request at the end of it, Julia temporised.

'I was in such a state that I left it in chambers by mistake,' she said, summoning up all her skills of advocacy before she began the explanation Anthony had asked her to make.

'He's not coming,' said Comfort before Julia could start. She was distressed to see that Comfort's slaty eyes narrowed into glimmering slits and sharp lines appeared from the sides of her nose down to her lips.

'That's right,' said Julia carefully. She went to sit on the red velvet-covered *chaise longue* that served as the model's couch. 'Apparently he can't bring himself to desert the destitute children of people he fought with and so he's accepted a job running an orphanage in Venice. He doesn't know how long he'll be doing it.'

Comfort's face seemed to shrivel as Julia watched her, and her mouth looked pinched and old.

'Comfort,' she went on, making her voice as gentle as she could, 'he begged us to understand . . .'

'Why did he write to you?' asked her sister-in-law sharply. 'And why won't you show me the letter? What else did he write?'

'Very little,' said Julia sadly. 'Just that he could hardly imagine what it's been like for us and he's sure we can't understand what his life has been like. I do wish . . . I think perhaps I do understand why he wants to finish the job, but I wish we could see him – just for a while.'

'What do you mean "finish the job"?' snapped Comfort, turning back to her gas rings, where a kettle had begun to sing. 'It's over.'

'The war, perhaps,' agreed Julia, 'but you know what a frightful mess it's left all over the Continent. Perhaps he just feels it isn't fair to come back until he's helped to clear it up.'

'Don't be so bloody reasonable!' Comfort burst out, sounding more American than she usually did. 'Have you any idea how infuriating it is to have to listen to you every day making excuses for people, explaining the most elementary facts to me as though I was an infant?'

'I'm sorry,' Julia said, breathing with difficulty as she absorbed the loathing in her sister-in-law's voice.

'Doesn't anything ever hurt you, Julia? Don't you ever feel anything at all? Is it impossible for you to understand anything about what real people feel?' Comfort went on, watching Julia's calm face with angry eyes.

Taking the tip of her tongue between her front teeth, Julia fought for control. It would do no good to burst into tears or to scream at Comfort that she shared all her misery, humiliation and rejection at Anthony's refusal to return to them. Just once or twice during the bitterest war years, Julia had allowed herself to put some of her distress into words. It had not helped at all, but only exacerbated Comfort's fury and led them both deeper into the unhappy solitude that had taken the place of the exciting friendship they had once shared.

'I understand all right,' she said, letting her tongue free at last, 'but since there is nothing we can do to magic him back here, it just seems more sensible to do as he asks and try to understand why he wants to stay.'

Comfort turned away and made a pot of tea with such jerky movements that Julia was afraid she might spill boiling water over herself. The tea made, she poured some into two cups, added a little milk to both, and brought one to Julia. Standing in front of her, Comfort said coldly:

'I don't know what's happened to you but you've changed. Anthony would never recognise you even if he did come back. You're so hard.'

Julia put down her cup after the first burning sip. Even the thought of wasting the milk ration could not make her stay any longer to listen to Comfort.

'I'd better go,' she said. 'Thank you for the tea.'

At the door she looked back, a faint pleading expression on her face. Comfort did not see it for she was standing by the window, her shoulders drooping and her head propped against the cracked glass. Julia wanted to say, 'You were my dearest friend: what have I done to make you hate me so?' But she could not. It wouldn't do any good.

Going slowly downstairs again to the small, dark-green study that had become her refuge, Julia tried to persuade herself that if she went on patiently accepting everything Comfort threw at her and never hitting back, then one day things might come right between them again. Hating scenes and arguments as she did, it never occurred to her that Comfort might long for a melodramatic battle of words, after which they could forgive each other magniloquently and construct a new friendship on the smoking ruins of the old.

Not until Julia was sitting at her desk, staring at the photograph of her husband that had stood there in its silver frame since the beginning of the war, did she let herself think of the most hurtful of Comfort's gibes.

Anthony looked so confidently back at her, with his most characteristic half-quizzical smile, that she could not believe he would find her hard. But it was true that she had changed in the six years since she had seen him. How could she not have? Quite apart from the horrors of the war itself, she had had to learn to live without him, afraid all the time of what might be happening to him; she had had to learn to live with Comfort's hatred, with Mark Heathwood's difficult love and her own inevitable response to it.

Julia pulled a piece of carefully hoarded writing paper out of its shagreen box and sat, pen in hand, waiting until she was certain what she wanted to say to her husband. The old days of scribbling luxuriously and throwing away sheet after sheet of paper until the letter was right had long gone.

At last she began to write. The ink had dried on the nib of her pen and so she had to find the bottle and dip the pen in it again to make the ink flow properly.

Dearest Anthony,

Your letter has arrived and I wanted to write at once to say that although I don't completely understand I can easily see why, having fought for so long for the freedom of Europe, you do not want to leave the most defenceless of its people in the straits you describe.

It would be wonderful to see you. Both Comfort and I miss you terribly. Is there any chance of your getting some home leave soon? I don't suppose either of us could get permission to travel to Italy for a long time yet.

She was rather upset when I told her your news, but I'm sure she'll calm down when she's thought about it. The war has been the most awful strain for her. Apart from the things everyone has had to put up with, she's rarely had enough time to paint and was hardly ever able to buy new brushes or any turps at all. You of all people will remember how unhappy she gets when she can't work properly. And all the rules that had to be imposed on us all to keep disruption to a minimum have driven her into a frenzy of frustration. . . .

I often think of the evening when we'd come out to Cumnor to dine with you for the first time and she wanted us to stay the night; when I said something about having to be back in college, she said superbly, 'Rules do not apply to me.' Well, they've had to these last five years, and she has hated it. Dragged away from the studio to work in photographic reconnaissance and knowing that I was allowed to go on doing my own work, she must have felt horribly frustrated. But the good news is that she is painting again, and soon that will wreak its usual smoothing for her and she'll be all right again.

Perhaps one day we'll be able to come to Venice to see you, and she can paint there. It would be wonderful. I miss you so much. Will you write and tell me about the children and your work? Even if I wouldn't be able to imagine the way you've had to live with the partisans, I'm sure I could picture your life now and I'd like to be able to do it. All I can think of at the moment are the paintings I've seen of St Mark's and gondolas on the Grand Canal – your orphanage can't be much like that. Do write when you've time.

London is very sad-looking now. All the craters have been filled in and the half-smashed buildings cleared, but the gaps are horrible and nothing will be repaired for years. Comfort seems to be able to find a weird, haunting beauty in some of the ruins she draws. At least you're spared seeing familiar, beloved bits of the city broken open and burned and scarred and left to rot. Perhaps by the time you're able to come back they'll have got on with the reconstruction. They've already started building little settlements of flat, boxy houses made from kits prefabricated in America. They look horrid, but whole villages of them can be put up within weeks.

With very much love, Julia.

# Chapter Four

On the evening of Monday 6 August Julia left chambers with Mark Heathwood and walked to a tiny restaurant they had always liked near the Aldwych. The proprietor coped with the apparently endless food shortages with imagination and created an atmosphere in his little dining room that was cosier than almost anywhere else. Even in the worst days of the fuel crises, he had managed to make it seem warm, and the food was better than in many grander places.

There was a red candle on each table when they arrived and the champagne Mark had ordered was waiting for them in its silver ice bucket. He was due to fly to Nuremberg two days later and, wanting to say goodbye to Julia in peace, had arranged the dinner a few days earlier. They dined off rabbit, but it had been carefully stuffed with prunes and bacon and gently cooked in a finely balanced sauce and was quite different from the humble, dry dish that was all Julia could produce from the same animal.

'I wish I could cook properly,' she said as she ate the last tender mouthful. 'Perhaps when it's all over and there's more time I ought to learn. I don't suppose we'll ever have a proper staff again.'

'With combined taxes at nineteen-and-sixpence in the pound, I don't suppose any of us will be able to afford servants,' said Mark bitterly. 'I'd assumed that it would be reduced in the next budget and gradually whittled down to a reasonable level once the war debts were paid –'

'If they ever are,' said Julia, interrupting him without conscience. He acknowledged her point with a tight smile.

'But now that Labour is in the saddle, income tax can only go up.'

They had already talked about the extraordinary way the British electorate had repaid their vast debt to Winston Churchill by voting the Labour Party into office. Even in his own constituency, where the Labour Party had declined to offer a rival candidate, an independent had polled over a third of the votes.

'I still can't understand it,' Julia said as she watched the elderly waiter removing their rabbit plates and bringing their sad pudding of bletted medlars and artificial cream to the table. 'The Labour Party! Wouldn't you have thought that they'd have let him finish the job? Surely until Japan surrenders . . .'

'It can't be long now,' said Mark, watching her with eyes that seemed to say all the things that he would not allow himself to put into words. 'He's been a supreme war leader, but perhaps they're right to think that he wouldn't be so good at organising the peace. Presumably they can't forget what happened after the last war. You're too young to remember it,' he added, smiling, 'but there was really appalling disillusion when Lloyd George's promises were ignored then and all they got for their sacrifices were depression and the dole.'

'Perhaps,' agreed Julia, plunging her spoon into the gently rotting medlar. 'These things do taste odd, don't they? But Beveridge will have to be paid for. . . . I suppose I am more bothered about what will happen to us all under Labour than about the old man's feelings . . . sorry though I feel for him at this moment.'

Mark finished his medlars and then drank the last of his wine, as though to take the taste away, before putting his glass down on the table and saying:

'Julia, there is something I want to ask you.' His tone, and the slight hesitation with which he spoke, told her that he thought he was about to annoy her. 'It isn't really any of my business, but . . .'

'You know that you can ask anything,' she said, smiling at him in friendship. 'I can't promise to say yes, but I promise to listen.'

'It's not that sort of question. What are your plans now?'

'My plans?' she said, looking just as puzzled as she felt. 'I haven't any except to go on working and trying to get the house patched up and perhaps even redecorated by the time Anthony comes home.'

'And then? When he comes home, I mean?' Mark asked. When he saw that she was waiting for him to put his question instead of guessing what it was and answering it on her own, he came out with it: 'Are you planning to have children?'

Julia lowered her eyes then, not out of embarrassment but to give herself time to think about her answer.

'I don't know,' she said slowly, looking up again. 'I'm not being coy. At the beginning it seemed so important to become established in chambers that the question did not really arise. Anthony was as anxious for me to succeed as I was, possibly even more so. We did sometimes talk about having a family, but there seemed to be so much time that it was never an urgent proposition. Then in the war, I was really glad that I had none.'

'Yours could hardly have been at an age when they would have been at risk,' said Mark mildly.

'Except from bombs or evacuation,' said Julia, remembering the agony some of her friends and clients had suffered. 'But now, it is true that I can't help thinking about having some. Why?'

Mark put both his elbows on the table and looked intently at her.

'Because I don't want you to waste everything you've worked for,' he said urgently. 'You're good, Julia, really good, and you could go all the way. And I don't just mean taking silk.'

At that Julia threw back her head and laughed. She had an attractive laugh, without either raucousness or shrillness, but he had rarely heard it. He smiled back in spite of himself.

'Aren't you forgetting a little something?' she asked when she had swallowed the last gurgle of amusement. 'I'm a woman.'

'I know. But things are changing already and they're going to change a lot more now,' said Mark. 'I ... I'd hate to see you throwing away that chance, just ...'

'Just to have children? Isn't that a bit dismissive? Without children, what is the point of it all?' she asked. 'No, don't bother to answer that. I can't promise you anything. Of course I want to make a success of my work, but I can't help recognising what it might be like to ...' Julia hesitated. 'To be a mother, too,' she said at last with a tiny, diffident shrug. 'Surely it needn't be either children or the Bar? It must be possible to combine them.'

'Perhaps.' Mark picked up his wine glass only to replace it when he saw that there was nothing left in it. 'And perhaps my terror is not so much that we will lose you from chambers but that I will lose you altogether,' he said frankly. 'You have made so much difference to my life that I find I hate the thought of your disappearing from it.'

'Mark,' said Julia carefully, 'have you ever thought that the reason we felt – feel – so much for each other is that we were thrown together at a time when both of us were rather unhappy? If Anthony had still been at St Michael's and Sylvia had been ... had given you what you hoped, wouldn't we have been no more than friends?'

He watched the familiar lines of her tired face, lit by the flickering candle flame and outlined by the dark-red wall behind her. Her dark-brown eyes were soft and her wide mouth looked rueful. Mark tried to be as objective as she had been, but all he could think of was how desperately he wanted her, how lonely he was going to be without her, how much he envied her husband – and how much he despised him for skulking in Italy instead of facing up to his responsibilities.

'That's too reasonable for me,' he said after a while, 'but you're probably right; you usually are. Julia, I think I ought to get the bill now and take you home. If I say any more, I shall certainly regret it and you probably would too.'

She nodded and they left it at that, sharing the bill equally between them as she always insisted. When the taxi drew up outside her house in Brunswick Square she turned to Mark and said:

'I shall miss you while you're away. I'll miss your company just as much as your advice and your support when I'm ground down by a miserable case. You have done an enormous amount for me over the years, taught me so much, and I'm really grateful.'

He had watched her through those years and tried to help her as she battled with both the prejudice of the more entrenched members of the Bar and the ritual and formality that she found so irritating. At first she had obviously been terrified in court, but she had covered her fear with a cold, unyielding severity that made nonsense of her critics' assumption that no woman could stand up to the rough and tumble of a hard-fought case. Unfortunately it had done little to endear her to juries. But recently, in the last couple of years or so, she had achieved enough confidence to relax in court and to show the judge and jury some of the grave charm that was one of her most appealing characteristics.

She had gradually won the trust of most of the solicitors who had instructed her and one of the silks who had led her in a long case the year before had confided to Mark that Julia Gillingham was one of the brightest and most reliable of the available juniors. The KC had not put the compliment directly to Julia, but he had given her the coveted red bag that all juniors wanted as a substitute for the blue one they were allowed to buy at the beginning of their careers.

'I'm glad if I've helped,' he said and kissed her hand. 'But you've done most of it yourself. You're a fine lawyer, and ... and a very good friend. Good night, Julia. I hope everything goes well for you.'

'Good night, Mark,' she answered. 'And good luck.'

She got out of the taxi and let herself into the big, quiet house. Walking upstairs to bed, she suddenly felt acutely lonely. Anthony was a thousand miles away in Italy, Comfort was almost as distant in spirit, and now even Mark was leaving London. When she was really busy, Julia could ignore her solitude, but when she was very tired and not supported by a framework of urgent tasks it seemed to gape in front of her like the mouth of some deep cave.

She walked into her study, snapped on the reading light on her desk and stared down at the photograph of her husband, trying – as she had begged Comfort to try – to understand him and his desire to live away from her. Julia had never felt that Anthony belonged to her in any sense at all, but before the war she had always believed that in some sense at least he needed her, which had made her need of him seem less frightening.

He clearly did not need her any longer, and she was left with the uncomfortable feeling that perhaps he never had, that what she had thought was his love for her might have been merely a reflection of her own for him.

Gritting her teeth, she told herself not to give up. What he had been through must have been enough to shake him badly. If he needed time to readjust to the idea of civilian life, then she should not hinder that readjustment by nagging demands of her own.

She walked out of her study towards Anthony's dressing room. As she crossed the passage she heard the sound of a wireless from upstairs and thought of going to the studio for solace in her loneliness, but it was too long since she had been able to rely on Comfort for that and so she went on into the dressing room.

Apart from fortnightly visits to air the room and do a little necessary dusting, Julia had not been in it since Anthony had left. That evening she opened the wardrobe doors to be assailed by a powerful smell of mothballs. Blowing the acrid smell out of her mouth, like a whale surfacing to breathe, she went to open the window and then returned to the rows of Anthony's suits and coats. But the sight of them did not bring him any nearer as she had hoped it would. Experimentally she touched the sleeve of one of the black coats he had worn with striped trousers in his consulting rooms, but it seemed dead, as though it had nothing to do with the man she remembered.

At the back of the wardrobe hung his old tweed jackets and one in particular, his favourite, ought to have reminded her of him. He had worn it whenever they had gone to Scotland or the Lake District for holidays. It was very shabby, made of ancient green tweed with leather patches on the elbows and covering the fraying edges of the sleeves. But even that smelled of mothballs and swayed gently on its hanger, empty and almost mocking.

A slight sound made Julia look away from the clothes and she saw Comfort standing in the doorway, her painty linen smock hanging open over a pair of disreputable grey flannel trousers and an old checked shirt of Anthony's.

'It doesn't help much, does it?' she said quite kindly.

Julia shook her head.

'I miss him, Comfort, so much,' she said directly, without thinking of their last conversation.

'Do you?' asked her sister-in-law more coldly. Julia turned away and shut the double doors of the wardrobe. When she turned back to face Comfort, she was struck all over again by how like she was to Anthony. Comfort leaned forward to examine her face in the plain antique mirror that stood on Anthony's mahogany chest of drawers, pulling little bits of oil paint from her darkened eyebrows.

'What makes you think I don't?' Julia asked.

Comfort shrugged.

'It's made no difference to you, his being away,' she said, still examining her face in the glass. 'You've just gone on working and firewatching and seeing that pompous ass Heathwood you're so fond of as though nothing had happened. It hasn't bothered you at all that Anthony was in such . . . such danger,' she added, turning away from the chest of drawers.

'Comfort,' said Julia, taking a deep breath, 'I don't know what you expected me to do. I had a job to do. It wouldn't have helped Anthony if I had become a neurasthenic and disappeared into a nursing home – and it would have ruined my chances at the Bar.'

'But as it is you've made use of every opportunity the war has brought and bumped up your annual income to what? Nearly four times the average for a barrister of your experience. The war has done you well, hasn't it, Julia?'

What she said was true, but the tone in which she had said it – both hostile and insinuating – hurt Julia badly.

'What's happened to us?' she asked Comfort. 'We used to know each other so well . . . and trust each other. Why have you decided that you don't know me at all?'

Comfort turned away and, without another word, disappeared into her studio. Julia sighed, wished that she had not broken her rule of never talking to Comfort about the difficulties between them and shut the window of the dressing room. Before she went to bed she ran the correct five inches of tepid water into the bath and tried not to remember the deep, boiling baths she had always used to relax in when work or exercise had tired her out.

The next morning, to her astonishment, when she reached the basement kitchen at breakfast time, she found Comfort standing in front of the cracked stone sink, surrounded by a wonderful smell of real, freshly ground coffee.

'Hello,' Julia said inadequately.

'The coffee is from my mother's latest parcel,' said Comfort without looking round. She was rinsing two large cups with hot water from the kettle. 'I thought we might share some for breakfast. And there's a tin of butter, too.'

'How nice!' answered Julia. 'I'll grill some toast. Did you sleep all right?'

'Not really,' said Comfort, turning round at last. Julia saw that her eyelids were swollen and the eyes themselves red.

'Oh, Comfort,' she said sadly as she put two slices of bread under the grill. 'He will come back, you know. He really will. When he can.'

'I suppose so,' she answered. 'I've written to say he must come back for Christmas at least and I'm trying to pull strings to get him on a flight, but . . .'

'Oh, you shouldn't have done that,' Julia began before remembering what a mistake it was to criticise Comfort. 'I mean, perhaps he'll think you're nagging him.'

'I think Anthony and I understand each other well enough to . . .' she was beginning when Julia hastily retracted what she had said.

'Listen,' she went on, 'isn't that the paper? Will you watch the toast while I fetch it?' She ran up the stone stairs to the hall to collect *The Times* from the mat by the front door. Ignoring the personal columns, she turned to the news and was reading it as she went back to the kitchen.

'Comfort,' she said from halfway down the stairs. 'Was there anything on the news last night about the bombing of Hiroshima?'

'Yes,' she said casually. She switched off the grill and put the toast directly on to the plates she had laid on the big deal table. 'An A-bomb. What does *The Times* say?'

'"Rain of ruin from the air",' Julia read from the headline.

'"President Truman announced . . . yesterday that the first atomic bomb had been dropped sixteen hours before by an American aircraft on Hiroshima."'

She skimmed the rest of the column, sat down at the table, and then read aloud again:

'"The Allies hesitated to use so great and awful a weapon . . . The atomic bomb, more surely than the rocket, carries the warning that another world war would mean the destruction of all regulated life." It is frightful,' she said.

'Not if it finishes the war,' said Comfort, pouring them each a cup of coffee. Julia took a mouthful and savoured the rare, rich taste as she swallowed it.

'What would you do without us Americans?' Comfort asked. Julia, who had often argued with her over the behaviour of many of the Americans stationed in England, smiled.

'I am very grateful for your mother's parcels,' she said diplomatically, but truthfully, too. Comfort laughed. They spent the rest of breakfast eating their crunchy toast and reminding each other of things they had done at Oxford and what Anthony had said to each of them about the other. By the time Julia had to leave for chambers, she was feeling happier and more relaxed than she would have imagined possible. She left the house murmuring to herself, 'the hour is always darkest before dawn'.

# Chapter Five

The fragile truce was damaged the following Friday when Julia incautiously criticised the Americans for dropping a second A-bomb on Nagasaki. The Japanese surrendered at once, and Comfort crowed with delight at her native country's unparalleled power. Julia shared her relief that the war really was over at last, but she could not help her instinctive revulsion at the devastation of yet another city full of people. But it took another American action to complete the break between the two of them.

On 21 August the new American President, Harry Truman, cancelled Lend-Lease, the long-standing arrangement organised by his predecessor to supply Britain with war materials and food. Britain was plunged at once into a financial crisis of quite desperate proportions.

Even thinking about it reduced Julia to a condition of dizzying rage and frustrated loathing for everything American. Knowing that Comfort would never agree with her, Julia said nothing about it when she met her sister-in-law on her way out of the house, but Comfort was not so restrained.

Comfort believed – and said again and again with ever-increasing bitterness – that America had financed the war, enabled the Allies to win it, and had no reason to go on paying now it was over. Julia, knowing that Britain had sacrificed a great proportion of its export trade (which had given American exporters a superb opportunity to increase their own markets and their fortunes) and had lost something like £700 million of assets during the war, believed that the Americans had a moral duty to help their ally. Lend-Lease had to end with the war, but no one in Britain had believed that it would be stopped so abruptly, with no warning and no period of adjustment.

'Besides,' said Julia to Comfort one evening as they shared a pot of tea in the studio, 'if they permanently reduce us to the level of poverty we've reached now we'll never be able to buy anything from them again, and, since the Continent is in a worse state than we, they'll be losing a lucrative export market – and probably plunging the whole world into a recession as bad as the thirties. It's so unsophisticated – as well as being cruel.'

Comfort finished her tea and then turned to her sister-in-law looking more hostile than Julia would have thought possible.

'Europeans are always saying that about Americans – as though we were all uneducated mid-Westerners – but you ought to know better,' Comfort said bitterly.

'Having shared a house with you, you mean?' said Julia in as pleasant a voice as she could manage. 'I've always thought you the acme of sophistication. But, perhaps unfortunately, you are not in a position to alter Truman's policy.'

'You're just plain ungrateful,' Comfort exploded. 'How I hate that British smugness! Thinking that the rest of the world owes you a living because of your traditions and your awful empire and your –'

'Then how can you bear to go on living here?' asked Julia quietly.

In the old days Comfort would have laughed, but there was no amusement at all in her face then. She got out of her deep, squashy armchair and stood looking down her bony nose at Julia, who lay on the model's couch, resting her feet.

'How could I possibly leave while Anthony is stuck out there?' she asked, sounding the h in the middle of her brother's name as though to underline her nationality. 'Besides,' she added in a spiteful voice, 'aren't you forgetting that I own one-third of this house? And that however rich you have become now, if it had not been for Anthony and me you would never have been anything but a junior solicitor in your father's firm?'

Julia covered her face with both hands.

'You know perfectly well that that was not what I meant,' she said from behind them. She took her hands away and looked up into Comfort's bitter grey eyes. 'You also know that I am well aware of everything I owe you – materially and otherwise. All I meant was that I am surprised that, feeling as you do about America, you do not prefer to live there.'

Comfort turned away, her shoulders tautly set under the thin rose-coloured shirt she wore tucked into her flannel trousers. Julia hoped that she was angry rather than miserable, but she could not be certain.

'I need to work,' said Comfort. 'Clear off, will you?'

'Yes, I'll go,' said Julia obediently. 'Please don't . . . Oh, I had a letter this morning; I'll leave it for you.'

Even before Julia had shut the door, Comfort had seized the letter and pulled it from its envelope.

Julia went slowly downstairs talking to her husband in her imagination as she did increasingly often.

'I'm sorry, Anthony. I try and try to keep her happy, but nothing works now.' On the first floor, she turned into her study to write to him directly.

His letters were becoming more relaxed each week as he told her in detail about his patients, about the rather miserable rooms he inhabited near the hospital, about the sad predicament of his housekeeper, and about the frightful state of Europe. It seemed that large numbers of officers awaiting demobilisation wangled their way into Venice and gave him vivid reports of the sights they had seen on the way.

Starving children lined the railway lines near Allied bases, crying monotonously for chocolate and cigarettes that they could barter for food. Bread was being sold by the slice in many parts of Italy, and the black market was everywhere. Soap was almost unobtainable. Anarchy threatened to overturn the few remnants of law and order. Girls were turning to prostitution in order to survive, and crime – from petty thieving to murder – seemed ineradicable. Collaborators were hunted out and treated with summary justice and sometimes without justice at all. Anthony wrote sadly that he had hoped the ending of the war would see the ending of cruelty, but it was quite clear that cruelty, too, was ineradicable.

Julia was able to write in perfect sincerity that, having read his letters, she understood better why he felt that he had to stay and help the children who were such pitiful victims of a war of which they were quite innocent. Having put that down, she also felt able to add that she missed him desperately and longed to see him, but she said nothing to suggest she knew of Comfort's efforts to get him home for Christmas.

She felt that her restraint was rewarded three months later when he announced that he would be coming back to London the day before Christmas Eve. Those months had passed quickly, because she was very busy indeed with a libel case, which she successfully defended, several trials for theft, grievous bodily harm and assault, in which she acted for the Crown, three divorces and an offer of the junior brief in an important murder trial that was due to be heard in the New Year. The KC who had been briefed was one of her favourites and so both she and her clerk were pleased. The silk's brief was marked at eight hundred guineas and, as his junior, Julia could expect to receive two-thirds of that sum.

Unlike most of the other silks with whom she had worked, James Norgrove always discussed the strategy of the case with his junior counsel and welcomed suggestions, instead of merely handing out menial tasks and keeping all the really interesting parts of the case to himself.

Because of his exemplary attitude to his juniors, the case involved Julia in a great deal of work. She not only appeared in the police court when the man was committed for trial, and dealt with all the necessary paperwork about the committal, but she analysed the solicitor's reports of his interviews with possible witnesses and drafted her own reports for James Norgrove on the ways in which he might use them, interviewed the two expert witnesses the prosecution would be calling, and visited the accused in prison to discuss his alibi and ask every question she could think of that the prosecution might throw at him in court. It was work that she enjoyed, but it took up a great deal of time while she was already having to work hard on all the cases that were being heard in the current term.

Her relations with Comfort improved, too. It was as though they had reached the nadir in August and then, as autumn started to crisp up the stuffy London air and turn the plane leaves yellow in the streets, the two of them began slowly to make friends again. Comfort was working hard too, making beautiful ink-and-wash drawings of the London ruins, as well as experimenting with a large abstract oil painting. Julia loved the London drawings, but was not at all sure about her reaction to the oil. Its colours sang and sizzled against each other, but the lack of form worried her, and she had no idea what to say about it. Fortunately Comfort seemed not to expect any comment.

They had begun to go about together in the few evenings when Julia had time between her cases and had sat enthralled at Sadler's Wells watching Benjamin Britten's *Peter Grimes*, which had opened in June; they went to the cinema, to the theatre and to occasional concerts. On other evenings, when they had eaten their miserable dinner of sardines or baked beans or the omnipresent and slimy Spam, they would retreat to the studio and listen to the wireless or talk about Anthony. There was a short recurrence of hostilities when the *Economist* published an article about the terms the United States was demanding for a loan of $375,000 million, which was desperately needed if Britain was to survive financially. The writer of the article shared Julia's views on the subject, and she allowed herself to read just one sentence out to Comfort over the breakfast table:

'"Our present needs are the direct consequences of the fact that we fought earliest, that we fought longest and that we fought hardest. In moral terms we are the creditors." You see, Comfort, it's not only me who thinks like that,' she said ungrammatically.

'I never thought it was,' said Comfort, hunching her shoulders defensively. 'You're just typically British.'

But they left the argument there, as though each thought peace was more important than forcing the other to admit defeat, and set about preparing the house for Anthony's return. Comfort began accumulating unrationed and unperishable luxuries and writing to her mother to beg for American delicacies. By the third week of December the larder was full of tins of outrageously expensive caviare and smoked meats, and there was even a pineapple, which had arrived from America just in time. Julia had not seen one since before the war and occasionally went to stare at its spiky dark-orange skin and try to remember what it would taste like.

Anthony's wine merchant had been persuaded to disgorge some carefully stored bottles of pre-war claret, which he promised would be 'drinking wonderfully now, Miss Gillingham.' Comfort paid the huge price, carried the bottles home to Brunswick Square and then took a Green Line bus out into the Surrey countryside to pillage the hedges and coppices for greenery to garland the ground-floor rooms. Julia's contribution in the time she could spare from her work was to give the house a thorough spring clean, which she knew Comfort would never think of doing, and overhaul the clothes that had been hanging in Anthony's wardrobes since 1939.

Comfort spent the entire day of his expected arrival downstairs, looking out of the window every half-hour, trying to read, pretending to mend her stockings and becoming more and more terrified that something had happened to prevent Anthony's arrival. Julia, on the other hand, went to chambers as usual and kept herself distracted with work on the murder case. She even went with her instructing solicitor to visit the defendant in prison, partly to ask him yet again to describe what had actually happened on the day his wife died and partly so that he would not feel completely deserted at Christmas.

The journey back to Bloomsbury from Brixton took far longer than she had expected and she grew colder and colder in the raw, foggy December afternoon. There were no taxis and she had to wait over twenty minutes for a bus, which broke down before it had even crossed the river. Along with the rest of the patiently grumbling passengers, Julia climbed down and joined the queue at the next stop. Fifteen minutes later another bus appeared, splashing their legs as it drove through a muddy puddle in the gutter, but it was so full that only the people in the front third of the queue were allowed on.

Julia ventured to protest, but the conductor called out that there was another one behind and she stood back, silently cursing. Eventually she saw another bus limping and shuddering out of the fog. When it drew up at the stop, she passed her heavy briefcase from her right hand to her left in readiness to grab the handle on the platform and haul herself up on to the bus when it was her turn. She was allowed on, but there were no seats left and so she stood with the briefcase between her feet, clinging on to the bar, for the rest of the forty-minute journey.

At half-past six, with a headache pounding behind her eyes, her back aching and her feet feeling as though they had been rasped raw with a hot steel file, she walked up the steps to her front door. Neither the shutters nor the curtains had been closed in the drawing room and she could see the glow of all the lamps and a flickering, dancing light that suggested Comfort had used some of the scarce coal for a fire. Julia knew that she would never have done that unless Anthony had arrived and pushed her key into the lock with quivering fingers.

Unlocking the front door, she was suddenly nervous. She had pined for Anthony's return and dreamed of it for so long that she was afraid of an anticlimax. The taunt Comfort had flung at her in the summer came back to her: 'He'll never recognise you, you're so hard.' What if he disliked what he saw in her? What if he had changed more than his letters had suggested? What if she disliked what she saw in him?

Until that moment she had never considered the last possibility, but it was too late even to think about it. The sound of her key in the lock had alerted Anthony and Comfort. Just as Julia was pulling off her hat in the dark hall, the drawing-room door opened. A spear of light flashed across the black-and-white marble checks of the floor. The door opened a little wider. Silhouetted against the bright yellow light was the tall, slim figure of a man. Julia could see nothing of his face, but the set of his shoulders and the carriage of his head were almost unbearably familiar.

'Julia?' The voice was oddly tentative, but she would have recognised it among a thousand others.

'Anthony,' she answered and knew her own voice was high and slightly shaking. 'How are you?'

He laughed at the banality of her question and said nothing, but he came towards her. As he got closer she could see even less of him than before with her eyes dazzled by the brilliantly lit doorway, but it did not matter. In the darkness she felt his arms going round her and his hands against her back pulling her towards him. The skin of his face felt warm and resilient against her cold cheek, but slightly scratchy, too. She pressed forward and lifted her hands behind his back to hold his head closer to hers. They were almost the same height. For the first moments they stood in silence, feeling the beat of each other's blood and relearning the sensations of the other's breathing and scent and touch. At last he pulled slightly away so that he could look her. Julia, her eyes having adjusted to the dark, could make out the outlines of his face and see the gleam of his eyes and the curve of his lips.

'Welcome home,' she said, breathless but happier than she had been for years. He moved his head forward again and kissed her. As his lips moved, hers opened. She felt completely overwhelmed, her knees weak and her mind blank. She let her hands drop from his head so that she could cling to his back.

'Are you two going to be out there all night?' Comfort's sharp voice from the doorway stiffened Julia's knees and started her mind working quickly.

'Of course not,' she said with deliberate gaiety. 'I want to look at him, and there's no light here. Come on, Anthony.'

He kept one arm round her waist as they walked together into the warmth and light of the drawing room. Julia had swept away all the dust and cobwebs that had accumulated during the war and stripped the dustsheets off the pale-yellow brocade chairs. She had polished the big looking glass over the white marble mantelpiece and Comfort had arranged a long dish of holly and ivy on it. The dark-green leaves of the ivy drooped over the marble and the red-berried holly fanned upwards against the gilded frame of the glass. Christmas garlands of fir and mistletoe and ivy, garnished with red ribbons Comfort had hoarded throughout the war, hung from painting to painting against the silver-grey walls, and there was a silver bowl of perfect Christmas roses on each of the semi-circular tables that stood in recesses on either side of the fireplace. There was a resinous scent in the air, which seemed to come from the garlands.

'It looks lovely, Comfort,' Julia said. The contrast between the room as it was then and the way it had looked when she had come back to it after her Bristol case was astonishing, and the contrast between its civilised welcome and the misery of the Brixton remand prison was such that she added: 'Aren't we lucky?'

Anthony hugged her and kissed her hair, but Julia was distracted by the sight of the fire. Despite the blissful warmth of the room it had only just struck her that wild extravagant flames were leaping in the grate.

'What have you done?' she asked, turning to Comfort with a face of horrified shock. 'There isn't nearly enough coal for a fire that size . . .'

Comfort's face closed in and her slaty eyes narrowed.

'That's not coal,' she said. Even before she finished her sentence, Julia guessed the truth and realised that the odd scent filling the room was the resinous smell of burning paint and not the garlands at all.

'It's the abstract. Doesn't the paint burn and crackle nicely?' said Comfort. The brittleness of her voice and the way she held her head, as though her neck had a steel rod driven through it, surprised Anthony, but he did not know enough about the abstract or the coal situation to understand all the unspoken messages that flashed between his wife and his sister.

'Oh, Comfort,' said Julia with real sympathy in her voice. 'Couldn't you have got it right?'

Comfort shrugged.

'I don't know why you're so worried. You never liked it. And it's giving Anthony some proper warmth for his homecoming.'

Julia looked at her husband, feeling almost ready to weep. Comfort had put such an enormous amount of work, not to speak of scarce paint and turpentine, into the painting that her burning it for him seemed like a deliberate sacrifice. Julia did not know what she wanted him to say to Comfort, but she knew it had to be something dramatic. He looked back at her, worried and unable to understand the signals in her brown eyes. Rather than make a mistake, he said nothing and so Julia turned away from him to face Comfort, who was still standing rigid by the fire.

'It's a wonderful fire,' said Julia. 'Like the old days. What a heavenly Christmas we're all going to have.' She had the satisfaction of seeing Comfort's shoulders relax slightly and a smile begin to open her face again. She was breathing a little faster than normal and her face was much pinker than usual. Julia thought she looked wonderful in her peacock-coloured dress.

'I must change,' she said hurriedly as she remembered the boxy black suit and plain white shirt she was wearing.

'Why bother?' asked Anthony, stroking her arm. 'We're not expecting anyone else, are we?'

'No,' said Comfort definitely. 'It's just us tonight. No guests. There's no need for Julia to dress.'

'Yes, I must,' said Julia. 'This smells of the prison. Besides with Comfort looking so stunning I feel at a serious disadvantage in my working clothes. I won't be long.'

Julia ran upstairs to her bedroom. The sight of Anthony's suitcase lying on the floor of his dressing room gave her a lurch of pleasure as she passed the open door, and she went on to her own room to strip off her clothes and wash away the prison smell and the grime that a long London journey always left on her skin and under her fingernails.

There were no fires in the bedrooms, and so as soon as she had washed she pulled her old grey woollen dressing gown round her shoulders, while she rummaged in her jewel case for her engagment ring. A large emerald surrounded by diamonds, it would have suited Comfort's colouring far better than Julia's and she rarely wore it. Then she turned to her wardrobe.

Everything she touched seemed to be either dull or far too formal for an evening at home, even one as special as Anthony's homecoming. At last she pulled out a long dress she had not worn since 1939. Made of thick, dull gold silk, it was quite high with long sleeves. She put it on, liking the luxurious sensation of the silk swaying about her legs, and then sat down at her dressing table to pull the pins out of her hair. As it tumbled around her face, she heard a footstep behind her.

Pulling aside some of the thick curtain of hair, she watched Anthony's reflection in the mirror. He came to stand behind her and put his right hand on her shoulder.

'You don't need to do this, you know,' he said, stroking her hair with his other hand. 'I don't need celebrations and special treatment. I've lived so long with everything reduced merely to a matter of survival that all this seems . . .'

'Exaggerated?' suggested Julia, not having considered that aspect of her desire to dress up for him. He smiled, but it was a rather painful effort.

'No,' he said, 'not that. But it's enough just to be home.'

Julia twisted round on her stool to look up into his face. She noticed at last how desperately tired he looked, how thin his face had become, and how badly his lips were chapped. There were far more and deeper lines around his grey eyes than she remembered and he had lost the confident sheen that superb health and fitness had always given him in the old days.

'Really?' she said doubtfully.

'Really,' he answered with determined certainty. Julia wanted to ask him all sorts of questions then, but she suppressed them all. If he wanted to tell her what had happened to him he would do so when he could.

'I can't tell you how much I've . . . wanted to see you back here,' she said. 'I know I've never been the sort of wife who made the care of her husband her life's work, but I do want to . . . to look after you, after all you've been through.'

'Hush,' said Anthony, stroking the hair away from her broad, white forehead, 'you are just the kind of wife I wanted. And I don't need looking after.'

Julia smiled up at him and then gently disengaged herself from his stroking hands so that she could turn back to the mirror.

'I'd better hurry up so that we can go down again. Comfort won't be pleased if we linger up here,' she said, brushing her hair energetically.

Anthony moved a little away to give her room to move.

'What's happened to her? I've never known her so edgy. . . . I couldn't believe that little scene about the fire,' he said.

Julia stopped brushing for a moment to think about the best way of explaining to him what had been happening in Brunswick Square during the war. At last she smiled at his reflection and said:

'I think I told you in one of my letters that she's been very unhappy, and she seemed to find me more and more tiresome as the war went on. Everything I tried to do to help her cope seemed wrong. When I asked her about her work she couldn't bear to speak to me, but if I didn't ask she accused me of not caring what happened to her. The cold gave her awful migraines and chilblains, which meant she couldn't work even when she had time. And she has suffered badly under all the restriction.'

Something in her husband's expression made her add: 'She was terribly unhappy, Anthony. It wasn't as trivial as it must sound to you.' He smiled ruefully at that.

'You always could see everyone's point of view,' he said. 'I must say that her sufferings do seem a bit trivial compared to what people in Europe are putting up with . . . Annunziata, for example.'

'Your housekeeper?' said Julia, applying a thin film of scarce lipstick to her mouth. She dusted a little powder over her face and then started to wind her hair into its accustomed roll and skewer it into place at the back of her head. 'Have you managed to get any news of her family yet?'

'No,' said Anthony, watching her. 'I think it's unlikely that they have survived, but getting any facts is horribly difficult. There are so many displaced people struggling home, stuck in camps and lingering in inadequate hospitals that it'll be months – years probably – before everyone has been accounted for.'

'What, none of her children?' Julia asked, looking at him in the mirror again. He shook his head and ran both hands through his short, blond hair.

'When I think of the agony people like her are going through – and the even worse agony of the ones from the Nazis' camps – Comfort's trials do pale into insignificance.'

Julia was silent for a moment. She understood exactly what he meant, but she felt as though she could not bear it if he hurt Comfort by telling her the same things. She stood up and faced him.

'She would be the first to agree with you if it was put to her like that,' she said. 'But it would make her even more unhappy to have to face it and to know that she had upset you. Can you try to put up with it?'

Anthony nodded slowly.

'Let's go down,' said Julia, tucking her hand into his arm. 'She's scoured London for delicacies for your dinner. Don't let's spoil it by . . .'

'No. All right,' he said and together they went down to the dining room, where Comfort was waiting for them by a table spread with an almost worrying amount of food.

Julia watched in admiration and pleasure as Anthony tucked into the feast without saying anything at all about the straits of the DPs or the starving women and children in Rome who were reduced to snatching food off peoples' plates in restaurants. They ate caviare and smoked goose breast and tiny fillet steaks before Comfort brought in the pineapple.

She had slit it down the middle, scooped out the flesh, cut it into squares and sprinkled it with half her sugar ration for the week, before piling it back in the thick, prickly shells, which she had laid side by side on a heavy silver dish.

'Goodness, that looks exotic!' said Anthony. 'You ought to draw it, Comfort, as a symbol of post-war luxury.'

They all helped themselves and as Julia put a spoonful of fruit into her mouth she remembered the slightly acid sweetness of it. Juice spurted into her mouth as she chewed and she savoured the unfamiliar taste.

After dinner they finished the wine and talked a little about Comfort's work and Julia's cases. She had a strong impression that Anthony did not want to say anything about his life in Italy, but when Comfort asked about Venice he talked readily enough about its buildings and the extraordinary feeling they gave anyone who had seen the devastation of Milan or Turin.

'You've said nothing about Rome,' Comfort said, draining the last of her claret. She turned to Julia. 'I've always loved Rome, because it's the place where Anthony and I had our first holiday after Father's death brought us together again. Do you remember it, Anthony?'

'Naturally,' he said with a smile that looked a little forced to Julia. 'We were still so strange to each other then, one American and one English, but . . .'

'But Rome taught us to know each other again, didn't it?' Comfort said and then without waiting for an answer went on: 'Have you been back? Seen that charming little hotel again? And the Albergo Sebastiani, and the jeweller's where you bought me my pin?' She touched a small gold stickpin she wore at the neck of her frock. Julia had seen her wear it so often that she had never even thought about its origins. It took the form of a coiled snake, gold with delicate green enamelled scales and a tiny scarlet tongue. Anthony said nothing.

'Has it changed much? Have you been back?' Comfort asked. Julia found herself gripping her hands together under the table, the nails of one dug into the palms of the other. She did not know why she felt so uncomfortable. When she looked at her husband she saw that his face was as cold and closed as Comfort's after a bad day's work.

'I've been back,' he said at last. 'Rome is nothing like it was then.'

Something in his voice made Julia change the subject precipitately. Later they all went to the gloomy kitchen in the basement to wash up and then agreed that they needed an early night. Anthony escorted Julia up to bed, but at the door of her room he hesitated.

'You must be awfully tired,' Julia said gently, hating the thought that he might stay with her and make love to her because he believed that she expected it.

'D'you know, I am rather,' he answered, obviously relieved. 'Would you . . .? I think I might sleep in the dressing room tonight.'

'Good idea,' she said, putting one hand on his shoulder and leaning forward to kiss him. 'Sleep well.' She turned into her room and shut the door so that he would not think that she was hoping that he would change his mind. Tired herself, she took off her clothes, carefully shaking out the gold dress before she hung it up.

Almost as soon as she had got into bed there was a knock at the door.

'Come in,' she said, surprised. 'Comfort! Are you all right?'

'I'm fine,' said Comfort, coming to perch on the edge of Julia's bed. 'I just wanted to make sure you were.'

Julia smiled at her.

'Yes, I am perfectly all right. A bit tired, but all right.'

'It's good to have him home again, isn't it?'

'Wonderful,' agreed Julia. 'Go to bed, Comfort. We all need our sleep. Will I see you in the morning? I have to be in chambers by nine. Someone's coming in to see me.'

'I'm not sure when I'll be up, but don't worry about Anthony. If he's still asleep when you go, I'll give him his breakfast.'

'Thank you,' said Julia, not quite sure why Comfort was making such a fuss about things Julia considered merely a matter of course. 'Good night.'

# Chapter Six

The next night was quite different. When Julia arrived home from chambers, tired and cold, she discovered that Comfort had gone out to dinner with the dealer who sold her work. Anthony took one look at Julia's face, which was greyish white in spite of the bitter chill in the air that ought to have whipped colour into her cheeks, and suggested that they share the remains of the previous evening's feast on a tray in front of the drawing-room fire instead of fiddling about in the dining room.

'That would be a relief,' said Julia, grinning at him. 'It's been quite a day. How was yours?'

Anthony shrugged.

'Odd,' he said. 'I didn't really know what to do with myself. Comfort produced an embarrassingly lavish breakfast and then took me up into the studio to show me the work she's done since I've been away. She settled down to work and I went to see my old consultant at St Michael's. He gave me lunch at the Savoy, which was good of him and then I walked, thinking . . .'

'How far did you get?' Julia asked when it became clear that he was not going to tell her what he had been thinking.

'St Paul's,' he said. 'It seems extraordinary that it should have survived when you look at how much has been lost.'

'There was one bomb there,' said Julia, 'way back in 1940, but it didn't do too much damage.'

'What was it like?' he asked. 'The Blitz I mean?'

Julia went to stand in front of the small fire thawing her fingers.

'Disagreeable,' she said at last, trying to be both realistic and moderate. 'Horribly noisy with the bombs and the fire engines, the ambulances and the ack-ack guns . . . and so uncomfortable! Trying to work in the cellar night after night and then trying to sleep. We made it quite cosy down there, Comfort and I, with camp beds and piles of eiderdowns and lamps. We used to take sandwiches and Thermoses of soup with us when the sirens went and settle down for the night.' She was silent for a while and then looked at him directly to say: 'It sounds so tame compared with what you must have been through, but it was foul at the time. Particularly coming up in the morning, wondering what damage you'd find and whether you'd hear during the day that yet more friends had been killed.'

'It doesn't sound tame at all,' said Anthony, but she thought he was being merely polite. He smiled. 'You look as though you need a drink. There's another bottle of claret, I think. Why don't you put your feet up while I go and forage for us?'

'You're very good to me,' Julia told him. When he had gone, she pushed off her heavy walking shoes and put her feet up on the sofa. The clock on the mantelpiece ticked gently and the burning coal in the fireplace hissed sometimes. Occasionally there was the sound of voices from out in the street and every so often a car would drive slowly by. Julia let her head fall back against the arm of the sofa and her eyes began to close. She opened them and blinked, but in a moment they were drooping again. After a while she stopped fighting and let herself sleep.

When Anthony came back, carrying a tray of food and a bottle of wine, he smiled slightly to see her abandoned to sleep. He put the tray down as quietly as he could, poured himself a glass of wine and lowered himself into an armchair where he could watch her.

He had been astonished at how little she had changed in essentials. There were more lines around her eyes and her face was thinner than when he had left, but her smile was as warm as ever and her brown eyes as fearless. She had obviously developed some much-needed confidence during the war, and her success had taken away the slightly abrasive determination with which she had tackled life in the old days, but she was still recognisably the girl in the photograph he had carried for so long. He thought that with luck and good judgment they might after all be able to rebuild a life together.

When she woke, so drugged with sleep that she hardly knew who she was or where, the first thing she saw was her husband, sitting at ease in an armchair with a glass of wine in one hand and a smoking cigarette in the other. When he saw that she was waking up he smiled at her.

'Anthony?' she said doubtfully and then as the sleep receded and her mind started to work again, she said it more certainly, adding: 'Sorry. I didn't mean to do that.'

'You were tired,' he said. 'You needed it. But now you need food.' He stubbed out the cigarette and pulled the tray towards him so that he could put a large spoonful of caviare on a piece of toast. He handed it to her with a plate and napkin. Julia ate it obediently and then saw that he was loading up another piece for her. She looked at him with a smile in which speculation and mischief were equally mixed.

'Since Comfort's out, I can perhaps confess that I'm not all that keen on this stuff,' she said. 'It's wasted on me. Why don't you have it?'

'I know you don't much like it, but it is very nutritious,' said Anthony with an answering smile. 'I watched you yesterday battling with your instinct to spit it out, and then I remembered the time I took you to New York to meet Mama. Don't you remember?'

Julia narrowed her eyes in an effort to bring her honeymoon back into her conscious mind.

'There was caviare on the first night out. Of course!' she said, laughing.

'And you never told me you didn't like it until you'd finished and could not help making a face when I offered you more,' said Anthony. 'You did promise me then that you'd never pretend to like anything you didn't.'

'Ah, but yesterday was Comfort's day,' she said. 'She'd taken such trouble that I didn't want to spoil it for her.'

'I know. You've been very good to her, Julia,' he said, far more seriously than when he had been teasing her about the caviare. 'It can't always have been easy. I am grateful . . .'

'You don't have to be. I just wish that she still liked me as she used to,' said Julia ruefully. 'It does hurt sometimes when she treats me as though we hardly knew each other – and disliked each other, too.'

'I think she does feel as she always did,' answered Anthony. 'She talked of you with enormous affection today. And now the war's over, she'll be able to show it again. How about some cheese to take the horrid fishy taste away?'

'Lovely,' said Julia, accepting his change of subject. They ate the cheese and the remains of the sugared pineapple and then Julia began to load up the tray to take it downstairs. Anthony stopped her, holding her right hand in his.

'Don't let's waste time with that,' he said. Julia looked surprised, but when he kissed her she responded without embarrassment.

'Shall we go upstairs?' Anthony said. Julia nodded and then laid her head on his shoulder. He put an arm around her and led her to her room.

The physical side of their marriage had always been quite happy, but neither of them considered sex the most important aspect of their relationship. Julia had been a virgin when they married and all she knew of lovemaking she had learned from Anthony, who was not very interested. Julia had always responded to his infrequent overtures, but she rarely made any of her own and had never minded that he chose to spend many nights alone in the dressing room. They had both been busy enough to need all the sleep they could get and she certainly slept better on her own than when they shared her double bed. When they did make love, it was the feeling of intimacy she enjoyed rather than the physical sensations of the act itself.

On that evening as they lay side by side, gradually relaxing together, it was his gentle endearments that she particularly liked, and the way he said again and again, 'if you knew how I'd missed you'. His stroking hands gave her a certain pleasure, but they sometimes tickled and did little to arouse her. When he did begin to make love to her, she could not help remembering the first time he had done so and her immediate thought, So that's it. I wonder what all the fuss was about.

But when it was over and he had cried her name and then buried his face in her hair, shuddering and almost sobbing, she stroked his head again and again and knew that she loved him.

'There, there, my love,' she murmured. 'It's all right, Anthony. I'm here. It's all right.'

He clung to her and said her name again and she felt closer to him than ever and full of love. She felt powerful, almost maternal, and desperately wanted to protect the rare vulnerability that he had shown. After a while he rolled away and apologised, which chilled her even though it did not surprise her. Two minutes later, lying on his back at her side, he was asleep.

Julia waited until his breathing was slow and even and then slid out of bed to wash and find a nightdress. Then she collected their clothes and laid them quietly over the chairs at the foot of the bed, found her book and got back into bed to read herself to sleep.

Sleep was just beginning to blur the eges of her mind and make her eyelids droop when she felt Anthony's hand on her thigh.

'Did I wake you with my light?' she asked, turning to smile at him. 'I'm sorry. I must have slept too heavily while you were getting supper to fall sleep again so soon.'

'I don't think it's that that's keeping you awake,' said Anthony. 'I was thoughtless. Come here, my love.'

Surprised, but willing to do whatever he wanted, she put down her book and turned towards him. He kissed her, stroking the heavy hair away from her face with gentle fingers. Then he let his hands stray to her neck and then her breasts, touching, stroking and moving away. Gradually her breathing began to change and her eyes widened. He started to make love to her in ways he had never done before and she responded as never before. At last he brought her to the very edge of complete pleasure and with a final lingering touch flung her over. Spiralling sensations seemed to split her mind apart. She understood at last why he had always called her name and why he had clung to her so tightly.

As the last tingling pleasure left her, she realised that she was gripping his hand and let it go.

'Anthony,' she said. 'I . . . Oh, thank you.'

'Are you all right?' he asked, kissing her forehead and brushing the hair out of her eyes.

'I never knew,' she said inadequately, not sure how to deal with what had happened. Anthony's lips smiled but she was saddened to see that his grey eyes looked worried. She waited for him to tell her why.

'It's still early,' he said after a moment. 'Would you like a cup of tea? All that salty caviare is making me thirsty.'

'Oh yes, please,' she said, glad of the opportunity to be alone for a while to put herself back together again.

When he came back, she was sitting up against banked pillows with her hair tidily brushed. Anthony handed her a cup of tea and stood by the bed in his dark-blue dressing gown, looking down at her.

'What is it?' she asked. 'Anthony, what's the matter?'

'I haven't been a very good husband to you, have I?' he said.

The bitterness in his voice appalled her and she contradicted him at once.

'Yes, you have,' she said. 'You've given me everything I ever wanted in life. You're tired and discouraged and unhappy. I know that and I wish that I could help. But whatever else worries you, you mustn't be anxious about me. I'm all right, Anthony. Please believe that. I love you. When your job in Italy is done we can sort things out and be happy again.'

'Can we?' he said. 'Can we ever go back to what we were before?'

'Why must we go back?' Julia asked, suddenly assaulted by the hopelessness in his voice. She knew that she had changed far too much to become once again the inexperienced, ambitious girl she had been when the war broke out, and she had no wish to do so. 'The war has done things to us all,' she said. 'We'll never be the same as we were then. But why does it matter? Can't we be happy as the people we are now?'

'I don't know,' he said. 'Happiness seems rather an alien concept just now. Oh, God, and now there's Comfort.'

Julia had not heard anything, but in the sudden silence after his announcement, she heard the familiar light tread on the stone staircase. The steps stopped on the landing outside. Julia could imagine Comfort staring at the open door of Anthony's dark dressing room and the line of light under the bedroom door. After a moment the steps started again and they listened to her going into the studio upstairs and then shutting the door behind her with a loud crash.

'What is it that's happened to make you think that happiness is so unlikely, Anthony?' Julia asked.

He shook his head.

'So many things,' he said. 'All part of the war. I can't . . . can't talk about them.'

'All right. I won't press you,' she said, feeling as though her insides were being torn out as she watched the despair in his eyes. He had seemed so secure the day before, but now he was letting her see a side of him that was completely unknown to her.

'I'm sorry, Julia,' he said, rubbing his eyes. 'I never meant . . . never meant you to see me like this. I'll go and leave you in peace.'

'Only if you want,' she said quickly. 'You don't need to hide anything from me.'

He looked at her and saw her smiling at him. There seemed to be love in her dark-brown eyes and trust and absolution.

'Come back to bed,' she said simply.

He got back into bed and when she had turned the light off, he clutched at her hand and said:

'It's so awful out there.'

'Then why don't you come back permanently?' she asked in a quiet, reasonable voice. 'There must be other people who could do the job, people who haven't fought for as long as you have. Surely you've done your whack now?' He let go of her hand and was silent for so long that she was afraid she had made him angry.

'I can't leave,' he said at last.

'Why not?' Julia asked quietly. There was no answer. Anthony's regular breathing deepened as though he was asleep, but she was almost certain that he was still awake.

# Chapter Seven

Julia woke the next morning with a feeling of unprecedented physical ease, as though every joint in her body had been unlocked, but with an echo of her husband's distress in her mind. She stretched luxuriously against the pillows and then lay still in the dark beside him wondering how to help him back to happiness. She wished suddenly that she had been able to find him a better Christmas present, something that might have made his life in Italy more comfortable perhaps, instead of the books she had chosen. Everything useful or desirable was rationed, except for antiques and works of art, and he could hardly have taken them back to Venice. She had thought that new books might help to pass his free time, but she was afraid that he might think them mean.

'Are you all right?' Anthony's sharp voice from her side made her start.

'Heavens yes! Why not?'

'You looked tormented. What were you thinking about?' he said, levering himself up against the padded headboard.

Julia smiled in relief.

'Your present,' she said with a small laugh. 'It seems horribly dull for the first Christmas we're sharing after so many years. I'd like to have made some wonderfully grand gesture, bought you a dozen warm, fur-lined overcoats or something.'

Anthony laughed then, too, and reached to hug her.

'You are sweet,' he said. 'But I don't need presents.'

They heard the sound of Comfort's footsteps on the floor above and nodded to one another.

'Yes, we'd better get up,' said Julia, flinging back the blankets.

The sudden cold on her bare legs made her shudder and she dressed as quickly as she could in a thick skirt of coppery-coloured tweed, a cream woollen shirt and a russet cardigan, fumbling with hooks and buttons and rubbing her hands to warm them.

'I'll go down and get a fire going,' said Anthony as he knotted his tie. Julia dealt with her face, noticing how much better the warm browns and reds suited her than the cold black-and-white she had to wear in court, and bundled her hair loosely back with a velvet ribbon. She followed him downstairs and met Comfort in the hall.

'Happy Christmas, Comfort,' she said cheerfully. 'You look wonderful in that dress. I don't think I've ever seen you in red before. It suits you.'

'Thanks,' said Comfort shortly. 'Oh and happy Christmas to you too.'

Julia's heart sank. If Comfort was in a bad mood then their chances of a happy Christmas were quite slim.

'Anthony's lighting the fire. I thought I'd go down and rustle up some breakfast.'

'I'd better do it if we're not to waste Mama's coffee. I don't suppose Anthony's had any decent American coffee for years,' said Comfort.

'Fine,' said Julia in a deliberately pleasant voice. 'Can I help? Or shall I just lay the table?'

'Whatever you like,' said Comfort over her shoulder as she turned down into the basement staircase. Julia followed her and silently collected plates and cups and cutlery to carry upstairs. She took them into the drawing room, where Anthony was still wrestling with the fire.

'I'm making rather a hash of this,' he said, looking round. 'Can you take over? I'd hate to waste any of your coal.'

Julia laughed. 'Yes, all right. It's such poor quality stuff these days that it's far more difficult to light than in the old days . . . At least that's my story: despite my serious lack of domestic skills, I cannot believe that I'm that much more cack-handed than the maids used to be.'

Anthony laughed, too, but there was a note in the laughter that made it sound unamused.

'You ought not to have to do all this,' he said, waving one black hand at the fire and then the heavy breakfast tray. 'God knows when you'll be able to have servants again.'

'I'm not sure we'll ever be able to,' said Julia. 'Never mind now. I thought we'd have breakfast in here instead of wasting the heat. Could you clear the card table and then lay it up with these?' She put her tray down on top of a low bookshelf and went to take her husband's place at the grate. With the skill of long practice she had the fire lit in a few minutes and was blowing it up with the bellows when Comfort came in with the coffee pot and a rack of toast.

'We've finished the butter,' she said in a despairing voice.

'Well that's not a major tragedy,' said Anthony lightly. 'It won't kill us to make do with marmalade alone. What a wonderful smell, Comfort. I haven't had decent coffee for ages.'

Comfort looked triumphantly at Julia, who was still on her knees by the fire, and then poured the coffee. It was left to Julia to return to the kitchen for the sugar and marmalade. Coming back, she could hear Comfort's voice but as soon as she opened the door it stopped. After an appreciable pause Anthony said:

'Well, I've got each of you two girls a small present. Do you want them now or after breakfast?'

'Now would be lovely,' said Julia, trying to ignore the obvious fact that Comfort had been talking about her.

'Oh let him have his coffee in peace,' snapped Comfort and then almost immediately added: 'I'm sorry, Julia. I'm not very good at Christmas. It's such a family occasion. Not having had a proper family I've never learned how to cope with it. Unlike you. You can't imagine how much I've envied your settled childhood and your two parents.'

'You've never said that before,' said Julia, looking at Comfort in astonishment. Julia found it extraordinary that Comfort should have envied anything so unlikely, because although her parents had been welded together by custom and conformity they could not have been more separate in every real sense. She could still remember the day when she had finally understood that.

Julia was thirteen at the time and had overheard her mother chatting to friends at a 'ladies' coffee morning' that had been arranged to raise money for the local children's home. All the ladies had been moaning about their husbands, although some of their complaints were not entirely comprehensible to the child who listened to them, but her mother had been the most bitter. Gone were the pretty tones and childishly caressing words that she used towards her husband; instead she spoke with bitter articulateness about his failings and his dullness and his meanness with money. Julia had sat on a corner of the stairs hidden from view, wincing at the loathing that she had discovered and for some reason desperately ashamed.

Not more than fifteen minutes after the last of the ladies – winding her foxes around her neck, her face freshly powdered and her lips carmined with lipstick – had left, Julia's father had returned home from his office for lunch. His wife, similarly repaired after her exhausting morning, stood in the doorway of her morning room, her arms outstretched. The caressing voice was back, the wheedling smile flicking up the corners of her red mouth, and she asked him for something. At that distance Julia could not remember what it had been; but it was probably money. It usually had been.

'Julia, darling, what's the matter?' Another caressing voice broke into Julia's thoughts. She looked up, wiping her hand across her eyes as though to push away the pictures her memory had conjured up, and saw Anthony looking at her with anxiety in his eyes.

'Nothing, Anthony,' she said, smiling at him in reassurance. 'For some reason I was reminded of a trivial but upsetting incident in my childhood. Not important. Sorry. Where were we?'

'We were just about to have breakfast and then open Anthony's presents,' said Comfort, pouring some coffee into her cup.

When they had finished, Anthony produced two identically wrapped parcels, which proved to contain almost identical angels, carved and gilded in Venice some time in the nineteenth century. Julia handed over her presents, three books for Anthony and a complete set of new paint brushes for Comfort, who reciprocated with one of her charcoal drawings of the ruins for Julia and a delicately coloured oil of the square at twilight one snowy evening for her brother.

There was a moment of peace as he and Julia admired the painting, but Comfort resumed hostilities within half an hour. Julia felt very close to Anthony and found herself wishing for almost the first time that they did not share the house with Comfort. She chided herself for her meanness and tried to be extra nice to Comfort to make up for it, but the effort showed and Comfort became more and more difficult. Whenever Julia expressed any opinion, whether it was about the chances of rationing being eased or the latest film they had seen together or even the policies being hammered out by the government, Comfort would contradict her. Anthony became visibly uncomfortable, but he said nothing to his sister until Julia had disappeared into the kitchen to roast the chicken that she had bought in default of turkey or goose for their Christmas lunch.

'Comfort,' he said, taking advantage of her absence, 'why are you being so beastly to Julia?'

Comfort hunched one thin shoulder.

'She's just so irritating these days ... so pedestrian and dull and reasonable. Imagine giving you three boring books for your first post-war Christmas! She hasn't any idea, doesn't understand that we –'

'I think she understands most things rather well. She's very sensible,' said Anthony, quietly interrupting her. 'But she's sensitive too and you're hurting her, you know.'

'Julia?' said Comfort with a hardness in her voice that shocked her brother. 'Nothing I could do would hurt her. She doesn't care a bit for me and just wishes that I wasn't here so that she could be alone with you.'

'That isn't fair, and you know it. She cares a lot for both of us and she does so much for us. .... Can't you try to be kinder? Or at least not so aggressive? Please, Comfort.'

'All right. But I think you're wrong. Oh I've got a present for you. Here.'

'But you've already given me that lovely painting,' he protested, accepting a small, rectangular parcel from her.

'That was a public present,' she said with a faint smile curling the edges of her mouth as she watched him unwrap the box. It contained a pair of heavy, smooth, gold cuff-links. Anthony looked down at them, wondering what on earth to say to his sister. He could not tell her that it seemed almost shocking for anyone to spend so much on something so unnecessary when all over Europe children like his patients were starving, dressed in pathetic rags and living in corrugated-iron shacks in makeshift camps.

'They're wonderful,' he said dully. 'You shouldn't have.' Then he looked up and caught her eye. 'But thank you,' he said making an effort to sound more cheerful. 'Thank you, Comfort.'

When Julia came back to say that lunch would be ready at one o'clock she found them sitting reading in silence. Comfort had the previous day's *Times* and Anthony was reading one of the novels she had given him. There was a faint smile in his grey eyes as he looked up.

'It's very entertaining, Julia,' he said. 'Thank you.' He wanted to add something about being glad that she had not been extravagant, but he could not with Comfort listening.

'I'm glad,' said Julia. 'And I love my angel. I'll hang it in my study, I think. The gold will look wonderful against those dark-green walls.'

'Good idea; the green needs something bright to lighten it,' said Comfort more pleasantly than she had spoken that morning. Julia responded with a smile and between them they managed to create a sweeter atmosphere. Lunch went well, even though it was spartan in comparison with pre-war Christmas meals, and afterwards all three of them went out for a walk.

Huddled inside her fur coat, Julia smiled secretly as she thought of childhood Christmas walks when she had always felt as though she had been stuffed so full of food that she could hardly move. It had been years before she had discovered the pleasures of self-restraint, but once learned it was a lesson she had never forgotten.

They walked across Guildford Street and down through Bloomsbury. As they passed Anthony's old hospital, Julia noticed that his face looked even more drawn than usual. Not certain whether it was regret for his old job or concern for his existing patients, she said nothing but she did slide her gloved hand into his crooked elbow. He squeezed her hand closer to his body and smiled at her, but he said nothing either.

Then they turned their backs on his past and wandered through the old familiar streets until they came to Gray's Inn.

'Has it survived?' Anthony asked as they crossed one of the roads leading into the Inn. Julia shook her head.

'The hall was bombed, but most of the rest is all right,' she said.

'How sad,' said Anthony, remembering the few occasions when he and Julia had dined there as guests of one or other of her colleagues. 'I suppose they'll be able to rebuild it eventually.'

'Yes, but no reconstruction can be as good as the original. It was built in 1556, you know,' said Julia.

'Yes, you told me –' Anthony was beginning when Comfort interrupted, saying in an irritable voice:

'It's bitterly cold standing around. Can't we get on?'

Without a word the others turned away from the ruin and walked out of the square. They took a great loop through the empty market at Covent Garden, past the opera house, up Endell Street, into Bloomsbury Street and right into Russell Street. Anthony stopped for a moment in front of the great grey portico of the British Museum.

'Well at least that's still here,' said Comfort, as though trying to make up for her lack of sympathy for the hall at Gray's Inn.

'Yes, in fact it is extraordinary how much has survived,' said Anthony, thinking of the complete devastation of some of the European cities. He had seen photographs of Nuremberg and Dresden and Cologne with their acres of rubble punctuated with the remnants of bombed and burned buildings. He had also seen and tried to deal with some of the casualties of the bombed cities of Italy. He felt Julia's hand on his arm again and knew that she understood some of the anguish he could not completely suppress.

He wished that he could talk to her about the things he had seen and had to do, and he knew that she wanted to hear about them, but for some reason he could not take himself across the barrier their different wars had erected between them. It might come down in the end, but it seemed solid and very high to him then.

'Tea, I think,' Julia said, and he realised that they were back outside his own front door. Comfort opened it and when Julia had gone down to kitchen to boil a kettle, she took his hand.

'What is it?' she asked, her face unhappy and her voice strained.

'I just can't help thinking of my patients. They're so young and so ill and they have so little resistance, Comfort. I don't know which of them . . .' His voice trembled slightly and he swallowed. 'I don't know which of them will have died by the time I get back.'

She drew back from him at once, dropping his hand as though it had hurt her.

'Do you hate me for making you come back?' she asked.

He put an arm round her shoulders and leaned his head sideways so that it rested on hers.

'Of course not. Never that, But . . .' he said, breaking off before he could put his caveat into words.

'But you can't wait to get back,' she supplied. 'I see.'

'Comfort, please don't make it more difficult than it already is. I feel torn in pieces by what I want and by what I have to do. There're you and Julia here and in some ways I long to be back with you; then there are those children there and they need me so much.'

'Do you think we don't?' came the quick question from his sister.

'It's not the same,' he answered. He put a hand on her cold pink cheek. 'Try to understand. They have nothing, and I care for them. There's no one else to care.'

'And that's really all it is?' Comfort said, peering at him as she sometimes peered at people whose portraits she was painting.

'All?' he asked, puzzled and a little worried.

'All that's kept you away from home? You haven't met someone else, who –'

'Certainly not, Comfort. Whatever you do, don't go upsetting Julia with idiotic suggestions like that. That's really silly of you,' he said angrily and moved away from her.

Comfort waited a long time before saying:

'OK. Good. I'm going up to change. Tell Julia I'll be down for tea in five minutes.'

'Before you go,' Anthony said, grabbing hold of her elbow, 'and while we're on that subject: did Julia?'

'What? Meet someone else? Anthony, that's ridiculous,' said Comfort, laughing. 'Of course she didn't. She spent the entire war working, talking her everlasting legal talk with that dreary KC in her chambers, and knitting . . . unpicking old sweaters and reknitting them into things she could wear now. Oh, and firewatching and queuing for rations and helping sometimes at rest centres for the blitzed. She even wanted to import some homeless people into this house.'

'I see,' said Anthony. 'It sounds as though she worked hard.'

'Of course she did,' said Comfort with a foot on the bottom stair. She looked over her shoulder at him. 'She almost made herself ill in 1941, doing far too much, and never getting enough sleep, but then she toughened up and stopped trying to do everything for everyone.'

He watched Comfort as she walked gracefully upstairs in her long mink.

'I made a cake, but I'm not sure it's worked out.' Julia's cheerful voice from the top of the basement stairs woke him out of his thoughts. 'I always read the recipe and do exactly as I'm told, but either I'm a congenitally rotten cook or there's something wrong with my eyesight. It never turns out right.'

'Poor Julia,' said Anthony. 'You shouldn't have to do the cooking as well as everything else. Comfort has just been telling me how hard you worked in the war, doing "everything for everybody".'

'Oh, what nonsense!' Julia exclaimed. She balanced the heavy tray on her left hipbone and took her right hand away to open the drawing-room door. 'Oh, good; the fire's lasted. I did no more than most Londoners. Come and have tea. We'll have to eat the cake even if it's disgusting: it's got the last of the fat ration in it and two whole tablespoons of dried egg, not to speak of an extravagant amount of golden syrup.'

'It sounds ... wonderful,' said Anthony with such a boyish grin that Julia knew he had been going to say 'disgusting'. Since she agreed with him and had no self-esteem about her cookery, she smiled happily back.

Anthony made love to her again that night and once more she found herself completely overwhelmed by sensations that left her gasping and almost afraid. Before she had recovered her usual discretion, she asked him the question that had been tormenting her ever since she had realised how unhappy he was.

'Anthony, are you lonely there?'

He looked at her then with such tenderness and sadness mixed that she almost burst into tears.

'No. There isn't time to be lonely,' he said simply. 'Up in the hills we'd had to live so hugger-mugger with each other that I used to long to be alone sometimes and so I cherish the little time I have to myself.'

'I'm glad,' said Julia. 'I was afraid that you might miss the friends you must have made there.'

'The best friend I had up there, David Wallington – did I ever write about him?' Anthony said. Julia shook her head. 'A young chap. He was parachuted in to join us very early in 1944 and organised supplies that made survival possible. He's stayed in Italy, too, working in Rome on various legal matters for the Occupation authorities, and he comes up to Venice whenever he can snatch a weekend or a week's leave. Then there's Annunziata, the children, the nurses ... Loneliness isn't really possible, although of course I miss you badly.'

'I wish I could go back with you,' she said, 'but ...'

'I know it isn't possible, Julia,' said Anthony quickly. 'Don't upset yourself about that. You've an important job to do and you've worked so hard to get where you are, you can't chuck it in.'

Julia looked at Anthony, thinking gratefully that there must be few husbands who would take such an enlightened view of their wives' careers.

'That's generous of you,' she said. 'But then you've always been generous. I wish I could help in some way.'

'You do,' he said, sliding down the bed and pulling the blankets up under his chin. 'Your letters help enormously.'

'I'm glad,' Julia said. That night she slept well.

When she had prepared breakfast the following morning and carried it into the drawing room, she noticed that Comfort's garlands were beginning to wilt and realised that they were almost at the end of Anthony's holiday. They had one more day and then he would disappear again and she would be left with Comfort. 'And your work,' she reminded herself bracingly and set about making the last day a good one.

It was. Comfort had recovered from whatever had been making her so crabby on Christmas Day, and the three of them spent almost as relaxed and cheerful a day as they had done long before the war when Anthony was working at the Radcliffe Infirmary and Julia and Comfort were at Somerville. They even began to make plans for when Anthony could come back to England for ever and they could repair and refurbish the house.

After such a day it was agonising for Julia to have to say goodbye to Anthony again. Due in chambers soon after ten, she had to leave the house at half-past nine. Comfort had stayed in bed late and so Anthony and Julia had the drawing room to themselves.

She looked at her watch for the tenth time and put down her coffee cup.

'I'm going to have to ...' she began.

'Leave,' supplied Anthony. 'I know. Julia, I ... It's been a wonderful holiday. Thank you.' He stood up when she did and put his arms round her.

'I've loved it,' she said honestly. 'And I'm so relieved ... so pleased that ... It won't be so difficult being without you now that we've remarried, if you see what I mean.'

'I think I do,' he said, stroking her eyebrows with one long finger.

'Don't stop writing those letters, will you? They keep me in touch with what's going on here.'

'I promise,' she said and then clung to him. 'Be careful of yourself, won't you?'

'I'll be careful,' he said and then took his arms away from her suddenly. 'And now you'd better go or we'll make each other maudlin. The war's over, Julia. I know I said some rather dramatic things the other night, but I'm perfectly all right.'

'All right,' she echoed. 'Good. Well . . .' she looked round the elegant room with its decaying garlands, trying to think of something suitable to say. In court she had never been so lost for words, not even during the most forlorn of cases. 'Well, goodbye, Anthony.'

He kissed her cheek and watched her go, blessing her common sense and her capacity to absorb and deal with difficult emotions. Without it, he thought, Comfort's terrifying swings from inspiriting happiness to aggressive melancholy could have made their life together unbearable. He hoped that she would become happy enough, now that she was painting again, not to put too great a strain on Julia's tolerance. He needed them both and would have hated to be made to choose between them.

# Chapter Eight

Julia had an hour-long meeting with James Norgrove, who was leading her in the murder case, and then returned to her desk to read through old cases to find precedents and authorities for the defence strategy they had planned. Glad to have something important to keep her mind off Anthony's departure, Julia was so absorbed in her work that when she was interrupted by a knock at the door soon after twelve she was irritated.

'Yes,' she called coldly.

'Julia, my dear, may I come in?' said a familiar voice. The door opened and Julia's expression changed as she recognised the long, lined face and tired blue eyes of Mark Heathwood.

'I didn't know you were back,' she said, smiling. 'Come in and sit down.'

'We've been let out for ten days,' said Mark, accepting a chair. 'Thank God.'

'Why? Is it awful?'

'Ghastly!' he said. 'The evidence of what they've done in those unspeakable camps of theirs is enough to justify the tribunal in itself, quite apart from the other charges, but it is unbelievably frustrating having separate prosecution teams from each of the four powers: what with the Russians determined to have every defendant hanged and the Americans . . .' He broke off, remembering that Julia's husband was half-American.

'Don't mind me,' said Julia. 'What have they been doing?'

'Apart from their apparently congenital logorrhoea, they're apt to say things – in court, mind you – like: "The voice you hear is the knocking of my knees. They haven't knocked so hard since I asked my wonderful little wife to marry me.'"

'You're joking,' said Julia, really shocked. 'In court? God, the Americans! And those are the people we're all so dependent on now. It seems ... Well, at least Keynes managed to get them to promise that loan for this summer, so we won't starve.'

'No,' agreed Mark, 'but in 1951 we'll have to start paying it back at – what? – $140 million a year until the year 2001, quite apart from this disastrous business of making sterling fully convertible when the loan comes through. There'll be an appalling run on sterling. But don't let's even think about the bloody Yanks. They've got all the power and the money now and we can't do a thing about it. I know you're busy, Julia, but could you manage lunch?'

Julia had a quick look at her watch and then smiled.

'If we go now and eat fast,' she said.

Mark laughed.

'Good. I'll see if Antonio has a table for us. May I use your telephone?'

'Please,' said Julia, beginning to pack up the papers on her desk.

They went to the small restaurant in the Aldwych and although the food was based on the usual war-time makeshift, Julia enjoyed herself. Mark told her far more about the trial in Nuremberg than he had allowed himself to write in his letters and gave her a vivid word picture of the court, packed with lawyers, judges, Nazis, journalists, photographers, translators, visiting firemen and brash young American guards. The French judges wore their traditional black gowns and lace jabots, the British and Americans ordinary striped trousers and black coats, but the Russians wore their military uniforms, and the contrast looked most peculiar, he told her.

'And the defendants?' Julia asked curiously. 'What are they like?'

'A very mixed bag,' he said. 'It's hard to generalise. One thing, though, they all hate being photographed and most of them put on dark glasses whenever the photographers come in. And they don't like being shown films of the camps. The first time, at least two of them burst into tears.'

'Does that suggest that they really did not know about them?' asked Julia, curiously.

'God knows. Perhaps it was just that being faced with what the reality looked like they were at last ashamed. Who can tell? But that's enough of Nuremberg,' said Mark as their meat plates were removed and the glorified rice pudding put down in front of them. 'How are you?'

'I'm perfectly all right,' said Julia.

'Really? You look awfully tired,' said Mark, noticing the dark bruises under her eyes and an unusual tension about her lips.

Julia shrugged.

'We've just had Anthony at home for three days, which was glorious, but he's gone again now, and I feel ... oh, I feel as I did at the beginning of a term at boarding school: unhappy, apprehensive, and quite unable to believe that the holidays will ever come again.' She took a gulp of wine and made a valiant effort to smile.

Mark thought how like her it was to try to camouflage her distress in frivolity.

'If only there were something I could do in Venice,' she said, putting her glass down again. 'I suppose I could go and live there with him. But much as I want to be with him, I can't just drop everything to do it. I'd wreck my career – and probably go potty if I had nothing to do, which wouldn't be much help to him.'

'I wonder,' said Mark, spooning some of the glutinous rice mould into his mouth.

'Well, I would,' said Julia. 'I've never not worked since I came down from Oxford, and I simply wouldn't know how to go on ... least of all now. I suppose in the old days I could have behaved like my mother and spent all day having my hair done, buying hats, interviewing the dressmaker and so on ... but not with the world in this frightful chaos.'

Mark swallowed the last sickly mouthful of his pudding.

'That's not what I meant,' he said. 'Kesselring's to be tried there by a military tribunal some time next year. I just wonder whether there might not be something you could do with that.'

'In Venice?' said Julia, her spoon halfway to her lips. She dropped it back on to her plate. 'How extraordinary. Why?'

'Didn't you know that it's been agreed that the lesser Nazis should be tried in the countries where their alleged crimes were committed? Kesselring was Hitler's C-in-C Italy, and Venice has been chosen. Since we're the Occupying Power there, it'll be a British tribunal that tries him.'

'Well, if it's a military tribunal I don't suppose there's much a civilian lawyer could do,' said Julia, suppressing the wild hope that had leaped in her mind. She doggedly finished her syrup-flavoured rice pudding.

'I don't know,' said Mark. 'Would you like me to talk to a few people?'

'I'd love it,' said Julia, giving up all attempts to pretend otherwise. 'More than anything in the world just now I'd like to be able to live with Anthony again.'

Mark's face tightened and he closed his eyes for a moment.

'I'm sorry,' said Julia. 'I didn't think.'

He shook his head.

'No, it's very right and proper that that's what you should feel,' he said. 'I just wish . . . Never mind. I'll see what I can do. I don't suppose it'll be a very long trial – unlike Nuremberg, which looks as though it's going on for ever – but it would mean a few months with your husband.'

'Thank you, Mark,' said Julia, really touched that after everything they had meant to each other he should be the one to make it possible for her to live with Anthony again.

Mark did as he had promised, and almost three months after their conversation in Antonio's dark little restaurant, a week after she and James Norgrove had succeeded in their defence of the alleged murderer, Julia was offered a job helping to prepare the case against Field Marshal Kesselring, who was to be tried for war crimes.

The status she was offered was fairly menial, but the job would at least allow her to live with Anthony for perhaps half a year. She weighed that against the briefs she would lose in London during those months, her clerk's probable rage and the distinct possibility that he would punish her when she returned to London by restricting her to work outside the courts. It did not take her long to decide that the risk to her work was worth taking for the sake of Anthony and their marriage, and she wrote to accept the job; but she said nothing to anyone in case Anthony decided to return to London after all. If that happened she would find a way to extricate herself from the war crimes office.

A week later the government nationalised the Bank of England and Julia began to think that six months or so out of the country might help her to keep her temper. It was true that they had also reduced the standard rate of income tax by a whole shilling in the pound, but that did not make much difference to someone like Julia who was paying nineteen-and-sixpence in the pound on everything she earned on the top slice of her income in combined income tax and surtax.

Trying to ignore the gloom she felt whenever she thought of what the Socialists were doing to her country, she concentrated on her work and tried to decide how and when to tell her clerk that she would be deserting chambers for about six months.

When she did eventually tell him in June, after it had become clear that Anthony was not going to leave Italy, her clerk was predictably angry. He told her that it would be a waste of her success in the winter's murder trial to run away before she could reap the full benefit from it. Julia explained that she would not be leaving London until the following November and tried to placate him by explaining that she felt she had done very little for the war effort and thought it her duty to use her legal expertise in the Allies' cause at last. She carefully avoided any suggestion that she was deserting chambers to be with her husband. It would have been the sort of wifely behaviour which her clerk and certain colleagues would have approved of in the abstract, but which they would also have taken as support for their view that women should not become barristers.

Eventually, after Julia had deployed her hard-learned skills of advocacy and persuasion for some time, her clerk grudgingly told her that he understood and even admired her 'sense of duty'. He added a rider to the effect that he might find it hard to persuade solicitors to offer her briefs when she came back again, but that he would do his best. Julia smiled with as much amiability as she could manage and went back to write to her husband.

Her letter reached Anthony almost exactly a year after he had sent her his first letter after the end of the war. He found it waiting for him when he got back to his digs after a particularly gruelling day at the hospital, and he sat at his desk, reading and rereading it.

'*Dottore*,' came Annunziata's voice, interrupting his difficult thoughts. He looked up.

'I'm afraid there is no news,' he said sadly, thinking of their very different circumstances and wishing that the letter he held in his hands could have announced the imminent arrival of one of her children rather than his own wife. Annunziata shook her head, and he saw that the grey threads were beginning to outnumber the black in her hair. Her gaunt face had filled out a little since she had started to work for him, but like most inhabitants of the occupied countries, she still looked years older than her age, which was forty-three. She was only one year older than Anthony, but a stranger meeting them would have assumed the difference to be more like ten or even fifteen years.

'No,' she said. 'I know that you would tell me as soon as you had news. But you look so sad. Is it the *poverini* in the hospital? Can I do anything to help?'

'I'm not sad at all,' said Anthony, pulling himself together as well as he could. He picked up Julia's letter. 'This has good news in it for me. My wife will be coming to work in Venice in the late autumn. Shall you mind looking after her as well as me?'

Annunziata's drawn face took on a lightness Anthony had never seen in it before and she went so far as to lay a work-hardened hand on his shoulder.

'That is wonderful,' she said. 'But she cannot come here. You must find better rooms, *dottore*.'

'I think I have,' he said. 'I meant to tell you. Signor Wallington has written too to say that he is coming here as well. He tells me that he has found a wonderful set of rooms over on the other side of Venice.' He rummaged in the papers on his desk and consulted a letter written in a firm, black hand. 'Yes, in the Campo San Maurizio, and he suggests that you and I share them with him.'

'And the Signora Gillingham, too?' said Annunziata a little doubtfully.

'I don't see why not,' said Anthony, sounding almost as tired and dispirited as he felt. 'He says this flat has five bedrooms and a huge *salone* and so it ought to be big enough. It belongs to a friend of his mother and he wants to rent it so that she should have some income, but it is too big for him alone. I suppose I'd better write to him and my wife.'

'Not until you have eaten,' said Annunziata firmly. 'I will fetch your dinner. Wait.'

Anthony, who had to make appallingly important decisions in almost every minute he was at the hospital, succumbed to the odd pleasure of doing as he was told.

'Will so large a flat be too much for you to manage?' he asked when Annunziata came back with the pasta she had cooked for him. She shook her head and even laughed.

'There is not enough to do here,' she said, 'and I have too much time to think.'

'Yes,' agreed Anthony, pouring himself a modest glass of wine, 'it hurts to think, doesn't it?' The housekeeper nodded silently, no longer laughing, and went away.

Anthony finished his pasta and, pushing his plate and glass away, he picked up his pen and set about the letters he had to write. The one to David Wallington was easy enough and he did that first.

My dear David,

How good to hear that you will be coming to Venice for the trial. I have just heard from my wife, who will also be working on it and expects to arrive here sometime in early November. From what you have written about the rooms in the Campo San Maurizio it sounds as though there would be plenty of room for all of us. Does that suit you?

I think you and Julia will get on all right. She's very sensible and not one to make a fuss about things that can't be helped and so the primitive bathroom ought not to fret her.

It struck Anthony as he reread that paragraph that it did not sound very complimentary about his wife and so he added a few sentences of description, explaining her standing at the Bar, so that David would not expect to be faced with some fragile tiresome siren. Then he started to tackle the more difficult letter.

My dear Julia,

What surprising news [he wrote laboriously]! I had heard of the Kesselring trial because David Wallington will be coming here for it too. I am glad that you two will meet, because I think you will like the boy.

He proposed to me some time ago that we should share a set of far more luxurious rooms than these over on the other side of Venice and I have already accepted. Would you be prepared to go along with that? I couldn't expect you to live here. As my housekeeper has just pointed out, there really isn't enough room and it's a pretty comfortless house. There are five bedrooms in the place David has found, which should give us all plenty of room.

Anthony reached for another sheet of writing paper and wrote, 'It will be pleasant to be able to show you Venice.' That did not sound enthusiastic enough and so he ripped the page in half and started again.

It will be wonderful to have you here. I can't wait to see you.
                                                Love, Anthony.

He hoped that Julia would not be hurt at the suggestion that they should share their digs with young David Wallington. He had never even considered the possibility that Julia would come to Venice and was dismayed at the prospect. Her presence in the city would mean a considerable adjustment to his life. No longer could he spend every moment of his time at the hospital, returning to his rooms merely to eat and sleep. He would have to start behaving like a husband again and he did not know whether he had the strength for that as well as the work he had undertaken to do for his orphans. It occurred to him that life might be much easier if he and Julia were to have another person in the house with them.

He addressed and stamped both letters and left them for Annunziata to post while he returned to the hospital.

Julia received his letter ten days later and was surprised by the tone of it. She reread it, noticing his exclamation of pleasure at her news and the way he had ended the letter, and decided that she was being over-imaginative.

'What does he say?' asked Comfort from the opposite side of the breakfast table.

'Ah,' said Julia, who had not told Comfort about the Venetian job. She explained and handed Anthony's letter across the table.

Making a superhuman effort not to give expression to her immediate jealousy, Comfort managed to say:

'I'm glad, Julia, for you and for him.'

'Thank you, Comfort,' said Julia, really touched. 'I won't insult you by asking whether you'll be all right alone here, because I know that you will.'

'I'll be fine,' agreed Comfort, thinking quite the opposite. 'Who is this Wallington boy he talks about? He's never mentioned him to me.'

'As far as I can remember, he's a much younger man who was with the same partisan group as Anthony. He told me that David Wallington was the best friend he'd made in the war. I hadn't realised before that he's a lawyer. Anthony always calls him "the boy".'

'Pretty tough on you to have to share your home with him,' said Comfort. Julia, who had been thinking just the same, merely smiled ruefully.

'Look, it's time for the news,' she said, leaning towards the wireless and switching it on.

Together they listened to an announcement that bread was to be rationed for the first time.

'Hell and damnation!' shouted Comfort, getting up from the table and flinging herself across the room. 'When is it going to stop? And don't you start being reasonable about this too,' she warned Julia.

'It would be pretty hard to be reasonable,' said Julia, thinking of VE Day and all the pleasure that peace had seemed to promise. 'Obviously we and the Yanks have to feed Germany, but it seems –'

'Bloody unfair,' finished Comfort, swearing far more than she usually did. 'Particularly since they're getting more than we are at the moment.'

'You're joking,' said Julia, thoroughly surprised.

Comfort shook her head, making the unkempt blonde curls fly about her face.

'No. I had dinner last night with a man from the Treasury and he told me.'

'Did he have much to say about what this government is doing to the economy?' asked Julia.

'No, he was either too discreet or too careful not to bore me,' answered Comfort with a smile. 'But he did give the distinct impression that he's worried about the loan.'

'Aren't we all?' said Julia. 'But don't let's argue again about that,' she added quickly.

Comfort came back to the table and poured some more coffee into Julia's cup.

'I'm beginning to see what you meant,' she said pacifically.

Julia looked up in delight, not because Comfort was agreeing with her at last, but because she seemed so much easier, so much more like her old self again.

'Do you suppose we'll ever be able to live a normal life again, Julia?' she said after a long moment.

'With Anthony back here or with unlimited amounts of food?'

'Both,' said Comfort, smiling her old familiar smile.

'God knows, I hope so,' answered Julia and then decided to confide a little. 'One reason I was so anxious to go to Venice was to try to persuade him to come home,' she said. 'He told me that the children there needed him so badly, but there are plenty here who must need him just as much.'

'I know,' said Comfort. 'I thought at the time that there was more to his determination to stay out there than he was telling me . . . He didn't tell you any more, did he?'

Julia shook her head.

'He's never told me anything more than he tells you,' she said with an easy smile.

Comfort tossed the curls back from her face.

'Do you mind?' she asked.

'No,' said Julia, not altogether truthfully. But with Comfort becoming more and more like the woman who had become Julia's dearest friend at university, she was not prepared to admit to jealousy. 'You're his sister . . . you've known him far longer than I. Why should I mind that you and he knew each other better than I could have done?'

'I'm glad,' said Comfort, her brilliant, slate-grey eyes softening. 'And I'm sorry that . . .'

'Hush,' said Julia, thinking that neither of them could cope with an emotional scene just then. 'The war's over now. Let's try to forget.'

Comfort said nothing, peering into Julia's eyes as though she were thinking of drawing her again.

'OK,' she said at last. 'And while you're out there you can try to find out what it is that keeps him in Italy and . . .'

'And get rid of it?' suggested Julia with a laugh in her voice.

'Well, I think you ought to try,' answered Comfort sternly.

'You know, I . . .' Julia was beginning when she caught sight of the kitchen clock. 'I must run. See you tonight. Are you in?'

'No. There's a party at Marcus's gallery. I've said I'll go. D'you want to come?'

'No, I don't think so,' answered Julia, buttoning up the jacket of her black suit and checking her face and hair in the mirror that Comfort had hung beside the big kitchen dresser. 'I find parties very lugubrious these days.' She seized her heavy black briefcase and hurried out of the room.

# Chapter Nine

Anthony's conviction that he would find the renewal of his married life easier with David Wallington in the house was shaken in August when David wrote to him from Rome asking him to testify at the trial for murder of one of the partisans who had fought with them in the mountains.

The man, whom they had known only as 'Paolo', had always been a troublemaker, but he had been a ferocious and loyal fighter, very brave and completely dedicated to ridding his country of the Nazis he hated. Anthony had heard nothing of him since leaving the mountains after the German surrender until he received David's letter.

> He's on trial for killing a collaborator – a man [wrote David] who went on from profitable dealings with the Nazis to playing a powerful part in the local black market. Paolo ran across him, I think by accident, and finding out who he was beat him up and got carried away. There is no doubt that Paolo killed him, but after what we all went through together, I feel it's our duty at least to testify to what he did in the war in the hope of a relatively lenient sentence.

David Wallington went on to explain when the trial was to take place and what would be involved if Anthony agreed to be a character witness. Even before he reached the end of his friend's letter, Anthony was angry enough to start writing his answer.

> Dear David [he wrote as calmly as he could],

How can you possibly think of giving evidence for Paolo? After the trouble he caused, and after what we both know of his quite uncontrollable violence, I think the longer he stays in prison the better. I would say that he is a danger to everyone who crosses him – and some who don't.

I know you'd fight to the death to protect the rights of any underdog you could find, but has it occurred to you that Paolo himself was probably involved in the black market and bumped off this other man because of current rivalry rather than as summary punishment for collaboration? I suppose that if it had happened at the time of the German surrender, when revenge seemed more important than anything else, I might have felt more inclined to help. But over a year later, his wretched temper should have cooled. All he had to do, if his victim was really a black marketeer, was report him, not kill him.

I can't testify for him, and I have to say that I'm surprised that *you of all people* are even considering it. The man is a liability and a thug. He ought to be locked up.

Anthony signed the letter coldly and hoped that it might persuade David not to intervene in the trial. There had been times during the war when both Anthony and David had wanted to expel Paolo from their particular band of partisans, but had been unable to risk it, since he had known too much about them all. Even David, who always believed the best about everyone he met, thought the likelihood of Paolo's going to the Germans to get his own back was too great, and they had put up with him until the war ended.

Anthony expected a protest from David and so he was not surprised to get another letter by return of post. In it, David wrote that he was not trying to persuade Anthony to testify against his will, but wanted to explain why he believed that he himself should do so, because he hated the idea of their being at loggerheads.

Everyone deserves a fair trial, whatever he has done. Moreover, we used Paolo's violence and thuggery whenever we went out against the Nazis. We'd never have got away after blowing up that supply convoy if it hadn't been for Paolo. You and I could have been picked up, tortured and even sent to a concentration camp. That seems to me to give us a duty to speak for him now. I don't intend to say anything beyond describing his courage in the fight to free Italy. There isn't anything else I can say. Obviously if I'm asked about his temper, I'll answer as you would.

Anthony thought that letter both critical and absurd, and he wondered what had happened to turn the cheerfully brave young officer he had known so well into a prig. David had always been unnecessarily influenced by his conscience and his devotion to the principles of fair play, but during the war he had at least allowed the demands of expediency and common sense to control his actions. They had trusted each other with their lives then, and without exchanging much information about themselves, formed a closer bond than any of their pre-war friendships had provided.

Anthony had admired David's gentleness as much as his fortitude and endurance in the often harsh conditions of their life in the mountains, and during the lonely months in Venice had looked forward to sharing his rooms with David. After reading David's letter Anthony's enthusiasm turned to profound misgivings.

He began to remember their few but violent disagreements and the occasions when David had done things he thought unjustifiably dangerous; to wonder whether, like so many others, David had been driven by the war to show talents and qualities that he would never bother to use in the ordinary life that peace would let him live. As the days passed and he became gloomier, Anthony even began to wonder whether the friendship they had shared had been no more than an illusion fostered by propinquity and shared danger.

He and Annunziata left the depressing house near the hospital at the end of August, when the heat was at its worst and the canal that ran beside the house was stinking like a primitive sewage farm. They both agreed that the new flat, with its huge, high-ceilinged rooms, was a distinct improvement. Anthony had no time to do more than look round the elegant apartment after he and Annunziata had followed the porter who was taking their luggage there.

As soon as Anthony had left to walk back to the hospital, Annunziata set about allocating bedrooms before telling the porter where to carry the cases and boxes. The biggest and most elaborate of the rooms she decided should go to Signora Giulia, and it seemed obvious to put the doctor in the communicating room next door. That left three rooms on the floor above, the biggest for the young Signor Wallington and the smallest for herself. There was only one bathroom and it was obvious to Annunziata's experienced eye that the plumbing was poor. She hoped that the Signora Giulia would understand and not expect American standards of gushing hot water all day.

Annunziata spent a blessedly busy day organising the new lodgings, sweeping cobwebs from all the corners and rearranging the gilded, painted furniture until the rooms looked as they should. They were beautifully cool even while she had the shutters open to blow the dust away and clear the air, and when she had finished everything, she sat at her ease in the small kitchen, waiting for the doctor to return for his evening meal.

As soon as she heard his step, she stood up and went out into the hall to welcome him and show him everything she had done to make his home comfortable. The sight of his face drove every thought of housewifery from her mind and she stood dumbly in front of him, the blood draining out of her face.

Anthony reached out to hold her, because she looked as though she might faint at any moment. She shook her head.

'Come and sit down, Annunziata,' he said, gently urging her towards the big salon. She obeyed him and waited, her eyes blank and her head bowed. Anthony had been accustomed to delivering bad news for almost the whole of his medical career and he had always found that the most difficult to give was an announcement of the death of a child, but nothing in his life had seemed as bad as the news he had to give Annunziata.

'Which one is it, *dottore*?' she asked, her voice hoarse, when he did not speak.

'Lucia,' he said quickly, not wanting to torture her by drawing out her anxiety any longer.

'What happened?'

'After she was caught, she was sent to Auschwitz,' he said, making himself look at Annunziata, although he could hardly bear the agony he could see in her eyes. 'The Red Cross has just received confirmation that she died very soon after she got there.'

Annunziata said nothing, but Anthony saw that she had gripped her hands together in front of her and was breathing heavily through clenched teeth. He wanted to comfort her, but there was no palliative to be given for the pain she was suffering.

'Thank you for telling me, *dottore*,' she said at last with the familiar heartbreaking dignity. 'May I go now?'

'Of course, Annunziata,' he said. 'You must do whatever you wish. And you must tell me of anything . . . anything I can do for you.'

She shook her greying head, which was now held proudly upright on her long neck. 'There is nothing anyone can do,' she said, smoothing her hands down over her apron. She looked down at it as though surprised to see herself wearing it, and then she wiped her hands. 'Your dinner is ready. Shall I bring it in here now?'

'You don't need to worry about that,' said Anthony, trying to help. 'I can get it later.'

'I would rather work,' said Annunziata. 'Now, or later?'

'Then now, please. Thank you very much.'

Anthony found it almost impossible to eat what she put in front of him, but he knew that his fasting would do nothing to help her, still less help her dead daughter, and he forced himself to finish everything. He then accepted Annunziata's offer of a guided tour of their new house and, since she obviously wanted it that way, tried to show no sign that the evening was any different from the others they had spent together.

When she had gone to bed he wrote to both Julia and David Wallington telling them what had happened so that neither should hurt or worry Annunziata with tactless questions or comments when they arrived.

David came first, in late September, and Julia followed five weeks later. She flew for the first time in her life and after the first moments of instinctive fear as the earth seemed to fall away from the aeroplane, she found it an exhilarating experience.

Sitting next to her was a tall, dark young man wearing UNRRA uniform. For the first part of the journey he sat absorbed in some papers, while Julia gazed out of the tiny porthole beside her seat and tried to identify the distant cities over which they flew and to imagine what the bomber pilots must have felt all through the war as they took their 'crates' to those same cities to dump tons and tons of high explosive on to them.

The aeroplane lurched suddenly and dropped down through the clouds so sharply that Julia felt as though her entrails were being sucked out of her body. She clutched the arm-rest of her seat and every thought was blanked out of her mind in a paroxysm of purely physical fear. The man who was sitting next to her looked up from his papers and patted her hand kindly.

'It's only the Alps, ma'am,' he said in a thick, creamy American accent that she would one day recognise as Virginian. 'You always bump a little bit over mountains.'

'Thank you,' said Julia, breathless but determined to display a proper British sang-froid. 'I was a trifle startled.'

He smiled, which seemed to lighten his heavy square face. Despite enormously thick dark eyebrows and a rounded pugnacious chin, it was a pleasant face, both intelligent and tolerant. Julia decided that she was justified in letting go a little of her assumed phlegm.

'I've never flown before,' she said. 'Are you a pilot? You seem to know a lot about it.'

'I was once,' he said, 'but there's not enough flying going on now to keep us all in business and so I'm grounded. I'm with UNRRA.' He gestured to his khaki uniform that carried no badges of rank or regiment and then said with a trace of bitterness in his voice: 'Life in Europe'd sure be easier if there were a few more planes. It's crazy. But a lot of things're crazy over here right now.'

'In what way?' Julia asked, becoming interested as well as polite.

'Beyond the impossible difficulties of feeding and housing all the DPs, I mean?'

'I just wouldn't know where to start, ma'am,' said the young American. 'I suppose the worst craziness is that we're trying to stamp out this damned, pernicious black market, because if we don't the relief supplies won't get to the people who they've been sent for. But in some places we have to let it go on, because without it even more people would be starving than are already.'

'It sounds an impossible contradiction,' said Julia frankly. 'Is that what you're involved with? Stamping out the black market?'

'Partly,' he said. 'We set up a Protective Service earlier this year to work with the indigenous police to deal with the black market in places like Italy and Poland. I'm seconded to the Italian section.'

'I can imagine that it's no sinecure,' said Julia.

'Excuse me?'

At that very American question, Julia smiled a little and explained what she had meant.

'It's difficult to see how it can be contained, though,' she went on, 'while there are such shortages of food and pharmaceuticals all over Europe.'

'I know,' said the American, apparently bearing no malice for her amusement, 'and there're plenty of other problems too: too many old scores being paid off and private battles fought. Stealing, lying, cheating and killing have all been seen as patriotic, anti-Fascist duties for too long, and it's hard to change that overnight.' He looked at her and saw that her strong face seemed suddenly very much paler than before. 'Are you OK, ma'am?' he asked.

Julia nodded and blew her nose vigorously.

'Yes, I'm fine,' she said without even trying to explain to him the realisation he had given her of the kind of world Anthony must have inhabited since his escape from prison camp. No wonder he had found some aspects of the Christmas she and Comfort had tried to give him difficult to accept. 'By the way, my name is Julia Gillingham.'

'Hi,' said the American. 'Jackson French. My friends call me Jack.'

'How do you do?' said Julia, apparently amusing him as much as he had earlier amused her. He ignored her question and went back to their previous conversation.

'But it's not only their guys. Our own don't help with their goddamned "liberating".'

'Is there much of that – looting, I mean?' asked Julia.

He nodded. 'Guys who've been in the firing line think it's their pay-off. The ones from the battle lines have rules, though. You never liberate anything from a house with people living in it, but you can do what you like with stuff from abandoned buildings. But some of the boys who weren't here for the real fighting don't follow the same rules. Some of them will take anything – from anybody. It's not so bad in Italy, but they think Germany's fair game to everyone – GIs, correspondents, photographers, the lot.'

Julia said nothing. There seemed to be nothing to say. After what Germany had done to the world, after the evidence of unbelievable atrocities perpetrated in the camps, after the painful struggle to stop them with all the deaths and agonies that that had entailed, private looting seemed almost trivial. But it shocked her all the same.

'Do they sell the stuff? If not, how do they get it home?' she asked.

'A bit of both,' came the answer. 'It's not a statistic to be proud of, but did you know that in July last year our people in Europe sent home a million dollars more than their combined pay? In just one month!'

And that at a time when Europeans are starving and we are mortgaging our future to the States to do what we can to feed them and try to create a peace that will last, Julia thought, but there seemed no point in saying it.

'We're nearly there,' said the American, leaning across Julia to look out of the porthole. 'What're you going to be doing in Venice?'

'I'm going to join my husband, Anthony Gillingham,' she said, 'He's been here since the end of the war.'

'I've heard a lot about him,' said the young man. 'He's doing a great job with those orphan kids.'

'Do you know him then?' Julia asked, her face alight with eagerness and healthier-looking colour.

'No. We've never met,' he said. 'But in the relief business you tend to get to know who the other guys are. Is he meeting you at the airport?'

'I hope so, but he may not have received my telegram about our ETA,' said Julia, relieved to think that the freedoms brought both by the war and by her age allowed her to accept such questions without the automatic suspicion drilled into her throughout her childhood and adolescence.

'Well I'll stick around then to make sure. If he doesn't show, I'll see that you get across to Venice.'

'That's extraordinarily good of you, Mr French.'

'Call me Jack.'

'Thank you. I don't know why you should take such trouble for me,' said Julia formally.

'No trouble, ma'am,' he said, looking surprised. 'Ah, now just you look down there,' he added as the aeroplane banked steeply.

Julia obediently hunched sideways again to look out of the porthole. There, below her, sparkling in bright sunlight was the most extraordinary sight she had ever seen: a sudden confusion of the familiar pink-and-white diapered front of the Doge's palace, then a space filled with people, red flagpoles, domes, a flash of blue and gold at the back and, in front of it all, the green-grey sea licking at the base of the glamorous buildings.

'Good heavens!' she said involuntarily. 'Good Lord! Even the paintings don't give you any idea.' The plane turned again and she could see nothing but the water. The brief glimpse of the city had been like some heavenly dream lost in a sudden awakening.

'We're coming in now,' said Jackson French. 'Brace yourself. Some of these guys of yours aren't so good at landings.'

Julia sat back in her own seat and braced herself, but it turned out not to be necessary: the landing was impeccably smooth. She twinkled at the American and he acknowledged her pleasure with a disarming grin, thinking how much less formidable she seemed than when he had first noticed her.

'OK, OK,' he said, 'some of yours are just as good as some of us. It's only that as a flyer you tend to be a bit critical.'

'That's all right, Mr French,' said Julia still teasing him a little, 'I can quite see how tiresome we "Limeys" are to you.'

They got out of the aeroplane both laughing and waited for their baggage to be unpacked, before presenting their passes and letters of authorisation at the military checkpoint. Then Julia, unable to contain her eagerness any longer, left the American standing by his baggage and walked into the hall to find Anthony.

The disappointment she felt when she had checked each waiting face was much sharper than she would have admitted to anyone.

'No luck then?' came the voice of the American.

'No,' said Julia calmly. 'Presumably he never got my telegram, or perhaps he's been kept at the hospital. Never mind.'

Before Jackson French could answer, a tall, broad-shouldered young man with a thin, lively face came hesitantly towards her. Seeing the American turn to speak to her, he checked, but then with an oddly appealing smile he walked on, pushing his smooth black hair back over his ears.

'Mrs Gillingham?' he asked in a very deep voice when he had reached her.

'Why, yes,' answered Julia in some surprise. 'Have we met?'

'No, but your husband asked me to come and pick you up. He's just managed to get hold of some scarce drugs and so he's had to do a couple of important operations this afternoon. David Wallington,' he said, holding out his hand.

'Good Lord!' said Julia, holding out her own. 'I mean, how do you do? Sorry to sound surprised. Anthony has always written about you as a "boy". I've pictured you quite differently.'

'We did tend to call him *"Il Nonno"*. He was probably just taking his revenge for that,' he said, adding when he noticed her looking blank, "The Grandfather".'

'Ah,' said Julia. 'I expect that's it then. Thank you for coming to meet me.' She shook hands with him and then turned to thank the American for his help and say goodbye.

'Anything I can do to help you in Venice, Mrs Gillingham, you just let me know,' he said before he touched his cap, grinned amiably at David Wallington and left.

'Don't look so surprised, Mrs G,' said the young man easily as he saw the surprise on her face. 'They're all astonishingly generous, but they haven't much idea of English notions of when it's decent to get personal.'

'I'm surprised my face is so transparent,' said Julia. 'I thought I'd learned to hide all emotions – at least in court. Now tell me, how is Anthony?'

'All right, I think,' said David. 'The boat's this way.'

'You think,' repeated Julia seriously. 'That sounds as though you're not sure. Is he ill?'

'Lord no! Tetchy and a bit depressed, I think. You'll cheer him up a lot. Here we are. Can you manage if I hand the cases down to you?'

Julia nodded and stepped gingerly into the damp-bottomed motor boat, wondering whether her scrupulously mended and polished shoes would suffer: she had no clothing coupons left and no chance of getting any more if they did.

David Wallington wondered what it was that was making her look so serious. Anthony had once shown him a photograph of her, but it was almost impossible for him to connect that smiling girl with the stern-faced woman he had met at the airport. He had been looking forward to her arrival, assuming that she would be able to soothe Anthony out of his difficult moods and make it possible for them to make peace with each other, but at that moment he was full of foreboding. He passed the luggage down to Julia and noticed a faint smile twisting her lips up at one side of her mouth.

Stepping down after her, he asked her what was amusing her. At that she smiled directly at him and although the smile was still lopsided he caught a glimpse of the laughing girl in the photograph.

'At myself!' she said. 'Ever since I discovered that the only way of getting from the Lido to Venice proper was by boat I've been envisaging a romantic, velvet-seated gondola rowed by a pair of operatic tenors.' Julia gestured at the peeling paint, the rusty engine and the thin film of viscous-looking water that clung to the inside of the boat. 'This is a lot more like reality.'

'Indeed,' said David Wallington, with the same appealing smile on his face. 'And it's no bad thing to have an unromantic arrival at Venice. It can be a bit overwhelming otherwise.'

Julia, who had been peering around the featureless flat grey water and sky all around her, looked back.

'How long have you been here?'

'Only since the end of last month,' he said, 'when I was transferred here from Rome. Permanently transferred that is; whenever I could wangle a week or even a weekend here I'd make sure I got it. I've always been inordinately fond of Venice.'

To Julia that casual announcement of love suggested a familiarity with the city that seemed alien to such a large, friendly, obvious young man and she asked him whether he had known Italy well before the war.

'My mother is Italian,' he said with a slight smile. 'Not Venetian – and in fact she always said she hated the place, thought it very sinister and peculiar – but I like Venice far more than Florence, which is her family's home. You look surprised.'

Julia searched his good-looking face for signs of foreignness, and then, when she saw him looking slightly surprised, apologised for peering at him.

'I was just taken aback,' she said. 'You seem so very English with your voice and those blue eyes; but now I do see that hair as smooth and dark as yours isn't very . . .'

'Now you've really insulted me,' he said, but there was laughter in his voice. 'I'm a half-Italian Scot – and there's not a single drop of beastly English blood in me!' Before Julia could comment on that he went on in a different voice: 'We'll be there in few minutes, but don't look round yet. The view of the Fondamente Nuove is disappointing to say the least. Look to your left and concentrate on the cemetery.'

She obeyed and watched the thin-looking grey water lap at the foot of a long, low peach-coloured wall that was topped with white stone. Dark-green cypresses reared up behind the wall, punctuating the tips and domes of the white mausolea that clustered among them. Delighted by the mixture of colours and shapes, Julia thought not only how odd it was to be ordered to gaze at a cemetery to avoid a depressing view, but also what a wonderful place it would be in which to be buried.

David turned the boat suddenly to Julia's right and, startled, she looked from side to side at the shabby buildings that towered over the small canal. Nothing could have been further from the brief, fantastical glimpse she had had of the Piazzetta. If it had not been for David Wallington's warning, she thought that she might have been struck with gloom, for the tall houses that seemed to crowd her on either side had no part to play in her dreams of the romantic floating city where she and Anthony might rediscover all the delights of a love that had been confiscated by the war.

'I'd thought of taking you ceremoniously down the Grand Canal, but then I realised that your first sight of it ought to be with Anthony and so we're going by rather a tedious way to avoid it all.'

'I can see why Anthony thinks a lot of you,' said Julia, touched by the young man's perspicacity and thinking that if he were to continue to be so sensitive to their feelings, his presence in their house might not be quite as infuriating as she had expected. 'That was kind.'

David said nothing, but turned the boat to her left again. Soon Julia lost all sense of direction as they crossed larger and smaller canals, turned first one way and then the other, turned she would have thought right back on their own wake. Every so often she caught sight of a graceful Gothic window, or some pretty carving on a doorway and she would sit more upright and peer about her, but what pleased her most as they plunged deeper and deeper into the city were the bridges: tiny most of them, built of the same sucked-peachstone brick as the houses, topped and edged with white stone, they arched over the dark-green water of the canals with delectable grace.

'Here we are.' David stopped the engine at a right-angled bend of the canal, tied the boat up to some railings and leaned over to heave Julia's baggage up on to the slippery white steps that led up to a little street. Then he got out of the boat and stood, one large hand outstretched to her. Julia took it and was heaved up almost like a suitcase herself.

'There is a water entrance to the house, but it's much more practical to leave the boat here and walk round to the front door. I hope you don't mind,' he said, easily picking up the bags and cases that had caused her such trouble earlier. 'Take the first on the right. I'm behind you.'

Julia obeyed and almost immediately found herself in a square, bounded on three sides by big houses, each with the pointed Gothic windows she had so much admired, and on the last by the smooth pale-grey façade of a neo-classical church. The relative modernity of the church might have disappointed her, but there was a thoroughly Venetian brick campanile leaning gently above and behind it, which consoled her. In the centre of the square, looking solid and practical, was a hexagonal stone well, with a domed cover of scratched black iron. A solid black spout curved away from one side of the well, water dripping from its mouth on to the shallow steps below.

'So this is the Campo San Maurizio,' said Julia, faced with the brick and stone reality of the place to which she had sent her recent letters. 'Which is our house?'

'This one,' he said, leading the way and putting her luggage down on the ground in order to unlock the big wooden door. 'We've the first, second and third floors. You carry on up. Anthony's probably back by now.'

Julia did not wait to see whether David followed her and in that moment she would not have cared if he had given away all her laboriously mended clothes and shoes to the population of the city. She climbed the stone staircase to the first floor, pushed open a pair of double doors that faced the top of the stairs and found herself in an immensely long room with a painted ceiling and many gilt-framed looking glasses. There seemed to be little furniture beyond a circular table with six matching chairs, a pair of hard-looking sofas and a selection of carved chairs, all with the gilt and paint peeling off them.

The size and battered splendour of the room dwarfed Anthony, who was standing by one of the windows at the far end, apparently staring down intently at something outside. Julia walked towards him, trying to slow her racing heart.

'Anthony?' she said quietly when he had not moved. He looked up and she was shocked to see that his face was even thinner and yellower than it had been at Christmas.

'Oh, there you are,' he said, as though they had seen each other an hour or so before instead of almost a year ago. 'Good trip?'

'Not bad,' she answered, trying to match his detached tone. She remembered that it had taken twenty-four hours before he had relaxed properly at Christmas. 'Are you all right?'

'So, so,' he said as she went to kiss him. He responded and patted her shoulder casually.

'How were the operations?' Julia asked, wondering if there had been some terrible disaster. 'David Wallington said that you'd had some emergencies.'

'Oh, they went all right. Now, why don't you sit down and rest your feet?' he said, obviously making an effort. 'Annunziata was planning to bring you some tea and I expect David has told her ... Ah, here she is.'

Julia turned to see a gaunt middle-aged woman setting a tray down on the big round table. Anthony strolled towards her, saying something in Italian that Julia could not understand. Then he turned to her and introduced her to Annunziata.

Julia shook hands with her, wanting to say something about the death of her daughter but quite unable to think of anything that would sound neither impertinent nor inadequate. Looking into those deep-set dark eyes, she could not help remembering the photographs and films she had seen of the concentration camps. Putting the memory aside, she merely said something about how grateful she was that Annunziata had looked after her husband so well.

'She doesn't understand any English,' said Anthony, looking mildly amused. 'Shall I translate?'

'Please,' said Julia, whose languages did not include Italian. She watched the other two as he translated her sentence and was curious to see that there was a faint flush in Anthony's cheeks as he listened to the housekeeper's response. Julia recognised the words, 'Signora Giulia' and 'Dottore', but nothing else. She looked questioningly at her husband. Shrugging, he translated what his housekeeper had said.

'She says that it has been both a pleasure and an honour to look after the doctor and she is pleased that his wife is now here to help make him happy again.'

'*Grazie, signora*,' said Julia, using one of the few phrases she had been able to mug up on the aeroplane.

'*Prego, Signora Giulia*,' answered Annunziata. Then she said something else, which Anthony told Julia meant that she was fetching a tea tray. Julia turned to him, seizing the opportunity of the housekeeper's absence to say:

'You're looking awfully tired, Anthony. Can't you. . .'

'Oh don't fuss,' he said irritably. 'All doctors are tired these days. It's nothing.'

'Fuss?' said Julia lightly. 'Did I ever do that?' Anthony managed to smile at her.

'No, you never did, thank God,' he said just as Annunziata brought in the tea.

# Chapter Ten

After they had drunk their tea alone in the large salon, Anthony pushed his chair back.

'I really ought to be getting back to the hospital now,' he said. 'Will you be all right here?'

'I'll be perfectly all right,' said Julia, drawing the straight brown eyebrows together over her nose as she did when a witness said something that did not fit the strategy she had planned for a case. 'But couldn't I come with you? I'd like a walk to stretch my legs after the journey and I'd love to see some of the children, not to speak of Venice itself.'

'Oh well, why not?' said Anthony after a surprisingly long pause. 'But wrap up well; it gets very cold at this time in the evening.'

'I can imagine,' said Julia, pulling down the jacket of her brown tweed travelling suit as she got out of her chair. The suit had been made for her before the war and was of such good quality that it had lasted well, but it was inevitably not as warm as it had once been. 'It was freezing on the way over from the Lido. I'll go and get a coat if you'd wait?'

Anthony nodded.

'Your room is the one directly over this,' he said, but Annunziata came out of the kitchen as soon as she heard Julia's step and escorted her up to the room. Julia almost burst into laughter when she saw the bed in which she was expected to sleep. It was immense, with a high, carved Rococo bedhead and curtains of tattered green-and-gold silk suspended from a heavenly choir of small gold putti. Comfort could have carried it off, Julia thought, but she with her warm flannel nightgowns and her square-chinned serious face and thick, straight, brown hair would look completely absurd in it.

Annunziata distracted her from the imaginary picture by saying something slowly and clearly in Italian. Julia knit her brows and tried to work out what it could be. Annunziata smiled, repeated what she had said even more slowly and made a pantomime of opening one of the suitcases David had left on the floor.

'Ah, yes, thank you,' said Julia, equally slowly and clearly, nodding at the same time. She fetched her heavy camel overcoat out of the bigger suitcase, smiled wordlessly at Annunziata, who was already busy taking frocks and skirts out of the smaller case, and went to join Anthony, resolving to learn the language as soon as possible. As she went downstairs, she put on the coat and pulled on her gloves.

'I'm ready,' she said, putting her head round the doors into the salon. David Wallington was standing by the table, drinking a cup of cold tea and he looked round to smile at her. Anthony stubbed out a cigarette, dropped the newspaper he was reading and picked up a coat he had left draped over one of the chairs.

'See you later,' he said coolly to David and then turned to Julia. 'Let's go. If we walk rather than taking the boat, you'll see more of Venice,' he said.

'Walk?' said Julia, forgetting that all the pretty bridges she had seen that afternoon must mean that pedestrians used them. 'I didn't know one could in Venice.'

Anthony laughed, transforming his face from a mask of tired and rather bitter anxiety to something much more like himself.

'It does seem odd, doesn't it? But in fact, it's much easier to get about the city on foot than by water – unless you've much to carry. Come on.'

He took her gloved right hand and hustled her down the stone staircase to street level. The way to the orphanage lay across St Mark's Square and there at last Julia found the grandeur that had been missing from her trip with David from the Lido airport. She and Anthony walked into the square from the southwestern corner. Julia tripped over an uneven paving stone and was so busy looking at her feet that she did not even realise that they had arrived until Anthony said:

'There!'

She looked up to see an immense paved area, marked with rectangular patterns of white stone as though for some esoteric ball game. On either side of her were straight rows of neoclassical buildings of dirty dark-grey stone, with a colonnaded arcade running beneath them. Julia found herself looking down the whole length of the piazza to St Mark's. She knew it from a hundred photographs, paintings and written descriptions and had expected to be as astounded by the reality as she had been by her brief glimpse of the Doge's Palace from the aeroplane; but this time she found herself disappointed. In the weird grey dusk all the buildings had an extraordinary thinness about them, as though they were two-dimensional, and the basilica itself looked like a series of stage flats for some ice-skating spectacular.

Julia turned to express something of her sense of anticlimax to Anthony, but he was not looking at her.

'Isn't it superb?' he said and she had not the heart to contradict him. 'Come on, Julia. We ought to walk slowly nearer and nearer so that you can see a little more detail with every step. David thinks it's best seen at this time of day, but I like a bit more colour myself.'

Julia obeyed and found that he was right: a little more was revealed to her as they drew ever nearer. The outline of the five domes sharpened and the stone carving above the arches blanched and revealed itself as the crisped foam of Ruskin's never-to-be-forgotten description. Gradually the gold and colours of the mosaics could be seen and the blood red of the two great flagpoles in front of the basilica. At last the Gillinghams stood only about ten feet from the central door into the narthex and Julia discovered that some of her disappointment had gone.

No longer dwarfed by the length of the piazza and the ordered severity of the colonnaded buildings on either side, the extraordinary church seemed mysterious and tantalising.

'Can one go in?' Julia asked, but Anthony shook his head.

'I should wait until David can take you. He knows so much about it that you ought to have him as escort for your first visit: I could only parrot what he's told me.'

When at last they left the theatrical scene behind and set off again for the hospital, Anthony tucked Julia's hand in the crook of his elbow and started to talk to her about the children he was taking her to see. As he talked, his voice relaxed and became warm and kind.

By the time they had reached the gates of the hospital orphanage, Julia had heard the case histories of nearly a dozen children. They meant very little to her until Anthony led her into the largest of the wards in his hospital and introduced some of the children to her.

The first ward they entered was long and cavernous, with a floor of alternating squares of apricot and cream-coloured marble, pale-grey walls and a high ceiling. Long rows of black iron beds covered with white blankets lined each side. Anthony led her down one side, speaking to a child here and smoothing the hair of another one there.

Many of them were attractive, with huge, wistful dark eyes, and occasionally one would smile brilliantly and answer a question of Anthony's or chatter incomprehensibly at him, but others lay still, looking desperately ill. Julia watched him comforting them and touching them and smiled at his tenderness. In the old days he had kept himself aloof from his patients, but he was so kind to these that he might have been their father.

They reached the end of the ward and Anthony had a word with a uniformed nurse sitting at a desk, and then took Julia on to the next ward, which was livelier than the first. Some of the children lay under their bedclothes, but others were out of bed, hopping about on crutches or playing in groups on the marble floor, and they crowded round Anthony as soon as they saw him, showing off their skills with the crutches and asking him for *dolci* and *cioccolatini*, which Julia understood without much difficulty.

She was as impressed by their cheerfulness as she was shocked by the fact that each one of them seemed to be recovering from an amputation. During one moment when Anthony was relatively far away from them, she said quietly:

'What's happened to them all? How did they lose their legs and arms?'

'Mines,' said Anthony briefly and with justifiable bitterness. 'Both the Germans and the Allies laid innumerable mines all over Italy. Hundreds of them have not yet been recovered or defused. These children have stepped on them when playing at the edge of a field or a wood. But they're the lucky ones. Most are killed. God knows when there will be enough money and skill to fit all these with artificial limbs. Come on.'

He said goodbye to his chattering, hopping patients and led the way out of the ward and Julia followed.

'Aren't we going in there?' she asked as they passed a pair of double doors. Anthony turned and shook his head.

'No; those are the TB wards down there. They have their own doctor in charge, and besides, I'm not having you exposed to TB if I can help it,' he said.

'Is there much tuberculosis?' Julia asked.

'Yes, a fair amount, and there's so little we can do for them. Streptomycin has miraculous results, but it's desperately scarce. I'd prefer it if we could get all the tubercular patients up into the mountains, but there simply aren't the facilities. Here we are, Julia. You'll like this lot.'

He led the way into a cheerful room, quite different from any of the wards they had seen.

'None of these is really ill any more, but they still need care,' he said before turning to greet the nurse in charge. Even before he had finished talking to her, a noisy group of children had clustered about Anthony, calling him *'Dottore'* and wheedling for sweets, chattering away and pulling at his clothes to draw attention to something they had made or drawn.

Julia watched in growing astonishment and pleasure as Anthony played and joked with them and handed out a few sweets, ruffled the dark heads and called cheerful remarks to the nurse at the far end of the room. Only one child did not join in the shouting, laughing, sleeve-tugging group around him and after a time, he deliberately went across to the chair in which she was curled, picked her up and cuddled her. Her name seemed to be Flavia and he murmured it over and over again. At last, she achieved a tremulous smile, put her skinny arms around his neck and tucked her small, dark head under his chin. Across her bowed head he looked at Julia.

He seemed to be asking her to understand why he had had to stay with the children, but Julia thought that she had understood that a long time ago. She watched the gentleness with which he coaxed Flavia to relax her hold on him, bending his handsome head a little to whisper to her. He seemed to be urging her to do something and eventually she lifted her head away from his neck, brushed her lanky hair away from her huge tear-stained eyes and said very quietly:

'*Buona sera, signora.*'

'*Buona sera*, Flavia,' answered Julia, wondering what could have happened to the child to reduce her to such a state of clinging terror. When he felt her relax, Anthony murmured something to her and put her down, saying to Julia:

'Come and meet Sister Caroline.'

Julia followed him and was surprised to be introduced to the fair haired nurse in English.

'How do you do, Mrs Gillingham,' she said in a cheerful American voice. 'We're all so glad you've been able to come. It'll do the doctor a lot of good to have you here.'

'Thank you, Sister ...' Julia was beginning when there was a fracas at the far end of the ward. The nurse looked at Anthony, but he shook his head and left to deal with it himself.

'He's had a difficult time here,' she said quietly to Julia, while they both watched Anthony's retreating figure. 'He needs rest, but he will never rest. I'm glad for his sake that you have come. I hope you can help him.'

Julia looked at her, noticing both the calm affection in her pale-blue eyes and the signs of hard work on her roughened hands. She looked thoroughly competent but kind as well and rather pretty.

It struck Julia that Sister Caroline might have had something to do with Anthony's decision to stay in Italy, which would explain his reluctance to allow her to go with him to the hospital. But even as she put words to the idea, she dismissed it. Surely if the two of them were in love, the nurse would never have spoken about Anthony as she had or so obviously welcomed his wife's presence.

'I expect you have helped him as much as he'd allow anyone to help,' said Julia, feeling her way.

The nurse smiled slightly but shook her head.

'That's it, you see,' she said. 'He won't allow it. But something is worrying him badly and I'm sure you'll be able to find out what it is. I can't.'

Julia did not explain that she had never been able to persuade Anthony to do or tell her anything he did not want to do or tell.

'I expect he has a great deal to worry about,' she said, gesturing around the big noisy ward.

'It's more than that, Mrs Gillingham,' said the nurse, slowly. 'Something has happened to him, damaged something in him. Haven't you noticed any change in him?'

There was an earnestness in her voice that got through Julia's defences and instead of choking off any more questions with her effective cold stare, she simply nodded. There was a rueful twist to her lips.

'Well that's settled them. Caroline, don't let them get too boisterous, will you? It's bad for them.' Anthony's voice stopped any more confidences between the two women.

'No, of course not, Doctor Gillingham,' said the American nurse. 'By the way, I am concerned about Alessandro. He . . .'

Julia turned away to let them have their professional discussion in peace. She noticed that the pathetic Flavia was sitting curled up in the chair where Anthony had left her, watching the other children playing. Her obvious loneliness troubled Julia, who walked straight over to the chair and knelt down on the hard, marble floor beside it. The child seemed to cower away in terror. Julia smiled and hesitantly put out a hand to stroke Flavia's hair, murmuring her name.

Flavia shuddered and shrank, pressing herself further back into the chair. Julia could not bear to leave her so afraid and so she persisted with her gentle stroking of the lanky, matted hair. She wanted to ask the child how old she was, but her rudimentary phrase-book Italian would let her do no more than say:

'How are you, Flavia?'

When the child opened her mouth at last to whisper the international 'OK', Julia felt almost as though the child had given her the welcome to Venice that Anthony had withheld.

'Good,' she said, still stroking. 'I'll come and see you again, if I may,' she went on in English, knowing that Flavia could not understand, but thinking that the sound of kindness in her voice might reach through the lack of a shared language.

'Well done, Mrs Gillingham,' came the quiet voice of the nurse from behind Julia. She looked round to see both Sister Caroline and Anthony standing watching her and stood up to face them. Anthony's face looked empty, but there was warm approval on Sister Caroline's and Julia smiled back at her.

'Can you find your own way back, Julia?' asked Anthony rather coldly. 'There are things I have to deal with here.'

'Couldn't I stay and help?'

'Not just now,' he said. 'We haven't time to see to you. I'll be back for dinner. Can you find your way?'

'I expect so,' answered Julia, determined to be accommodating. 'But if you were to sketch me a quick map it would help.'

With an irritability she would not have expected, Anthony turned and stalked down the long ward to Sister Caroline's desk, pulled out a piece of paper and started scribbling on it.

'You see what I mean?' said the nurse quietly to Julia. 'It's so unlike him to behave like that, but it's been happening more and more recently.'

'Yes, I do see,' answered Julia, worried and yet at the same time relieved to think that it had not been she who had caused Anthony's odd mood. He came back with his hastily drawn map and gave it to her.

'Thank you, Anthony,' she said, taking it, 'and thank you for bringing me here. Goodbye, Sister Caroline. I hope to see you again soon.'

They shook hands and Julia left the hospital to pick her way through the dark narrow streets back towards the Campo San Maurizio. It was considerably more difficult than she had expected. The route she and Anthony had taken from St Mark's Square to the hospital had seemed almost straight when they were walking together, but as Julia tried to retrace it, it seemed twisted and difficult. She kept discovering that she had made a wrong turning and had to turn back on her tracks. The openings off the main streets all seemed to look the same and there were times when she tried two or three before she found the right one.

What little daylight there had been had gone and the few lamps hanging from the sides of houses were quite inadequate. Stopping underneath one to check the map, Julia felt a tingling shock as she heard footsteps close behind her. Reminding herself that she had walked unafraid through the completely lightless streets of blacked-out London all through the war and managed to find her way to all sorts of places, she folded up the map and set off boldly, ignoring any possible pursuers. But as she strode forwards, she could not help remembering what the American she had met on the aeroplane had told her about crime in Italy and the lack of any effective controls.

The footsteps seemed to follow her whenever she turned a corner, and they echoed disagreeably from building to building so that she could never be quite sure how close they were. Coming at last to a small bridge that looked familiar, Julia peered at the small white sign that gave its name and consulted Anthony's map yet again. The footsteps stopped and Julia turned sharply round. There was no one behind her. The steps started again and seemed to be retreating. With an explosive sigh, Julia gathered her common sense and set off again.

At last, unmolested and apparently unfollowed, she came to a yellow sign with an arrow directing her to S. Marco and she speeded up to emerge, sweating with tension despite the cold, into the great empty square. Even the pigeons had gone. The lonely space seemed almost more frightening than the close, dark streets had done.

Deliberately distracting herself from her irrational fears, Julia thought about the child she had just left and wondered again what had happened to make her so withdrawn and afraid. Julia had never considered herself at all maternal, but the protectiveness that the child had aroused in her and the response she had called forth when she eventually spoke brought an instinctive smile to Julia's wide mouth. She thought she could understand what mothers must feel. 'Happy mothers', she said to herself, amending the proposition as she remembered her own childhood.

Memories of Flavia carried Julia across the square, out into the widish street that led away from it across the bridges and through the squares until she came at last to the house Anthony had rented. Relieved and yet ashamed of her childish fears, she let herself in through the front door and climbed the stone steps up to the first floor. She was surprised to notice how tired she was and decided to sit for a while in the salon before going upstairs to her bedroom to change.

Walking in through the double doors, she found David Wallington sitting on one of the sofas, a pipe in one hand and an Italian newspaper in the other. He stood up as soon as he noticed her arrival and quickly asked whether she minded his pipe.

'Not at all,' she said, pulling off her comfortable old brown felt hat. 'It's such a friendly, domestic sort of thing that it's very comforting.'

'Are you in need of comfort, Mrs Gillingham?' he asked, looking at her through his thick, dark eyelashes. She was surprised that he should ask so personal a question after their short acquaintance and simply looked at him with the expression that her colleagues would have recognised. David was rather taken aback and shrugged slightly.

'Did Anthony not come back with you?' he asked.

Julia shook her head. 'Something important kept him at the

hospital,' she said, betraying none of her feelings. 'He said he'd be back for dinner.'

'Well, that won't be for a while. Would you like a glass of wine?' David asked.

Julia carefully reminded herself that it was hardly David's fault that Anthony had hurt her and that it was as much Anthony's fault as David's that he was sharing their temporary home.

'Why not? I'll just nip upstairs and get rid of these,' she said, trying to sound friendly as she gestured to her heavy overcoat and walking shoes.

While she was up in her room she scribbled a letter to Comfort, telling her about the hospital and about Flavia, adding:

The children so obviously adore him that it's easy to see why he felt he had to stay with them until someone else could take over their care. I really don't think you need to worry about his motives or about mysteries or conspiracies. He is most desperately needed here and clearly feels – as he told us – that he has a moral debt to this country.

She signed the letter and stuck it in an envelope so that she could post it the following day. Collecting a book she had brought with her so that she would not have to make conversation for too long, she then went downstairs to have a drink with David Wallington.

They talked amiably enough about the international situation and the trial on which they would both be working, and Julia allowed herself to relax a little. She found David both charming and amusing, and he asked her no more unsuitably personal questions, but she wished that he were somewhere else.

For his part, he discovered that she was not quite as formidable as she had seemed at first and that beneath her seriousness there lurked a sense of humour and a warmth of interest in other people. Despite that, he still found it hard to connect her with Anthony. There was nothing in Mrs Gillingham's gritty intelligence and common sense to match the mixture of passionate commitment, powerful anger and inexplicable sadness that made her husband's friendship at once so important and such a challenge, and nothing in her pleasant looks to compete with his extraordinary handsomeness. David wondered how they had ever come to marry.

Attempting to find out more about her, he asked Julia what she was reading.

'I'm rereading the *Sonnets from the Portuguese*,' she said readily, picking up the thin, floppy, brown-leather book.

'I don't much like Elizabeth Barrett's stuff,' said David, wrinkling his nose.

'Perhaps you prefer her husband's,' suggested Julia, and then in a voice of deliberate casualness, which made David smile, quoted: '"That's my last Duchess painted on the wall, Looking as if she were alive ..."'

'Not really,' he admitted with a laugh. 'I like novels better than poetry.'

'So do I normally,' said Julia with a slight smile, 'but I was moved to read these because ... Never mind,' she finished, not knowing him well enough to say what she really meant: I was moved to read them because they were written by a woman out of passionate devotion to her husband.

'You must know Italy very well,' she said to change the subject.

'Only parts,' he said. 'My mother used to bring my brother and me to her house at Fiesole every summer. It was never as much home as Scotland, but we both got awfully fond of it, and made a lot of friends among the other families there.'

'Where is your brother now?' asked Julia and then wished she had not as his face seemed to close down as though shutters had been put up over his eyes. It was a stupid question to have asked any young man of fighting age after such a war. She watched David make an effort to answer.

'He's in Scotland now and all right, they think,' he said slowly. 'But he had a bad time in Changi.'

'I'm so sorry,' said Julia at once. 'It was crass of me to ask.'

'No, no, please don't worry, Mrs Gillingham,' said David, seeing that she really minded having upset him. 'He is getting better now, although still pretty weak, I gather.'

'Don't bother with the "Mrs Gillingham",' said Julia, trying to make amends for her insensitivity. 'Do please call me Julia.'

'All right. Thank you very much. Can I pour you some more wine?'

'I think not,' she said and looked down at her gold wristwatch. 'Do you know what time dinner is likely to be?'

'Half-past seven,' he said.

'Then I think I'll go and have a bath if there's any water,' she said. David's expression seemed to say, 'You'll be lucky.'

'I see,' said Julia. 'Well, I'll try. See you later, David.'

'Yes, indeed,' he said, getting up and watching her as she walked to the door. It seemed strange to him that so tall a woman could move with such easy grace, and he wondered whether she had always carried herself so well or whether she had had to work to achieve such unselfconscious assurance.

David thought that he had never met a woman who could talk so well and yet demand so little in return, and it occurred to him that it might have been that combination of attributes that had attracted Anthony in the beginning. Although Julia had obviously considered his first question impertinent, she had not appeared to mind when he disagreed with her quite robustly and she had tried neither to drag the conversation round to herself nor to draw compliments from him. Perhaps it was because she was so much older, he thought as he refilled his pipe and picked up the paper again, that she seemed so different from the women he had known in London before the war.

# Chapter Eleven

Julia had her bath in tepid water and then hurried to dress in a warm woollen frock. Despite the winter underclothes she had on and the thick material of the dress, she was still cold and she wished that there were a fire in her room instead of the stove that was warm enough to the touch but seemed to do nothing to temper the icy chill of the marble floor or the echoing space of the room. There were no curtains at the windows, only external shutters, and no carpets. Despite its magnificence the room seemed comfortless as well as cold.

Julia looked longingly at her thick grey dressing gown, which she had often worn over her clothes at home during the worst winters of the war. If she had been about to dine alone with Anthony she might have worn it, but David Wallington's presence irritatingly imposed a certain formality on her.

Having done her face and hair, she went downstairs and was relieved to see Anthony standing next to the stove, a glass of wine in his hand. He smiled when he saw her.

'Did you manage to sort everything out?' she asked, walking towards him.

'Yes,' he said, holding out a hand to her. Julia took it briefly in hers and he exclaimed at its coldness.

'As David almost warned me, there wasn't any hot water for my bath,' she said, 'and I think I'm colder even than I was before it.'

'I'm sorry,' said Anthony. 'I'm afraid the boiler is erratic.'

'It's all right,' Julia said. 'I'm used to it. I don't know when I last had a proper, deep, hot bath.'

'I'm glad you got back all right,' he said a little stiffly. 'I. . .'

'Never mind,' said Julia pre-empting whatever excuse he had been going to make for sending her off so abruptly. She did not want to embark on such a subject with David listening to them. 'Here's Annunziata with supper.'

She left the two men and went to help Annunziata unload her tray and lay the table. There was some quite ordinary-looking cutlery, pretty porcelain plates and really magnificent wine glasses. The clear glass bowls were the shape of well-opened tulips and the elaborate stems had flecks of pure gold caught in the glass.

'I've never seen glasses like these before,' said Julia, holding one up to the flame of one of the candles on the table. The light caught the gold and sparkled.

'They were made at Murano,' said David, who had followed her to the table and was helping to lay out the plates. 'I often think that most modern Murano glass is unbelievably ugly – far too elaborate – but these are nice, and they're nice to drink out of, too.'

He waited until Julia and Anthony had both sat down before pulling out his own chair. Annunziata handed Julia a deep dish filled with ribbons of white pasta in a wonderful sauce of tomatoes and mushrooms and what tasted to Julia like cream. David correctly interpreted her expression of doubt, surprise and pleasure.

'Yes it is cream,' he said. 'Annunziata has been planning a special dinner for you ever since Anthony told us you were coming.'

'How kind,' said Julia. 'It is delectable – particularly after sardines, sausages and powdered egg, which is what I've been used to at home. Will you tell her, please?'

Anthony translated Julia's compliments. Annunziata thanked her and left them to their food.

'How is London?' asked David courteously while Julia was still trying to think of something to say and wishing that she and Anthony could be alone together. 'I haven't been back since I was sent out here after the Italians surrendered.'

'Much the same,' said Julia, putting down her fork. 'Battered and bloody but quite unbowed. People seem to be losing their patience with queues and rationing. Most of us thought naïvely that once the war was over life would get back to normal in London – not progressively worse the further we got from VE Day. But you probably don't want to hear about that.'

'I suspect he does,' said Anthony with an edge in his voice that surprised Julia. 'David has a particular interest in the feelings of Londoners – particularly the feckless poor.'

Julia looked at David, and was about to ask a question, but Anthony forestalled her. She ate another mouthful of pasta and listened.

'Yes, he plans to nurse a London constituency until the next election.'

'Really?' said Julia, rather amused. 'What made you decide to go into politics?'

'He wants to change the world,' said Anthony, again in that edgy voice. 'You see, my dear, he is going to stand as a Socialist.'

'Good Lord!' said Julia before she could stop herself. 'I mean, how interesting.'

David laughed and raised his glass as though in a toast. It was not clear whether it was a mocking salutation to Anthony's contempt or a more serious one to his own parliamentary hopes.

'Anthony seems to think that adherence to Socialism is a sign of pathological lunacy,' said David, 'instead of a reasoned decision based on the past performance and the future ideals of both major parties and the needs of the great majority of the people. He can't accept that what I want for the country is more likely to be achieved by the Labour Party.'

Anthony snorted in derision and proceeded to shock Julia with his bitter mockery of David's ambitions. They seemed misguided to her, but she would never have allowed herself to give expression to such overt contempt. There had been many times in the past when Anthony had appeared to be unaware that his sarcasm sounded much crueller than he meant it to be, but Julia had the uncomfortable impression that this was different. He seemed positively to want to hurt – or at least needle – David, who seemed perfectly harmless to Julia, if rather in the way.

'And what is it that you want to achieve?' she said kindly.

'Simple little things,' said David, his lean good-looking face breaking into a cheerful smile. 'Things like plenty of food for everyone, proper family allowances, no more slums, really good free education for all children irrespective of their parents' means; excellent free medical care for everyone ...'

'But why free for everyone?' asked Julia, no longer trying to be kind. 'That's the aspect of the National Health Service Bill that I simply cannot understand. What on earth is the justification for allowing people like Anthony and me to have free doctoring? There are so many people who need so much and can afford so little that it seems madness.'

'Precisely,' said Anthony. 'But that's only one of the lunacies. They're simply making doctors servants of the bureaucrats – we'll be wasting our time filling in forms instead of caring for the ill. Interfered with at every turn, subject to pettifogging rules written by civil servants who know nothing whatever of medicine. It's outrageous.'

'But, Mrs Gillingham ... Julia I mean,' said David Wallington, ignoring Anthony. He swallowed some pasta, planted both elbows on the table and swivelled in his chair so that he could look directly at her. 'Unless people like you and Anthony – articulate, demanding, informed – share the national health and education, the rest of the population who are none of those things will never get a fair deal.'

'Nonsense,' said Anthony. 'What will stop them getting a fair deal as you call it is the interference of the State.'

'The State is likely to produce a better service for the people than self-interested groups like –'

'You sound quite implacable,' said Julia, surprised at the change from ingenuous young man to determined theorist.

'He is,' said Anthony coldly. 'He's an idealist and all idealists are wreckers. They are so infatuated with their dogmas that they can never see the human cost and reality of what they do.'

David flushed, but to Julia's admiration he did not even try to answer. He was obviously angry, but instead of arguing he calmly ate the rest of his pasta and then poured some more wine into her glass. The dark purple-red looked superb against the gold-flecked glass in the candlelight.

'How far have you got?' Julia asked him temperately. 'I mean has the party allocated you a particular constituency yet?'

'Not yet, although I'm in correspondence with Transport House,' he said, 'and it looks as though I may get one in South London if the selection committee approve. The member there has warned them that he's likely to retire at the next election, but they haven't got as far as selecting a new candidate luckily. I hadn't got going quickly enough for the last election, but I have hopes for next time.'

'Only next time,' said Anthony with obvious satisfaction, 'Dalton will have made such an unholy mess of the economy and Bevin will have antagonised the Americans beyond bearing, aggravated the Russian situation and completely ruined any possibility of a solution to the Palestine problem, and the electorate will get rid of the Socialists. All your friends will be out on their ears and you won't have a hope of getting elected.'

'Anthony!' said Julia, allowing herself to sound angry at last. It was none of her business whether the two of them quarrelled or not, although she disliked seeing her husband needling anyone so unnecessarily, but she thought it ill-mannered of him to stage an argument on such an occasion. David was obviously inhibited by her presence from giving as good as he got.

'Well they have already started to wreck the economy,' said Anthony. 'This idiotic business of agreeing to make sterling convertible as a quid pro quo for the American loan is going to cause an appalling drop in the value of sterling as soon as it comes into force.'

'Well that was the price of the loan. The Americans would never have given way and the money was desperately needed,' said Julia, trying to make peace.

'Only because the Socialists promised so much extra in the way of welfare to get themselves elected. And we'll be paying the price for decades,' said Anthony. He reached for the carafe of wine and poured some more into his glass, splashing some over the edge.

'Not entirely,' said David quietly. 'Most of the money is needed to finance the policing of the Palestine Mandate, the sorting out and support of Greece against the Communists, and the assistance to every other country that might otherwise look to Russia for food and arms.'

Julia thought it time to change the subject and asked Anthony whether he had heard from his mother recently.

'She's apparently very well,' he said, 'although she keeps trying to make me persuade Comfort to move back to the States, which is tiresome.'

'She must miss you both,' said Julia gently.

'Hardly me, my dear,' came the dry answer. 'After all, she left me with my father when I was six and never troubled about me then.'

Realising that she had chosen an unsuitable subject for diverting them all, Julia tried once more and succeeded in getting Anthony and David to talk in reasonable amity about what sights she ought to see while she was in Italy.

Later, when Anthony escorted her up to her bedroom, she asked him why he had ever invited David to live with them since he so clearly found him unbearably irritating. Anthony shrugged.

'We were friends in the war – great friends – as I told you,' he said, shutting her bedroom door behind them. 'Although I always did get irritated with all his half-baked, sentimental Socialism.' He struck a match to light the candles on either side of the bed. The dim light they threw looked warm and welcoming. 'When he wrote to suggest that I move in to this flat with him, it seemed a good idea. But he's changed.'

'I rather liked him when we were talking before dinner. What on earth did he do to make you so angry with him?' asked Julia.

'It doesn't matter,' said Anthony irritably. 'But he behaves so charmingly and seems so ingenuous and innocent that one can be quite taken in. Don't be, Julia. He's not the simple friendly boy he seems. He can be utterly ruthless and do the most damaging things without a second's thought ... He's really very dangerous under all that easy friendliness.'

'But . . .' she started when Anthony took her in his arms.

'But don't let's talk about him any more. He's not important now you're here,' he said, stroking her back and kissing her. Julia leaned against him, pleased that he seemed to want her.

They made love, happily enough but without great passion, and afterwards lay side by side in the ludicrously grand bed, talking comfortably of nothing very much in the candlelight until Julia said:

'Anthony, in the old days we used to talk about starting a family one day. Don't you think now would –?'

'What a moment to pick!' he said before she could get any further. 'No, Julia, I don't.'

'But why?' she asked.

'With the world in ruins, parentless children starving all over Europe, too many mouths to feed . . . Why on earth now?'

'I suppose,' said Julia, who had flinched at the unexpected impatience in his voice, 'because between them the war and losing you for so long have taught me that having children – your children, I mean, not just children in general – matters . . . that we haven't all that much time left and that we ought to make the most of it.'

'What do you mean "not much time"?' Anthony asked quickly with an odd inflexion in his voice. Julia pushed herself into a half-sitting position so that she could look at him and try to understand what was making him angry.

'Just that I'm thirty-two, which is old to be starting a first baby,' she said after a moment.

Anthony blinked and then shook his head slightly.

'Perhaps, but you've plenty of time. It's no more dangerous at thirty-six than at thirty-two,' he said, which struck her as being rather clinical in the circumstances.

'I really would like to try,' she said, smiling and not letting his reaction make her sound irritable.

'For God's sake, Julia,' he said even more impatiently than before, 'this is the worst possible moment.'

'Very well,' she said and slid down under the bedclothes. She reached for her book, but changed her mind and blew out her candle instead. After a moment she felt Anthony's hand on her shoulder.

'I'm sorry, my dear,' he said. 'I spoke too roughly. It's just that when you've seen as many damaged children as I have . . . children with no hope at all, you . . .'

'It's all right,' she said, turning to face him with all the immediate generosity that was so much part of her character. 'I'm not sulking. I was just a bit taken aback by what you said, but we can't expect to understand each other as easily as we once did.'

'No,' said Anthony, pushing back the blankets. 'And I think we're both pretty tired. Sleep well, Julia.' He got out of the bed and bent to kiss her forehead before disappearing into the connecting bedroom.

It took Julia some time to get to sleep that night, and she was still heavily asleep the next morning when Annunziata knocked on the bedroom door. Getting no answer, she opened it and called loudly:

'*Signora, signora, svegliarsi!*'

Julia lifted eyelids that felt as though someone had laid heavy coins on them all night and saw the black-clothed housekeeper standing just inside the door. With her brain sluggishly beginning to work, Julia sat up.

'*Buon giorno*, Annunziata,' she said, trying to push the sleep out of her eyes. The woman came a little closer and tapped at her wristwatch. She was still too far away for Julia to be able to see its face, but she understood at once, looked at the clock on the table at her side and flung back the bedclothes.

'*Grazie*, Annunziata,' she said hurrying over to the painted wardrobe in which her clothes had been hung the night before. '*Capisco*. I understand.'

The housekeeper smiled and went out to return two minutes later with a tray of breakfast. Julia, dressed by then in her underclothes and dressing gown, was on her way to the bathroom. She thanked Annunziata and asked clumsily where Anthony was. Annunziata made it clear that he had been gone for some time and was at the *ospedale*. Julia went to wash.

When she came back she poured herself a cup of coffee, grimaced as she recognised the bitter taste of a familiar substitute and tried to decide what clothes would be most suitable to wear to the Tribunale di Giustizia. After some thought, she plumped for the black suit she would have worn to court in London. If it turned out to be too formal, she could always wear something more countrified the next day, and it would never do to appear over-casual on her first day in a new job.

When she had buttoned up her plain ivory silk blouse and shrugged her shoulders into the square-shouldered black jacket, she walked over to a long looking glass that hung between the windows to do her face and hair, sipping the disgusting ersatz coffee and eating a tired roll as she did so.

Once her dull-brown hair was brushed back and pinned into her customary French pleat, Julia thought she looked depressingly severe. All the previous day's colour had left her skin and with her eyes still puffy from sleep, her face seemed dull and stodgy. Thinking that perhaps some colour or sparkle on her clothes might help, she rummaged in her small jewel case for a gold chain set with pearls and garnets, which her grandmother had left her, and hung it round her neck under the collar of her shirt. The gold and the dark red of the garnets improved the general effect a little, she thought as she hurriedly finished her breakfast.

Having put on a black hat and slung an overcoat around her shoulders, she went down to the salon to find David Wallington, who had promised to escort her to their office.

'Goodness, you look tidy,' said Julia as she noticed his impeccably pressed khaki uniform. He looked much older, more practical and infinitely less approachable than he had done the day before. For the first time Julia thought that she could imagine him being as dangerous as Anthony had suggested, but she was disconcerted to notice that he wore the ribbon of the MC on his tunic. No one had told her that he was brave.

David laughed easily.

'I don't think flannel bags and an old tweed coat would quite suit the majesty of a British military tribunal,' he said, gesturing to his uniform with a self-mockery she liked. 'Even the preparatory stages of it.'

'We probably ought to go, oughtn't we?' said Julia, leading the way downstairs to the street door.

'What a pity!' exclaimed David as he pushed it open and saw the thick, damp mist that seemed to fill the square. 'Venice can look so ravishing on a sunny morning and I'd planned to show you the prettiest route to the office. But there's no point now.'

'Never mind,' said Julia. 'We can concentrate on the case instead. Oh no, before we do that: do you know anyone who could give me Italian lessons? I can't bear the uselessness of not being able to communicate with people here, particularly Annunziata.' She huddled herself deeper into her camel overcoat to avoid the chill fog that hung about the buildings like a thick, clammy shroud.

'Yes, there are lots of people. I'll think who'd be best,' said David. 'We turn right here, into the Campo Santo Stefano. It's the largest square in Venice after St Mark's. They used to hold bullfights here.'

'How extraordinary to think of Venetians having bullfights. I'd never have associated anything so cruel with them.'

'Good heavens, Mrs G!' said David, stopping in his tracks.

Julia was amused by his expression of theatrical surprise and could not help smiling in response.

'Have I said something peculiarly silly?' she asked without worrying about it.

'Astonishingly,' he answered with a cheerful grin. 'But it's hardly fair of me to tease. Why should you know anything about Venetian history? They did some amazingly cruel things here – of which bullfights would have been about the least. One of the reasons why the Venetians were so successful for so long was that they were utterly ruthless.'

'Ruthlessness need not imply cruelty, surely?' she said, serious again.

'No, it ought not to,' agreed David. 'Unfortunately it often does.'

They were both silent, thinking of what had been done by the ruthless and the cruel during the past six years. Julia remembered that David's brother had been a prisoner of the Japanese.

'Is it much further to the court?' she asked to distract them both.

'No, about another ten minutes. It's a very simple route, but I'll draw you a map for when you have to come and go on your own. By the way ...' He broke off and when she looked at him she thought that he was ashamed, which seemed odd after their easy teasing a moment earlier.

'What's up?' she asked without finesse, treating him as she would a colleague in chambers.

He looked surprised and then oddly relieved.

'It's just that I am rather bothered about your job,' he said. 'It's ludicrous for a barrister of your experience and standing to be doing a job junior to mine.'

Julia laughed a little bitterly.

'But, David,' she said with exaggerated clarity. 'I'm only a woman. I know my place.'

'Nonsense!' he said energetically. 'Oh, I know you're mocking me, but it is an idiotic thing for anyone to believe ... That being a woman makes you automatically subordinate, I mean.'

Julia stopped dead, an expression of pleasure in her warm brown eyes.

'You've been away a long time, haven't you?' she said at last. When David looked puzzled, she went on: 'There are a great many people at the Bar who think precisely that. You should hear some of the comments about "girl barristers". It's ... refreshing to discover that you don't share their views.'

'I certainly do not. I never did,' he said, 'but if I had, what I learned with the partisans would have told me how wrong I'd been. The girls were just as brave and full of endurance as the men.'

'Were you surprised?'

'Only at their physical toughness,' said David. 'I don't mean they were all paragons, but the villains and the slackers were equally distributed among the sexes.'

'I'm glad,' said Julia. 'I wish I could believe that the war would have taught everyone that. But listen, David, you needn't worry about the job. I would have taken almost any kind of work that brought me here to be with Anthony again.'

'Thank you,' he said simply. 'I'm glad of that. He's needed you badly.'

'By the way,' said Julia, changing the subject abruptly, 'I'm not actually certain what it is that I'm to be asked to do.'

'Ah, well it's awfully simple – the sort of thing a new pupil might be set to – sorting through statements, making a précis, suggesting which might be used for the prosecution.'

'That's fine, David. Don't worry about it,' said Julia.

# Chapter Twelve

David led her down a claustrophobic little alleyway that led ultimately to the Rialto. Crossing the bridge, they made their way to the court building, a Renaissance palace that lay between the fish and vegetable markets.

'We use the back way in, although like all the Grand Canal palaces it was built to be entered from the water. Come on, I'll show you our offices and introduce you to the rest of the team.'

When he had shown her the cloakrooms and the temporary tea room on the first floor, he took her on up to a large light room at the top of the building, where a small group of young English military lawyers were sitting over their papers. David introduced Julia to them and then showed her to a laden table overlooking the Grand Canal.

'This must have been your doing,' she said, looking from the pretty view back up at him. 'Thank you, David.'

'I thought that the least we could do was ensure that you had something decent to look at,' he said. 'Now, these are your files,' he went on, pushing them to one side of her table. 'They consist of statements taken by British military police sergeants just after the war from people who witnessed German actions against the partisans. As I said outside, what we need you to do is plough through them picking out the ones you think we ought to use, and reducing them to a single page . . . then we'll have to decide how convincing they are. It's become clear that in the immediate aftermath of the German surrender some fairly exaggerated stories were taken down and believed.'

'I can imagine,' said Julia. 'I take it that part of the charge against Kesselring is going to be that the Germans used excessive force?'

'That's right. I don't think that there'll be much trouble proving it, given that we've orders of Kesselring's –' He broke off and turned away from her to call: 'Martindale!'

'Yes?' said a tubby-looking man from the other side of the room.

'Have you got a copy of Kesselring's partisan orders?'

The lawyer scuffled among his papers and then held some out to David. He brought them back to Julia's table and handed them over. Julia skimmed the translations of the Field Marshal's orders in the way she had learned during her first few weeks in chambers, picking out the essentials at a glance. In growing surprise she read out:

'"I will protect any commander who exceeds our usual restraint in the choice and severity of the methods he adopts against partisans . . . a mistake in the choice of the means to achieve an objective is always better than failure to act or to be neglectful. . ."' She turned over the pages to the second order.

'Good God!' she exclaimed. '"Should troops, etc., be fired at from any village, the village will be burned down . . . Nearby villages to be held responsible for any sabotage to cables and damage inflicted to tyres." That's outrageous. . . . The villages might not have had anything to do with the sabotage.'

'Precisely,' said David. 'And there were undoubtedly plenty of cases when villages were destroyed for acts of sabotage carried out by people completely unknown to the inhabitants.'

'I see. Thank you. I'll get on with it then.'

'Good. Let one of us know if you have any problems,' he said, 'but I don't suppose that you will.'

He left her and she set to work. Despite her good intentions, she was irritated and distracted by the noise the other lawyers made riffling through their papers and asking each other questions. In London she had had a room to herself for at least some of the war. Nevertheless she read through statement after statement, appalled by the things she read and yet curiously relieved that at last she was learning about the kind of life Anthony must have lived with the partisans. She read of actions to blow up ammunition dumps, power lines and railways, to ambush supply trucks, and generally harass the Germans and make their tasks as difficult as possible. She read, too, of the revenge the Germans had taken for such sabotage.

Just as she was absorbing details of a particularly brutal reprisal at Udine, where women and children were mown down by German machine-gun fire, she felt a touch on her shoulder and flinched.

'Sorry to give you a shock,' said David Wallington, 'but I've got to go out to a meeting now and I'm not sure when I'll be back. Will you be all right?'

'I'll be fine,' Julia assured him, 'but I would like to ask you one or two things . . . not only about these files but about what happened to your group, so that I can put these into some kind of perspective. Would that be all right?'

'Perfectly,' he said, but as he turned to go, Julia thought that she caught a wary, almost suspicious, expression in his blue eyes. Puzzled, she turned back to her files, making notes of questions and requests for clarification as she read.

At twelve-thirty she lunched on dry sausage rolls with some of the other lawyers in the tea room on the floor below their office and heard what they had been doing during the war. Her own stories of firewatching during the Blitz and helping at 'incidents' were tame in comparison with accounts of life behind the German lines, and she felt rather a fraud to have joined them knowing so little of war at first hand. They did not seem to mind that, though, and sounded interested in all she could tell them of the war in London and the buildings, squares and churches that had survived the bombing. What clearly interested them even more were her accounts of legal London and what she thought of their chances of getting tenancies when they eventually got back.

From them she also learned about the progress of Kesselring's interrogation in London. He was being held in the 'London Cage' and questioned by Lieutenant Colonel Scotland, who would undoubtedly be one of the principal prosecution witnesses. Scotland had been surprised that Kesselring made no attempt to deny what had been done during the Italian campaign or to try to evade responsibility for it, but his acceptance ought at least to make the case easier to prove.

Julia also heard that the other main charge against Kesselring would be his responsibility for the killing of 335 Italian men and boys in the Ardeatine Caves outside Rome. She already knew that they had been shot in reprisal for a bomb attack that killed thirty-two or -three members of the SS in the Via Rasella in Rome.

After lunch she went back to her files, faced with a clearer picture of life under Nazi occupation than she had ever had before. It must have been peculiar for the Italian people, she thought, to have been allies of the Germans until 1943 and then suddenly subject to their full ferocity. Squeezed between the Nazis in the north of the country and the invading British and Americans in the south, some of them must have regretted the change.

No wonder people like Jackson French were finding it difficult to impose law and order on the population. For a part of it at least he must represent not the liberators of the country, but merely another set of enemy invaders against whom any action was justified.

For some reason Julia found it easier to work that afternoon. She had decided to read right through all the files first, flagging those that she thought would help to build the prosecution's case, and then start preparing her précis. Hearing the sounds of departure all around her at five o'clock, she looked up and was surprised to see that it was so dark outside that she could see only shadows across the Grand Canal.

Determined not to have a repetition of her uncomfortable walk back from the hospital the previous day, she had put a prewar tourist map of Venice in her bag that morning, together with the batteryless dynamo torch she had carried through the blackout in London.

Despite the map, she took several wrong turnings on the short walk home and found herself in more than one dead end. By the time she reached the Campo San Maurizio, she was thoroughly irritable. She was also tired and very cold. There were no lights on in the big salon and so she went on up the stairs to her bedroom, feeling a bit bleak. She had relied on Anthony's being there to take away the slight sting of his early-morning departure.

After a few minutes' thought, Julia changed out of her dark suit and high-heeled shoes into a pair of trousers, a thick corduroy jacket and stout walking shoes. Tying a scarf round her head in place of her hat, she set off across Venice to meet Anthony at the hospital. Once again she felt the unpleasant sensation of being followed as soon as she reached the far side of St Mark's Square, but she ignored it and reached the hospital without being accosted by anyone.

An orderly sitting at a desk inside the front door said something to her in Italian and she responded simply:

'Dottore Gillingham?'

The answer was an incomprehensible flood of excited speech, but Julia got the distinct impression that Anthony was not available. She then asked for Sister Caroline, at which the orderly smiled, nodded and pointed down the main corridor. Relieved to think that she would at least be able to communicate with someone, Julia made her way to the long ward.

'Mrs Gillingham!' came the American nurse's cheerful voice in welcome. 'How good to see you.'

'Thank you, Sister,' said Julia. 'Is my husband about? The man at the desk tried to tell me, but I couldn't understand him.'

'He's operating, I'm afraid. Was he expecting you?'

'No,' said Julia, shaking her head. 'But my working day ended much earlier than I had expected and, being at a loose end, I thought I'd come and escort him home.'

'He doesn't usually leave until after seven,' said the nurse dispassionately. Julia looked at her watch. It was only just after six.

'Well now I'm here may I chat to some of the children?' she asked. Sister Caroline gave immediate permission and Julia walked straight over to the chair where Flavia was sitting huddled and silent while the other children played and fought with each other all around her.

'Flavia,' she said softly, going to kneel on the floor beside the chair. She did not try to touch the child, but simply stayed there, saying her name occasionally and talking very gently in English. It did not seem to her to matter whether Flavia understood her words or not. When Flavia made no response at all, Julia edged a little closer and briefly touched the child's head. Then she waited.

'*Buona sera, signora,*' whispered Flavia at last without looking up. But when Julia returned her greeting and lightly stroked her hair again, she did look up to produce a small, tentative smile.

Julia felt almost as triumphant as she did when she won a complicated case, and she settled herself more comfortably on the hard floor beside the child. Within ten minutes Flavia was smiling more naturally and within twenty she was sitting on the floor beside Julia, playing finger games with her. They could neither of them understand what the other was saying, but they were communicating in other ways and giving each other a great deal of simple satisfaction.

'You're very good with children, Mrs Gillingham,' said Sister Caroline from behind Julia. Julia turned back to smile up at her, but Flavia climbed back on to her chair and turned her face away.

'I came to tell you that Doctor Gillingham is just coming out of theatre,' said the nurse, looking ruefully at the bent head of her charge.

'Thank you,' said Julia, getting up. 'I'll come again tomorrow, Flavia,' she added softly. 'How would I say that in Italian, Sister?'

Sister Caroline translated the sentence and Julia repeated it slowly and carefully. Flavia waited until she heard the sound of the nurse's retreating footsteps and then shot another quick furtive smile through her hair. Julia followed the nurse back to her desk at the far end of the ward.

'You must have had lots of experience with children,' she said as Julia sat down in the visitor's chair.

'Alas, no,' she said. 'I've never had time to get to know any, and I'm only just beginning to realise what I've been missing.'

'Well take it from me, you have distinct talents in that direction, and –'

'Julia!' Anthony's voice ripped into the warmth with which Sister Caroline had surrounded Julia. 'What on earth are you doing here?'

Both women looked at him in surprise. He sounded not merely irritable but actually angry as he stood in front of them in his loose white coat.

'I just came to see if you were likely to be coming back for dinner,' said Julia pacifically, thinking that something must have gone wrong with the operation he had just done. 'And as you were tied up I stayed to play with little Flavia for a bit.'

'And succeeded in getting a very good response from her,' said Sister Caroline, obviously doing what she could to ease the tension between the other two. Julia noticed it and was relieved to have that extra confirmation that her suspicions of an affair between Anthony and the nurse had been wrong.

Anthony took Julia's elbow and ushered her out of the ward. In the dim passage outside, she pulled her arm away from his gripping hand and rubbed it. Anthony turned to face her and she saw that his face was white and accusing.

'Julia, please don't ever do that again,' he said in a voice that bit.

'But Anthony, what possible harm could it do?' Julia asked, astonished.

'First, untrained personnel in a hospital are a positive danger to the patients. Second, you do not speak Italian and I am not prepared to put up with the confusion that you could cause the staff and children. Third, there are virulent infections in this hospital and I do not want you exposed to them,' he said, ticking the points off on his very clean fingers.

Julia's face softened as he warned her of the infections.

'There are not enough facilities or drugs to cure the patients we have here without perfectly healthy people exposing themselves unnecessarily,' he went on, destroying the softening effect of what he had said earlier.

'But, Anthony,' Julia said, unable to let such a violent diatribe past without argument, 'if there are infections here then you are exposed to them daily and consequently must expose all of us in the Campo San Maurizio to the same germs. It would make no difference if I –'

'Will you just accept that it is dangerous for you to be here and I cannot have my staff distracted by entertaining you?' he said as coldly as though she were a stranger.

'Very well,' said Julia just as coldly. Furious though he had made her, she was not prepared to plead with him. 'I don't understand what is making you take such an extraordinary attitude, but you are in charge.'

'Exactly. Now, I have to stay here this evening; I shan't be back for dinner. I'll see you later,' said Anthony and turned abruptly back into his ward. Never in all their life together had he spoken so dismissively to her.

Julia was left to pick her way back through the sinister alleyways, puzzling about what could have made her husband behave so unlike himself. It was not until she reached the far side of St Mark's Square that she began to connect his coldness with Comfort's. Both of them had the power to make her happier than she had ever expected; and both of them could plunge her without warning into solitude. Reminding herself that they were the two people she cared most about in the world, she accepted that the solitude was the price of the happiness and knew that it was a price worth paying.

She was cheered when she reached the Campo San Maurizio to find the lights blazing in the salon, Annunziata cooking dinner, David Wallington smoking his pipe over the newspaper, ready to pour her a drink, and – best of all – a pile of letters from England.

David handed them to her and tactfully picked up his paper so that she could read them unembarrassed. There was one from Comfort, she saw as she riffled through the pile, one from Mark, one from her mother (which surprised her) and even one from George Wilson, whom she had not seen for nearly a fortnight before her departure for Venice. She opened his first and read a lively account of his latest case, the infuriating behaviour of their clerk and the bleakness of chambers without her. Julia was touched by that, although she did not believe it.

Mark's letter was much the same except that it included a fervent expression of relief that he was back in London after a tormenting year in Nuremberg and wished that she had stayed in London. Reading that, Julia let herself acknowledge the thought that had been teasing her for some hours: that she might have made a serious error in coming to Venice.

'Not bad news, I hope.' David Wallington's deep voice, sounding a little hesitant, broke into her gloomy thoughts. Smiling slightly, she shook her head.

'No. Just news from two colleagues, which makes me feel a little homesick for my own familiar life,' she said, picking up the glass of wine he had poured for her. 'But never mind that. Was your meeting successful?'

'It was fine,' he said. 'And on my way back I called on an old acquaintance of my mother's to find out if she would consider teaching you Italian.'

'How good of you, David,' said Julia. 'Will she?'

'Yes indeed, and she put a counter-proposal to me, too, that you might consider helping her to teach English to a group of refugees who are living under her protection here,' he said.

Remembering Anthony's summary refusal to allow her into his hospital, Julia thought she might well accept the proposition, but she was far too cautious to do so without knowing more about it. She explained her reservations and agreed to go with David to meet his mother's friend on their way back from the office the following day. Julia picked up her remaining two letters and then pushed them into her handbag to read later.

'David,' she said with sudden decision.

'Yes?'

'What is the matter with Anthony? He's so irritable and he never was before ... not just before the war, but when he came home on leave last Christmas. And it's not just with me. He was snapping and sniping at you yesterday.'

'I think ...' he began, looking oddly nervous. Before he could say any more the door opened and Annunziata came back with a huge blue-and-white porcelain tureen of bean soup and a basket of bread, which she put on the table.

Julia thanked her laboriously in Italian and then went to the table with David. As soon as Annunziata had watched them take their first appreciative mouthfuls of the pleasantly filling soup, she left them and Julia turned to David.

'You were about to tell me about Anthony,' she said. 'You must know him so much better than I by now that I am sure you can explain.'

'It's true that his temper is on a much shorter fuse than it was before,' he said carefully, 'but I think that is only because of all the difficulties he has at the hospital, trying to get drugs for the children and equipment for the operating theatre. He's under an enormous number of pressures there, and I think they perhaps make it difficult for him to think about anyone else's problems. And I don't think he's recovered yet from . . . well, from the things that happened in the war.'

'That sounds quite likely,' said Julia. She took a spoonful of soup, thinking that it might be likely but it did not help her much.

'Don't let it hurt you, please,' said David suddenly. Julia looked at him in surprise. 'I know it's none of my business,' he went on hurriedly, 'but it's just the war. It's made all of us unlike ourselves . . . much better in some ways; very much worse in others.'

'Yes, I'm sure it has,' she said at last. 'But what did happen to Anthony then? He wouldn't talk about it when he came home last year and I don't like to remind him by asking.'

Once more David's face took on an expression of half-nervous obstinacy that made Julia suspicious. Anthony's warning flashed into her mind and she wondered what on earth this apparently charming, brave young man could have done to provoke it. A man who, stranger though he was, seemed to mind that she should not be hurt.

'All I know, you see,' she said, 'is that he escaped from the camp and ended up fighting with partisans. From the things I've been reading today I realise how terrifying that could have been, but I can't help thinking that if I knew more I'd be able to understand him better.'

David could not resist that plea. If anyone was going to be able to bring Anthony back to his senses, it was likely to be his wife, and the more she sympathised with him, the better. David decided to tell her about the organisation of the partisan camp Anthony helped to build and about the partisans themselves: men who had fled to the hills to escape deportation to Germany, Communists who had been fighting Fascism for years, escaped prisoners and probably a few deserters too; and the girls, many of them still in their early teens, who acted as couriers between the groups and often ran frightful risks to get food for the partisans.

He told her, too, about his own arrival in the camp after a parachute drop in which his radio operator was killed.

'Was that why we never got any messages to say that Anthony was alive?' Julia asked involuntarily. David shook his dark head.

'It just wasn't safe to transmit that sort of information, even in code. He did not dare let anyone know who he was, you see, because of what happened before he reached the partisans.'

Julia asked him what he meant and he told her all about Anthony's escape. He and two friends had cut through the wire of their prison camp one night soon after Italy had surrendered to the Allies and before they could be transferred to Germany. They managed to get to the nearest railway station before the alarm was sounded. Train hopping, hiding during the day, walking at night, scrounging food where they could, they had made their way painfully up Italy towards Switzerland. One of his friends was caught on a foraging expedition to a small village just north of Rome, but the other reached the foothills of the Alps with Anthony just as the autumn was changing into winter.

They found shelter with a family of peasant farmers, who refused to let them risk a mountain crossing while the weather was so uncertain, shared everything with them and hid them from the occasional German patrols. One of their children fell frighteningly ill and Anthony let them know that he was a doctor. The child recovered quickly, and word of Anthony's skill leaked into the surrounding countryside and scarcely a week passed without someone appearing at the farmhouse for help.

Eventually the small band of ill-organised local partisans came to hear of him and summoned him to help treat a man who had been terribly beaten by the Gestapo. They had rescued him, but had no facilities to treat his injuries. Anthony went willingly, did what he could for the man, looked over some of the others who had been wounded or ill, and gave advice on all sorts of problems from the treatment of gunshot wounds to the prevention of constipation, which most of the partisans suffered because of their restricted diet and their lack of fluids.

When he got back to the farmhouse where he had been hidden, he discovered that someone had betrayed his hosts. The farmhouse had been burned to the ground, the livestock driven away, the surrounding land devastated, and the farmer, his family and Anthony's fellow escaper had disappeared. Anthony went straight back up into the mountains to work with the partisans and discovered later that the entire family had been tortured and subsequently shot. What had happened to his friend from the camp, he had never discovered.

'I know it must seem hard for you to have been left in ignorance for all that time,' David said, assuming that it was resentment that was keeping her quiet. 'But he really could not. . .'

'No, no. I understand that,' said Julia with a smile. 'And I do understand now why he feels that he owes the people here so much but . . .' She broke off, trying to apply as much analysis and intuition to the problem as she would to any case.

'But what?' asked David, frowning.

'I don't understand why he should have changed so much . . . why he should snap at yu and needle you as he did last night.' And, she added silently to herself, why he should look at me as though he hated me.

'You needn't worry about me,' said David seriously. 'Anthony disapproves bitterly of my politics and he thinks I indulge my conscience at the expense of other people without costing myself anything. That's all. It's a point of view.'

'I don't think that is all,' said Julia, watching his face and finding confirmation of her suspicions in his narrowed eyes and down-turned mouth, 'but I won't press you. Is there any more soup in that dish?'

They discussed inconsequential things after that and Julia went early to bed to lie awake thinking of Anthony and of how she might repair the holes that had appeared in the fabric of her marriage. She heard him coming back at about midnight and was not surprised that he went straight into his own room. When she had heard him undress and get into bed, she turned over on her face and willed herself to sleep.

But she did not get much rest, waking often after tormenting dreams of children wounded and dead. Once she woke feeling as though a child had just been pulled out of her arms. She could still feel the weight of its hard head against her arm and the half-pleasurable, half-painful tug of its gums on her breast.

She got out of bed, then, and walked about the bitterly cold room, banishing the memory of the dream. She had never to her knowledge held a very young child in her arms and had obviously never fed one. The sensations she had dreamed were imaginary. No one had torn a child away from her. Anthony had requested her not to interfere with his patients and had ignored her small success with the difficult but appealing Flavia, but that was no reason for her to wake in the night, aching and almost weeping with deprivation.

So she rationalised as she walked silently up and down the room in her bare feet, growing colder and more sensible with each turn, until at last she thought she might sleep again and went back to bed.

# Chapter Thirteen

The following day when the office closed at five o'clock, David did as he had promised and took Julia to meet his mother's friend, Giovanna Sassanta. She lived, as he explained, on the same side of the Grand Canal as the court but in an area known as the Dorsoduro. David enlivened the walk there with snatches of Venetian history, and entertaining snippets of information such as the fact that until the first Accademia Bridge was built in 1848 many people lived their entire lives without once crossing the canal and that even in 1946 there could be found Venetians who had never seen St Mark's.

Julia was interested, but she could not help thinking that he was using his knowledge of Venice to stop her from asking any questions about the woman they were going to see and so she interrupted him mercilessly.

'Tell me about this Signora Sassanta,' she said.

'Ah,' said David, slowing down as he walked beside her. 'I had hoped that you could meet her first. What do you want to know?'

'Anything,' said Julia. 'Why are you being so defensive? Was she a Fascist?'

'She? No; well, never an active one in any case, and she was always against the Germans. In fact, she did good and very valuable work for the partisans, financing some groups and helping out in all kinds of ways,' said David. 'But her husband was a different matter. He supported the Germans and bitterly resented the Badoglio government that surrendered to the Allies in 1943.'

'I see,' said Julia, adding acutely: 'And you thought that I would refuse to have anything to do with her?'

'Not exactly,' said David. Julia thought from the sound of his voice that he must be smiling. 'But I did think you might be a bit shocked and prefer someone else.'

'What happened to her husband?' asked Julia, reserving judgment until she had met the *signora*.

'He was shot by partisans just after the Germans surrendered,' said David. 'Giovanna was there when it happened. It would take a lot to get over seeing your husband machine-gunned in front of you, whatever his politics,' he went on. Julia silently agreed but continued to reserve judgment.

They walked on in silence through low lintels into covered passageways, across little squares and past leaning towers, half-tripping sometimes on uneven paving stones. Julia seemed to smell decay all around, not just the familiar rotting vegetation and sewage from the canals, but mildewed paint and decomposing wood and crumbling stone. In the darkness the city seemed secretive and rather sinister. The contrast between the miasma of decay and the strength of David's deep voice beside her was peculiar and unsettling.

At last they turned a corner and stopped in front of a shabby old palace. David turned to grin at Julia in the dusk and hammered on the front door.

'Sorry it took so long,' he said as they waited to be let in. 'Are you worn out?'

'No, merely cold and rather confused,' said Julia. 'I suppose that one day I'll learn my way about this place.'

'Good heavens, yes,' said David. 'Ah, Giovanna, *come stai?* This is Signora Gillingham. Julia, Signora Sassanta.'

The two women shook hands and Giovanna Sassanta invited the other two up to her apartment on the second floor. She must have been in her early fifties, a short, stoutish woman who gave an impression of unshakeable confidence and authority. She spoke fluent, if heavily accented, English and after a few polite remarks came straight to the point in a business-like way that Julia appreciated. They negotiated for two lessons a week, for which the *signora* asked only a tiny fee, and then she asked whether Julia would consider teaching English to some refugees who were also living in the house. After some thought Julia agreed to give two-hour lessons each Wednesday and Saturday evenings for nothing.

There were six of them, living on the lower floors of the house with their children, and Julia was taken down to be introduced, while David stayed upstairs. Signora Sassanta called each of the women by her Christian name and referred to Julia simply as Signora Giulia, explaining that it would be easier for all of them if they did not have to bother with unfamiliar surnames. Julia, watching the thin, wary, dark-eyed faces of five of her prospective pupils, agreed. She thought it would be difficult enough remembering one name for each of them until she had got to know them.

Only one of the women stood out enough for Julia to be certain of being able to put the right name to the right face. Introduced as Raffaella, she looked quite different from the others. Where they were dark-eyed and brown-haired, she was fair, with a light, slightly sallow skin and pale greenish-blue eyes. Dressed like the others in dingy black, she somehow managed to look completely different. Her eyebrows were plucked into high arcs above her eyes while theirs were shaggy and unkempt, and she looked both younger and less tired than the others, but there was more to it than that.

It was not until Julia had said goodbye to the six women and gone upstairs again to collect David Wallington that she realised that the main difference was that Raffaella looked healthy and far better fed than the others. She was very slim, but her skin was smooth and clear, the whites of her eyes very white, and her blonde hair was glossy. She looked well cared for and far from destitute.

'Who are those women?' Julia asked David as they walked towards the Accademia Bridge.

'I don't know specifically,' said David. 'I've never seen or spoken to any of them, but I know that Giovanna houses and feeds them because they are alone and without resources. Apparently some are widowed, others deserted; what they all share is that they have no one else to support them.'

'And perhaps have had trouble with people hunting down collaborators?' suggested Julia.

'Perhaps,' answered David quietly. 'But the war's been over for nearly eighteen months. There has to be a stop to revenge at some time. Someone has to draw a line and start again. Giovanna is trying in a small way. It seems to me worth doing.'

'I rather agree,' said Julia, judiciously.

'And you must remember,' added David, before she could say anything else, 'that not all the so-called partisans who killed and looted after the war had had anything to do with resistance to the Germans; nor were all their victims collaborators.'

Julia said nothing and after a few minutes David courteously found another subject for them to discuss.

'How are you liking Venice?' he asked.

Julia took a moment to think about her answer. She was not going to tell him that she had never expected to feel lonelier living with Anthony again than she had done in London during the war and that she was still afraid she had made a terrible mistake in coming to Venice.

'I like the quietness,' she said after a while. 'And the fact that the only collapsing buildings have been ruined by time and not by bombs. I like the oddness of it, too, although sometimes it seems almost frightening. I find it theatrical and unreal, but that's probably because it is still strange. When I've been here a few weeks, I'll be able to answer you better. And you?'

'I love it all,' he said, sounding more relaxed than she had yet heard him. 'The sadness of it, the glamour, the pinnacles and the fretted windows, the statues, the colour of the bricks, the mucky canals, the dead ends, the slinking cats, the paintings, the history, the romance, the . . . the allure of it all.'

'The voice of a lover,' said Julia, sounding warmly amused and David laughed. He liked her frankness and her amusement, too.

'Yes, I suppose it is,' he said and was about to ask her about her tastes when she said:

'Ah, Anthony must be at home.' They had reached the house in the Campo San Maurizio and there were lights flickering in the windows of the first-floor salon. David was conscious of disappointment as he watched Julia go straight up into the salon.

Before she could say anything to Anthony, he greeted her with an immediate apology for his outburst of the day before.

'I'd had a hellish battle to stop a post-operative haemorrhage and I wasn't sure I'd succeeded. But it was no excuse, Julia. Will you forgive me?'

'Of course,' she said, taking both his hands between her own. David stood in the doorway, forgotten by both the others. 'It surprised me a bit at the time, but even then I understood. Don't worry about it, Anthony.'

He leaned forward to kiss her and David backed quietly away.

'How is Flavia today?' asked Julia a little later. She had felt bitterly guilty that she had not been able to redeem her promise to visit the child again. Anthony seemed to have forgotten that Julia had ever met his favourite patient and he talked happily of the things she had said and how she was just beginning to allow Sister Caroline to come close to her. Trying to suppress her residual annoyance that Anthony had never allowed her to help with the child or even acknowledged that she had managed to reach through Flavia's defences, Julia listened in silence.

'But that's enough of me and my hospital. How is your work going?' said Anthony, at last remembering his wife as more than an audience.

'So so,' said Julia. 'It's a little frustrating to know that however well I do my part in preparing the case, I shan't be able to have any say whatever in the trial itself. Still, it's a military tribunal. I can't expect to be part of it. And I'm going to make the most of my time here and learn Italian properly.'

'That sounds excellent,' said Anthony, getting up off the sofa. 'Perhaps you won't be too bored here after all.'

'Not at all,' she said, pleased that he should have been worrying about her. 'In any case, it's quite nice to live at a slower pace than we did in the war.'

Her conviction that he did not want her in Venice lessened and gradually life became easier. Having been professionally involved in several matrimonial cases since the war, Julia knew that their difficulties in readjusting to married life were far from unique, and she worked as hard on repairing her marriage as she did on preparing her part of the case against Kesselring. She never risked arousing Anthony's anger by going to the hospital again, although she often thought about Flavia and the way the child had obviously trusted her. Julia hoped that the child would have forgotten her promise and not feel betrayed by her continuing absence.

Anthony repaid her patient labours with friendliness, showed interest in anything she told him about her work, and was ready enough to talk of his own, but there was a distance between them that there had not been before the war. He never revealed anything of what had happened to change him so much, and as the days drifted into weeks Julia gave up trying to find out; there seemed to be no point.

Gradually, as he realised that she was not going to probe into the past or nag him to return to London, Anthony grew more relaxed and managed to accept her presence in Venice, and even to share her bed sometimes. The modest happiness Julia had glimpsed the previous Christmas seemed to be coming within their reach at last as the New Year approached.

There was only one main shadow left between them. Despite making love to her rather more often than he had ever done in the old days in London, Anthony was determined not to conceive a child.

Julia continued to dream her agonising dreams of fulfilment and unbearable loss, but she said nothing about them. Sometimes watching the controlled desperation in Annunziata's eyes, Julia asked herself caustically why she was so anxious to have children when they laid one open to such pain, but although there was no answer to her questions, the need remained. It ate into her so badly that she even found herself unable to look at the innumerable paintings of the Madonna and Child that hung in every Venetian church she entered.

Letters from Mark and George Wilson helped her to regain a sense of proportion by keeping her in touch with her own world, relaying all the gossip of legal London, accounts of particularly interesting cases that never reached the Law Report in *The Times*, and the reactions of her colleagues to the manoeuvrings of the Labour government.

They seemed to be getting home affairs more or less under control, George wrote one week in December, and the public appeared to have accepted the increasingly austere life that was imposed on them as all available resources were directed to the export drive, but foreign affairs were a different matter. The Russians and the Americans were causing serious anxiety as they battled for supremacy; the demands for Indian independence and a separate Muslim state were growing uncontrollably; the situation in Palestine looked utterly intractable as the government tried to effect a compromise between the conflicting needs of the Arabs and the Jews, and Ernest Bevin was thought not to be handling it well.

Julia read the letters with a mixture of interest and regret that she was so cut off from direct news. Paper shortages still meant that *The Times* was skimpy, so that even when they managed to get hold of it, it was unsatisfying. She often discussed George's gloss on the news with David, who was anxious to know what informed members of the public thought of all kinds of questions, so that his frequent letters to his sponsors at Transport House and the likely members of the selection committee in the constituency he hoped to represent at the next election would be as impressive as possible.

He wanted to know Julia's views and those of her friends on the international situation, on whether the British would put up with austerity for long enough to get the country back into economic stability, and on less important matters such as the different talents of the patrician Hugh Dalton and the proletarian Ernest Bevin, whether many people believed that Dalton would have made a better foreign secretary than Bevin, and whether they really thought that the King had intervened because he so disliked Dalton. He also wanted to know what the majority of people in Britain thought of the Americans.

When he asked her that one morning just after Christmas as they were walking to their office, Julia smiled.

'To give you a single example: almost the only unifying view on

Palestine,' she said, 'is that it is monstrous of President Truman to publicise his demands that the British allow unrestricted immigration into Palestine while suppressing the fact that he refuses to increase the quota of visas for Jews who want to get into America. From some of his pronouncements you'd have thought he was the only person in the world with sympathy for the Jews, but he won't give any practical assistance. That is thought to be typical: massive power, massive wealth, but not a corresponding sense of responsibility; free with advice but unnecessarily tight with money.'

'Don't most people at home accept that there should be a Jewish homeland?' David asked, surprised and ignoring the Americans for the moment.

'Nearly everyone agrees that there must be reparation made for what the Jews suffered in the war, but not everyone believes it is fair to banish the Arabs from Palestine to make room for them. And these continual attacks by the Irgun and the Stern Gang are turning opinion against the Jews,' said Julia.

'I know,' agreed David gloomily. 'It's an impossible situation.'

As they talked on their way to and from the office every day, Julia had discovered that David was not nearly as doctrinaire and fanatically left wing as Anthony believed, and she grew increasingly to respect his ideas. She liked him too and as she and Anthony grew happier together, Julia lost most of her irritation with David's presence in their home, but she never let herself forget Anthony's warning. He had not repeated it, and seemed much less inclined to criticise and provoke David, but Julia was too cautious to trust anyone described in the terms Anthony had used of David.

She sometimes asked him about his war, as though that might have helped her to see him more clearly. He talked easily enough of Anthony's achievements but very little of his own. Once when Julia pressed him, he reluctantly explained that he had been sent to Italy by an intelligence organisation and was therefore bound to secrecy.

'David, I am sorry,' said Julia at once. 'I'd never have nagged you to tell me if I'd known.'

'It's all right,' he said, with his familiar smile. 'You couldn't have known and I had begun to feel churlish stalling whenever you showed interest in what I'd done.'

'I've met one or two people from SOE since it ended,' she said slowly, 'and they have described some of the things they had to do.'

'It wasn't SOE,' said David shortly. Then, apparently regretting his curtness, he added: 'It was a small group run by an extraordinary man called Suvarov and set up to monitor the political affiliations of resistance groups. At first it was simply staffed by researchers but as the war developed it became clear that direct intelligence was needed and a few of us were sent in to work with partisans.'

'How extraordinary!' said. Julia. 'I've never even heard of its existence.'

'Very few people have, and Suvarov has always wanted to keep it like that. I ought not to have said anything even now, but I know that I can trust you not to talk about it,' said David seriously.

'Yes,' she answered, wishing that she could be as confident in him; 'you can trust me.'

She also could not quite bring herself to trust Giovanna Sassanta. She was an excellent teacher and under her tutelage Julia made quick progress with her Italian. They got on well together, too, and always had plenty to talk about, but Julia could not escape the feeling that Giovanna was less than frank about her real feelings towards the Allies.

Giovanna was fanatically opposed to Communism and to that extent shared the American and British ideas of how the postwar world should be shaped, but it was clear that she bitterly resented what they had done to her country as they fought their way up it from Sicily to the Alps and also the way in which they had been administering it since the Germans had been defeated.

The two women talked a lot, sometimes in slow, careful Italian, but more often in English, and Julia grew to like Giovanna so much that she wanted to banish her doubts. One day as they were sitting in the shabby, cold, uncomfortable sitting room at the end of her lesson, Julia felt that she knew Giovanna well enough at last to ask what it had been like to live with a man who believed in something as alien as Fascism.

'It was not quite like that,' said Giovanna, rightly assuming that her pupil's ideas of what it had been like to live in Italy before and during the war had been formed only by the foreign press. 'Roberto was a good man, kind and pragmatic, and he was my husband.' She got up and fetched a photograph from a table between two windows and showed it to Julia. The leather-framed photograph showed a middle-aged man wearing spectacles; his hair was receding and he was dressed in a dark suit. To Julia he looked almost nondescript, neither good nor bad. There was nothing she could say about him.

'He never denounced anyone or damaged anyone,' Giovanna explained patiently, trying to banish the obvious doubt in Julia's brown eyes. 'It's easy for you English in your island, where everyone is innocent because no one had to choose, but here it's different. Roberto was not political. He pursued his business, looked after his workers as well as he could, and – how do you say it? – he turned the blind eye to my activities.'

'You mean he knew about them?' said Julia. 'Wasn't that dangerous?'

Once again Giovanna shrugged. 'Everything was dangerous under the Fascists – let alone the Germans. Roberto thought that we could protect each other. Whichever side won, one of us would have the right contacts to ensure the other's safety.'

Giovanna laughed then, and Julia winced at the bitterness of the sound. She did not know that Giovanna was remembering the day that masked men claiming to be partisans had burst into her house and forced their way to her husband's study. He had been sitting at his desk and she had just gone in to ask him something. When the door was flung open and three young men with guns stood there, Giovanna had gone straight to her husband's side. Before she could say anything, the first man had shot her husband at point-blank range while he sat at his desk.

She had been quite unable to believe what she was watching. It seemed to happen so slowly that ever since she had castigated herself for not speaking, not flinging herself on the young man with the gun before he could fire.

Giovanna shuddered suddenly, thinking of the blood and tissue that had sprayed from Roberto's head down the front of her skirt and the mocking greeting of one of the masked young men.

'We apologise, *signora*,' he had said, 'that it has taken us so long to rid you of this Fascist pig. But we have been busy in the town.'

Giovanna had gagged then and nearly fainted as she clung to the big desk, trying to keep upright until they had gone. But they had not gone until they had stripped her house of everything of value that they could find and carry away. She gasped again at the memory, feeling the same terrible powerlessness, the fear, the disgust and the desperate anger.

'Are you all right?' Julia's cool, English voice brought Giovanna back to the present. She looked almost in disbelief at the shabby furnishings of the house she had rented and the sagging bookshelves behind the upright figure of her intelligent, sympathetic, but probably prejudiced English pupil.

'Say it in Italian, please,' she said to give herself time to bury the memories again. Julia struggled, reached for her pocket dictionary and eventually produced an acceptable Italian sentence. Giovanna manufactured a smile.

'*Bene*,' she said. 'You have done well, and you learn quickly.'

'You're a good teacher,' said Julia. She looked at her watch. 'May I drop in downstairs before I go? I promised to lend Raffaella a book. She learns quickly too, much more so than any of the others.'

'Ah, yes, I can imagine it. She seems intelligent.'

'Giovanna,' said Julia slowly, 'how much do you know about her? I mean, has it ever struck you that she is not quite the same as the others?'

'Of course it has,' came the calm answer, 'but that doesn't matter. She came here afraid and in need. I don't ask questions of any of them. What does it matter now what happened before? The partisans killed Roberto, because he belonged to the wrong side. It didn't change anything for them; it did them no good. Between them all the different sides have wrecked Italy. Someone has to rebuild something, put people's lives together again without digging around for reasons to hate.'

'I see,' said Julia. 'But ought you not to find out about her?'

'No,' said Giovanna categorically. 'Even if I wanted to, how could I? The only name I know her by is "Raffaella". It's unlikely that it is her real name and even if it were how would it help me to find where she comes from?'

'But what about her identity papers? Ration books?' Julia asked.

Giovanna shrugged and her heavy eyelids drooped over her black eyes.

'She had none when she came. But they are not always ... necessary. They can be ... replaced.'

Julia was not certain whether Giovanna was telling her that she had bought forged identity papers for Raffaella and she was careful not to ask. Giovanna's gibe about the 'innocent English' had been enough to stop Julia from feeling any right to moral superiority. When they had said goodbye to each other, she went down to look for Raffaella to hand over the book she had brought. She knocked on the door.

'*Entra*,' called Raffaella and Julia went into the small bedroom to find her sitting by a window with her child in her arms.

She was trying to persuade her baby to eat little squares of bread that looked as though they had been dipped in milk. There was a lamp on a chest beside the window seat and its yellow light poured down on her smooth blonde hair, making it shine and pointing up the contrast between its luxuriance and the shabbiness of her cheap black dress. But what Julia noticed most of all was the tenderness with which Raffaella held her baby and the gentle smile on her small mouth. Trying not to remember her tormenting dreams and needs, Julia almost backed out of the room, reluctant to disturb the two of them.

'Signora Giulia,' said the girl, looking up from her child at last. She dropped the last soggy piece of bread back into the painted bowl beside her and picked up a clean rag to wipe his milky lips. 'How good to see you. Is that right in English?'

'That's right,' answered Julia, smiling. 'You are making very good progress at your English conversation. I have brought you the book.' She put it down on the window seat beside Raffaella.

'Ah, thank you,' she said, stroking the child's furry head in a casual, happy way that made Julia's insides clench. It seemed absurd to feel bitterly jealous of a girl hardly out of her teens, who was saddled with a fatherless child in a country that was three-quarters ruined. But, absurd or not, jealousy was just what Julia felt and it disgusted her.

The child was as attractive as his mother, with big eyes that were less green than hers, although his hair was dark. He smiled a lot and gurgled happily when she held him up and kissed him.

'Would you like to hold him, *signora?*' Raffaella said suddenly as she caught the expression of longing on Julia's usually calm, firm-chinned face.

'I?' said Julia in a tone of surprise, but her arms had already arranged themselves to receive him. Raffaella tightened the blue shawl in which she had wrapped him and handed him over. Julia sat down on a hard wooden chair that Raffaella brought her and looked down into the baby's face. He seemed quite content within the arms of an inexperienced stranger and suddenly smiled up at her, opening his mouth and crinkling up his blue-grey eyes. Julia thought that there was a flash of intelligence in them, but she dismissed the idea as nothing but sentimentality.

'How old is he?' Julia asked, looking away from the child into the pretty face of his mother and noticing that her mouth was a quite different shape from his. Hers had a short upper lip, while his was both bigger and more evenly closed.

'Eighteen months,' answered Raffaella, having counted through all the English numbers up to eighteen so that there could be no misunderstanding. 'He is very greedy, and bigger than that.'

'But charming,' said Julia, taking hold of one of his hands and revelling in the sensation of closeness when his small fingers gripped hers.

'Like his father,' said Raffaella, holding out her arms. With some reluctance, Julia handed the child back. Jealous herself, Julia was aware of the passionate envy that Raffaella might feel of someone in her position and she had no wish to sound like Lady Bountiful, dispensing charity and demanding confidences in return. She did not want to ask any indiscreet questions, and yet if Raffaella wanted to talk, Julia did not want to stop her. She compromised with an interested smile.

'Signora Giulia,' Raffaella said after a moment of obvious indecision.

'Yes,' said Julia encouragingly, noticing with surprise that there was a calculating expression in the pale-green eyes that looked across to hers.

'Can you help me to go to England, and . . . to live?' Raffaella asked.

'I think that's a bit unlikely,' said Julia, quite taken aback. 'I have no powers to do anything like that. Why England? Wouldn't America be a better place for you to start again? There are so many Italians there and it's a place where –'

'I do not like Americans,' said Raffaella bitterly. Julia, still feeling sore about the way the United States exercised their enormous power to coerce and criticise her country, could not prevent a sympathetic smile forming on her lips. Raffaella brightened at once.

'I just do not know, Raffaella,' said Julia slowly. 'I will try to find out if it would be possible to get you to England. I expect it will be difficult. You are wise to practise your English while you wait,' she added, no longer surprised that Raffaella always had a question prepared at the beginning of each lesson about some aspect of English life and often begged for books and extra work. None of the other women had ever shown so much interest.

'*Grazie, signora*,' said Raffaella, letting her heavy eyelids hide whatever expression there was in her pretty but slightly protuberant eyes.

'Well, goodbye,' said Julia, getting up. She could not resist going to stroke the child's head for a moment and closed her eyes as she felt his warmth under the palm of her hand. 'I shall see you on Wednesday as usual. Will you give my regards to the others, please?'

'*Certo*,' said Raffaella, watching her over the baby's head.

Julia walked home through the shabby streets of the Dorsoduro, using her torch in all the unlit alleys and squares. She knew the way well enough by then to turn left and right by instinct and as she walked she tried to think of ways in which she might be able to help Raffaella.

When she reached the Accademia Bridge, Julia leaned for a while against the parapet, looking down to the Grand Canal towards Santa Maria della Salute. It was very cold, but everything looked so wonderful that she was prepared to put up with it for a while. The moon had risen while she was in Giovanna's house and now lit the black water of the canal with sliding pools of whiteness. It fell, too, on the palaces on either side, catching the coloured marble inlay of one and the eccentric funnel-shaped chimneys of another, and bathed the entire white dome of the Salute so that it stood majestically pale against black sky and black water at the head of the canal.

A small motor boat chugged through the canal beneath the bridge, sending the water slapping against the palaces and splintering the moonlight on the water into a hundred flashing fragments. Julia leaned her elbows on the uncomfortable parapet of the bridge and acknowledged the allure of Venice that she had resisted in her first, depressed reaction to the city. She was happier than she had been when David Wallington had told her how much he loved the place and she was prepared to admit the pleasure it could give.

As soon as she reached the house in the Campo San Maurizio Julia went straight up to her bedroom to drop her Italian text books and take off her hat before joining the men in the huge, cold salon for dinner. But when she walked into the room she had the distinct impression that she was interrupting something very important.

Her husband was sitting at one end of the gilded sofa with his head in his hands and David Wallington was standing in front of him, talking very quietly. He stopped as soon as he heard Julia's step and turned his head, revealing a bleak and worried face.

'Are you all right, David?' she asked, suddenly anxious. 'You look terrible.' He nodded his dark head and she expelled the breath she had been holding. Then David moved aside so that she could see her husband. When he did not speak, David said:

'Anthony's had some very bad news. I'll get you a drink, old man.'

'Have you, darling?' said Julia going to her husband's side at once. She sat down on the sofa and when David had walked out of the room took one of Anthony's hands in hers. It was clammy with sweat and he withdrew it at once, but he did not cover his face again. She saw that his skin was grey and as sweaty as his palm; his eyes looked bloodshot and his mouth pinched. Every other thought was banished from her mind by concern for him.

'What's happened, Anthony?' she asked. He turned to look at her and she could not be sure whether it was anger or dislike that distorted his face.

'Flavia's dead,' he said, looking away again.

For a moment Julia could not speak as she tried to control the maelstrom of wildly different emotions that swirled in her mind. At once relieved that the news was not worse for Anthony personally and sad that the appealing, unhappy child was dead, she wished that she had been able to do more to ease Flavia's torments and resented Anthony's prohibition all over again.

'What happened?' she asked when she could be sure that her voice would sound gentle again.

Anthony straightened his spine and then leaned against the rigid gilt back of the sofa, looking up at the frivolous painted ceiling.

'It doesn't matter. All that matters is that she's dead.'

'I'm so sorry, Anthony,' said Julia. 'But you mustn't let yourself hurt like this. You know better than anyone that there's never a guaranteed cure for any serious medical condition. And –'

'For God's sake! Don't try to comfort me,' he said bitterly through clenched teeth. Taken aback, Julia got off the sofa and went to stand at one of the long windows looking down at the canal. It seemed such a short time ago that she had been happy. The darkness of the water reminded her of Flavia's huge, frightened eyes and the reflected light of the moment when she had at last smiled and spoken. Julia turned her back on the moonlight.

'Anthony,' she began again, but before she could say any more, David Wallington came back, carrying a tray with a bottle and three glasses on it. He put the tray down on the table, which, Julia saw, was already laid for dinner, and opened the bottle. He poured out three glasses of wine and took one to Anthony.

'Here,' he said carefully. 'You need a drink.'

'To drug myself into insensibility?' said Anthony. 'I thought you always believed that I ought not to give them those drugs. Shouldn't you be delighted that I'm feeling like this about the consequences?'

'No of course not,' said David carefully. He went to fetch a small table and carried it to the sofa so that he could put Anthony's drink on it within reach. But Anthony ignored it, got up and announced that he was going to have a bath.

'I hope there's some hot water for him,' said Julia. 'David, what was all that about?'

'It's a bit complicated,' he answered. 'Why not come and sit down?'

Julia did as he suggested and waited.

'Come on, David,' she said, putting all the authority of her five years' seniority into her voice. 'I know that you don't like breaking confidences, but I'm only going to put my foot in it with Anthony if I don't understand what's been going on.' He looked at her, unhappy and pleading, but she did not let him off the hook.

'You probably know that penicillin is desperately scarce?' he said at last. Julia nodded impatiently. 'Well, in certain emergencies, Anthony has bought it on the black market – out of his own money. He did that this time when the child got meningitis. She died soon after the first injection. Anthony thinks that the drug must have been adulterated – or fake.'

Julia was silent as she absorbed the horrible implications of what David had said.

'Oh poor Anthony,' she said slowly. 'No wonder he couldn't bear to be comforted. He must feel as though he killed her himself.'

# Chapter Fourteen

Anthony did not return to the salon that night and so Julia knocked on his door when she went up to bed.

'Come in,' he called in a resigned voice. She went in to see him lying on his bed in the dark. He was still fully dressed and there was a cigarette smouldering unsmoked in the ash tray by his side.

'Well?' he said disagreeably. 'I suppose David has told you about my illegal drug running?'

'Anthony,' said Julia carefully, 'don't build up a great drama where there isn't one. Flavia's death is quite bad enough without that.'

'Good heavens!' he said, swinging his feet over the side of the bed and switching on the light. 'Don't tell me you – my excessively law-respecting wife – think I was right to buy black-market penicillin?'

Julia fetched a chair and brought it to Anthony's bedside.

'No,' she said, not prepared to lie even to comfort him, 'I don't but I can understand precisely . . .'

'How gratifying for us both that you understand,' he said. Julia winced at the sarcasm.

'I hadn't meant to sound patronising,' she said when she could. 'Don't let's quarrel about it. I came because I hate you to be unhappy and I thought that perhaps I could help. We used to talk sometimes in the old days when you had had a tragedy at the hospital and it seemed to help you then.'

Something in the reasonableness of her voice or her good intentions reached Anthony. Through the agony he recognised what she was offering him, but it was something he could not accept. He stubbed out the cigarette and wiped both hands over his face.

'I'm not really fit for human consumption tonight, Julia,' he said, trying to sound less angry. 'And there is nothing on earth you could do or say to make me feel less ghastly than I already do. I loved that child and I killed her. The fact that she might have died anyway, that she was living in terror and misery that are now over, that ... oh, all the rational consolations you are no doubt ready to hand out: none of them can touch what I feel now. Go to bed and leave me alone with it.'

'All right,' said Julia, getting up to put the chair away. 'But if you –'

'No, Julia,' Anthony said, sounding at the end of his tether. 'Don't say any of it. Just go away.'

Julia left and went to lie alone in bed, wondering how to help him and why she could not and what had happened between them to make him so unreachable. She wished that she could understand him as easily as the witnesses she cross-examined in her professional life. None of her carefully developed rationality could stop her feeling as though he had hit her, and none of the real compassion she felt for him could stop her feeling angry about it.

The next day when Anthony came back from the hospital he announced that he had arranged a funeral for Flavia at three o'clock the following Saturday afternoon and expected that Julia and David would be there. Both of them agreed at once, prepared to do anything that might make him feel less desperate about the child's death.

Anthony had chosen a small shabby baroque church close to the hospital for the service, and they all made their own way there separately. When Julia arrived, dressed in her black London suit and best hat, she was surprised to see that the church was almost full and that many of the mourners were children. David was sitting beside Anthony in one of the front rows of chairs, dressed in uniform, and Annunziata was there too. As Julia walked up the aisle to join them, she recognised Sister Caroline from the hospital as she passed and assumed that the rest of the congregation were Anthony's colleagues and patients.

There were two large vases of flowers in front of the steps up to the sanctuary and between them lay a small, white coffin on trestles. Red candles stood in the massive gold sticks around the altar and the priest who waited there was dressed in black vestments.

'Am I late?' she whispered to Anthony as she slid into the chair beside him. He shook his head. A choir of small boys filed into their seats in the sanctuary and Julia was touched to see how many of them had sticks and crutches. They, too, must be Anthony's patients.

The priest came forward and began what Julia slowly realised was a full requiem mass. The scent of the incense that was blown in great smoky drifts across the church made her feel faint and the unfamiliarity of the Roman Catholic service made it seem even longer than it was. Julia tried to feel appropriate emotions, but all she could think of was how inappropriate the endless, heavy service seemed for the death of so young a child, and all she could feel was a strong conviction that if Anthony had cared so much for a strange child, he ought not to be so adamantly opposed to their having their own family.

She looked sideways at him during the mass itself, while the Catholics among the congregation took communion, and lost her anger as she saw the misery in his eyes and the whiteness of his face. He had clamped his bottom lip between his teeth, and when she looked down she saw that his fists were clenched. Julia looked away, unable to watch so much pain without offering help he would not accept.

At last the mass was over and Anthony edged out of the row of chairs to pick up the little coffin and carry it down the aisle himself. His shoulders were taut and his face paler then ever and set in bleak lines. Exchanging a surprised and anxious look with David, Julia picked up her bag and followed. When they walked out of the church into the little grey square, they found that Anthony was carrying the coffin towards a purple-draped, black motor-boat that was tied up by the stone steps down to the canal.

'Come on,' he said. Julia and David obeyed, and joined Anthony and the priest. The boat set off through the small backwaters towards the Fondamente Nuove and out across the lagoon to the island of San Michele. Julia remembered how David had pointed it out to her when he had first brought her to Venice and how she had thought it the ideal place to be buried. Now, all she could think of was the child who had lived in the body that lay in the coffin. Rain started to fall, lightly at first and then in such solid, relentless drops that it beat up the surface of the water and made it hard to see more than a yard or two ahead.

Julia found herself shuddering at the thought of what would happen to the body itself and wishing that she could believe in some kind of afterlife. Brought up as a Christian, she had mislaid her childhood faith at some stage in her growing up, almost without noticing it, and now she regretted it. There had been so much death in the last six years that it seemed almost indecent to mind so much that this one child was dead, but Julia could not help herself.

She felt something being thrust into her gloved hand and looked down in surprise to see that David was offering her a large handkerchief. Until that moment she had not realised that she had tears mixed with the rain on her face and quickly mopped them.

When the burial was over and they had all returned, wet and cold, to Venice, Anthony announced curtly that he was going to the hospital. Annunziata said that she had shopping she must do and so Julia and David were left to go back to the flat together.

'Thank you for your handkerchief,' Julia said when they were alone. 'I'll get it washed and give it you back. I'm sorry to have made such an exhibition of myself.'

'You didn't do any such thing,' said David quietly. 'It was a very natural reaction. In fact I . . .' He broke off and Julia hurried to fill the difficult silence.

'I'm not sure whether I was really crying for that poor child,' she said, not wanting him to think her more altruistic than she was, 'or for Anthony or for myself. I . . . I so much want to help him, but all I manage to do just now is irritate him.'

'As I do,' said David. 'Please don't let it make you unhappy.'

Julia was so surprised that she stopped. David stopped too and turned to face her in the rain, which was slowly beginning to slacken.

'I just mean that there's been enough unhappiness over all this without your suffering, too,' said David. 'I know you can't simply turn it off, but I'm sure when Anthony recovers he'd hate to think of your remembering the things he said when he was half out of his mind with misery.'

Julia watched David as he stood silhouetted against the low grey sky, looking solid and dependable. For once she forgot that she was older than he and more experienced in everything except war, she forgot Anthony's warnings and her own resistance to David's charm and she let herself acknowledge for the first time that in him she had found a person who seemed in some way a reflection of herself. She felt that she knew him well and ought to be able to trust him, too.

'Thank you,' was all she said.

'For nothing,' he answered. 'It's only common sense.'

'I think that perhaps that's one reason I feel so grateful,' said Julia with a rueful smile on her wide mouth. 'Both Anthony and Comfort get horribly irritated when I try to do for them what you have just done for me and I ... I wonder,' she added in quite different voice. She started walking again.

'Wonder what?' asked David falling into step with her.

'Oh, just whether I could get Comfort to come out here to stay for a bit. She might well be able to get through to him. She ... they ... she always used to be able to reach him in his blackest glooms, when I could only offer things he did not want.'

'Are they so very close?' asked David as they reached the empty expanse of St Mark's Square. 'When he got back from London last year he gave me the distinct impression that he found her rather tiresome.'

'He was a bit annoyed with her then,' Julia admitted, watching the way the pigeons scuttled away from them through the puddles, only bothering to take to the air when escape became inevitable.

'But yes, they're very close. Much more so really than brothers and sisters who have been brought up together.'

'I hadn't realised that they had not,' said David, coming to a halt outside the plate-glass windows of Florian's café. 'I say, would you like a cup of coffee or something? There's no particular reason to get back home, is there?'

'None that I know of,' said Julia, thinking how extraordinary men were. Anthony and David had spent two years living in close proximity in the greatest danger and yet they had obviously never discussed their families. 'And it might even stop raining. Yes, I'd love a cup. Thank you.'

David pushed open the door for her and they went in out of the rain, taking off their coats and shaking the wet off them. Julia loved the elegant old café, with its painted walls and hard, red-velvet seats. No one hurried you there, even if you chose to spend all morning toying with a single cup of coffee. After the bustle and discomfort of wartime restaurants in London, Florian's seemed a haven of half-forgotten leisure.

As usual it was full of Allied officers on a 'swan' from their tedious post-war postings around Italy, mixed with a few Venetians, who were reading newspapers, chatting or simply idling their time away looking out of the windows that overlooked the square. David exchanged greetings with half a dozen men in uniform and introduced Julia to each one. She was rather amused to see one or two knowing glances cast in her direction and, as soon as she and David were settled at their own table out of earshot of any of his acquaintances, she said with a smile:

'I think one or two of your friends are wondering what's happened to make you pick up such an eccentric sort of popsie.' To her surprise, and amusement, David took it seriously.

'I do apologise,' he said formally. 'I ought to have made it clearer that you were here with Anthony.'

'Oh, don't worry, David,' said Julia. 'I only mentioned it because I thought it was funny. Now, what shall we have? I think I'd like hot chocolate, if they have any.'

David turned to give their order to the white-coated waiter who was hovering by their table, and before he had finished Julia's attention was caught by a familiar, drawling American voice. She looked up to recognise Jackson French.

'Why if it isn't Mrs Gillingham from the plane,' he said, seeing her watching him. He levered his long, heavy body up from behind the little white-marble table where he was sitting and strolled over to her.

'Mr French,' she said, holding out her hand. 'How nice to see you again so soon. This is Major Wallington, an old friend of my husband. We're all sharing the same digs here in Venice. David, this is Jackson French of UNRRA.'

'We met at the airport of course,' said David, nodding a little stiffly to the American. 'How are you, French?'

'Fine, just fine,' he answered.

'Are you here for long?' Julia asked, suddenly remembering his job and its possible implications for her husband. The shock of Flavia's death and Anthony's reaction to it had overshadowed the significance of his revelation about buying drugs on the black market.

'I fly out tomorrow,' he said pleasantly. 'We've had reports that a big batch of penicillin has been lifted from the depot in Klagenfurt and it's said to be on its way into Italy. We want to get hold of it and the "liberators" before it's been divided up and possibly adulterated and distributed to God-knows-where. Good to see you both. So long.' He raised a hand and retreated to his own table, collected his companion and left the café.

Julia had avoided looking at David while the American was with them, but once he had gone she said quietly:

'What would happen to him if it were discovered?'

'Anthony? God knows . . . Probably not much, but it wouldn't do his reputation any good at all either here or in London, which is unfair since what he's done has always been wholly altruistic. It's not as though he's profiting from the black market: simply spending his own money to make good the deficiencies of the legitimate distribution system.'

'I know all that,' said Julia. 'But if someone really is messing about with the penicillin, the authorities ought to be given every chance of catching them. That's far wickeder than any black marketeering.'

'I know,' said David. The waiter arrived just then with a heavy silver tray of cups and pots. He arranged it on their table and David poured out Julia's hot chocolate and then his own coffee. 'Anthony and I have argued about that. But he won't do anything about it and I can't bring myself to report him. The one faint gleam of light in this whole horrible murky business is that he's unlikely to go to the black market again.'

'And so we just ignore it?' said Julia, holding her warm cup in both hands.

'I can't see that we have any realistic option,' answered David sadly. 'Besides, Anthony has a virtually unanswerable criticism of anyone who suggests to him that it is illegal to buy black-market drugs and that he ought to uphold the law, and be seen to do so, particularly now when it has been so badly threatened for so long.'

'Really?' said Julia, interested and a little worried. 'And what is that?'

'That we are in the process of prosecuting a man for obeying the laws of his own country when it would have been more humanitarian to have disobeyed . . .'

'Ah, that,' said Julia, who often thought about that particular dilemma. 'Yes. It isn't answerable, although there are a lot of answers one could try to make. But it doesn't alter the fact that he might have information that could help identify the criminals who are selling lethal drugs.'

'I know,' he said. 'But all I can bring myself to do is to try to persuade him. You may be able to do more.' As he spoke Julia looked so troubled that David made an effort to change the subject.

'You were just about to tell me about Anthony and his sister when I interrupted you,' he said in a quite different voice.

Appreciating his attempt to distract her, Julia smiled and drank some hot chocolate.

'Yes,' she said, 'you asked me if they were close. I think that because of their rather peculiar lives they are much closer than siblings in any normal family.'

'I hadn't known that there was anything peculiar,' said David. 'Not that I want you to tell me anything . . .'

'Don't worry. There's nothing at all secret about it. Their parents split up when Anthony was six and Comfort two. Their mother took Comfort back to Pittsburgh and brought her up as a rich American, while Anthony lived with his English father in rather straitened circumstances in Cornwall. They met again at their father's funeral when Comfort was twenty-one and just becoming determined to live in Europe, where she thought her painting would have a better chance than in the States.'

'How extraordinary it must have been!' said David. 'Meeting as complete strangers and yet, according to the photographs Anthony has shown me of Comfort, they look almost exactly the same.'

'Yes they do, although their characters have quite big differences. Anyway, they became the firmest of friends. I imagine that he took the place of the father she'd never had. Comfort moved in with Anthony and when he took a job at one of the Oxford hospitals, she decided to go with him and take a degree there. That's where I met them.'

'I'd wondered about that,' said David with a smile as he remembered his surprise at Julia's complete unlikeness to her husband. 'And so you were friends with her first?'

'Yes. She was quite a bit older than the rest of us, but she took me up and included me in most of the terribly glamorous life she and Anthony lived out at Cumnor.'

Julia stopped then, thinking back to the idyllic years they had spent as first Comfort and then Anthony had made friends with her and introduced her into a world quite different from anything she had known.

They had made her feel both valuable and valued, which was an intoxicating sensation to the young provincial girl who had been brought up to think of herself as a poor substitute for a son by her father and as a tiresome and unsatisfactory rebel by her mother. Anthony and Comfort had also made Julia feel that she fitted into their world of internationally acclaimed artists and connoisseurs, scientists and writers. Dazzled by their friends as much as by the style in which they lived, Julia had thought that the Gillinghams were the physical embodiment of every virtue. By the time she had learned to know them well enough to see their failings, she loved them both too much to care.

'They were wonderful to me,' she said, blinking, unaware that her face had softened and her mouth curved into the gentlest, most delightful smile David had ever seen on her lips.

'Anthony's a good friend,' David said. 'And so if his sister is anything like him, I can understand how you must feel about her.'

'Apart from that,' said Julia, still smiling but in her more familiar lopsided way, 'there was her extraordinary generosity. She seemed positively to want me to fall in love with him. Most women who cared as much as she does about their brothers would have had some reservations about a usurper.'

'But you were hardly that, were you?' said David. 'I mean, you didn't exactly take him away from her. You all share your house, don't you?'

Julia nodded. 'It seemed both practical and the best thing to do. After all, we did before Anthony and I married and so it would have been odd, as well as horribly unkind, to leave Comfort alone afterwards – when she had become my sister . . . in law at least.' She drained the last of her rich, thick hot chocolate. 'I'm sure she'll come here when she knows how much he needs her, and I hope you'll like her.'

'I'm sure I shall,' said David. 'After all, you do.'

He got up and called the waiter so that he could pay their bill, leaving Julia taken aback by his choice of words.

As soon as they got home again, she went up to change out of her damp clothes and to write to Comfort, begging her to come to Venice to help Anthony. Julia said nothing about the black market or the possibility that the penicillin Anthony had injected into Flavia had been adulterated, but she did explain about his devotion to the child and his unhappiness.

I seem unable to give him any kind of consolation [she wrote], and you were always so good at cheering him up in the old days. Couldn't you come? I know it's difficult to get a place on an aeroplane, but you managed to get Anthony home last Christmas. Do try, Comfort. I miss you so much and Anthony needs you.

Julia had to wait three weeks for an answer, weeks during which Anthony became more and more distant from her. He insisted on sleeping alone and left the house before either Julia or David were up each morning, returning silent and exhausted long after dinner. He seemed to talk more to Annunziata than to either of the others, meeting all their overtures with monosyllabic coldness. Knowing how unhappy he was – and how guilty he felt himself to be – Julia did not resent his silences or his long absences from the house, but she was hurt by them and longed to be able to help.

David watched her, admiring the way she put up with Anthony's patent hostility without ever snapping back at him and most desperately pitying her. Her predicament made him angrier with Anthony than he had ever been and shook the foundations of his friendship as nothing else had done. How anyone could treat a woman like Julia with as much coldness as Anthony did was something that David could neither understand nor forgive. It seemed to him that Anthony ought to put the war behind him, difficult and unpleasant though it had been, and make a fraction of the effort Julia made every day to keep their life together amicable.

As Anthony became increasingly hostile, Julia found herself turning more and more to David, until she had to face the fact that she had allowed herself to grow dangerously fond of him.

Something in David had woken her to a knowledge of her own needs. She was not sure whether it was his generosity, his quiet courage, his unfailing care for people or the knowledge he had of his own character and his acceptance of it, but something in him had made her recognise that there were parts of her own self that had been too long denied. It occurred to her forcibly that it was nowhere written in stone that she should be the Gillinghams' devoted protegée and emotional punchbag for ever. She owed both Comfort and Anthony a great deal, but it suddenly seemed to her as though she had been paying the debt for too long and with too much interest.

Appalled at herself and her disloyalty, Julia reminded herself that she was married. However high the interest on her debt, she had undertaken to pay it and must pay to the end. David had shown her a self that cried out to something it had recognised in him, but she knew that she had to ignore it all. She understood at last she was falling in love with him, but with that realisation came the knowledge that she must stop herself before she did any more damage.

'Never mind,' she told herself energetically. 'Treat it like a cold: ignore the symptoms and they'll clear up in time.'

Her letter reached Comfort by the last post on a raw January day, when she was just leaving the house to go to an exhibition sponsored by her own dealer. Comfort stuffed the envelope in her crocodile handbag, straightened her hat and hurried out to find a taxi.

Until he had invited her to the exhibition, Marcus had not told her that he was supporting a small group of refugee artists, mostly from Eastern Europe, but as soon as he did she badgered him to introduce her to them. It had never occurred to her that Julia's departure for Venice would leave her lonely and she was unprepared for the depression that settled on her as the winter began to bite. The painting DPs promised a diversion at least from her accustomed life of queueing for rations, trying to work in the freezing studio, battling with the consequences of the transport strike, and seeing friends who seemed to be just as miserable as she was herself.

When she reached the little gallery in Chelsea that Marcus considered adequate for the new painters, she looked eagerly at the twenty-four paintings he had hung. Only a few interested her at all, but there was one that seized her imagination. It was a small landscape, desolate and snow-covered, and yet indescribably beautiful.

'Like it, Comfort?' Marcus's slightly nasal drawl woke her out of her silent contemplation and she turned with an eager smile.

'Very much,' she said. 'Whose is it?'

'Tibor Smith,' he answered. 'Come and have a glass of tea and meet him.'

'Glass of tea?' said Comfort as they walked to the far end of the room, where a few people were huddling round a paraffin heater. They looked discouraged and almost abject. Comfort, who thought that she had had enough discouragement of her own, decided to back away, but Marcus gripped her wrist and insisted on introducing her.

Later he also insisted on sending her home in a taxi with Tibor Smith as her escort. Comfort insisted that she was quite capable of going on her own, but the Hungarian kissed her hand with such an air and begged to be allowed to go with her in such an attractively accented voice that she smiled on him and let him take her home.

By the time they reached Brunswick Square she liked him enough to invite him in for a cup of 'English' tea and felt a rare sense of embarrassment as she took him up through the big house to her studio and learned that he and the other five painters were camping together in the three small rooms over Marcus's second-best gallery.

A week later she offered him the use of Julia's rooms on the first floor and a space in the studio in which to paint. It was only after he had moved in and she was handing him her ration book so that he could go and do the necessary queueing for her food that she rediscovered Julia's letter, tucked in a pocket of her bag. While Tibor went off into the bitter cold outside, she huddled over her scanty fire and read of Anthony's need for her.

When Comfort's belated reply reached Venice, it gave Julia a welcome distraction and a faint hope that there might soon be an end to Anthony's deliberately solitary unhappiness. Comfort wrote that she would come to Venice as soon as she could, but that that probably would not be until late February.

I've written to Anthony, of course [she ended her letter], and I'm pulling all the wires I can find to get a flight sooner, but it does not look hopeful. I have to go to Paris early in the month to see Bob Storrington, who is making arrangements for a big exhibition of my stuff there and it may be possible to come straight on to Venice. I'll let you know. Thank you for telling me.

With that Julia had to be content and she settled down in the freezing cold of that most bitter winter to wait out the time until Anthony could be freed of his load of guilt and depression and she could rid herself of her unsuitable affection for his friend.

# Chapter Fifteen

The trial of Field Marshal Kesselring opened at ten o'clock on 10 February in the dark-panelled courtroom under the slogan *'La Legge è Uguale per Tutti'*. David and Julia and the other court personnel had been in their appointed seats for an hour and a half before the proceedings began. The important visitors filed in after them, and then the members of the press corps. When they were all settled, the President of the Court, the four colonels who made up the tribunal and the Judge Advocate General appeared, followed at last by the prisoner. Kesselring, impressive and solid-looking with very short silver-grey hair, was unmistakably a very senior Prussian officer.

Watching him, Julia remembered Mark Heathwood's descriptions of the favourable impression Kesselring had made when he gave evidence at Nuremberg. She was interested to know how his lawyers would conduct his defence since he had made no denials of his actions and ideals during his London interrogation, but the prosecution case would come first.

The prosecutor rose to give the opening address, but before he could begin Kesselring's chief defence lawyer, Dr Hans Laternser, asked the court to grant an adjournment. He had arrived in Venice from Nuremberg only the previous day after two nights' travel. He had had no time to confer with his client and only twelve hours to study the charges.

After much discussion and with obvious reluctance, the court was adjourned for a week.

The trial was resumed a week later, only to be adjourned once more after the opening proceedings and the prosecution's opening address, setting out the charges. The Field Marshal was to be tried on two counts: the first, that he had been responsible for the killing of 335 Italians in the Ardeatine Caves outside Rome and the second that he had incited his troops to act with unnecessary force against the partisans.

On Wednesday 19 February the trial at last began in earnest with the cross-examination of Lieutenant Colonel Scotland. There was a light moment that morning, when the prosecuting lawyer asked his witness a question about the organisation of the German army. Dr Laternser immediately rose to protest that the witness had never been in the German army and therefore could not properly be asked or answer any such questions.

Prosecuting counsel then said quietly to his witness:

'Colonel Scotland, were you ever in the German army?'

To the astonishment of almost everyone in the court, the answer came in the affirmative. Later, Julia discovered that the German army in question had been in South Africa and that Colonel Scotland's appointment had ended some years before the Great War.

His evidence was also remarkable for his insistence that Kesselring had exaggerated his own importance as Officer Commanding Troops in Italy, and was therefore not in fact responsible for the atrocities of which he stood accused. It was curious, Julia thought, to hear the chief prosecution witness speaking so forcefully in favour of the defendant.

It was not until the following Monday that the affidavits on which Julia had worked so hard and for so long were presented to the court. It had eventually been decided to limit the statements to accounts of atrocities alleged to have been committed only between June and August 1944, so that they could be tied precisely to Kesselring's orders.

Very few witnesses had been found who were prepared to come to court to repeat their statements in the flesh, but some did and their words were translated first into English and then into German, causing some confusion as to the precise meaning of what they had actually said. The translations were not the only technical difficulty: there were only two shorthand writers in the court and they were hard pressed to keep up with the proceedings, causing the court to be adjourned more than once so that they could transcribe their notes.

After the affidavits one of Kesselring's subordinates, a man named Krumhaar, was cross-examined about an operation in which he had had twelve men from the village of Burgo Techino shot because two of his men had been severely wounded by 'terrorists' during a parade through the town. The bodies of the executed men had been left in the main square for twenty-four hours to serve as a warning to the rest of the inhabitants.

Krumhaar's examination was completed by Wednesday and on the following day the court was adjourned once again, leaving only one more prosecution witness to take the stand. Julia spent that Thursday very much at a loose end. She was not accustomed to having nothing to do. In London, even if a case were delayed because a witness had not presented himself or the judge was ill, there was always plenty of work waiting for her in chambers. In Venice she had nothing beyond the one case except for learning Italian, teaching English, sightseeing and trying to be patient with, and understand, her increasingly morose husband.

By then she felt that she had seen enough paintings, churches, marble floors and medieval palaces to last her for a long time. She could hardly descend on Giovanna Sassanta's house without an appointment, and Anthony had made it abundantly clear that he did not want her to cross the threshold of his hospital. Comfort was due to arrive soon, but had not yet specified the day.

Deciding to use up some of the time writing letters, Julia wondered how married women without either little children or work managed to fill their empty hours. For the first time she felt a faint stirring of compassion for her own mother, whose obsession with her appearance, shopping, flirtation and gossip Julia had despised for as long as she could remember. When she had written to Mark Heathwood and to George Wilson, asking whether he had managed to find out whether Raffaella had any chance of getting permission to live in England, Julia pulled a new sheet of writing paper towards her and wrote a chatty, cheerful letter to her mother.

Just before she had finished it, Annunziata came into the salon with a telegram addressed to Julia. Conditioned by the war to expect only bad news from those familiar yellow envelopes, she opened it reluctantly. Comfort had sent it from Paris to say that she would be arriving in Venice in the evening of the following Saturday. The telegram ended with an unnecessarily extravagant extra three words: 'Missed you vilely'.

When Anthony arrived spent and ill-looking from the hospital later that evening, Julia handed him the thin yellow sheet and was relieved to see a lightening in his dark-grey eyes and a faint smile on his thin lips. He made the effort to say something pleasant to his wife and they drank a glass of wine together for the first time in weeks.

The following morning Julia accompanied David to the gloomy courtroom again with a sense of relief. After the last prosecution witness had given his statement, Kesselring's defence counsel rose to give his opening address. Julia listened to it with professional interest, expecting the usual Nazi defence of obedience to superior orders. In fact it became clear that a considerable part of the defence was going to be that of justification, that the laws and usages of war permitted reprisals to be taken against hostages.

When the proceedings were adjourned for lunch, Julia collected the notes she had been conscientiously making and pushed them into her briefcase, before looking for David to see whether he wanted to have lunch with her. He seemed to have escaped before she had and so she made her way out of the court alone, trying to decide whether to lunch in the tea room upstairs or to go out to a restaurant.

'Julia!' David's familiar deep voice called out to her as she walked into the hall and she felt herself smiling involuntarily. 'Julia, come and meet a friend of mine. He and his wife have just arrived here.'

She walked a little reluctantly across the hall to where David was standing beside a thin, dark man in civilian clothes. As she got closer to them Julia thought that she had never seen a man with such brilliant dark eyes or so saturnine and yet handsome a face. He exuded both power and a compelling attraction. Julia wondered who on earth he could be.

'Suvarov,' said David, 'this is Mrs Gillingham, who is here in Venice with her husband. Julia, this is Peter Suvarov, whom I knew during the war.'

'How do you do?' said Julia, realising that she was shaking hands with the man who had sent David to fight with the Italian partisans. She tried to remember the little he had said about Suvarov, but all she could think of was that without him neither she nor Anthony would have met David. She often worried about her feelings for David, but the thought that she might never have known him made her feel almost ill.

'Are you here for the trial?' she asked Suvarov, trying to stop herself from thinking about those feelings.

'Not really,' he answered in an intriguingly accented voice. 'I'm here on a belated honeymoon. My wife and I are staying at the Danieli, but she's not been feeling well and urged me to take up the offer of an observer's seat here.'

'I do hope it's nothing serious,' said Julia politely, thinking that it was rather hard on his wife to spend her honeymoon feeling ill while her husband sat in on a war crimes trial.

'No, no,' said Suvarov. 'She just feels rather under the weather sometimes. David and I were wondering if we could take you out for a spot of lunch. Will you come?'

'You must have so much to talk about that you can't possibly want a stranger,' said Julia. 'Perhaps another time?'

'I very much hope so,' said Suvarov seriously. 'What about this evening? Perhaps you and your husband would come and dine with us? David is coming and my wife would be so pleased if you would too.'

'That's extraordinarily good of you. I'd like to come very much,' said Julia. 'I'm afraid that my husband is often caught up at the hospital and so I simply don't know whether he will be free.'

'Never mind. We'll see him if he is and not if he isn't,' he said with a relaxed informality that charmed her. 'Until tonight then,

Mrs Gillingham,' said Suvarov. 'Well, David, we'd better be off if we're to be back in time for this afternoon's session.'

After that the question of Julia's lunch was settled and she went straight back to the Campo San Maurizio to warn Annunziata that neither she nor David would be in for dinner. Food was far too scarce for Julia to bear the thought of wasting any. Annunziata agreed that Anthony was unlikely to waste time going out to dinner with the others even if he did return in time and promised to cook something quickly for him if he appeared wanting a meal.

'Annunziata, are you all right?' asked Julia when the question of dinner was settled, relieved to be able to talk to her at last with reasonable fluency.

'Yes, *signora*,' answered the housekeeper, but the weariness was horribly evident in her voice.

'Is there no news?' said Julia with pity in her eyes.

'No news. They must all be dead,' she said.

Julia took Annunziata's hand at once and said with desperate urgency:

'No, that is not true. When my husband was lost people told me he must be dead, but I would not believe it. And he was not dead. While there is no news, there is hope. Please believe that, Annunziata.'

The woman clung to Julia's hand and broke down for the first time, weeping and pouring out a torrent of Italian that Julia was incapable of translating for herself. She just waited until the storm was over, when she pulled a clean handkerchief from her sleeve and handed it to Annunziata, remembering with a tiny moment of irrepressible pleasure the time when David had done the same for her.

'You are kind, Signora Giulia,' said Annunziata, tidying her face and hair and standing upright again. 'So kind.'

'Hope is all any of us has now,' said Julia carefully choosing her words to make certain that they meant what she wanted them to mean.

Annunziata looked directly at her then and nodded.

'You are right to hope, *signora*,' she said as slowly. 'The doctor will get well again soon.'

'Thank you,' said Julia. Then, catching sight of her watch again, she added: 'I must go, Annunziata. Will you be all right now?'

Annunziata nodded her head gravely and held open the door for Julia, who returned to the court wondering how much else Annunziata had seen and understood in her unobtrusive way.

That evening Julia dressed for dinner with unusual care and even did her hair in a new style. Giovanna had recently taken her shopping among some of the newly reopened antique shops in the city and had persuaded her to buy a pair of small tortoiseshell combs. When Julia had washed and dried her hair, she borrowed a pair of old-fashioned curling tongs from Annunziata and curled the tips of her thick hair under so that it lay sleekly against her shoulders. Taking wings of it back on either side of her face, she anchored them with the combs and stood in front of the looking glass to assess the result.

It was not a style that she had affected before, but she decided that it suited her better than the severe chignon had ever done. The fullness around her forehead balanced her square chin and the waterfall of glossy brown hair softened her angular bones and made her look younger than usual.

The only evening dress she had brought with her was the colour of well-polished copper, which added a little colour to her pale complexion, but it was not going to be warm enough and so she took the mink that had been part of her trousseau from the wardrobe and slung it around her shoulders. The colour was not good with her frock, but warmth was more important than aesthetic perfection and so she ignored the clash.

She went downstairs to find David waiting for her, dressed in uniform, with his British warm over one arm.

'No sign of Anthony?' she said. Not much to her surprise, David shook his head. 'Never mind. Annunziata's promised to make him something if he comes back hungry.'

They walked towards St Mark's Square together in comfortable silence, knowing each other well enough by then not to have to make bright conversation or comment on the weather or the buildings they passed. As they were walking into the square, David did venture to ask whether Julia had yet got over her aversion to St Mark's itself. She laughed.

'Not really. It just doesn't seem to be my idea of a church – so gloomy and full of galleries and mosaics and nooks and crannies and that horrible cold incense smell,' she said.

'I know,' said David cheerfully teasing her, 'you think a church should be like an English Gothic cathedral or a little whitewashed village church with moth-eaten Peninsular War banners fluttering from dry-rotted lances.'

'I suppose I do,' said Julia. As an only child, she had had no experience of that kind of affectionate teasing and she rather enjoyed it. 'Certainly it should be gentle and simple or a place of cold, airy silence.'

They set off across the square and as they were passing Florian's, Julia said:

'Will you tell me a bit about the Suvarovs? He seemed an interesting sort of man this morning.'

'He is,' said David with a hint of reserve in his voice.

'That sounds as though you don't altogether approve of him,' said Julia. 'And yet you seemed to like him.'

'I don't and I do, if you see what I mean. He's a Russian émigré – came out just after the Revolution, although he had been part of it himself, and I don't think he's ever really settled down to ordinary life. The war was just what he needed, and the kind of secret department he was given could have been designed for him. He was brilliant, both at seeing what had to be done and at making people want to do it at whatever cost to themselves.'

'Yes I see,' said Julia, thinking that he sounded positively dangerous. 'And his wife?'

'I've never met her. He was married before – for a long time – to a woman who had an incurable disease. She died last year, leaving him a considerable fortune. Within a month he was married again.'

'Hence the "belated honeymoon" he talked about,' said Julia. 'What sort of woman is she, the new wife?'

'I know very little about her, although she worked for him in the war too. She's said to be the daughter of a English general and apparently very beautiful ... a good bit younger than him, of course.'

'Do you know,' said Julia, shivering in the cold wind as they turned into the Piazzetta, 'that's the first time I've ever heard you sounding censorious.'

David acknowledged the gentle criticism and tried to justify himself.

'They were obviously carrying on long before the first Mrs Suvarov died, and I ... No, you're right: it's not fair to judge when one knows nothing of the circumstances. Let's just say it seems a bit questionable and leave it at that.'

'What sort of work did she actually do?' asked Julia, still surprised by David's unusual severity.

'I'm not sure,' he said in an oddly formal voice, 'but there were some fairly odd stories going the rounds about her. I think she mainly collected information for him on foreigners living in London ... by slightly questionable means. But she's said to be brave, tough, and very bright.'

Expecting to meet a hard-faced predatory bitch after David's warning, Julia discovered instead a delicately pretty fair-haired girl, who was obviously in love with her saturnine husband. She wore very little make-up and a thoroughly modest frock. It was not until she stood up to shake hands that Julia saw that she was pregnant. Her dark violet-blue eyes looked tired to death, and from the way she moved it was clear that her back and her ankles ached badly. She produced a smile of immediate friendliness as she shook hands with Julia.

'I'm sure you ought to be sitting down,' Julia said as soon as the introductions had been made.

'I know I look a complete wreck,' answered Felicity Suvarov with a mischievous gleam in her remarkable eyes, 'but I don't feel quite as bad as I look.'

'Just tired,' said Julia burying her immediate and very unfair jealousy in sympathy.

'I must say,' answered the pregnant girl, 'that I had never expected to be as tired by anything as I was during those awful nights in the Blitz when sleep seemed something one would never have again – but this is worse!'

Delighted to find in her Venetian exile someone else who had spent the war in London, Julia sat down beside Mrs Suvarov.

'Wasn't it hideous?' Julia said. 'I used to think sometimes that if I didn't have a proper night's sleep I'd never be able to work again. Were you in one of the services?'

As Felicity blushed, Julia belatedly remembered David's disapproval of his chief's wife and wished that she had kept her questions to herself.

'I was in the FANY at the beginning of the war,' Felicity said, recovering her complexion, 'and then I was seconded to Peter's department . . . a kind of research assistant.'

'That must have been interesting,' said Julia and then, because it was obvious that Felicity did not want to talk about her war experiences, began to swap anodyne reminiscences with her. As they talked about the perils and amusements of the blackout, Julia became more and more intrigued by Peter Suvarov's ravishing bride. She talked with all the unconscious confidence of a woman who has seen and understood the effects of her beauty on other people for years and yet there was an individuality about her that Julia had not expected, and a strange wistfulness.

When they went into dinner and she was sitting beside Peter Suvarov, Julia took pains to draw him out and discovered him to be quite as attractive a character as his wife. The conversation between the four of them ranged from the trial and Venice itself to the difficulties besetting the people who were trying to build a better, more humane world than the old one on the wreckage left by the war. Suvarov had much to say about the territorial ambitions of Marshal Stalin and David interrupted at one moment to ask whether Suvarov had ever met him.

'Oh yes . . . but he was a bit of a joke in those days just after the Revolution: the Georgian peasant. We all thought that Trotsky could have run rings round him, but it was Stalin who survived to wreck the last few hopes of the Revolution and now to swallow up Eastern Europe.'

Remembering that Peter Suvarov had, himself, taken part in that Revolution, Julia asked him about the Russians' probable intentions. He did not think that their ambitions extended far into Western Europe but he thought it had been a serious error to let the Russians take Berlin and establish themselves there. It became so clear that he was not optimistic about the possibilities of a peaceful settlement with Russia that Julia said:

'Well at least they haven't got the A-bomb. Provided America doesn't pull out of the alliance completely, that ought to give us all some protection.'

'It won't be long,' said Suvarov gloomily. 'And they'll never rest until they've caught up with the States.'

Julia noticed that Felicity looked towards her husband with an air of almost maternal concern, as though afraid of the effect of the conversation on him, and it struck Julia that he probably still had many relations in Russia.

'It must be strange,' she said slowly, 'to have been part of the Revolution and then to find yourself on the opposite side from people you fought beside.'

He nodded.

'But even that is not as hard as recognising that the sum of human misery has probably been increased by what we did, incredible though that would have seemed to us then.'

'Do you think that Socialism in itself necessarily increases human misery?' asked Julia with conscious naïvety, watching David from under her dark eyelashes. He knew precisely what she was doing and made a face at her, but they both listened in real interest to what Suvarov had to say.

'No more than any other creed,' came the cynical answer. 'As always, it depends on the motives of the leaders who operate it and the ability of the mass of the population to challenge them. Any political system that refuses to allow dissent becomes a tyranny.

But if young David gets himself into Parliament, I expect he'll do as good a job on the government back benches as he would in opposition.'

Felicity asked David then about his ambitions and when he had admitted them, she said:

'Don't your family disapprove a bit?'

David's lively face took on an expression in which regret and determination were almost equally mixed.

'Yes, alas. My father in particular loathes the idea, but. . .'

'But one cannot rule one's whole life by what one's father thinks,' supplied Felicity with considerable feeling. Julia found herself wanting to get to know her better, quite certain by then that whatever there had been between Suvarov and Felicity while his first wife was alive it had not been the kind of affair David had assumed.

'Exactly,' said David, grinning at her, 'and I shall go on trying to show him that Socialism is a fairer and much more just system than Capitalism.'

Julia said drily that she thought that free Capitalism with an adequate system of social welfare for all those who could not make their own success in it was probably the fairest workable system, and then laughed as she saw David's expression.

'You look as though you were going to be sick,' she said.

David managed to laugh, too, although his mind was no longer on the subject of politics at all. All he seemed to be able to concentrate on was the small dimple that appeared to the left of Julia's mouth whenever she smiled her rather lopsided smile. He suddenly wondered whether she smiled like that because she could rarely allow herself the full release of a complete smile, but must always keep one side of her lips tucked under control. He also wondered with equal suddenness what on earth was happening to him.

Liking Julia as he did, admiring her stringent intelligence, her honesty, the unexpected humility that would never let her give advice unless she was asked for it, and her unfailing reasonableness, it had never occurred to him that he might be falling in love with her. The sudden recognition of his state horrified him.

Julia Gillingham was the wife of his best friend. She showed every sign of being absorbed in her difficult life with her husband and would probably be ... David realised that he had no idea what her reaction to his state would be. She would never mock it, he was certain of that, and he could not believe that she would be shocked, because she was far too experienced and sensible to waste energy on such a useless emotion; but it would probably distress her, and she had enough distress to absorb without his adding to it.

He knew so little of women that he felt as though he had woken up to find himself halfway across a vast mountain in a blizzard without map or rope or compass. His one serious love affair had happened in the first year of the war with a girl younger than himself whom he had thought he loved. Only when they actually got to know each other had he discovered that it was the idea of loving her that he had fallen for and not the girl herself. Since then he had been attracted to several women, and discovered both the intoxicating pleasures offered by some of them and the speed with which fulfilled desire died. But never had he felt for any woman the things he felt for Julia Gillingham.

Watching her, he became aware of an extraordinary pain at the thought that she could never know how much he felt about her.

'...don't you, David?' Her kind, low voice broke into his thoughts and made him jump.

'I'm sorry, I was miles away. What were you talking about?' he said, smiling involuntarily at the faint amusement in her brown eyes.

'It doesn't matter,' she said gently. He seemed oddly *distrait*, she thought, and wondered whether their teasing about his political ideas could have upset him. Wanting to protect him, she took charge of the conversation then, turning it to subjects that could have no personal connotations for him, subjects like the efficient way that the British government had persuaded the Americans to take over responsibility for Greece and its defence against Communism, which they could no longer afford, and their less effective attempts to involve the Americans in the Palestine troubles.

When they had exhausted politics, Julia asked David whether

he had seen the recent report in *The Times* about the Allied commission which had been investigating Italians who had helped escaping prisoners of war.

'No,' he said, a little puzzled. 'I missed it. Why?'

'Apparently it's coming to an end,' said Julia, 'and the commissioners have found that a great many of the Italians they tried to reward for what they did have refused to take any money at all. When you think what they risked that's amazing.'

'Not really,' said David. 'We've come across the same thing all over Europe. People risked everything to help escapers and want nothing in return. It helps to remember that whenever one's faced with the horror stories about betrayal and collaboration and the black market.'

After that they ignored the war and its grisly aftermath and talked about nothing very important: new books, the latest films that had been shown in London since Julia had left and about the BBC's new Third Programme.

After a time David relaxed and joined in, complimenting Felicity, chaffing her husband and turning often to Julia to remind her of earlier conversations they had had or to ask her opinion. She enjoyed herself and acknowledged a disloyal thought that if Anthony had been there she would not have had nearly so much fun.

At last the party broke up when Felicity announced that her spine felt as though it were about to collapse and that she must go to bed.

'We must go, too,' said David, quickly standing up. 'Court in the morning. Will you be there, Suvarov?'

'Unless Flixe needs me,' he said, looking at his wife with a mixture of protectiveness and adoration that made Julia think back to her own honeymoon and wonder whether Anthony had ever looked at her like that.

'Would you like to do a little gentle sightseeing one day?' Julia asked her and was touched by the way Felicity's face lit up. 'The court is endlessly being adjourned and I could easily come and collect you once we've been let out.'

'I'd love to. How kind of you,' said Felicity and they agreed to a tentative appointment for the following morning.

'Isn't that when your sister-in-law is due to arrive?' asked David.

'She won't get here until the evening,' said Julia, 'so I'll have plenty of time.'

They said goodbye to each other, and then Julia and David walked out into the freezing darkness. Julia turned the big collar of her fur coat up round her face and David took her arm. Despite the bitter weather they strolled slowly along the Riva degli Schiavoni as though neither of them could quite bear the thought of the evening's ending. Looking across the lagoon towards San Giorgio Maggiore, Julia saw that the moon was almost full and hung, huge and round, just over the Palladian dome.

'I know it's a cliché,' she said, standing with David's hand in the crook of her arm, 'but it really does look as though it were floating, as though it might be washed away by the next tide.'

His hand tightened slightly as he agreed with her, and she longed to turn and face him, pull his head gently down and kiss him. The impulse was so strong that she could hardly believe that he did not feel it too. Her blood seemed to race through her arteries, and she knew that she was breathing more quickly than usual. Exercising all the self-restraint of which she was capable, she pulled herself away from his hand and pointed across to the Giudecca.

'I haven't been over there yet,' she said. 'What's it like?'

Relieved that he had apparently not betrayed himself and yet wishing that she had not moved away from him, David told her about the history of the old Jewish quarter of Venice. The topic lasted them all the way back to the Campo San Maurizio and it was not until they were climbing the stairs up to their respective rooms that he let himself say:

'I loved this evening. Thank you for coming with me.'

'Ah, David,' said Julia, before she could stop herself. Then she straightened her shoulders, smiled briskly, and went on: 'It was fun, wasn't it? Just a pity that Anthony couldn't be there, too.'

At that salutary reminder of her husband, David nodded and turned abruptly to climb the stairs to his bedroom.

# Chapter Sixteen

The next day Julia woke with all the trivial but uncomfortable symptoms of a developing cold, and she wondered whether she had caught it dawdling by the edge of the icy lagoon. She thought of staying to nurse it in bed, but then remembered her promise to Felicity Suvarov and made herself get up. Julia felt better once she was on her feet and when she remembered that Comfort was due to arrive that evening cheered up even more.

Comfort had been in Paris for a fortnight, officially to sort out details of an exhibition of her paintings, and she had taken the opportunity to replenish her depleted wardrobe and see as many of her old friends as she could find.

There were still plenty, although some had not survived the Nazis' ferocity and others had died in the orgy of vengeance that had been unleashed after the liberation. Comfort met some rebuffs from people she had counted as her friends, who resented their allies' safety from occupation almost as much as the damage they had inflicted on France as they pushed the Germans back after D-Day. But most of the people she telephoned were happy to see her.

With them she talked, looked at the latest exhibitions, ate in tiny restaurants in the Quartier Latin that smelled deliciously of garlic and wine and smarter ones in the Champs-Elysees, wandered about the city marvelling at how little physical damage the Nazis had done, and had a marvellous time. Only a few of her friends had been active in the Resistance, but it was clear that neither they nor anyone else much wanted to talk about the choices they had all had to make. That suited Comfort, because she was sick to death of war stories and all she wanted to do was forget the whole horrible business and somehow get her life back on to its prewar footing.

Buying her new clothes helped, with all the half-forgotten luxury of choosing the models in Dior's grey-and-gold salon and returning for fittings as the suits and dresses were moulded to her figure. After the depressing makeshifts to which she had been reduced by British rationing, the sensation of wonderful materials against her skin was almost as pleasing as the *vendeuse*'s comments about 'Madame's wonderful figure' and striking face.

The finished clothes were delivered to the hotel on her last morning in Paris only an hour before Bob Storrington was due to collect her for lunch. Comfort tried on all the clothes and decided to wear the black suit. It would be perfect for lunch in Paris and, although it was not really suitable for travelling, it would at least ensure that she looked as she ought for her reunion with Anthony. Having seen herself properly dressed again, she could not bear the thought of confronting him in the skimpy, shabby, ready-made clothes of wartime London.

Sitting in front of the looking glass, making up her face, she hoped that Anthony was all right and not quite as heartbroken as Julia seemed to think he was. It seemed unlikely that he could be as devastated by the death of a single patient as Julia had made out in her letters, but then she had never really understood him. Probably, Comfort thought, as she blotted her lipstick and bared her teeth to check that there were no lipstick smears on them, Anthony had simply not felt like explaining his feelings to Julia and she had misinterpreted his silence. Certainly the letters he had written home had made no great fuss about the child's death.

There was a knock at the door. Checking her face in the glass, Comfort smiled in satisfaction.

'*Entrez,*' she called, still sitting at the dressing table, and turned her head with impeccable grace to welcome her guests.

The two men who came in were old friends of hers, rich American connoisseurs who had made their home in Paris before the war and left only just in time. As far as Comfort knew, they had returned to the States for the duration, although in fact they had been in London for part of the time, working for the Free French, and back in France for most of the rest. After the liberation they had found their old apartment undamaged, moved back in and set about recreating their old life of searching out young artists, arranging exhibitions for them and building up their own collection of European art. To Comfort, they seemed as anxious as she to ignore the war and they had put themselves out to entertain her during her visit.

The previous evening they had insisted on taking her to the cinema, ignoring her protests that she would rather see the Molière play at the Comédie Française, to watch Jacques Prévert's film *Les Enfants du Paradis*. It had been made in 1942 but had not been shown until the Nazis had been banished from the country. The two men had told Comfort that she would just love it. Planning to despise the film as a poor substitute for classic drama, Comfort had actually found it touchingly romantic, but oddly disturbing too.

'So what did you think of the film, Comfort?' asked Bob Storrington, peering over her slim shoulders into the looking glass and repositioning his silk tie. 'You refused to say last night.'

'It was hardly a refusal,' said Comfort, amused to see that the war had done nothing to reduce either his unfailing elegance or his vanity. 'It was just too much to absorb straight away.'

She stood up to get her little black hat, perched it on the side of her sleek fair head and skewered a pearl-tipped hatpin through the felt. Long suede gloves and a new handbag completed her ensemble and she stood waiting. Bob whistled.

'You look beautiful!' he said. 'Doesn't she, John?'

'Much more like herself than in those dreary London clothes,' said his companion with an engaging smile. 'Well, Comfort?'

'Well what? Oh, the film. You were right: I loved it. I loved the sadness of it and the staginess . . . and the tragedy of their loving each other so much that they could not be happy without each other or even manage to make anyone else happy, despite all their niceness and good intentions.' She stopped and stared at her own face in the mirror.

'And?' said John, surprised that the usually articulate Comfort should phrase her approval in such pedestrian words.

'And I loved the ending,' she added quickly, turning back to face them with her familiar, brilliant smile in place, 'with the hero playing himself for once in a crowd of clowns, as though he could only be real in an unreal world and vice versa. . . . I think that's what I mean. But you'd need Julia to reduce all that raw feeling to accurate words.'

'We knew you'd like it,' said John, satisfied. 'I'm glad you didn't miss *La Princess d'Elide* too much. And now to lunch. I wish you could stay a bit longer. We've hardly had time to do anything, and now that you're looking so wonderful. . .'

'But I can't,' said Comfort, her eccentrically beautiful face softening. 'It's been too long already.'

They took her to a small, perfect restaurant, where she had never been before, and fed her on soup and fish and meat and cheese, all of a quality and in quantities she had only dreamed of during the war. As she finished the last morsel of a perfectly running Brie, she said, sighing:

'There have been times since it ended when I gave up hope of ever eating food like this again.'

'Only the lucky rich can do it,' said Bob. 'But since you are just as rich as us . . .'

'Richer probably,' said John, raising a smile from Comfort, who liked her assets to be appreciated just as much as her talents and her looks.

'. . . you ought to come and live here,' Bob went on, ignoring his friend's interruption, 'and leave your brother and his good, dull wife to their sober lives.'

Comfort put down her wine glass with a snap, her smile shrinking like a jersey boiled in washing soda.

'Julia is not dull,' she said through her teeth.

'Oh my!' said Bob, looking at her more seriously than his voice would have suggested, 'you have changed your tune. What's happened?'

'Nothing,' said Comfort, who had been unable either to forget or justify some of the things she had said to Julia during the war. She hunched one shoulder. 'You've never properly appreciated her.'

'And you have?' said Bob, nibbling at the last of his cheese.

'Not always,' said Comfort, with rare honesty. It would, she felt, atone for the things she had said and mean that she did not have to talk to Julia about them. Much more happily she went on: 'But that's because I'm not as sensible as she is – or as kind, or. . .'

'"Sensible", "kind",' said Bob as the waiter removed their cheese plates and substituted a wonderfully fragrant apple tart. Tasting it, Comfort thought that it was as different from English apple pie as champagne was from soda water.

'In fact dull,' Bob went on, watching her with a cynical smile. 'And as you well know you find dullness just as awful as we do. That's why you love us so much.'

She laughed, half pleased and half resentful, and finished her apple tart.

'You ought to move back here,' said John. 'Do think about it. We need people to fascinate us. And unlike some others, we understand you.'

'I can't,' said Comfort, liking the word 'fascinate'. 'And anyway Anthony understands me . . . Needs me too. Besides . . .' She broke off, unaccountably reluctant to tell them the rest, although she had made no secret of it in London.

'Aha,' said Bob, twinkling at her, 'so now at last we come to it. There's a new man in your life, isn't there? I told you so, John,' he added in a stage whisper. 'We heard that you've even got him in the house.'

'Well yes and no,' said Comfort with a quick, almost self-conscious smile. 'There is a painter, whose work I really admire. . .'

'It's just his work, honestly,' said John to Bob. 'There's nothing naughty about it at all. She'd never. . .'

'Shut up, both of you,' said Comfort, really laughing. There were very few people who were allowed to tease her, but these two could just get away with it. 'His work and him. He's a charming Hungarian, who had such trouble with the Communists that he had to get out. I've rented Julia's rooms to him while she's in Venice and he paints up in my studio.'

'And . . .' prompted John. 'Come on, Comfort, tell all. We're horribly short of gossip.'

'Well I don't want you two gossiping about me,' said Comfort, her lazily amused voice sharpening until it sounded almost vicious. The two men, who were used to her, turned and raised their eyebrows at one another. Suddenly Comfort did not find their double-act funny any longer. She looked at the gold watch that hung loosely on her thin wrist. 'I'm going to have to leave soon if I'm not to miss my plane,' she said.

'Oh, you must wait for coffee,' said Bob, sobering and turning to signal to the young waiter. Comfort agreed and enjoyed it when it came, but the sparkle and fun had been taken out of their conversation by the unfortunate choice of the word 'gossip'. When they had all finished the coffee, Bob got up to pay the bill, leaving John to apologise for his misplaced piece of mockery.

'I'll forgive you,' said Comfort, 'although considering the trouble you caused me with your wretched tittle-tattle in the old days, I ought. . .'

'What do you mean, trouble?' asked John, completely serious at last. Comfort looked at him, surprised to see him without his mocking smile, and then she shrugged.

'When you started prattling about that man I sometimes saw here before I ever went up to Oxford,' she said. 'Anthony got to hear the story and in the usual way of gossip heard a greatly exaggerated version and was seriously upset. I never want to face that sort of thing again.'

'Comfort, I –'

'Don't apologise again. I'll forgive you if you find me a taxi that will take me back to pick up my baggage and get me to the airport on time.'

'Consider it done,' he said, with a faint echo of his usual theatrical flourish. He left the cosy little restaurant to reappear a few minutes later with the announcement that her taxi was at the door and that he and Bob would go with her as far as her hotel. The head waiter opened the door and Comfort preceded the two men out, enjoying the way her long black skirt swung about her legs and showed off her slender ankles and new, high-heeled shoes.

She did not notice the raggedly dressed, exhausted-looking woman who was carrying a heavy basket across the road towards her, until she heard the bitterly articulated:

'*Salope!*'

Outraged, Comfort looked at the woman, drew herself up to her full height, looked down her beaky nose and began to cross the road towards the waiting taxi. More obscenities followed just as the two men were hurrying to catch up with Comfort, and then the woman stopped dead in front of Comfort and spat in her face.

The disgust she felt almost paralysed Comfort for a moment, before she started to fumble in her bag for a handkerchief. Bob caught her by the shoulder and used his own to wipe her face, while John turned on the woman and let loose a volley of dismissive French. She turned away and he, too, came to Comfort's side, urging her towards the taxi. A sharp blow hit her between the shoulder blades and she wheeled round to see the woman who had spat at her leaning down to pick up another stone.

Without waiting for anything else, Comfort ran to the taxi, pulled open the door and almost flung herself inside.

'Why? Why?' she said, her face bitter with fury, when the two men got in beside her.

'It has been happening a bit,' said John soothingly. 'It's not you, Comfort; it's the clothes. There's a pretty strong feeling that while materials are so scarce it's not fair for the rich and privileged to wear things like that when the rest of the population can hardly even get their shoes repaired. It happens over food, too. She saw us coming out of the restaurant and . . .' He stopped, shrugged his shoulders and left the rest to their imagination.

'She was vile,' said Comfort, recovering fast as she took in the impertinence of anyone's venturing to question her expenditure or appearance. 'And probably mad.'

'Or desperate,' suggested Bob, who knew rather more than Comfort did about the straits to which many Parisians had been reduced by the war. He toyed with telling her a few home truths, but then decided it would do no good. Truth had had to go by the board in the work he had been doing during the war and there seemed no point on insisting on using it again. Comfort was Comfort, he reflected, and no one had ever been able to change her. As he had once said to John, you took Comfort as she was or you ignored her, and he enjoyed her enough to put up with her.

She caught her aeroplane easily and spent the journey thinking about Anthony. It seemed outrageously unfair that after so long she could not have him to herself and she hoped that his lodger would be tactful enough to leave them in peace during her visit. Anthony had written that Julia seemed to like him, and so perhaps she could keep him out of their way. At the thought of Julia, Comfort's fine eyebrows contracted above her bony nose. Ever since Julia had acknowledged that she needed Comfort's help to make Anthony happy, Comfort had known that somehow she was going to have to make it up to Julia.

At that moment, Julia herself was walking across Venice, thinking happily of Comfort's arrival. Having escorted Felicity Suvarov around St Mark's cathedral, Julia had gone back to the Danieli hotel and shared some lunch with her. As they talked about the war years and about what the future might hold for them both, Julia found herself liking Felicity more and more, although she was astonished at the freedom with which Felicity was prepared to confide in her about everything except her work during the war. Julia, accustomed for years to keeping her own counsel, listened but did not reciprocate.

She learned among many other things that Felicity had known Peter's first wife quite well and admired her desperately as she struggled with her increasing disability and urged her husband to live as freely as he could.

'She must have been an extraordinary woman,' said Julia, trying to imagine living her life in a wheelchair and knowing that her attractive husband was falling in love with someone else. It would take superhuman charity, she decided, to forgive, let alone encourage him.

'She was,' said Felicity, her beautiful face glowing. 'The first time I met her, while I was working for him, I think she knew that I had fallen in love with him and yet she was kinder to me than anyone I've ever known. D'you know, in a way I feel as though I have to take care of him for her.' She laughed a little self-consciously. 'I know that sounds revoltingly sentimental.'

Julia smiled, enjoying Felicity's ingenuousness as well as her readiness to laugh at herself, but she looked at her watch and said:

'I'm going to have to go and give my regular Saturday afternoon lesson to my refugees.'

Felicity hauled herself out of her chair, admitting that her doctor had ordered her to rest after lunch every day and they said goodbye to each other.

Julia set off towards the Dorsoduro, beginning to feel really ill with a headache pounding behind her left eyebrow, smarting eyes, a rasped throat and a nose that felt as though it were stuffed with hot, wet flannel with a few pins in it, but even so she decided to give her lesson. On her way to the house she stopped off in the Campo San Maurizio to see if Annunziata had everything she needed for the dinner she was preparing to welcome Comfort, and discovered that the English post had arrived with a letter from George Wilson.

Julia opened it and read it as she made her way towards the Accademia Bridge. George wrote that he was not optimistic about the possibilities of getting Raffaella permission to emigrate to England.

There are so many cases of genuine, unbearable hardship [he wrote] that unless your protégée can produce some family connection here, I don't see how you'll be able to swing it.

Julia waited to give Raffaella the bad news until she had delivered her lesson, led a halting conversation in English about the future of Italy, handed out the previous week's exercises that she had marked, and set the work for the next lesson. While the other women were packing up their books, she turned to Raffaella.

'May I say hello to your son?' she asked.

Raffaella's green-blue eyes sharpened.

'Of course, Signora Giulia,' she said, standing up gracefully. 'Will you come now?'

Julia followed her to the private bed-sitting room, where her child was happily playing in his cot. Raffaella lifted him out and turned him to face Julia.

'He looks very well, Raffaella,' she said carefully. 'And getting bigger all the time.'

'Have you news, *signora?*' asked Raffaella, dumping the heavy child on the floor at her feet.

'Not very good news, I'm afraid,' she said and read out what George Wilson had written. She had to translate one or two words into Italian.

'But I have a family connection,' said Raffaella at once.

'You have?' said Julia, surprised. 'But why did you not tell me that at once?'

A faint colour appeared in Raffaella's pale cheeks and the clever eyes were veiled. When she looked up again, they were clear and slightly pleading. She gestured to the child playing on the floor.

'His father is English,' she said.

'Ah,' said Julia, thinking that she understood why this particular piece of information had been withheld. 'But not your husband?'

Raffaella shook her blonde head.

'He was . . . no: he wanted to marry me,' she said. 'He said so. But my brother made . . . was difficult. And he had to went.'

Julia sat down on a hard chair beside the child.

'Had to go,' she corrected. 'Well, I think you had better tell me the whole story. It might help.'

Raffaella sat on the bed and proceeded to explain her history in a mixture of broken English and fast, graphic Italian to Julia. Her headache seemed to be getting worse and worse, and Raffaella's command of English slipped as she grew increasingly excited. Her voice seemed to get shriller, too, and her hands danced in front of Julia's painful eyes as she gesticulated more and more wildly. After fifteen minutes or so, Julia thought that she had grasped most of the story.

Raffaella and her elder brother had had to flee to the mountains after some unspecified trouble with the Germans and had joined a local band of partisans. He had found a niche at once with the men, but she told Julia that she had been unhappy for months, struggling with the other women to force local villagers to disgorge food, humping it back up to the camp and preparing it under extraordinarily difficult conditions. There were days when the leaders of the band refused to let them light any kind of fire in case German patrols found them and yet they somehow still had to produce food that the men could eat.

She seemed to skate over the next part of her story, but Julia grasped the salient part, which was that one of the English officers who fought with the Italians had fallen in love with her, promised to marry her and secretly made love to her. It was clear that he made her life happier than it had been, but she still had to put up with the desperately uncomfortable conditions and go out on her terrifying foraging expeditions. On one of them she was picked up for questioning by the Germans.

Julia flinched as she heard that and wondered how she herself would have stood up to the kind of life Raffaella was describing.

The Germans had no idea who she was and the villagers from whom she had been begging food had not betrayed her and she was allowed to go without suffering anything much worse than a slapped face and an hour's sarcastic, sneering interrogation. After that, she told Julia, she was even more afraid of leaving the doubtful sanctuary of the partisans' camp, particularly as she had begun to feel rather ill. When she belatedly realised that she must be pregnant she could not tell the Englishman, because he was away from the camp leading an action against an important German supply dump.

Unfortunately other people in the camp had by then also realised her condition and someone had told her brother. Berserk with rage, he had called her a slut and worse and demanded the name of the father. Frightened for the Englishman, because she well knew that her brother had an uncontrollable temper, she did not tell him anything. Then he started beating her.

Raffaella described her injuries in indignant Italian, ticking each one off on her fingers, but Julia could understand only something about cracked ribs and something about her eyes. Even that was bad enough.

'Did you not tell him about the Englishman?' Julia asked slowly, trying to imagine a world in which an illegitimate pregnancy could provoke such a punishment.

Raffaella lifted her chin proudly and shook her head.

'He would have killed him,' she said slowly in English and then reverted to Italian again. Struggling through the cotton wool that seemed to have been stuffed into her brain, Julia found that announcement of savagery almost impossible to believe. While she was framing a question that would not sound insultingly doubtful, Raffaella went on telling her story. She told Julia that she had put the blame for her child on to one of the Germans who had arrested her. Her brother was disgusted and called her a filthy collaborator, but at least the Englishman was safe. Only his return stopped the beating her brother gave her.

The Englishman had her carried to her makeshift tent so that her wounds could be attended to, and then he heard the story from her brother. When at last he came to see her, he obviously believed in the story of the German and she was too proud to tell him the truth. He gave her physical protection, but never showed her any affection again. After the liberation he saw that she escaped her brother's clutches and got to Rome with enough money to keep her and have the baby safely.

'And was it enough?' Julia asked, trying to make sense of the story.

'No,' answered Raffaella and then went on to tell Julia with no self-consciousness at all that she became a prostitute in Rome, where the dollar-rich American soldiers were prepared to pay a small fortune to a good-looking, elegant girl. All was apparently well until her brother followed her to Rome, discovered her whereabouts and threatened to kill both her and her 'half-German' baby. To save both their lives, Raffaella had left her lucrative work in Rome and fled to Venice, where Giovanna had taken her in.

'But why?' said Julia, feeling stupid. 'Why should he have wanted to kill you?'

'He is mad,' said Raffaella flatly. 'The war was perfect for him: he could beat people and kill them and be proud of it. He hated me because he had to be ashamed of me. He called me a *puttana* . . . you understand?'

Julia nodded.

'So he could not be proud any more. They mocked him. It made him mad and he wanted to kill me. If he finds me again,' said Raffaella at last, her greenish eyes dilated in apparently genuine fear, 'he will try again to kill me. I have to go. And there is nowhere to go except to England. Perhaps there I can find his father and we will be safe.'

She dropped a hand on the child's dark head and stared pleadingly at Julia.

Julia was not at all sure that she had followed all the details of the story, and did not believe everything she had been told, but she did accept that Raffaella was genuinely afraid.

'Do you know where this Englishman lives?' she asked.

Raffaella shook her head.

'But I could find him,' she said.

Julia did not feel up to assessing the likelihood of that just then.

'I will write to England and ask,' she said carefully, finding it increasingly painful even to speak. She had had many colds during the last few years, but this one seemed much the worst. It seemed to be affecting her brain as much as her breathing. 'I must go, Raffaella. When I have news I will tell you.'

Then she went upstairs to tell Giovanna that she thought she would not be able to stay for her Italian lesson, because she felt so ill, and took herself painfully back across the Grand Canal to her temporary home. By the time she reached the Campo San Maurizio, she felt so tired that she was almost afraid she would have to climb the cold stone stairs to the first floor on her hands and knees.

There were lights in all the windows and as Julia slowly walked up the stairs, she could hear the sound of cheerful voices from the salon. Mingling with that of David was Anthony's, sounding far happier and more relaxed than she had heard it for weeks. Forgetting Raffaella's story, almost forgetting her headache and her cold, Julia pushed open the double doors to see the two men standing around the stove, glasses in their hands, laughing.

'Hello,' she said hoarsely, pleased to see them at ease with each other again.

'Julia,' said Anthony. 'Good God! Are you all right?'

She nodded.

'I've just got rather a cold,' she said.

'Come and get warm,' said David almost at the same time as Anthony was saying:

'You ought to have a hot whisky and lemon. I'll see if Annunziata's got any lemons.'

'I'll go,' said David, putting down his glass and hurrying out of the room.

'Did you get her?' Julia asked. 'Is she all right?'

Anthony nodded. He had promised Comfort that he would tell no one about the woman who had spat at her and called her filthy names.

'Yes. She's upstairs dressing,' he said. 'She wanted to impress you with some new clothes she bought in France.'

'Oh dear,' murmured Julia, looking down at her baggy tweed coat and skimpy straight skirt. 'I don't think I've got the energy to change.'

'No, much better recruit your energies,' said Anthony, just as David returned carrying a jug of hot water and two slices of lemon on a plate.

'There's no sugar left,' he said almost as though it were a major tragedy.

'Don't worry,' said Julia. 'I'll just have whisky and hot water then.' She lay back against the hard sofa, sipping the drink when

David brought it to her and swallowing with difficulty. She was roused only by the sound of the door's opening.

'Comfort!' Anthony's voice opened Julia's eyes and she saw her sister-in-law standing in the doorway wearing a most remarkable dress. The tightly fitting bodice was cut quite low over Comfort's small bosom. The waist was dropped, emphasising the long elegant lines of her figure, and the huge, spreading skirt fell at least six inches below her knees. The astonishing garment was made of some smooth material in a mixture of very dark greens and blues which flattered her blonde hair and made her slate-coloured eyes even more ravishing than usual.

'You look absolutely stunning,' said Anthony. 'Come and have a glass of wine and meet David Wallington.'

Julia glanced sideways at David, feeling very much at a disadvantage in her old brownish-grey tweeds. She expected to see him gazing at Comfort in the admiration she deserved, but in fact he was looking down at Julia.

'Are you really all right?' he said with a seriousness that made the familiar question matter. Julia nodded and pulled herself up from the sofa.

'Darling Julia,' said Comfort, sounding at her most American and her most caressing. She held out her arms.

'I can't kiss you,' said Julia hoarsely, 'because I've got a foul cold. But it is wonderful to see you, Comfort.'

'Never mind the cold,' said Comfort, putting her arms around Julia and laying her smooth cool cheek against Julia's hot one. She whispered: 'You do know how much I really care about you, don't you?'

'I know,' said Julia, pulling herself back. 'It's all right, Comfort. There's no need for great drama.'

Comfort was hurt and showed it. Julia thought that her cold must be softening her brain. Nothing was more calculated to put Comfort in a bad mood than a piece of unnecessary criticism like that.

'This is Anthony's David Wallington,' said Julia, deciding to ignore her mistake. 'David, this is Comfort, of whom you have heard Anthony and me speak so often.'

'Yes indeed. How do you do?' he said, holding out a large hand. Comfort shook it and murmured something formally polite, but she looked him over in rather obvious disdain, tilting back her small head to see his face. It seemed that she was not impressed for, having completed her examination, she turned ostentatiously away to follow Anthony to the table where the wine stood. They stayed there, talking quietly together until Annunziata came in to lay the table.

Anthony introduced Comfort, who immediately started talking in fluent, fast Italian, which made Julia feel as inadequate and insular as she had ever done at Comfort's university parties. It also made Julia angry, pointing up the unnecessary rudeness of Comfort's dismissal of David.

Julia made no effort to talk then, because her throat hurt so much, but later, over dinner, she felt that she had at least to try. It became obvious as soon as Annunziata handed round the soup tureen that Comfort was deliberately trying to exclude David from the conversation and show him how *de trop* he was. Julia deliberately turned to him to explain the significance of Comfort's private jokes and fill in the background whenever she mentioned the name of one of their friends whom David could not know. After a moment he unobtrusively laid a hand on her knee and said:

'Don't try to talk. It must hurt so much. I'm all right.'

Julia smiled at him and then looked across the round table at Anthony as though to persuade him to get Comfort to behave better, but either he misunderstood her signals or did not care enough, for he sat, watching his sister, laughing at her jokes and joining in her reminiscences.

By the time dinner was cleared, Julia thought that she had never felt so tired. When Anthony suggested that they all go for a walk to see St Mark's by moonlight and have their coffee in Florian's, Julia shook her head.

'Honestly, Anthony,' she said with a sigh, 'I think I'll be better in bed. This wretched cold is making me feel bloody. Would you mind terribly if I stayed at home?'

'No, of course not, Julia,' said Anthony, smiling at her with more sympathy than he had managed to show for weeks. 'I'll look in when we get back and see if you need dosing with anything. David?'

'I'll stay and keep Julia company until she goes to bed,' David answered easily enough. 'I've a stack of papers to read before the next sitting. Next time perhaps, Miss Gillingham,' he added, turning politely to Comfort.

'Perhaps,' she answered, smiling freely at him for the first time that evening.

When they had left, Julia wondered whether to say anything or not, but David seemed to have no such inhibitions.

'Phew!' he said. 'What had I done to make her so cross?'

Relieved to have the matter out in the open, Julia took a sip of wine to ease her throat and tried to explain her wayward, difficult, fascinating, beloved sister-in-law to him.

'She is probably afraid that if Anthony likes you too much she will be excluded,' she said slowly through the pain. It seemed far more important that David should understand and not be hurt than that she save her throat. 'I still find some of the things she does difficult to understand even after all these years, but I have grasped her conviction that people have only a finite quantity of affection to give and her terror that if Anthony lets anyone new have any she will have that much less for herself. She has always been rather possessive of him, except oddly enough as far as I'm concerned.'

'Presumably because she's possessive of you, too,' said David quickly.

Julia looked at him doubtfully. For so intelligent and perceptive a man, that was an oddly silly thing to say.

'I? Oh, no, David. You're wrong there,' she said.

David got up from his chair and prowled around the room. Julia thought that she had never before met anyone who exuded such restless strength and yet could be so gentle in his dealings with other people. Once again she wondered what it was that he had done in the war to make Anthony so angry.

The glass in the long windows rattled suddenly as a gust of wind battered them, and all the six candles on the round table guttered in the draught.

At last David came back and stood looking down at her. He seemed to loom over her and she instinctively moved back in her chair with a jerk.

'I am sorry, Julia,' he said, withdrawing. He found a chair and pulled it beside the sofa. 'I always forget how overpowering my size can be,' he added as he sat down.

'Please don't misjudge Comfort,' she said seriously. 'Anthony and I both love her, and if you and she fight. . .'

'I won't fight her – why should I? But I'm afraid she may fight me. I'll try and stay out of your way while she's here.'

Julia put the desolation that suddenly thrust itself into her mind down to her cold and said that she thought she ought to go bed. David stood up at once.

'I shouldn't have kept you talking. I am so sorry,' he said, holding out a hand to help her up. Julia took it and tried not to cling.

'I'll go and ask Annunziata to fill you a hot bottle,' he said. 'I don't think you ought to get into a freezing bed in your state. I'll get her to bring it up to you.'

'Thank you, David,' said Julia. 'Good night.'

'Good night.'

She left him to pull herself up the bannisters to bed, thinking back to the inordinately exciting first summer when Comfort and Anthony had rented their house outside Oxford and she had fallen in love. He had often been on duty at the hospital, and then Comfort and Julia would lie on long cushioned chairs on the terrace, breathing in the lemon scent of the immense magnolia that sprawled up the old red brick of the house and talking about him and about what life might be like when they all left Oxford. Julia had felt like a character in a fairy tale, whisked out of humdrum existence and given a glimpse of perfection.

'Where did it all go?' she asked herself.

# Chapter Seventeen

Julia felt worse and worse all the next day, but managed to hide it from the others. David left the salon straight after dinner on the excuse that he had letters to write and, half an hour later, Julia went up to bed early, leaving Comfort and Anthony alone.

After a poor night's sleep, punctured by weird dreams from which she emerged coughing and aching in every joint, Julia woke on Monday morning to a suspicion that she might be really ill. She found Anthony eating breakfast alone. He took one look at her and put his hand to her forehead again.

'Back to bed, Julia,' he said in a kinder voice than she was used to in Venice. 'You're a clot to have got up. You're ill. Come on. We'll bring your breakfast up.'

'I'm not sure that I want any,' she said and inside her skull her hoarse voice grated against the pain. Anthony put an arm gently around her shoulders and urged her upstairs back to bed as though she were one of his charges from the orphanage.

On the stairs they passed Comfort, dressed in filthy old trousers and a sweater from which floated festoons of draggled wool. In spite of the squalour of her clothes she looked almost as superb as she had done in her ravishing French dress.

'Are you all right?' she asked, peering into Julia's half-closed eyes.

Before Julia could even shake her head, Anthony had answered for her

'No. I'm putting her back to bed. Rout out Annunziata, would you, Comfort, and get her to bring up a tray of breakfast. No,' he added turning back to his wife, 'you must have something. Just an egg if we've got one and some coffee – the caffeine will at least cheer you up.'

Whether it was the caffeine or Anthony's taking so much trouble over her, or perhaps merely the result of laying her aching, pounding head back on the pillow, Julia felt slightly less uncomfortable in bed and she told Anthony so when he came back to take the tray away.

'Now, will you feel safe enough with Annunziata? I have to get to work and so must David. Comfort can sit with you, if –'

'Oh no,' interrupted Julia, her voice still intolerably painful. 'She's on holiday. I'll sleep. But tell David . . .'

'Don't talk, darling. It'll only hurt your throat worse. I've told him and he will explain your absence in court. I'll squeeze a minute or two to come back at lunchtime, and I'll bring some things for your throat then. Meanwhile, have you got plenty of aspirins?'

Julia nodded. Anthony bent down to kiss her hot, tight forehead. She wanted to cling to his hands and say, tell me it's still all right between us, tell me you still love me, tell me we can have a child one day.

Even in her weakened state, she knew that her desperate need was irrational, but that made it no less important. Why motherhood should have become such an obsession she could not imagine, but she did understand that whatever was the matter with her was contributing to her misery. She wondered how long ago it had begun and how many of her difficulties could be put down to whatever was the matter with her.

'What have I got, Anthony?' she whispered, trying not to betray any anxiety. He watched her face carefully.

'I think it's just a bad cold, my dear; but in this climate and with all the infections flying about, I'll keep a close watch on you,' he said calmly. 'Don't be afraid. It's not too serious whatever it is. You'd be a lot iller if it were. All right?'

She nodded, her eyes locked on his, begging for reassurance and support. He smiled at her with such confidence that she felt comforted.

'Try to sleep,' he said. 'That's the best thing for you. Sleep. There's nothing to worry about.'

Julia laid her head back but did not shut her eyes until he had left the room.

The hours until lunchtime limped past. Annunziata looked in to Julia's room at fairly frequent intervals to turn her pillows or sponge her hot face, but would not let her try to talk. Sometimes Julia slept, dreaming of horribly twisted versions of real life so that it was hard to tell when she was awake and worrying and when asleep and tormented. The pictures Mark had created for her of the Nuremberg trials figured in her dreams and so did the bomb sites of war-torn London. Comfort was there, and Anthony. There was terror and pain.

The ache in her head got worse and she began to imagine a pain under her breastbone. Julia knew that it could not be real because it brought with it even more horrible visions, in one of which Comfort and Anthony had her pinned to the ground and were hitting her with garden rakes with specially sharpened tines.

In the dream all three of them were in the garden of the house outside Oxford. The occasion was an immediately recognisable lunch party, after which Comfort and some of the other guests had gone off to swim in the nearby river, while Anthony and Julia had sat together, digesting and beginning to explore the edges of the feeling that was growing between them.

On the real occasion, Comfort had arrived back from the river and had stood in front of them both, her blonde hair a mass of tangled curls, each curl spangled with water. Water dripped off her hands, too, and her severe black bathing dress. The sun lit the drops and sparkled in sharp bursts of white light; but some of the drops caught and fractured the light so that Comfort appeared to be the source of a million tiny rainbows. The picture in Julia's dream was so vivid that she could feel the sun on her face, and even in sleep her eyes screwed up as though against the glare. But suddenly reality was distorted and in her dream she was pulled to the ground and the two of them began digging at her chest with the rakes.

She woke at last, sweating and trembling, and struggling to breathe, one hand pressed against her front, to see Comfort standing at the foot of the bed. For a moment, Julia could not bear even to look at her, but at the sound of Comfort's voice, as gentle as it had ever been, Julia opened her eyes properly.

'Wake up, Julia sweetie. It's a dream. Wake up.' Comfort's hands were clenched over the carved, gilded footboard of the bed and her big grey eyes were anxious when Julia could at last focus on them. Her responsibility for Comfort brought her back to her senses. Swallowing against the swollen tenderness of her throat, she tried to speak. No sound came out and so she swallowed once more and tried again.

'It's all right. I'm awake now. Thank you,' she managed to say.

'You're much worse, aren't you?' said Comfort, her voice sharper.

Julia nodded, feeling a pain shooting up her neck. She closed her eyes, too tired even to try to reassure her sister-in-law.

'I'm going to send a message to Anthony. Have you a fever?'

'I think I must have,' whispered Julia. 'Don't worry him.'

'You need him just as much as those orphans. Don't be afraid of him. He loves you,' said Comfort, and Julia believed her as she had believed her all those years before when Comfort had been urging her to fall in love with him. Julia tried to ignore the sensations of fear that her nightmare had left behind.

She lay back, exhausted, hearing Comfort leave the room and then speak quickly but very quietly in Italian, presumably to Annunziata. Julia had no energy to do anything but wait. She could not shake off the effect of the dream despite Comfort's kindness, and her muscles still trembled. Her chest ached sharply, too, just as though someone really had been hitting into it. A fat tear seeped out from under each of her eyelids, but she was too tired to wipe them away. She just lay, sore and afraid until Anthony came back.

He touched her burning forehead with firm, cool hands, put a thermometer between her dry lips and later pulled down her nightgown to tap her bare chest with two fingers of each hand. Julia felt too ill to be interested in what he was doing, and in any case her mind came and went as the waves of fever rose and fell, but she heard Comfort say:

'What is it? I see you've reached some kind of diagnosis.'

'Pneumonia,' he answered softly. 'Poor Julia.'

'You'd better get her to the hospital,' said Comfort.

Julia opened her eyes again and saw Comfort looking around her as though she expected to see men in white coats with a stretcher appearing through the walls. To Julia's immense but unspoken relief, Anthony shook his head.

'She'll do better here, Comfort. There's Annunziata to look after her – and you, if you'll stay – and –'

'Of course I'll stay,' she said impatiently. She gripped his wrist. 'It's not dangerous is it, Anthony?'

For a moment he was very still. Julia felt too tired and afraid to speak, but she lifted her heavy eyelids again and looked at him. He saw her expression and smiled confidently.

'No, it's not dangerous. All right, darling?' Julia slowly nodded her head once against the pillow. He went on: 'I'm going to collect some things from the hospital to make you more comfortable, but first I've got to lift you up. There's some fluid in your lungs and you'll breathe more easily if you're propped up.'

Julia let them haul her up and stuff extra pillows behind her head, but the pain sharpened and she was hard put to it not to swear at them for hurting her. The dream came back to her in all its horrible force and the tears re-emerged.

'It's all right,' said Anthony, stroking her face with his fingers. Their coolness was a relief on her burning skin, but the weight of even that light stroking seemed to hurt. Anthony seemed to understand and he took his hand away.

He took Comfort out of the room with him and answered her question more honestly.

'It is extremely dangerous,' he said. 'She's badly run down anyway – like most of us since the war – and has very little resistance.'

'Isn't there anything you can do?' asked Comfort, her slaty eyes darkening and her nose looking sharp as she absorbed the shock.

'There must be. You can't just leave her like that and wait. Anthony, you must. . .'

'Oh, yes,' answered Anthony. 'There are many things we can and will do. And there's penicillin, which is infallible . . . but yet again the Medical Procurement people at UNRRA have delayed the latest delivery and we've none left.'

'Well you must get some,' said Comfort at once, clutching his right arm. 'Who's in charge? Is there a telephone number? Shall I call them?'

'I'll deal with that,' said Anthony, noticing that there were tears in Comfort's big grey eyes, 'but I want you to stay here with her. She ought not to be left, and if her breathing gets worse, prop her up. If you're frightened, send a message for me. All right?'

Comfort nodded, but her face was distraught. Anthony had always known that she loved Julia, but after the things Comfort had said at Christmas he had not expected her to be thrown into quite such terror. He did not know that her vivid imagination had given her a convincing picture of Julia's death.

'Keep calm,' he ordered. 'You'll do no good at all to Julia if you get hysterical. I'll be back as soon as I can. Go and sit with her.'

Comfort obeyed and spent the next two hours sitting beside Julia's bed, watching her as she slept and bathing her face with cool water whenever she started to thrash about and mumble in delirium.

'It's all right, Julia,' she would whisper then. 'I'm here. Don't die. We need you. Don't die. It's all right.' The monotonous litany sometimes seemed to soothe Julia, but more often made no impression at all on her obviously terrifying dreams. Soon after three o'clock, she calmed down and seemed to be sleeping more naturally. Comfort leaned back in her chair in momentary relief.

Annunziata opened the door quietly and checked to see that Julia was asleep before walking silently to Comfort's chair and whispering that there was a visitor for the *signora* downstairs.

'I can't leave her,' said Comfort, equally quietly. 'Can't you ask them to go away?'

Annunziata shook her head.

'He is a friend of the *signora* and of Signor David. Please talk to him. I will sit with her,' she said. Eventually Comfort yielded her place to the Italian and went downstairs to the salon, where she found a slim, middle-aged man with a lined face and grey-streaked dark hair, whom she had never seen before.

'Annunziata says you're a friend of my sister-in-law,' Comfort said rather abruptly.

'Peter Suvarov,' he said, holding out his hand. Comfort shook it automatically and introduced herself.

'I wouldn't have troubled you, Miss Gillingham,' said Suvarov, 'but that your housekeeper said that Mrs Gillingham is seriously ill. Is there anything that I can do?'

'God knows,' said Comfort, having lost all her *savoir faire* in the face of Julia's terrifying illness. 'My brother is trying to get hold of some penicillin. Apparently that's the only infallible thing for pneumonia, and . . .'

'She's got pneumonia?' said Suvarov. 'Good God! Poor Mrs Gillingham. I mustn't keep you away from her, but will you tell her that my wife and I are very concerned? We both liked her so much.'

'Everyone does,' said Comfort, forgetting the times when she had been driven to distracted cruelty by Julia's unfailing matter-of-factness – and by her concentration on other people. 'How well do you know her?' she asked aggressively.

Peter Suvarov looked at Comfort and recognised the shock and fear in her eyes. He urged her to sit down on one of the hard, gilded sofas for a moment. Shrugging her superb shoulders, Comfort sat down and waited for his explanation.

'You look as though you need a bit of a rest,' he said. 'We hardly know her at all. I knew David Wallington well during the war, and he introduced us. We all four had dinner together one night while your brother was at the hospital. That's all. But when I heard from him that she was ill, I had to . . .'

'I see,' said Comfort more politely as she stood up again. 'When she is well enough I'll tell her about your visit.' And then to her supressed rage she realised that she was crying. She could not convince herself that Julia would ever be well again.

Peter Suvarov smiled, his eyes crinkling up at the corners and his bitter mouth relaxing, and handed her a handkerchief.

'This is ridiculous,' said Comfort, muffling her face. 'I don't usually cry in front of strangers.'

'This is hardly a normal time. Cry away. I'm not one of those men who are terrified by female tears. . . . A lot of people wept over me in the war – and not women only.'

'The war, the war, the bloody war!' said Comfort, screwing up his handkerchief and giving it back to him. 'I hate it. It made us all behave like lunatics but no one except me seems to want to forget it. Why can't you all shut up about it?'

'I suppose,' said Suvarov, paying no attention to her rudeness or the incipient hysteria in her voice, 'because it was so important . . . not just fighting it, but being part of it, doing one's best and living more intensely over a longer time than one had before.'

'Never mind. I'm sorry. I must go back to her,' said Comfort a bit more calmly. 'I've been away too long.'

'Of course,' said Suvarov. 'My wife and I are leaving Venice next week. May I call before then to see how Mrs Gillingham is?'

'If you want,' said Comfort gracelessly, already halfway to the door. 'Can you see yourself out? I can't. . . I'll send Annunziata.'

She went out, leaving Peter Suvarov to wait for a more rational assessment of Julia's state from Annunziata. He knew enough Italian to understand what she told him of Anthony's diagnosis and prognosis, and to ask her to tell David Wallington that he had called. Annunziata nodded and said slowly:

'The young *signor* will be very unhappy.'

'I know,' said Suvarov, adding in English as he picked up his hat. 'That's why I want him to know he can talk to us. That young woman won't be much help and the doctor is hardly a suitable confidant in the circumstances.'

Julia was dreaming again when Comfort got back to her bedside and her skin felt hot and dry. Comfort changed the water in the bowl she had filled earlier and sponged Julia's face and neck and hands and arms again. But it seemed to worry Julia and she cried out:

'No, Comfort, no, please,' as though Comfort were actually hurting her.

Increasingly worried, Comfort dried Julia's face as gently as she could, threw the water away and went back to her chair to watch. Anthony returned soon after five o'clock with the news that there was no penicillin in the city at all, but that he had telephoned everyone he could think of who might supply it and had sent a telegram to UNRRA headquarters.

Julia came round just as he was erecting a kind of tent over her bed. A tall, brown iron cylinder with a wheel and a dial at the top stood beside him. Really frightened, then, she tried to sit up, croaking his name.

'Lie back, Julia,' he said at once, coming to push her shoulders back against the pillows. 'Don't be afraid. It's just oxygen to help you to breathe.'

'You won't go away,' she whispered, clinging to his hand.

'Only if I have to,' came the reply. 'Comfort is here and Annunziata. They both know what to do. Lie still, Julia, and try to breathe.'

'It hurts,' she said, sounding almost as surprised as complaining.

'I know it hurts, but it will start to hurt less now. Breathe slowly and carefully. We're getting the stuff you need and there's nothing to be afraid of.'

A small conscientious smile lifted the left-hand corner of her dry lips.

'Well done, Julia,' said Anthony. 'That's the stuff. Keep your spirits up. Now, I know you don't feel like food, but you must try some of the soup Annunziata has made. She'll bring it to you in a few minutes and it'll help you keep your strength.'

Julia tried to obey, as she tried to do everything he demanded of her over the next few days and as she tried to keep her misery and pain and fear from all of them. For much of the time she was delirious, but there were lucid intervals, during which she was slightly comforted to understand that the nightmares that had tormented her were products of the disease and not of reality.

Dreams of Comfort and Anthony and David mixed with memories of the war and became tangled up with the figures on the painted ceiling above her bed and the work she had been doing for Kesselring's trial. Sometimes she dreamed that she stood in the dock of some great court, accused of terrible crimes, at others that she was having to use all her skill to free Anthony of a capital charge and failing. Gallows loomed in the shadows of her dreams and dead babies and famine, and a blonde woman with sly green eyes. Only the strong figure of David Wallington seemed to promise any kind of help and she called out to him. But he never came.

Anthony spent as much time with Julia as he could, but there were patients at the hospital who were iller even than she and at times he had to leave her with Comfort and Annunziata. Comfort's anguished determination to make up for her earlier coldness made her far more interfering than Annunziata, whose calm gentleness provided the only moments of real respite for Julia. Sometimes during her lucid moments, she thought that Annunziata could not have been kinder if Julia had been one of her daughters.

Only David never seemed to come. Julia knew that he might have been in the room while she was unconscious, but his absence during her times awake began to fret her. They had become such friends that it seemed unnecessarily unkind of him to stay away. One evening, when the pain of her laboured breathing had become very bad, she lay watching Comfort as she sketched something on a big white pad. The intensity of Comfort's concentration was almost palpable and Julia lay as still as she could and breathed as carefully as her sodden lungs would allow so as not to disturb her. Then Comfort looked up, her eyes narrowed and peering. Julia tried to smile, but it was a poor effort. Comfort bent her head again and added a few quick pencil strokes to her drawing. Laying down both pad and pencil on the floor, she looked up again.

'So you're awake. How do you feel?'

Julia thought for a little while and then produced one word: 'Bloody.'

'You poor thing,' said Comfort, leaning over to check the pressure gauge on the oxygen cylinder. 'How –?'

Just as she said that, Julia had started her own question.

'How's David?' she croaked.

'Very cross that Anthony won't let him in to share the nursing,' said Comfort drily. 'What help he thinks he could give, I can't imagine. A great clumsy hulk like that in a sickroom!'

Julia closed her eyes, so that Comfort should not see the sudden dislike that she felt. The emotion was so unlikely – and such a betrayal – that Julia wanted to believe that she had never felt it. She heard Comfort pick up the sketch pad again and simply lay, letting her draw whatever she liked.

There were no other distractions from the difficulty of breathing, the pain, the falling over chasms of unconsciousness, the dreams and miserable awakenings until Anthony appeared well after eight that night to give his wife an injection. Julia was so far out of her usual self-control that she whimpered at the prick of the needle.

'It's all right, my love,' said Anthony, wiping the puncture with a spirit-soaked swab. 'We've got some penicillin for you at last. You'll be all right again in no time now.'

She rolled her head sideways on the pillow and murmured, 'I'm so sorry.' She had not meant Anthony and Comfort to hear, but something must have been audible.

'Did you hear that?' she heard Anthony ask.

'She was mumbling so,' answered Comfort. 'But it seemed to be an apology. She's always hated being a nuisance.' Julia's shoulders tightened, and almost at once she heard her husband's voice:

'Julia's not a nuisance, Comfort. I only hope to God she's not in too much pain. Pneumonia is no joke, you know. But she'll be all right now. With this drug it's only a matter of time.' His shoes squeaked on the hard floor and Julia heard him walk towards the door. Comfort, believing Anthony without reservation, knew that Julia was no longer in any danger and went back to her chair and her sketches with the anxiety draining out of her.

The penicillin injected into Julia's veins four times a day killed the infection inexorably, and within three days the oxygen tent had been removed and she was sitting up in bed waiting for her meals with real hunger. She no longer needed a constant attendant by then and Annunziata and Comfort came and went as they chose. At last Anthony allowed David in to the sickroom.

He came, looking as he always did, huge, a little untidy but with a smile of great sweetness on his lean face, from which the tan had almost completely faded. Julia was pleased that he did not tiptoe or whisper, but spoke in his normal voice.

'So, the miracle drug did its stuff,' he said cheerfully. 'Thank God. I hope you haven't had too beastly a time.'

Julia pushed the lank, greasy hair off her forehead and smiled up at him.

'It could have been a lot worse; but I'm sorry about the penicillin.'

'Good God why?' demanded David, looking astonished. 'Without it you'd . . . you might have . . . you'd have taken far longer to get well.'

'I might have died, you mean,' said Julia in the first lawyerly voice of her convalescence and then was sorry when she saw his face. 'But, David, I might not have. People do get over pneumonia, and . . .' Her voice faltered, but then strengthened: 'I hate the thought that my illness took Anthony back to the black market.'

At that David leaned forward and stroked her horrible hair. Thinking of its dirty stringiness, Julia could not help flinching. David quickly removed his hand and sat back in his chair.

'There was no question of that, Julia,' he said. 'After what happened to Flavia, he would never have risked injecting illegal penicillin into you. This came to Venice officially.'

Julia said nothing, but from the way she relaxed into the pillows David realised how worried she had been.

'Yes,' he said slowly, still looking at her in that peculiar way, 'you really are rather a remarkable person.'

'Nonsense, David,' said Julia, 'there's nothing remarkable about me. I'm as ordinary and self-interested as the next person.'

He shook his head, but did not speak. After an apparently unbreakable silence, Julia decided that she would have to say something else and so with considerable truth, she told him that she had missed him.

'Did you? I missed you almost intolerably. Not even being allowed to come and see you – if it hadn't been for the Suvarovs I think I'd have gone mad.'

'Felicity,' said Julia, suddenly remembering the morning they had spent together just before she fell ill. 'Did she catch it?'

David shook his head.

'She was fine when they left,' he said, 'and Anthony explained that pneumonia is very quick to develop. She'd have shown symptoms long before they went. They both sent their love to you,' he added, remembering the day when he thought that Julia was going to die and had gone to them in despair.

'What is it?' she asked, seeing his face harden in front of her. She held one of her hands out to him. 'David, what's happened?'

He took her hand between both his own, turning it palm upwards and gazing down as though he were a fortune-teller, searching the damp pinkness of her flesh for answers to all sorts of impossible questions.

'I wish to God I knew,' he said, but he could not look at her, because he did know.

# Chapter Eighteen

As she slowly regained strength, Julia began to be able to think of things beyond her own physical state, and whenever David came to see her she urged him to tell her what had been happening at the trial. He took care never to stay with her for more than twenty minutes, obeying both the spirit and the letter of Anthony's orders, but he tried to give her a clear account of the eight days Kesselring had spent in the witness box, watching her face all the time for signs of boredom or exhaustion.

Julia's questions about the line the defence lawyers were taking were as acute as anything she had ever asked David, and they filled him with relieved delight. The sharpness of the terror he had felt during her illness had revealed to him just how much he loved her, and once she began to recover he had been afraid that they would never again be able to talk simply as friends. The easy, informed arguments they had about the Kesselring case proved him wrong: as they talked, the two of them might have been no more than friendly colleagues. David began to think that it might be possible to go on living in the same house as Julia and Anthony without either betraying himself or suffering unendurable frustration.

One day he reported that the defence had claimed that partisan warfare was contrary to the Hague Convention, that the Germans therefore had every right to take reprisals against the partisans, and that any excesses on their part were explained if not justified by their horror of what the partisans did.

'"I am a hero of the resistance. You are an irregular soldier. He is a terrorist",' Julia suggested.

'I know. Double and treble standards. And it is hard not to think

226

of one's own horror at some of the things that the Irgun and Stern Gang are doing in Palestine, for instance,' David said after a long silence.

'True,' said Julia, 'but in Palestine the British army does not burn villages, hang hostages and leave their bodies in village squares for days at a time as a warning, whatever horror they feel at things like the bombing of the King David Hotel and the murders of those sergeants. You can't deny that the Germans' actions were excessive.'

'Believe me, I don't,' said David seriously. 'Although if you read the American papers, you can see that they have been accusing our troops of committing "atrocities" in Palestine. No, I just have doubts about the legitimacy of some aspects of these trials.'

'Such as?' asked Julia, who had had her own doubts for some time.

'Outlawing the defence of following superior orders, for one,' said David, noticing that Julia was beginning to look tired. He got up to go, saying: 'But we can keep that for another time. You ought to rest.'

Julia denied feeling the least bit tired and she pressed him to explain what he meant.

'It is difficult to justify when you think of that British officer who was convicted for refusing to obey orders to take part in the assault on Le Havre because his superiors had not allowed the German commander to evacuate the French civilians first,' said David. 'They say that twelve thousand French civilians were killed there in the preliminary bombing, let alone during the actual fighting. The man who refused to take part was court martialled, cashiered and sentenced to a year's hard labour. To me that puts us in a difficult position when trying Germans, whose crime was obeying their superiors' orders, whatever our horror at what those orders led to.'

Julia nodded. It was a piece of official hypocrisy that had often worried her. She let her eyes close for a moment.

'I really must go,' said David. 'I've worn you out and worried you. Anthony would strangle me if I caused a relapse.'

'No he wouldn't,' said Julia. She had meant to be comforting, but even to herself the words sounded depressed. David looked down at her as she lay against the white pillows, pale and thinner than ever, and thought how much easier it would be to keep himself in check if her husband treated her with the gentleness she deserved.

'Tell me once how you're really feeling,' David said, 'and then I will leave you in peace.'

'So so,' said Julia, looking up at him from her pillows and smiling at the affection and the anxiety in his face. 'Physically almost all right again, though a bit weak, but I get gloomy and exaggerate all sorts of minor difficulties into terrible tragedies.'

'I expect that's just convalescence,' said David, longing to take her in his arms and comfort her.

'That's what Anthony says,' she said sensibly. 'Thank you for coming in. It's cheered me up no end to be reminded that I do have work and a brain and something to do when I'm allowed up again.'

David looked rather odd as she said that, but he left so quickly that she could not ask him anything about it and picked up her book to absorb the time until Annunziata brought in her supper.

It dawned on her as she was eating the liver and polenta an hour later that there was something different about Annunziata. There was a light in her dark eyes that Julia could not remember seeing before her illness and yet there was sadness too. When Annunziata came to collect the tray, Julia asked her tentatively whether she had had some news.

'My son is alive,' said Annunziata, her dark eyes gleaming in the candlelight.

Julia got out of bed, took the tray back from Annunziata, put it down on the chest of drawers and hugged her.

'I'm so glad,' she said in Italian. 'When did you hear? When is he coming home?'

Annunziata, who had accepted the hug, made Julia get back into bed and then told her the whole story. Anthony's regular enquiries of his colleagues around Italy had at last borne fruit and Annunziata's son had been discovered in a Roman hospital recovering slowly from serious wounds to his head and spine. He had been caught in an explosion at Monte Cassino. His dog tags had been blown off in the blast and the head wound had severely damaged his memory so that no one had any idea of his identity. Patient care had gradually restored his mind until he had been able to remember who he was.

'And the spinal wound?' asked Julia carefully. 'Can he walk?'

Annunziata stood absolutely straight and with all the dignity that Julia so admired in her shook her head.

'I'm so sorry,' Julia said, thinking of all she had read and heard about the battle at Monte Cassino.

The Allies had found their way to Rome blocked there by Germans who were using the ancient Benedictine monastery as their base and flung a series of attacks against it. By the time the British, the Americans, and the ultimately successful Rifs from North Africa had made their assaults, the monastery was almost completely destroyed for the third time in history. The first had been during an attack by the Saracens in the Middle Ages and the second during an earthquake.

Giovanna Sassanta had given Julia a rather different view of the fighting in the Cassino valley from the one she had gained from the British newspapers at the time. Trying to explain her husband's loathing of the Allies and all they stood for, Giovanna had told her that there had in fact been no German or even Italian troops in the monastery and that its destruction had been unnecessary. As she listened, Julia had not been able to escape the thought that Giovanna must have shared more of her husband's convictions than she had admitted.

Annunziata, who had so personal a reason for resentment, made no such criticisms. She told Julia only that the doctor had been wonderful in finding her son and in promising to let him live in the Campo San Maurizio.

'The hospital say he can't be moved for two months yet,' said Annunziata, picking up the tray again, 'but then *il dottore* will arrange everything. He is a good man, *signora*.'

'I know he is,' said Julia. 'I'm glad that he has been able to help.'

She looked forward to his usual visit that evening, but he did not come, and it was Comfort who appeared at half-past nine to remake Julia's bed and see that she had everything she needed for the night.

'Is Anthony all right?' Julia asked a little wistfully.

'He's fine,' said Comfort, 'but he had to go back to the hospital after dinner. So I'm his deputy.' She sat down on the edge of Julia's bed and offered to brush her hair.

'I can do that,' said Julia. 'But can you move over a bit? You're sitting on my feet.'

'Sorry,' answered Comfort cheerfully, moving down the bed. 'What would you like to do tomorrow? Anthony left instructions that you could get up for a couple of hours if you felt up to it. Shall I hire a gondola and take you up the Grand Canal to the sound of trumpets?'

'Oh, Comfort, you are wonderful!' said Julia, happy that Comfort was her old extravagant affectionate self again. 'You know very well how I'd hate that. Besides I don't think the gondoliers work in the depths of winter. What I'd most like to do is go to the court to listen to what's happening in the trial, but. . .'

'No. Anthony said no work and no court for at least another week,' said Comfort, relieved that she would not have to accompany Julia to anything so dull. 'We could go and look at pictures, or walk to Florian's for a drink, or just sit downstairs and talk. Whatever you like.'

'I'd love to get out of the house for a bit,' said Julia, plumping for Florian's. The walk there took only about ten minutes and she thought that even with the frightening weakness in her legs that she had discovered the first time she got out of bed she ought to manage that distance.

She did, but only just, reaching the café breathless and with her knees trembling. Comfort piloted her to the nearest seat and hailed the waiter to order a brandy. Julia lay against the hard, red velvet back of the bench, staring up at the painted walls around her.

Before the brandy came a familiar American voice penetrated Julia's tiredness and she sat up straighter.

'Why Mrs Gillingham! How good to see you up and about again. I'd heard you were sick.'

'Mr French,' said Julia, holding out her hand. 'Thank you. I may say that my recovery is wholly due to your organisation's producing some penicillin just in time,' she added. 'Thank you for that too.' She watched his heavy dark face and wondered why it looked rueful.

'Yes, I heard about that too,' he said. 'Doctor Gillingham sure burned the wires between here and headquarters when he was trying to get it.'

'And with reason,' said Comfort, coming back with the brandy.

'Ah, Comfort, this is Jackson French of UNRRA. Mr French, this is my sister-in-law, Comfort Gillingham, a compatriot of yours.' Julia watched in amusement as Comfort's spectacular looks and casual elegance had their usual effect on the young man. She was also amused to see that Comfort was shaking his hand and even inviting him to share their table. Her immediate antagonism to David Wallington had led Julia to expect her to display a similar hostility to Jack French.

During the course of their conversation, to which Julia listened with only half her attention as she sipped her brandy, she learned that Jackson French was likely to be posted to London to play a part in the winding up of UNRRA later in the year and that Comfort herself was due to leave Venice in two days' time 'now that Julia is getting well again'. Comfort gave Jackson French her address and told him to be sure to call her when he got to London.

'Is the black market conquered then?' Julia asked him during a pause in the others' talk.

'I don't suppose it'll ever be that,' he said with resignation. 'But supplies are beginning to get through in better order than before. The new penicillin factory is almost finished and the Italians we've been training to run it are due back from Canada any day now. Food is still a problem, of course, after last year's dire harvest.'

'And presumably,' said Julia, who had been reading the backlog of newspapers that had accumulated during her illness, 'the appalling winter will have done for this year's as well.'

'I guess so. But the new organisation will have to handle that. I'm heading Stateside when I've done my bit in London. When are you going back, Comfort?'

'I'll never go back,' she said. 'I've become too European. Besides, the part of my family I care about is here now,' she added taking Julia's hand for a moment.

That evening, knowing that David was dining out, Anthony came home in time to have dinner with Comfort and looked in to talk to Julia before changing out of his hospital clothes.

'Comfort says you took a walk today. How do you feel after it?' he asked, untying his tie and pulling the cuff links out of his shirt.

'Rather feeble, actually,' Julia admitted. 'And absurdly inclined to self-pity.'

'That's convalescence,' he said. 'And it'll last for a while yet. I've been thinking that you ought to get away from here for a bit, but I don't quite see how I could leave the hospital just now. But. . .'

'Please don't worry about it,' said Julia, childishly hurt that he was not prepared to let her needs take precedence over his work, but struggling as usual to be reasonable.

'But,' he went on, 'David has suggested that we should all borrow his mother's house outside Florence at Easter. Would you like that? You ought to be strong enough by then to cope with the journey, and I can try to organise things at the hospital so that my assistants can cope.'

'I'd love it,' said Julia, feeling more cheerful. 'How kind of David – and his mother!'

'He's a good friend,' said Anthony. 'Angry though he's made me in the past, he is a good lad. Well I'll tell him it's on then. Good.' He walked through the communicating door into his own room, leaving it open while he dressed. When he was ready he came back into her room, shutting the door behind him on his way down to dinner.

'You look very miserable,' he said kindly, pausing by her bed. 'Can I help?'

Julia manufactured a smile.

'Yes,' she said. 'You can give me permission to wash my hair. I tried to get Comfort to help me and she refused without your say-so. Please? It feels unspeakable.'

'Of course you can,' said Anthony, laughing. 'I'll ask Annunziata to bring you hot water and towels first thing tomorrow morning.'

'Good,' said Julia. 'And you could answer a question, too, if you will.'

'If I can,' he said.

'I've been wondering about David,' said Julia casually, as though the question were not of the utmost importance to her. 'You reminded me a minute ago of your original warning about him. What was it he did to make you so terribly angry with him before I came?'

'It doesn't matter, Julia,' said Anthony with a return of the impatience he had shown so often before she got ill. He even pulled back his cuff to look at his watch. 'No one who wasn't with us in the hills could possibly understand what it was all about and it's over now. I've just about managed to forgive him. Let's leave it there. It really isn't any of your . . . concern.'

'Fine,' said Julia and watched him go. She wished that she could ask David what Anthony had been talking about, but she obviously could not. Everything David had shown her of himself had made her love him and yet she believed that he had done something unspeakable. The two sides of the equation did not balance and she could hardly bear the implications of that.

Comfort left Venice two days later, promising to write to Julia every week and to do her best to put the house in order for their return. Her departure left Julia depressed. Seeing how low she was, Anthony decided that she needed to get out of the house and gave her reluctant permission to spend half of each day in court. David escorted her there on her first morning and was touchingly concerned for her, insisting on taking a cushion for her to soften the hard seat on the press benches and urging her to promise to leave the stuffy, dark-panelled room if she felt faint or troubled.

'A little faintness would be nothing,' Julia said, 'compared with the excruciating boredom of spending all those empty hours in the house. How women who don't have professions manage to keep themselves sane I cannot imagine!'

'You could never give up the law, could you?' asked David.

'I suppose I could,' said Julia, thinking of the children she longed for, 'if there was something equally important I had to do. But to sit around in a house, organising bazaars, having my hair done, that sort of thing? No, I couldn't do it. That reminds me,' she added, 'I wanted to say how kind it is of you and your mother to arrange this Easter holiday for us.'

'It is a real pleasure, believe me,' said David, smiling down at her. 'And Mama has written to say how grateful she is that we'll be able to see how the old house has stood up to the war and cope with any disasters for her.'

'She must have missed it,' said Julia.

David's smile faded.

'Yes,' he said.

'I think the war must have been hard on her ... particularly while Italy was still part of the Axis; not least because there was a camp for Italian prisoners of war just beyond our gates in Scotland. She never said anything about it when I went up there for my last leave, and she's never written about it since, but I can imagine a little of what she felt. Fiesole has always seemed very like home to me too,' he added with apparent irrelevance.

They threaded their way through the vegetable market, full of dull early spring vegetables instead of the mounds of tomatoes and aubergines and peppers and artichokes that Julia longed to see and buy, and reached the Tribunale di Giustizia a few minutes later.

Julia was touched by the number of people who congratulated her on her recovery as she made her way with her cushion to her allotted seat at the end of the press benches, and gave several brief accounts of her illness to people who asked. The court might be in a foreign country, there to try a citizen of yet a third nation, but it was her element and she was relieved to be back in it, even though she could take no active part in the trial.

The proceedings began in their customary stately way and then a Colonel Beelitz was called as a defence witness. He was there to explain to the court that he and the other officers had tried to control the Nazi leaders' demands for gross reprisals for the deaths of the Germans in the Via Rassella. Hitler had apparently demanded that fifty hostages should be killed for every dead German soldier, and Himmler had wanted whole areas of Rome to be cleared and their inhabitants deported.

Julia was so interested in the cross-examination that she almost disobeyed Anthony's instructions to go back to the Campo San Maurizio for lunch and spend the afternoon in bed, but, remembering how weak she had felt the previous evening, she did as he said. Once she had taken off her black suit and was lying in bed dressed only in her underclothes and dressing gown, she admitted to herself that she was so tired that she might not have lasted out the afternoon in court without fainting.

She slept until Annunziata came to call her soon after five with a bowl of *zabaglione,* which Julia had never tasted until her illness. It seemed to her a wonderful invention, making far more of a single egg than any British concoction, easily digestible, tasting rich, sweet and thoroughly sustaining. She insisted on sharing it with Annunziata, who looked even more gaunt than she had done before the news of her son's survival, and then got up.

For a miracle, almost boiling hot water poured out of the taps into the bath and Julia let herself have a really deep bath for once, lying there dreaming about the day when her life might be whole again and weaving plans to make it so, until the skin of her fingers and toes crinkled and the water felt cold. Stirring it around herself, she looked down at her long body, noticing how her illness had removed the last spare flesh. Her ribs were clear, her hipbones stuck out like mountains on a desert relief map, her thighs were straight and looked even longer than usual. Remembering the struggles she had had in the early days of her married life to avoid putting weight on her waist and hips, she laughed.

Relaxed and without the miserable depression of the previous few evenings, Julia pulled herself out of the water, rubbed herself vigorously with the hard, thin towel Annunziata had left there for her and went to dress.

Twenty minutes later, wearing her grey-flannel trousers and mole-coloured jersey and with her hair casually tied back in a velvet ribbon, Julia walked into the salon, only to be brought up short by the sight of David staring blankly at a yellow form in his right hand, a tumbler of whisky ignored and tilting in his left.

Pretending for a moment that she had noticed nothing wrong, Julia poured herself a glass of vermouth and then turned to face David. His thin face was yellowish-white and his whole body seemed somehow diminished. His blue eyes stared at her blindly and when she gently said his name he gave a start, spilling whisky over the crumpled telegram.

'David?' she said again, just as quietly, putting her glass down on the table again. 'Is it very bad?'

He made a tremendous effort to bring himself back into reality; his hands shook and he swallowed twice as he tried to speak; then he passed his right hand, still clutching the telegram, through his dark hair. Feeling the strange texture of the paper in his hair, he brought his hand back in front of his face, and his dazed eyes focused on the telegram. He could not bear to talk about what had happened and so he handed it to Julia and went to sit on one of the excruciatingly uncomfortable gilded chairs by the window while she read it.

Julia smoothed out the single sheet of paper.

Your father and Jonathan killed in motor accident yesterday stop Funeral tomorrow stop Desperate to see you stop Arriving Fiesole Maundy Thursday stop Mama.

Julia looked from David to the telegram and back again. At first he sat looking at his feet, and she could not think of a thing to say. All the obvious expressions of sympathy were wholly inadequate. Knowing how much his brother had meant to him and how happy Jonathan's slow progress towards regaining his health had made him, Julia could hardly say, 'I'm so sorry they're dead.'

Then David looked up and, as though the desperate misery in his eyes had called out to her, Julia went and knelt on the hard, icy floor at his feet, reaching up with both hands. She put them on his broad, bony shoulders.

'David,' she said, 'my dear, dear David.' He looked straight at her, and she could tell from the way his lower eyelids were drawn up at the inner corners and his nostrils distended that he was trying not to cry. He leaned forward until his head was lying against her shoulder. His need for comfort overrode every other consideration and Julia cradled his head with one arm, stroking his thick, soft hair with the other hand. His hands clutched at her back.

Julia could feel the cool, faintly bristly skin of his cheek against her face and she was bitterly ashamed that in the middle of his awful pain she was conscious of the pleasure of it. When he rubbed his face briefly against her shoulder, when she felt his warm breath against her neck, when his big hands pulled her closer to him, she felt all her senses responding and had to work hard to keep her breathing slow and even and her hand light as it stroked his hair. Ashamed of her response though she was, she would not pull away from him while he needed her; that would be even worse.

At last he relaxed his grip on her back and pulled himself up to sit straight in the purgatorial chair.

'I'm sorry, Julia,' he said a little stiffly. 'That was unforgivable.'

'No it wasn't, David,' she answered kindly. 'It was very natural, and I'm glad I was here.'

'I must go and telegraph Mama,' he said suddenly. Julia removed her hand, but he did not stand up. After a moment's pause, Julia asked if he wanted her to go to the telegraph office for him. He shook his head.

'No, the air will do me good. Don't keep any dinner for me.'

'You must eat, David. I'll get Annunziata to keep something hot in the kitchen and then if you'd rather not be bothered with us tonight, you can have it there – or in bed, if that would be better,' said Julia, her heart feeling as though it were held in a tightening vice as she saw his misery.

He gripped her wrist suddenly, so hard that she almost cried out.

'It's not that I don't want to be with you, Julia. God forbid! I don't want to eat, that's all. Oh Lord, that must be Anthony,' he said.

Julia had heard nothing.

'Will you tell him for me, Julia?' he begged, getting out of the chair at last. 'I don't want to have to talk.' He knew it was not fair to lay everything on her while she was still so weak, but he trusted her implicitly and there was no one else.

'All right, David. Go and send your telegram, and then come back and try to have some food when you can,' she said.

He nodded, released her hand, and walked quickly to the door. With his hand on the knob he half turned back to her.

'I'm glad you were here,' he said in a strangled voice and then went out.

Julia rubbed her eyes with a handkerchief and then went to retrieve her drink. She had just taken a mouthful of the rather sour wormwood-flavoured wine when Anthony came breezily into the room.

'I say, what on earth's the matter with the Boy David?' he asked, seeing his wife.

'There's been a most frightful accident,' she said and Anthony stopped quite still just inside the room. 'His father and his brother have both been killed. He asked me to tell you, I think because he can't bear to talk about it. He was reading this when I got here,' she went on, holding out the telegram.

Anthony came to read it, then automatically folded it up and put it in the breast pocket of his black coat.

'Poor boy,' he said with more tenderness than Julia had heard from him since the crisis of her illness. 'Well that puts the lid on the Fiesole plan. We obviously can't go thrusting ourselves on that poor woman now.'

'Heavens no,' agreed Julia, thinking about the Easter plans for the first time that evening. 'Lucky that he's already got permission to go. I wish there was something we could do to help him, though.'

Anthony put an arm around her shoulders and she looked at him, surprised but pleased that he had managed to touch her again.

'You always did believe it possible to cure other people's unhappiness,' he said. 'But the truth is that however sympathetic or kind one is, one can't ever do anything to prevent someone else hurting.'

'Except perhaps listen,' said Julia, who believed passionately in the ability – and obligation – of friends to help.

'I doubt if David'll talk. He's a very private man, Julia. Don't be too hurt if he shuts us both out now,' said Anthony.

'I'm old enough to wait without being hurt for people to let me in again,' she said lightly, hoping that he had listened to what she said and understood its application to himself.

David did not in fact begin to relax his reserve until nearly a week after the telegram had arrived, when Julia judged it a suitable moment to say that she and Anthony would be making other plans for Easter. For a second or two David looked stricken. He said nothing, but just stared at Julia, the hurt twisting his sensitive mouth.

'But, dear David,' she said pitifully, 'you can't want us interfering at such a moment. We'd be desperately in the way. Your mother will want you to herself.'

'Would you really hate it so much?' he said at last, and then hurriedly added: 'Of course you would. I'm sorry.' He tried to smile, but it was a poor effort. 'Of course you must go somewhere else.'

'I shouldn't hate it, David; not if you needed me,' said Julia, telling the unadorned truth.

Anthony, predictably enough Julia thought, decided that his patients needed him too much for him to take any kind of holiday over the Easter weekend, but he made no objection to David's formal request to take Julia away to stay with his mother.

# Chapter Nineteen

Anthony escorted Julia and David to the railway station on the Thursday before Easter and while David went to buy the tickets, Julia seized the opportunity to ask her husband to do a small errand for her.

'One of my Italian teacher's refugees has been badgering me to find out whether she could get permission to live in England,' she said. 'I've always thought it unlikely, but I've just heard from George this morning that it is impossible. Her claims are just not strong enough. Would you take her the message for me? It seems very unfair to leave her hoping when there is no hope.'

'All right,' said Anthony, shrugging. 'If it's that important, I might as well go straight from here. Why not give me the letter – unless there's anything private in it – and the woman's address.'

'There's nothing private,' answered Julia, 'although I would quite like the letter back when you've shown it to her.'

'All right,' he said, kissing her cheek as David came back towards them with the tickets. 'Now, don't let poor David's tragedy wear you down. You're still convalescent and you need to rest.'

'I promise to follow all your instructions,' said Julia with illusory meekness. Anthony laughed and touched her cheek briefly. Julia smiled to see him happier than he had seemed before her illness.

'I'll miss you,' she said. 'All right, David, I'm coming. Goodbye, Anthony.'

He held open the train door for her and heaved their two bags up to David.

'Take care of her, old man,' he said and slammed the door shut.

'Of course I shall,' said David through the open window.

'I'll see you both on Monday night, then,' said Anthony, turning away.

Julia spent most of the journey between Venice and Florence trying to decide exactly what to say to David's Italian mother. He had told her enough about his parents' passionate devotion to each other for Julia to feel desperately sorry for her.

They reached the railway station at Florence just after four. David jumped down on to the platform and put up his hands for the baggage. Julia handed it down to him. When he had dumped their two canvas bags on the ground, he reached up again to help her down from the high train.

Once again the touch of his hands on her wrists made her insides lurch with pleasure.

'How do we get to Fiesole?' she asked and was pleased to hear that her voice sounded entirely passionless.

'A friend of mine who's working in and around Florence said he'd meet us in his jeep if he could make it,' David answered looking round. 'If not, it'll probably have to be the bus.'

They walked out of the station and stood, blinking a little in the bright sunlight. Julia was just thinking how wonderfully refreshing it was to be in the middle of a real city, with town noises and roads and motor cars, when it dawned on her that her baggy brownish-grey tweeds and old felt hat were far too countrified. She had put them on without thinking, because they were what she had always worn for travelling outside London, but she began to wonder what David's mother would think of them and to wish that she had put on her good black coat and skirt instead with one of her London hats. A shout from David made her start.

'Bill!' She turned to see David waving. 'There he is, Julia; so you won't have to walk to the bus. Good.'

Julia looked in the direction of his waving arm and saw an equally tall man in UNRRA uniform stride along towards them. When he reached them, David introduced him to Julia and she shook hands and then turned aside as Bill said something gruffly about how sorry he was. David clapped him on the shoulder and simply said:

'I know. Thanks. Have you really got transport?'

'Yup. Over here, and luckily it's almost legitimate. I've got to get over to a village out on the Bologna road and I can easily drive there via Fiesole. Seen Florence before, Mrs Gillingham?'

Julia answered civilly and resigned herself to half an hour's polite conversation. She did not see much of Florence as they roared through it in the jeep, just a muddled impression of large buildings and a broad dark-green river, but as they began to drive up the steep, swooping hill to Fiesole, David's friend said:

'If you look back in five minutes or so, you'll see the best view in the whole place.'

From the back seat of the jeep came David's voice, as light and teasing as Julia had ever heard it. She was so pleased that he was able to talk so frivolously that she hardly distinguished what he was actually saying.

'It's even better from the terrace of my mother's house. Don't you look back, Julia; mustn't spoil your appetite for views of Florence.'

She did turn her head then, but only to smile at David and marvel that he could look so happy; but even as she watched his face seemed to grow colder and he nodded. Irritated with herself for reminding him, Julia turned back to face the front and said nothing more until Bill had dropped them outside a big yellow house on the edge of Fiesole. She thanked him and waited while David invited him in for a cup of tea. Julia was interested to see an expression of faint embarrassment cross Bill's face.

'Thanks, David, but I've bent the rules enough; I really ought to get on to the village and see to this wretched food distribution. So much goes missing that we've got to find out why. It may simply be inefficiency at this level, but it could be worse. These damned black marketeers are everywhere; they siphon the stuff off as soon as it comes into the country, at the various stores and again at the local distribution points. They're even sending it out of the country – to Yugoslavia and France.'

'Really,' said Julia. 'But that must be in huge quantities to make it worth their while. How do they get so much out of the country?'

Bill looked at her for a moment.

'It's not certain, but there's a suggestion that they have stolen British army trucks and uniforms and, with forged documents, pass themselves off as official convoys. It's not generally known, but they've got at least 60,000 tons of grain away like that,' he said

'Profitable business,' commented Julia.

'Yes indeed. The profit is roughly ten or twelve thousand lire per hundredweight,' Bill said drily. 'Whoever put up the money for the scheme has made a fortune. We've got to stop it before UNRRA is wound up. So long. Goodbye, Mrs Gillingham.'

David hauled their luggage off the back seat and Bill drove off.

'That scale of operation does make Anthony's black marketing seem quite trivial, doesn't it?' said Julia as they watched the jeep disappearing in a cloud of dust.

'I've always thought so,' said David. 'And after all he's done it for the most altruistic of reasons – unlike Bill's quarry.'

'Yes,' Julia said with an expression on her face that he could not quite read, 'but the law is the law and one can't decide to apply it only to those whose motives and characters one dislikes. It has to apply to everyone equally, however "good" or "bad" or else. . .'

'It becomes a very bad joke,' David said. He smiled at her and picked up their luggage. 'Come along and meet Mama.'

Julia followed him through a tall, wrought-iron gate and waited on the weedy gravel in front of the pale-yellow walls of a large square villa as he pulled a long, iron bell. Within a very short time, she heard the sounds of bolts being drawn back. The heavy, dark double doors opened and in their shadow stood the most striking woman Julia had ever seen.

Dressed in comfortable-looking tweeds that were as old and baggy as Julia's but did nothing to disguise her tall slimness, Allegra. Wallington had David's smooth dark hair and elegant hands, but there was no other resemblance between them. Where his face was angular and spare, hers was a flawless oval, and her round eyes were very dark. The lines that radiated from their corners did nothing to detract from their brilliance, but in some curious way made her look approachable, despite her immense style.

To Julia's eye she seemed to wear no powder or lipstick, but then she hardly needed any. Her skin was a pale olive colour but absolutely clear and her magnificent eyes gave her face all the definition it needed. She looked desperately tired, but there were no obvious marks of grief on her face.

'Mrs Gillingham,' she said in a voice that carried only the faintest Italian accent, 'how very good of you to come and stay with me.' She held out her hand and Julia shook it, saying:

'It is charming of you to have invited me, Mrs Wallington. Particularly now.' Julia wanted to say something more direct about the accident, but could not imagine how to approach the difficult subject in the face of such easy courtesy. All she could think of to do was to step aside so that David and his mother could greet each other.

'David,' said his mother, very gently, and then added a sentence in Italian. Julia heard the name 'Jonathan', but she made a determined effort not to translate the Italian words, knowing how much the two of them must need privacy. David answered in the same language and then reverted to English.

'Is much of the house habitable? Where have you put us, Mama?' he asked cheerfully.

'Upstairs,' she answered, linking arms with Julia. 'Come on up, Mrs Gillingham, and I will show you your room. It's not been too bad, David. Germans were billeted here, but they seem to have treated the place with considerably more decency than they did the people.'

There was no easy way to answer the bitterness in her voice, and Julia remembered what David had said about his mother's probable feelings during the war and tried to imagine what it must have been like for Mrs Wallington, stuck in Scotland, knowing only a little but guessing all too much of what was happening to her own country – and to her two sons.

'It's over now, Mama,' said David gently. 'I know that doesn't make what's happened any better, but it is finished . . . We just have to rebuild and make sure that it can never happen again.'

'I know,' she said. 'Forgive me, Mrs Gillingham. You must be so bored with war talk. Here we are.'

She opened a door and ushered Julia into a shadowed room on the second floor. Unlike the apartment in Venice, this room was decorated in the English style and furnished with two plump single beds covered in chintz counterpanes. There was even an armchair that actually looked comfortable. Julia had difficulty in suppressing a sigh of relief.

David dumped her bag on the floor by the bed and then went to open the shutters, letting some real light into the room through the yellowing lace curtains. It allowed Julia to see the glowing rose colours of the chintz and also to notice the shabbiness of the well-washed paintwork and the cracks in the ceiling.

'I promised her the best view of Florence from here, Mama,' he said over his shoulder as he wrestled with the catch. 'Ah, that's better. Julia?'

Julia went to stand beside him on the minute balcony and stared down across the valley. There, spread out below her in the late afternoon sun, was Florence. In the foreground were small green fields dotted with clusters of red-roofed houses and the dark spires of cypress trees; further back was the great mass of the city itself, with the cathedral's rust-red dome rising unmistakably in the very centre of the view. Julia could make out dark-green stretches of the river as it wound between the ochre and terracotta of the buildings. Beyond the city rose a line of gentle hills, looking blue-grey in the distance.

'It's wonderful,' she said, turning back into the room. 'Mrs Wallington, I can't tell you how amazing it feels to be here – in all this space – instead of shut up in Venice.'

David's mother smiled then and her lovely face looked suddenly young and for a moment hardly tired at all.

'Haven't I always said it was a dank, sinister, unhealthy place, David?' she said. 'I think our guest is very intelligent.'

David responded to the teasing by walking over to his mother, putting an arm around her thin shoulders and dropping a kiss on to her smooth hair.

'Yes, Mama, she is; and yes, you have always said so. But Venice is full of wonderful things, and even for you I won't pretend to dislike it.'

'You always were a stubborn creature,' she said with a charming tenderness in her voice. 'From the moment they told me that you were a breech baby I knew I'd have trouble with you.' Turning to Julia, she went on, smiling still: 'Haven't you found him stubborn too, Mrs Gillingham?'

Julia, delighted to see that the affection between them was solid enough to allow such teasing, said, as though she were considering some knotty legal problem:

'Stubborn? I wonder . . . I've certainly become aware that I wouldn't like to cross him, particularly on a matter of principle.' Julia looked at David then and was a little surprised to see that he was not laughing as she had expected. Instead he was standing with his head on one side, looking seriously at her. Mrs Wallington laughed.

'I said you were intelligent,' she commented. 'But this is all irrelevant. Mrs Gillingham, I've become Scottish enough to need my tea and I'm sure you'd like some after that horrid train. I think it's just warm enough to have it on the terrace. Will you come down when you're ready?'

'Thank you,' said Julia. 'Tea would be wonderful!'

They left her to unpack and she was pleased to find a jug of warm water wrapped in a towel on the washstand. Having scrubbed the train's grime from her face and hands, she searched for a comb to deal with her hair. It had been far easier to keep it tidy, she thought, in the days when she wore it pinned up; the style she had taken to suited her better – and made her look and feel years younger than she was – but it was a terrible nuisance.

Amused by her burgeoning vanity, she dawdled over the unpacking to give Mrs Wallington plenty of unencumbered time with her son. It seemed to Julia to be the height of good manners to have greeted a stranger with apparent pleasure under such circumstances and then to have included her in the family teasing, but she wanted to make certain that they could forget their manners and talk freely to each other without having to bother about her.

When at last she made her way downstairs towards the terrace, she could hear their voices speaking in English. Slowing down, she listened in case they were in the middle of a talk too personal to be interrupted; but it soon became clear that they were discussing the house and the various improvements that might be made once Europe had reached some kind of normality again.

Much relieved, Julia walked out through the open French windows on to the terrace. At the sound of her step, David pulled himself out of his chair and smiled at her. His mother turned and smiled too.

'Mrs Gillingham . . .'

'Oh please call me Julia – if you wouldn't mind,' said Julia. Mrs Wallington inclined her head in an extraordinarily graceful gesture of acquiescence.

'Julia, come and sit down and have your tea,' she said, pouring another cupful. Julia sat down and took her tea and a small almond biscuit.

'David tells me that you have been very ill,' said Mrs Wallington. 'It's that terrible place, you know. How anyone could have expected you to get properly well there I cannot imagine! And David says that your husband is a doctor: he ought to have sent you straight up to the mountains.'

'I wasn't as ill as that,' said Julia, laughing slightly. 'And he has so many patients with much worse ailments that he took quite a robust view of my case.'

'Well, now that you are here, you must stay until you are really well, mustn't she, David?'

David leaned forward to replace his tea cup on the table and then he straightened up.

'I think she ought to do exactly as she wishes, Mama. After all her husband is in Venice – and she hadn't seen him in all the war years,' he said.

Julia was horrified, thinking that the last thing David's mother would want to hear just then would be about another woman's wish to be with her husband. Her sympathy for Mrs Wallington helped her to ignore the realisation that it was an enormous relief to be away from Anthony and with people who produced an atmosphere of such calm and ease that she felt immediately at home with them.

'Of course she must, David,' came the gentle reproof, 'but she will get well much more quickly in Fiesole than in Venice. And I want her to know that she is welcome in my house for as long as she wishes.' David put a friendly hand on his mother's knee, and Julia thanked her.

'There are many things to see in Florence, too,' said Mrs Wallington. 'David will take you about and show them to you: he knows so much about it all.'

'He was certainly the most wonderful guide in Venice,' Julia said, smiling at him.

'You flatter me, both of you,' he said, and again Julia was amazed that the pair of them could appear so cheerful. 'Julia, I hope that you will let me take you down into Florence for dinner tonight; if we went early, we could stroll a little first and look at one or two of the best exteriors.'

Julia looked from one to the other, strangely at a loss. She wanted to say that she would quite happily go and dine on her own in Florence so that they could be alone together, but Mrs Wallington pre-empted her.

'Unfortunately I cannot join you, because I am expecting a very old friend of my family, who has been here all these years,' she said. Julia smiled her thanks and then turned to accept David's invitation.

Her conscience at peace, Julia set off for dinner in a mood to enjoy herself. She and David decided to catch the bus down into Florence and then try for a taxi home. As they were waiting at the bus stop in the main square of Fiesole, about five minutes' walk from the house, she said carefully:

'David, I hope your mother didn't think me dreadfully insensitive —'

248

Before she could complete her sentence, he interrupted her.

'Why on earth should she have thought anything like that?' he demanded, sounding almost angry.

Julia touched his forearm lightly.

'Hush,' she said.

'Sorry.' David sounded much more like himself. 'But what do you mean?'

'It's very difficult. I just . . . it's just that I wanted to tell her how sorry I am about . . . about what happened to your father and brother but, not knowing her, I didn't want to say it in a way that might upset her. And so I didn't say anything.' Julia ended her little speech looking at her feet. When David said nothing, she waited and then at last looked up at him. There was an expression in his blue eyes that she did not completely understand, and so she lifted one eyebrow.

'You are kind, you know,' he said rather helplessly. 'I don't think I realised quite how kind until they were killed.' He seemed to be trying to pull himself together and just as the bus appeared at the mouth of the square, he murmured: 'Don't worry about Mama; she will have understood what you were thinking, and in any case I can tell her if you'd like.'

'Would you?' said Julia over her shoulder as she climbed up into the bus. 'That would be awfully good of you.'

They found seats side by side and silently agreed to talk no more about the tragedy. Instead, David pointed out landmarks they passed and eventually Julia led him on to talk about his childhood holidays at Fiesole. The first time he had to include his brother's name in an anecdote, his voice hardened a little, but soon he was talking much more easily, telling her of picnics and expeditions and even fights they had had with each other and with the Italian sons of their mother's friends and relations.

'Was it difficult getting to know them?' Julia asked, as the bus creaked round a particularly sharp hairpin bend. 'Didn't they treat you as strangers?'

'I suppose they might have done at the beginning,' he said, 'but by the time I can remember we had become part of the place really. Mama had brought us every year, and we somehow fitted in.'

'Did your father not come?' asked Julia, curiously. He shook his head.

'Partly because of the estate; there was always too much to be done. But mainly because he didn't like the place and believed that he didn't like Italians. How he thought he could love Mama so much and dislike her friends and relations on the grounds that they were Italian, I don't know. And he did love her,' said David and then was silent.

'How did they meet?' Julia asked, not sure whether he wanted to talk or not. It seemed that he did want to, for he answered her question far more fully than he need have done.

'It was quite funny in fact,' he said, a real smile lighting in his eyes. 'Some neighbours of ours in Scotland had unnaturally cosmopolitan views about the best way to bring up their daughters and they had all been sent to stay with family friends in both Paris and Florence when they were about seventeen.

'One of the daughters, Fiona, who was always known as "the pretty one", had struck up a great friendship with Mama, who had been invited back to Scotland. Now, Fiona was thought to be a suitable bride for my father – just the right age, pretty and vivacious enough it was thought to appeal to a man who was beginning to be known as a confirmed bachelor.' He stopped then and Julia supplied a prompt.

'And he caught sight of your mother and fell desperately in love,' she suggested.

'Not at all,' he answered, the grin coming back to his lips. Julia smiled back, not sure what she was about to hear, but very much enjoying his pleasure in the tale.

'No, he had been toying with the idea of proposing to Fiona, whom he had known all his life and whom he liked. But just before he could get the words out, she begged him to do her a tremendous favour. My father was a generous man, and so he cautiously agreed to do what he could. After a while she explained that she was in love with someone else – not hopelessly ineligible, but not nearly as suitable as my father – and her parents had refused to allow her to see the man. She therefore proposed that my father should pretend to fall in love with her difficult and very homesick Italian friend so that it would be clear to her parents that there was no hope of getting him for Fiona.'

'Pretty rough on your mother if it hadn't worked out,' said Julia.

'Oh, no, Fiona had already squared Mama, who had agreed to play her part. What no one had expected was that my xenophobic father should find himself first sorry for the poor little foreigner and then gradually – but quite irreversibly – falling in love with her. She took much longer.'

'What a nice story,' said Julia. 'But what happened to Fiona?'

'That's where everything gets especially satisfactory! She grew tired of her less-than-suitable young man just as quickly as her parents had predicted and then in no time at all fell in love with – and married – the elder son of a duke.'

'And so everyone was happy,' said Julia, smiling again and not giving voice to her suspicion that perhaps the young homesick Italian might have been happier if her besotted husband had managed to forget his dislike of foreigners and their countries. It seemed very hard that she should have had to uproot herself completely while her husband could not even be bothered to accompany her on holidays to her own country.

'Here we are,' announced David as the bus pulled up outside the cathedral. 'Come on – and don't worry too much about Mama. She got over her homesickness pretty quickly and he used to come over here with her every year until we were old enough to come instead.'

'Ah, David,' said Julia, sighing as she waited for him on the pavement. 'I'm not used to having my mind read, you know.'

'No,' he agreed swinging himself down beside her. 'Do you mind?'

'Not really,' she said without thinking about it. 'In fact it's rather restful. Provided that,' she added as though drafting a contract, 'you don't do it all the time.'

He laughed. 'I can only do it when we're in the middle of a conversation and you look at me speculatively and then say something anodyne in a voice that is so deliberately empty of judgment that I can practically feel the strength of will you are exerting to keep it so,' said David with the hint of a laugh in his deep voice.

Julia wrinkled her nose as she looked up at him.

'I didn't know I was so obvious,' she said, and he answered quickly:

'Well you are used to living with two very self –'

'Careful, David,' she said.

'Self-absorbed people,' he finished.

'But I love them,' said Julia. It was an article of faith. 'And they are – and always have been – very good to me, even if they can't read my mind.'

They were walking along a smallish road to the left of the extraordinary green-and-white-striped cathedral and David suddenly stopped and put both hands on Julia's shoulders. She felt the familiar shivering pleasure at his touch.

'Would you rather I simply agreed or told the truth?' he asked.

Julia closed her eyes, partly because that was a question she did not want to answer and partly because she thought it might help to stop her flinging her arms around his neck and saying, kiss me, oh please kiss me.

'Julia?' he said softly.

Correcting her instinctive move towards him, she made herself open her eyes and slightly shook her head.

'I don't know, David. I love them.' Her voice sounded exhausted even to her own ears. With an expression on his face that suggested he could not fight any longer, David pulled her towards him and slowly stroked her head and back. Julia let herself lean against him. She heard the steady beat of his heart under her cheek and felt his hand stroking her hair again and again.

'I know you do,' he said at last and with an obvious effort. 'And they love you, too. Anyone would.'

No longer sure that she could believe it, but still determined to make the best of her marriage, Julia managed to pull herself away from David. When they were once more walking side by side in the dusk, Julia said gently:

'You said I was kind, but so are you.'

'Not really,' he said, sounding very sombre. 'I just find myself getting so angry ... I'm sorry. I'm a bit stirred up just now and find myself unable to control those feelings that ought to be controlled.'

'Don't be sorry,' Julia said with an effort. 'But hadn't we better eat?'

'Yes. Bill recommended a restaurant – it's just round here.'

She followed him into a tiny, brightly lit room that was suffused with the most delectable scents of cooking. They were shown to a little table, where they would have to sit side by side. Julia pushed her way to the further chair and sat down, wondering how to make herself small enough to avoid touching David every time she moved or breathed. As soon as he sat down it was clear that there was no room for modesty. His arm lay against hers from shoulder to elbow and there was nothing they could do about it.

Julia sat, listening to his carefully controlled breathing, feeling his arm tense against her. She made a deliberate effort to relax: they would both have blown up if they had had to sit like that all evening, she thought. As soon as her muscles had slackened, she could feel a corresponding movement in him, and his voice was almost normal when he asked her what she would like to eat.

'Something light, I think,' she said, looking blindly at the menu. 'I find I'm not terribly hungry.'

'Nor I,' he said, and called the waiter.

# Chapter Twenty

Later that night, when they had returned to his mother's house, David suddenly said:

'I lost control a bit this evening. I won't do it again and I'm awfully sorry.'

'For nothing, David,' said Julia, knowing that it was her fault and not his that they had got so near the brink.

'So long as you aren't angry with me,' he said quietly. 'I don't think I could bear that.' It was all Julia could do then to wait until she could be certain of her voice.

'I'm not angry, David,' she said at last. 'Far from it. I wish –' Before she could find an expressible desire, he interrupted.

'No, it's all right,' he said quickly. 'I know. I'm just sorry that my absurd . . . No, never mind. Good night.' He left her so abruptly that she could not have stopped him even if she had known what to say. She stood looking after him as he strode down the corridor towards the opposite end of the house.

At last she turned into her luxurious, English-style bedroom and lay down, fully dressed, to try to decide what to do about David. If only there were some way in which she could let him know that his feelings for her were not something for which he needed to apologise without landing them both in a situation from which they could not retreat. She was married and that was that. There could never be any resolution of her love for David, but she did not want him to think that his feelings were unwanted or unreciprocated.

The next morning, having hardly slept, she went down to breakfast feeling dreadful. Her head did not precisely ache, but it felt hollow and somehow precarious; and she found it hard to make her muscles work so that she felt as though she might trip over her own feet or walk into the furniture. Mrs Wallington took one look at her and put down her own coffee cup.

'Julia, you look terrible. I knew that they had not given you enough time to recover from the pneumonia. I think you should go straight back to bed and I shall bring you a tray of breakfast presently.'

'You're far too kind to me, Mrs Wallington,' said Julia with real feeling. 'But I'm quite all right really: I just didn't sleep very well. I'll be fine as soon as I've had some breakfast.'

Her hostess looked carefully at Julia's face and then pressed her:

'I don't want to nag, but I do think you ought to take better care of yourself. You are very pale and there are huge bruises under your eyes. Would you hate a day in bed so much?'

Tired to the point where she felt that her eyes might fall out of their sockets, Julia could not repress her instinctive relief at the prospect of a day's rest and Mrs Wallington saw it.

'Go on. Off with you. I'll tell David when he comes down so that you don't need to worry about whatever plans you've made with him. Breakfast in five minutes or so.'

'Thank you very much,' was all Julia could say. She walked heavily upstairs again, relieved to have a chance to think through her options undistracted by his physical presence. Reaching the haven of her bedroom, she stripped off her clothes again, wrapped herself in her dressing gown and got back into bed. She had hardly settled herself against the pillows and let her thickened lids slide back over her aching eyeballs when she heard a knock on the door. Wishing that Mrs Wallington had not staggered up all the stairs with a heavy breakfast tray when her guest was unlikely to be able to eat anything very much, Julia called out, 'Come in.'

The door opened and David stood there, a tray in his hands. Without a word he brought it to the table beside her bed and put it carefully down. Straightening up, he took deep breath and, without looking at Julia, said:

'I am desperately sorry to have upset you so. Mama thought you were just tired, but it's more than that isn't it?'

'A bit,' she said, and she watched him walk to the end of the bed. There he turned, looked at her and gripped the bedstead with both hands.

'I am sorry,' he said again. 'I've tried to stop it, but I haven't been able to. I know it's unfair of me and horribly troublesome for you, but please believe that I'm not going to start importuning you – or anything like that. I ought never to have hugged you last night or said any of those things.'

'Oh David,' she said, her voice quivering with the very effort needed to keep it calm. 'I've tried too.'

'Yes I know,' he said, and at that she looked directly at him. His eyes looked so unhappy that she could hardly bear it, but before she could say anything more he had plunged on: 'It must have been obvious and I'm sorry for that too. You've been very gentle with me, which makes it even worse; perhaps if you'd been more brutal I could have managed to stop . . . but then you would never be brutal. I know that.' He attempted a smile, but it was a poor effort.

'David, stop, please,' said Julia, getting out of bed. She stood about four feet away from him in her ungainly dressing gown. 'You mustn't think . . . Oh, Lord! This is so difficult. I'm not usually stuck for words,' she went on, thinking of the successful extempore speeches she had made in court when her clients had led her into all sorts of impossible positions.

'Please don't think that you are the only one who has been trying to suppress those sort of feelings,' she said at last, plumping for simplicity.

For a moment she was afraid that David was going to ask her what on earth she was talking about and tell her that she had completely misunderstood his elliptical declaration, but he did not. Instead he silently walked the few feet between them and put his arms round her. Once again she leaned against him and felt his hands clasped at her back. Then she felt him laying his cheek on her hair. His heart was banging against his chest wall so hard that she could feel it thudding into her as well.

'Do you mean that?' he asked at last, his voice astonishingly gentle in contrast to that violent physical sensation.

'Yes,' she said simply. 'I've tried not to, but I can't help it either.'

His arms tightened on her back for a moment and she felt him raise his head. She looked up at him and before she could say anything else he had kissed her. With her battered instincts singing 'At last, at last, thank God!', Julia kissed him back.

'We need to talk about this,' he said when at last they broke apart.

'I know,' she answered. 'And it's almost impossibly difficult.'

'Yes, my dear, dear love, it is,' he said with a tiny smile on his lips. 'I think probably we ought to leave it until you have had some sleep. You look exhausted; Mama was right about that. Do you think you could sleep?'

'Now?' she asked, her own lips curling into a smile. 'Yes, I think I could now.' He left her and set about smoothing the sheets of her bed with touchingly serious clumsiness. Then he turned back the top sheet and blankets.

'In you get,' he said. Julia obeyed, amused at his fatherliness, and lay back on the pillow. He stood, looking down at her until she reached up to lay one hand on his thigh.

'I'm so glad that you know at last,' she said.

He covered her hand with his own.

'Yes. Astounding though it feels, Julia ... But I mustn't start now. Try to sleep, if you can.'

He closed the shutters and, leaving the breakfast tray behind, crept out as though she might already be asleep. In fact she lay in the warm, dark-grey shadows of her room quite at peace for the first time since she had come to Italy. Whatever was to happen in the future, she loved and was loved and for the moment that was enough.

Hours later she woke to the same sensation of calm fulfilment. After all those months of fighting the knowledge that Anthony did not want her much, it was a heavenly feeling. She and David could not do anything about it, of course, but it was wonderful.

Moving with extraordinary ease, as though all her muscles and sinews had been somehow loosened, Julia got herself out of bed and into her clothes and then went to open the shutters. It was not until she saw the colour of the light – deep warm gold that she realised how long she must have been asleep and looked at her watch. It was half-past five. Too happy to feel ashamed of being such a poor guest, too relaxed to worry about anything at all, she found her shoes and went downstairs to the terrace.

There was only David, sitting at ease in one of the basket chairs, in front of the tea tray.

'Is your mother out?' asked Julia, standing in the French window.

He turned his head lazily and smiled before standing up and explaining that as it was Good Friday his mother had gone to church with some old friends and was likely to have dinner with them as well. Julia sat down in the chair next to David's and let him pour her a cup of cooling tea.

'No, no, this is fine,' she said as he suggested making a new pot. 'Did you sleep?'

'For a while,' he answered, 'and then I went out to have lunch with Bill. I don't think I was quite as tired as you. . . Ah, Julia.'

'I know,' she said, answering his tone rather than his words.

'You see,' he went on as though they had been talking all afternoon. 'I had no idea until this morning that you were in the same state as I.'

'You must have,' said Julia, reaching across the space between their chairs to touch his hand. 'I felt as though I was announcing it the whole time: by the way I watched you, and talked to you, and could hardly manage not to touch you – stroke your head, brush your arm, hold your hand ... I was horribly afraid then that you must know and hate me for my disloyalty to Anthony.'

'Anthony,' he said and brushed a hand across his face. 'Yes, we must talk. Do you feel up to it?'

'Yes,' answered Julia. 'I think so. But I'm not quite sure what there is to say. I am his wife and you are his best friend, and neither of us could . . . I can't leave him, David.'

'No, I know that,' he said at once. 'I'd never ask it of you. And in any case, I'm in no position to . . . to marry. I have no idea what I shall be doing even this time next year; I haven't any achievements or even firm plans that I could offer you. I may have to spend a lot of my time in Scotland now – perhaps even look for a Scottish constituency – and your work is in London.'

Julia was relieved that that was out of the way and that David's announcement had been so definite.

'And neither of us could be happy deceiving him – could we?' David went on.

Julia got up from her chair so fast that the basketwork shrieked. She walked to the edge of the terrace and leaned on the balustrade, looking out over Florence. The roughness of the lichened grey stone under her hands and wrists helped her to keep her mind under some sort of control.

The city spread out below her looked so calm, almost as calm as she had felt such a little time before. She stared down at it as though the pattern of domes and towers and roofs could tell her what to do.

'No, I don't think so,' she said at last. 'I should never have . . . But then why not? Isn't it rather a waste of all we feel to ignore it? Anthony once told me that he thinks "bodily fidelity is wholly irrelevant",' she quoted bitterly.

She turned back to face David and hated to see a reflection of that bitterness in his blue eyes.

'I ought never to have kissed you or let things get to this stage,' Julia admitted. 'Older than you, married, female: it was up to me to keep us on the straight and narrow. But I couldn't bear you to think that you were feeling all that on your own. I wanted you to know how important you are; how much I care about you – value you; and . . .' her voice quivered and stopped, but then she took another breath and finished her declaration steadily enough: 'and how much I want you.'

David poured himself another cup of tea and drained it, although it was quite cold by then and horribly tannic.

'That makes it much more difficult, you know, than when I thought it was only me,' he said.

Julia looked up at the cloudless sky and felt the last of the day's sun on her face.

'But more honest,' she said, still gazing upwards. 'And I hope that there's some good in that. Is it so important that we become more than platonic lovers?'

David was silent for so long that she had to look at him in the end.

'Half of me says "no, of course not",' he said, smiling a little.

'And the other half?'

'Minds like hell and has the most appallingly prehistoric instincts,' he went on. 'But that's absurd really, because as soon as I've . . . made love to anyone before – and it hasn't been that often – I've lost most of the feeling that led me there straight away, if you see what I mean.'

'Yes, I think I do,' said Julia sadly. Anthony had once seemed to want her badly, but that had hardly lasted even through their honeymoon, and he seemed to have seized on any excuse since Flavia's death to avoid sharing her bed.

David saw the effect his words had had on her and quickly tried to take away the sting.

'But I have never loved anyone as I love you,' he said, truthfully.

Julia was about to say something else when they both heard the sound of his mother returning.

'Perhaps it's just as well,' murmured David and then in a quite different voice he said: 'Mama!'

Julia took one look at her hostess's face and decided to make some more tea. Picking up the tray, she carried it out to the kitchen and put the kettle on the small bottled-gas stove that stood beside the huge, cold, black range. When the water boiled she made more tea in the silver pot, refilled the milk jug, found clean cups and a plateful of almond biscuits, and carried the tray back to the terrace.

She was surprised to see the two Wallingtons sitting opposite each other, about eighteen inches apart, apparently concentrating hard on something that lay between them. Moving towards the table to lay down her load, she almost laughed when she saw that they were playing cat's cradle. She put down the tray, poured out three cupsful of tea and sat watching them.

'Pound of candles, Mama!' David exclaimed. 'Well done!'

Mrs Wallington's tight face relaxed a little as David leaned forward over the criss-crossed string that her hands held taut between them. David's long fingers plucked carefully at two of the lines, swung them over the outlying strings and took the whole pattern back from her hands to form a new one within his. She gazed at the new arrangement, absent-mindedly reached for the tea Julia had placed near her elbow and drank. As though the heat of the liquid burning her lips reminded her where she was, she looked away from the cat's cradle and made her eyes focus on her guest.

'Julia,' she said, as though she were just waking up. 'How good of you to make tea. Thank you.'

'It was a pleasure,' she said, a little worried by both the intensity of Mrs Wallington's earlier concentration and her current vagueness. 'You're both a delight to watch at that,' Julia went on. 'I've never got beyond the first two or three rounds.'

'My husband taught me when we were first married,' said the elder woman, licking her burnt lower lip. 'The concentration always helped when I was feeling homesick.' She released her lip from between her teeth and Julia was horrified to see a speck of blood on it. As though aware that her control was slipping again, Mrs Wallington turned back to the disciplined criss-cross of string and concentrated with almost palpable force. David looked up then and Julia nodded her head in the direction of the drawing room, meaning (as she knew David would understand) that she wondered whether she should leave them alone. He answered with a minute shake of his head and she obeyed, sitting on to watch the fantastic skill with which they wove and rewove their patterns, each keeping the strings taut and symmetrical even as they transformed them into a completely new shape. Neither spoke and Julia understood that David's mother was on the very brink of breaking down; any little thing might tip her over into outright despair.

Julia, who had come to understand a little of Allegra Wallington's character in the short time they had spent together, was as anxious as David to prevent that happening. David had obviously always known and Julia had learned that, whatever feelings were churning around inside his mother's mind, it was vital for her that they remained private.

David was holding the strings in a pattern Julia had never seen before. His face seemed to show nothing except benevolent interest, but Julia could tell from the way that he was carrying his head and a certain tension in his body that they were approaching a crisis point.

Allegra leaned forward a little and delicately laid her fingers and thumbs on either side of the cradle. She performed a complicated manoeuvre, which Julia could not follow at all, and brought her two hands up between the strings held by her son. At once the carefully constructed cradle collapsed; there was no longer any pattern, merely an ugly mass of tangled string hanging from his hands.

Allegra leaned even further forward, tears waterfalling down her thin, pale-olive face, until her head was resting on top of the string in her son's hands. Julia got up from her chair as quietly as she possibly could and left them alone. As she reached the French windows into the drawing room she–heard Allegra's voice, ugly and distorted by an immense sob:

'How can I bear it without him, Davy?'

Hating the thought that she was eavesdropping, Julia still could not force herself away and half turned to see David gently pushing his mother upright again. Julia watched him take a handkerchief from his trouser pocket with one hand while shaking the debris of the cat's cradle from the other. Instead of simply handing his mother the handkerchief, he held her chin with one hand and wiped the tears from her cheeks. Only when she had managed to stop crying and he had dried her face completely did he even attempt to answer.

'I don't know how, Mama, but I think you will. And . . .' He broke off and Julia knew that he was trying to decide how far to let his honesty take him. His shoulders were taut under his jacket.

'And terrible though it is, Mama, isn't it better to feel like this now than never to have known what it was like to love someone so much?'

Tears starting into her own eyes, Julia waited, not wanting to walk away while they were both silent. 'Wouldn't it be better to love like that for a little while than never to know what it is like?' she asked herself silently. She had spent most of her own childhood trying to persuade her parents to fall in love with each other and known how little they really cared for each other or for her, but until recently she had not realised how little real love there had been in her own marriage.

'E vero, mio figlio', said Allegra at last in an aching voice that seemed to express both infinite sadness and acceptance. 'Yes, that is true.'

Julia went to sit in the kitchen, trying to stop applying what she had just heard to her own situation. It seemed very important just then to remember exactly what she had felt for Anthony at the beginning. The difficulty was that the memory seemed to be inextricably linked to her friendship with Comfort. Searching through her mind the only emotions she could recreate from that time were a dizzying pleasure that someone as sophisticated, cosmopolitan, successful and confident as Doctor Anthony Gillingham should appear to want anyone as dull and provincial as she had been and a kind of a triumph that she could present Comfort with Anthony's declaration of love. Comfort loved him so much herself that his admiration of her friend was a kind of justification of the friendship itself. That was it, Julia said to herself, as she sat at the big scrubbed table in the Florentine kitchen, all those years and a thousand miles away.

A heavy step on the stone-flagged floor made her start.

'It's only me, Julia,' said David as she turned. 'I've been looking for you all over the house.'

'Sorry,' she said, smiling at him. 'I just thought I'd better keep out of the way. How is your poor mother?'

'As you saw. I've given her some of the Veronal her doctor prescribed and she's gone to bed. Are you all right?'

'Why?'

'Your eyes have gone dark, and your mouth looks thinner and you're pale again; I've noticed that that always happens when you're unhappy,' he said.

'I suppose that I've just been recognising that the sort of feeling your mother had for your father is . . .' she paused as she searched for as unemotive a word as possible. 'It is so very different from what I feel for Anthony. But I'm sorry, David, I oughtn't to be bothering you with all this at such a time. You must be missing them both so much.'

'Yes,' he agreed. 'But it's in a different compartment from you and me. I don't ever want you to think that what I feel for you is a response to –'

'Don't, David,' she said, getting up from the table. 'I know it's not.'

He stood looking at her in silence for a few moments and then gave a funny little smile, ruffled her hair and said:

'Now, you haven't had anything to eat all day – except for that biscuit – and you must be starving.'

'Not really,' she said with a rueful smile. 'All this emotion seems to be doing instead of food.'

'Nevertheless, we must both eat. Mama made me promise to feed you before she agreed to go to bed. She said that there was pasta, a couple of eggs and a little ham,' he said, looking around the big, empty kitchen. 'And since neither of us is Catholic, there's no bar to any of that.'

'I'm afraid my cooking doesn't extend to much more than scrambled eggs or sardines on toast,' said Julia, feeling thoroughly useless.

'Don't worry,' he answered with the first real amusement of the day, 'mine does.'

Watching him finding the food and preparing and cooking it

with deft and practised skill, Julia marvelled at his practicality. When they had eaten, sitting companionably at the kitchen table, she told him how impressed she was by his unsuspected talent.

'It is time that someone began to look after you for a change, Julia,' he said seriously. 'You've done a long, long stint, haven't you?'

They managed to part that night with no more than a friendly kiss, but the following evening when Mrs Wallington again went early to bed was more difficult. Once again David and Julia ate together in the kitchen at the scrubbed wooden table. David had lit two squat candles stuck in pottery sticks, and they provided the only light in the room. The rest of the great kitchen was huge and empty around them; the small oval of warm candlelight seemed to hold them together.

At first they talked easily about David's chances of demobilisation, and the kind of law he would practise when he eventually got back to London, and his prospects of fighting a reasonably safe seat at the next General Election, but inevitably that led on to Julia's plans.

'I don't know, David,' she said at one moment when they had finished their pasta. 'One thing these workless weeks in Venice have taught me is that I need my profession. I should go quite dotty without work, and there is none for me in Venice now. I am going to have to go back to London pretty soon.'

'And Anthony?'

'God knows. Do you think he can be persuaded to leave his orphans?' said Julia. When David did not answer, she went on: 'After all, I suspect that you know him far better than I have ever done.'

David sat looking down at the empty wine glass that he was turning round and round between his hands. He wanted to tell her the whole story then, but he was afraid of what she might think.

'I don't think I do,' he said instead without looking up.

Julia, not wanting to have to think of Anthony any longer, got out of her chair and prowled about the big dark kitchen. David watched her in silence for a while, wondering what she was thinking, longing to persuade her to forget her husband, longing beyond everything to make love to her.

Julia stopped by the cold range and ran her fingers along its surface. Suddenly she lifted her hand and examined the brown, greasy deposit that her fingers had picked up and grimaced in disgust. She went to the stone sink, scrubbed her hands under the single cold tap and set off on her perambulations again, slowly circling the big pine table, moving in and out of the gibbous pool of light shed by the candles.

'What I can't understand,' she said at last coming to a stop again behind David's chair, 'is why he married me at all and why he. . .'

'I suspect because he loves you, even though he doesn't always show it,' said David, trying to be fair. 'And . . . Oh Lord, Julia, I'm finding this desperately difficult.'

The raw, rough feeling in his voice was so obvious that Julia forgot all her determined restraint of the previous evening and put her arms around him as he sat at the table, laying her head on his.

'Oh David, my darling,' she said. 'I'm sorry.' He twisted in his chair so that he could look at her, and she leaned down and kissed his forehead. His skin felt very soft and cool under her lips. He turned back and put his hands over hers as they lay across his chest.

'All my most prehistoric instincts are coming to the surface,' he said at last, his voice breathless and the words coming out syncopated. 'I don't think I can talk any more about your husband. I need you too much.'

Julia's own needs rose to answer that despairing cry so powerfully that all her carefully nurtured detachment melted away. With her conscious mind telling her what to say and do, her emotions rebelled and she heard herself say something quite contradictory to its orders:

'David, I think we'd better go to bed.'

'Do you mean that?' he said. Standing up, he examined her face with extreme care.

'Yes,' said Julia. 'What harm can it possibly do anyone if we don't let it invade our lives? Tonight, here, now, we can't hurt anyone by making love.'

In all her suppressed longing for David, Julia had never imagined such gentleness as he gave her that night or such freedom. When he had shut the door of her bedroom behind them both, he came to stand in front of her and stroked her face with one finger, tracing her eyebrows, the semi-circular curve of the bones under her eyes, the diagonal lines of her cheekbones, and her lips. Light though his touch was, she found it infinitely exciting and when his fingertip reached the centre of her lips, she opened them and felt his finger on her tongue.

Through his increasingly deep, ragged breathing, he said her name once, twice. She felt his other hand cupping her head and, releasing his finger, she leaned forward until she lay against his chest.

'Yes, David,' she said, answering his unspoken plea. 'I'm here.'

Putting both hands on her head so that he could tilt it up towards him, he said:

'I can hardly believe it, Julia. Are you really sure?'

'I'm sure, David. Come to bed.' Taking his hand, she led him to the bed and lay down.

'Julia,' he said, dropping on his knees beside the bed. Before she could do more than smile up at him, he had kissed her eyes, her lips, the soft skin of her neck just below her ear, and then he began to unbutton her clothes.

The delicacy of his touch as he stroked her was such that Julia could hardly feel it at all, and yet it aroused in her a longing for him that she had never before experienced. His face was so unguarded that if she had not loved him as much she would have been afraid for him.

Gradually, as her need became overwhelming and his stroking intensified, she lost all her feelings of protectiveness for him, forgot that she was older than he, forgot everything except his touch, his strength, his love for her and her passionate longing to give him everything. In that giving she found completion and happiness beyond all expectation.

Afterwards, as she lay curled in the crook of his arm, with her head tucked underneath his chin, he said:

'I won't be able to regret this, whatever happens. It's meant too much.'

Hardly able to move at all for the blissful heaviness of her limbs, Julia tried to make her mind work enough to answer him.

'We shouldn't either of us have anything to regret, David,' she said at last, and found that it was true. What they had given each other, dramatic though it had become at the end, had been the inevitable physical manifestation of what had happened between them weeks earlier. It was both an acknowledgement and an easing of the exquisite – almost intolerable – tension that had been built up between them.

They slept then, tucked up around one another, waking several times during the night, but rarely for long enough to do more than acknowledge the other's presence. It was not until soon after six o'clock that David carefully uncoiled his long body. Julia woke, smiling.

'Go back to sleep, Julia,' he said, very quietly. 'I'm just going back to my own room.'

'Must you?' she said, still half asleep and not thinking of anything at all except David. She brought her right hand up out of the bedclothes and held it out to him. He took it in both of his and smiled down at her.

'I think so. . . . It seems important not to worry Mama with this just now,' he said. Julia loved him for that protectiveness, too, and pulled her hand out of his to let him go.

'Try to sleep a bit more,' he said. 'You look very tired.' He stood looking down at her as she lay with her hair spread out on the pillow, her eyes still half shut by the heaviness of sleep and her lips smiling. 'I know that we can't let this mean anything more than itself,' he said at last, 'but it has made . . . you have made me very happy, Julia. Whatever happens, don't forget that. . . please.'

'I won't forget,' she said.

# Chapter Twenty-One

They said very little to each other on the journey back to Venice, both lost in their own thoughts. Julia was battling with the temptation to make more of what had happened than was justified. She had told David that they could hurt no one by making love, and she knew that to make that true she would have to banish the knowledge of her love for him to the back of her mind and to think of their few short days together as no more than an oasis in the middle of some desert journey. Those days had given her so much that they ought also to have given her the strength to carry on her journey.

The temptation might have been harder to withstand if David had not told her that he could not have married her even if she had planned to leave Anthony. Leaning against the hard back of the seat, swaying with the movement of the train, Julia watched David from under her half-closed eyelids. He was not looking at her and his face was bleak. Julia turned to look out of the window at the green fields and picturesque villages that flashed by the train's dusty windows, trying to school her mind and emotions into recognising that she had left the oasis behind her for ever. She had not expected to find it so difficult and suddenly she shivered.

David turned his head as the movement caught his eye and he looked at her doubtfully. She smiled a little ruefully and after a moment he looked away again.

Gritting her teeth, Julia tried not to regret falling in love with him. It seemed to her then in a moment of uncharacteristic melodrama and self-pity that she might have been picked out by fate as a lesson to other women who chose to exercise their brains and talents beyond their traditional sphere. Unexpectedly successful in her professional life, she seemed doomed to make a ludicrous mess of the rest. 'Lucky at work; unlucky at love', she misquoted derisively to herself and regained a little of her normal common sense.

David had said that he would never regret what had happened and that seemed sensible. There was no point in regretting something that could not be undone by all the contrition in the world.

A half-cynical smile twisted her lips as she thought of the Easter mass she had attended with David and his mother. If only she were a Catholic like Allegra, she would be able to confess, accept whatever penance was imposed and be given a chance to start again as though she had never made love with him at all.

David saw the twisted smile and the calculation in Julia's brown eyes that had so recently looked at him with love and wondered what she was thinking. She did not look happy. He hoped that it was the future that was making her sad and not the past they had shared. If only she were not married, he thought, things would have been so much easier. They could have taken as much time as they needed to explore their feelings and desires and work them out, instead of leaving each other not only unsatisfied, but with a tantalising glimpse of what might have been.

They reached Venice a little before five o'clock. Julia suddenly thought that she could not bear to go quietly back to the Campo San Maurizio with David as though nothing had happened, to meet Anthony perhaps at the front door and have to answer cheerful questions about Florence.

'Would it be too much of an imposition to ask you to take my stuff back with you?' she asked rather formally.

'No, of course not,' said David, taken aback by her tone. 'But aren't you coming?'

'I think I ought to drop in on Giovanna's protégées,' she said with a bright smile. 'I asked Anthony to give one of them a message before we left last week and I ought to go and see her myself. See you at dinner?'

'Yes, yes indeed,' said David, watching her turn and stride away from him through the thin crowd. After a while he pulled himself together, picked up their bags and went to get a boat down the Grand Canal.

Julia walked slowly out through the twisting streets of yellow and cream and brick houses, across small squares, past insignificant churches and across the little backwaters until she came to Giovanna's house. She rang the front-door bell.

Giovanna opened the door herself, looking short and square and as sensible as ever. Julia found that it was a relief to be able to go back to an aspect of life that was unchanged by what had happened between her and David. She greeted Giovanna and answered her questions about Florence without difficulty. When Giovanna offered her a glass of wine, she accepted and they sat talking of nothing much for a while, before Julia said:

'In fact I really came to see Raffaella, because I thought I ought to amplify the message I sent to her last week.'

Giovanna looked surprised.

'But she's gone,' she said. 'She left on Saturday, taking the baby and all her things.'

'Did she say where she was going?' asked Julia almost sharply, afraid that Anthony might have delivered the bad news in an unnecessarily insensitive way, or even exercised his talent for withering sarcasm on her. Giovanna shrugged and put her wine glass down on a small table at her side.

'No. And I asked no questions,' she said repressively.

'Of course not,' said Julia, trying to control her irritation. 'But anything might happen to her. Oughtn't you at least . . .? I beg your pardon. It's none of my business.'

Giovanna's expression told Julia how much she agreed with that statement but that she was too polite to say so.

'It is worrying, though,' Julia said. 'Had she ever told you about her murderous brother?'

'Yes,' said Giovanna. 'I had not realised that she had told you. She came to me last Friday morning to say that she had seen him near here and had to leave. I didn't try to make her stay. Have some more wine.'

Julia allowed Giovanna to refill her glass, but she did not drink. After a while Giovanna said more kindly:

'Don't look so worried, Giulia. Raffaella came here when she wanted shelter that she could not get elsewhere. I expect that she has now found some more. I couldn't make her stay: this is neither a school nor a reformatory. If she needs us again, she'll come back.'

'She's so young.'

At that protest, Giovanna laughed. There was an unpleasant note in the sound.

'She took care of herself in Rome, after all. She's one of those who will always find someone to look after her. Don't worry about her. Drink your wine.'

Remembering the shortages, Julia obeyed and then got up to go.

'So, until Wednesday,' said Giovanna. Julia nodded and said goodbye.

When she got back to the house, there was no sign of Anthony. She unpacked the bag that David had left in her room and then walked down to the salon. He was sitting there reading but after one look at her face he put away his book.

'Julia, something's happened,' he said. 'What is it?'

She almost laughed at that question. Of course something had happened: they had made love to each other, shared everything with each other. It seemed odd that he should not understand how cataclysmic an event it had been for her. Perhaps it had not been so important for him. She looked at him and some of the protective cynicism she had assumed disappeared. There was no longer any hardness in his face. He looked as concerned and affectionate as he had ever done. She could feel the muscles in her face relax and sat down on the hard sofa.

'What is it?' said David again. 'Can't you tell me?'

'Of course I can,' she said, laying a hand on his knee for an instant. 'It's just rather worrying. I told you, didn't I, that one of Giovanna's refugees wanted me to find out whether she had any chance of moving to England?'

'I don't think so,' said David, moving a little closer to her on the uncomfortable sofa.

'I thought I had,' she said, trying to ignore the physical sensations his closeness brought her and concentrate on the subject of Raffaella. 'Never mind. I've been making enquiries for her and I had a letter just before we left that made it clear she hadn't a hope. Anthony agreed to let her know for me and I went there just now to talk to her. . .' She broke off.

'Well?' said David. 'Was she unpleasant? That seems rather unfair: it's hardly your fault.'

'No, it's not that,' said Julia, frowning at the opposite wall. 'She's disappeared.' She looked back at David, whose face registered nothing but rather puzzled interest.

'She's had a frightful time, and . . . I'd better tell you the whole story or you'll never grasp it,' said Julia, smiling a little at his bemused expression. She told him what she had heard of Raffaella's history and watched his face registering shock, disgust, and sharp, unmistakable anxiety. That surprised her.

'And so you see,' she finished up, 'there she is with a half-English baby and nowhere to go. This Paolo – the brother – may not have done anything to her yet, but she was so terrified of him that I am worried about her.'

David had stood up and got his pipe out of his pocket. He spent rather a long time filling and lighting it. When it was smoking properly he turned to look at her. His face had been wiped of all expression beyond a mild superiority.

'Julia,' he said with an inflexion in his voice that sounded a warning. With his head thrown back, his long legs apart, one hand on his pipe and the other tucked into his jacket pocket he reminded her of a barrister about to embark on a piece of doubtful reasoning on behalf of a beleaguered client.

'Yes?' said Julia warily.

'I don't think that you ought to pay much attention to stories like that,' said David. Julia stiffened. Whatever they had shared it was not for him to tell her what to believe or what not to believe. 'This young woman confessed to you that she is a prostitute, and the obvious reason for her disappearance is that she has merely reverted to that way of life. You have no reason to believe anything she has told you and it's most unlikely that any of it was true. I really do think that –'

'Thank you for your advice, David,' said Julia, interrupting him with no expression in her voice at all. She stood up. 'I think I'll go and have a bath before dinner.'

She left him looking after her with a worried expression. When she turned back at the door, he forced a smile, wishing that he had told her everything long ago.

Walking upstairs to find out whether there was any hot bathwater, Julia tried to account for David's odd reaction. Until then he had never shown himself to be anything other than sensible, intelligent, tolerant and kind whatever they discussed or did. The tone of dismissive patronage – and contempt – with which he had talked of Raffaella shocked her, because it was so unlike the man she had thought he was, the man she had come to love.

It was not until she was washing herself in the tepid bathwater that she thought of Raffaella's child, with his smooth dark hair and his blue eyes, and a possible reason presented itself to her. She dismissed it at once on the grounds that just because David had shown less than his usual benevolence there was no reason to believe him guilty of fathering a child on an Italian girl and abandoning her. There must have been hundreds of partisan bands in North Italy and as many Allied officers. It would have been a ludicrous coincidence for David's band to have been the same as Raffaella's. And yet, a voice in Julia's mind said, he knew Giovanna because of her involvement with the partisans; perhaps Raffaella knew her for the same reason. Perhaps David had introduced Julia into that household so that he could have a conduit for information between them without compromising himself by going there in person.

Anthony's original warning came back to Julia and she tried to remember the precise words he had used. They had been something like: 'You may think that he is charming and ingenuous, but he is capable of doing the most destructive things.' Could Anthony have been thinking of Raffaella when he had said that?

Julia got out of the bath and dried, half thinking herself stupid to have allowed her emotions to lead her into believing David possessed of almost every virtue and half castigating herself for believing that a man she loved so much could have been guilty of what had been done to Raffaella. David had confided to her that making love to women usually killed his desire for them. Was he one of those men who despise women who allow themselves to be seduced? Was it possible that she could have fallen in love with a man who thought like that?

It seemed unlikely and yet she had to admit that experienced though she was in most aspects of life, love was something of which she really knew very little. Until she had met David the only man she had ever loved was Anthony: perhaps after all the difficult feelings she had for him were in fact more real than the dizzying sensations, the longing to protect, and the sense of completion she felt with David.

Wishing that she had ignored all feelings of delicacy and asked Raffaella for the name of her lover when she had the chance, Julia dressed slowly. She took trouble with her face and hair so as to absorb as much time as she could before she faced David again. Just as she was admitting to herself that she really would have to go down to dinner she heard Anthony's voice greeting Annunziata.

'Hello, my dear!' he said when he saw Julia coming downstairs. 'You look better. How was Florence?'

'Fascinating,' she answered in a matter-of-fact voice. 'So different from Venice. I wish I knew Italy better.'

'We never came, did we, in the old days?' he said, holding open the salon doors for her. 'When things have settled down properly you and I and Comfort must have a kind of grand tour.'

There it was, thought Julia, a reminder of the long history she shared with Anthony. Despite his lack of interest in making love to her or having children with her, he clearly believed that their marriage was solidly rooted and was still making plans for the future.

Together they went into the salon to share an uncomfortable dinner with David. That something else had happened to worry Julia was obvious to him. She was far more formal and conversational than she had been for months. But whenever David looked directly at her she avoided his eyes and spoke to her husband instead. He assumed that she felt guilty – as he did – for what they had done and regretted it, which he did not.

As soon as dinner was over, Julia announced that she was going to help Annunziata with the washing up and then going early to bed. David insisted on carrying the heavy tray of dirty crockery to the kitchen for her and as he put it down he said quietly in English:

'Julia, please don't let it make you unhappy. Nothing that's happened need –'

'I find myself in rather a muddle,' she interrupted, speaking carefully and as quietly as he. 'I need a bit of time to sort things out before I know where I am. All right?'

'Yes, of course,' he said, withdrawing a little way. 'You know I'd never press you to . . .'

'I know, David. Thank you,' she said. When he had gone, she smiled at Annunziata in relief. Together they cleared the kitchen and Julia led Annunziata on to talk about her son. She seemed glad of the opportunity and confided that she had already made him six new shirts and that Anthony was helping to get hold of a modern wheelchair in which her son could have some measure of independence.

'Why don't you go to visit him?' asked Julia. 'He isn't due to leave the hospital for some time and it must be possible. I'm sure Doctor Gillingham could arrange it.' Annunziata's face seemed to crumple. She mopped her eyes on the dishtowel in her hand and then apologised.

'Don't worry about that,' said Julia, puzzled. 'Is there some reason why you can't go?'

'Not if you will allow it, *signora*,' said Annunziata.

'I'll speak to my husband at once,' said Julia, surprised that Anthony had not thought of it himself. Annunziata took both Julia's hands in hers and said slowly and clearly so as to be certain that Julia understood:

'Signora Giulia, you deserve to be happy.'

It was so clear that Annunziata knew that she was not that Julia was tempted for a mad moment to pour out her whole story and ask Annunziata's advice.

'Thank you,' she said instead, clasping Annunziata's hands for a moment. 'We'll all be happier when we can put the war behind us.'

The next morning Julia awoke with her mind beginning to take precedence over her emotions again. It seemed abundantly clear to her as she lay in the cool light of early morning that she must extricate herself from the Venetian imbroglio as soon as possible. David had told her that he and she could have no future together and so whatever connection there was between him and Raffaella was really irrelevant. Anthony had made it equally clear that he did believe he had a future with his wife. Her only option was to go home and ignore everything that had happened in Venice, and wait for him to follow her. The practicalities of her escape took very little time. The colonel in charge of the Kesselring case made no trouble about her leaving, since he had already found a substitute for her, thanked her for all the work she had done and told her how sorry he was that she had been ill. The man at the airline office found her a seat on a flight leaving three days later, and she sent off her telegrams.

It seemed to her as she was walking back to the Campo San Maurizio that she ought to tell Anthony at once and altered her course for the hospital. She had never set foot in it since the day he had accused her of interfering with his patients and expelled her, but telling him that she was leaving Venice would be easier there than in the house, where they might be interrupted by David at any moment.

As she reached St Mark's the rain started to fall, despite the growing warmth of the weather. It seemed to her that she had hardly ever seen the city in clear sunlight and she wondered whether she would have liked it better if she had. She felt tired, as she so often had after her illness; tired, useless and a fool. If she had only been content to make the best of her life as it was, she would have been in a far better state.

When she reached the hospital she was disconcerted to be told that Anthony was not available. With a vivid memory of her last visit, Julia then asked for Sister Caroline and made her way to the long ward where Flavia had once struggled with her terrors.

Sister Caroline greeted Julia with reserved friendliness and disclaimed any knowledge of Anthony's whereabouts.

'Can I help?' she asked.

'Not really,' said Julia with a smile. 'I came to tell him that I have to get back to London soon. That wretched pneumonia has rotted up my job here and there's nothing really to keep me.'

'Nothing?' said the nurse rather severely.

'No,' said Julia, suddenly so tired that she dropped into a chair beside the nurse's desk. She knew what Sister Caroline meant and, remembering how kind she had been the previous November, tried to explain.

'I'm no good to him here,' Julia said after a while. 'I might as well go back to London, where I am of some use to my clients at least.'

'You sound very much like a convalescent,' said Sister Caroline more kindly. 'Don't let your physical weakness drive you into doing things you will regret.'

'No. No of course not,' said Julia, recovering herself and wondering what had happened to her to make her confide in strangers and make her brain feel so woolly. 'Well, goodbye, Sister. It's been a great pleasure. I wish that I'd been allowed to help a bit more.'

'Goodbye, Mrs Gillingham.' They shook hands and Julia made her way out of the hospital.

Having walked right across the city it seemed silly to turn straight back again and so she decided to look at the little Scuola of the Dalmatians that David had talked about on one of their sightseeing expeditions soon after she had arrived in Venice. One of the Carpaccios there was his favourite Venetian painting, he had told her, and she had never seen it. Julia pulled the little guide book from her handbag and plotted the simplest route.

Losing herself several times in the unfamiliar alleyways that seemed much older and darker than their counterparts on the other side of Venice, Julia walked slowly towards her destination. About halfway there, she felt suddenly faint and rather sick, and she sat down to rest for a while on the stone steps of a tiny bridge, leaning her head against the rough brickwork of its walls.

Five minutes later she was recovered enough to wipe the clammy sweat from her face with a handkerchief and look around her. She was surrounded by shabby houses. Black and green algae marked the walls for about two foot above the dark-green water of the canal, and above that damaged mushroom-coloured plaster flaked and cracked off the old peachy bricks. There was one house where someone had put pots of plants just outside a window on the first floor and their new leaves were the only fresh-looking thing in the whole scene. Everything else seemed on the point of decay: the grilles across the lower windows were rusty and bent out of shape; the main door had once been painted green, but only traces of colour remained and the lowest planks were beginning to rot; even the poles where boats tied up looked as though they were in danger of collapse.

Stuffing her damp handkerchief back in her handbag, Julia started to get up, but when she heard the sound of a window opening, she waited, not particularly wanting to advertise her pallid face and dishevelled hair to any strange-Venetians. She heard a light, sweet, familiar voice singing in Italian and twisted her neck to look at its owner.

There, looking as pretty as always and far better dressed, was Raffaella, casually watering the plants on the tumbledown balcony. Julia sat back against the brickwork of the bridge, relieved that the girl was all right after all, but puzzled and affronted that she should have just disappeared without a word. After all, Julia had been to considerable trouble for her. Raffaella dumped her watering can on the floor and turned, murmuring a scolding. A moment later she stood up again with her son in her arms.

In that moment Julia hated Raffaella: for her plucked eyebrows and her fine blonde hair; for her pretty voice and little hands, her slender figure and above all for her dark-haired, blue-eyed baby. There was no real evidence that he was David's child, but Julia was becoming more and more convinced that he might be, and she was shaken by a storm of jealousy that appalled her. Rage and shame and resentment and thwarted love churned around in her, making her feel sick again.

When she heard the window shutting again, she got up and began to retrace her steps to the hospital. All desire to see David's favourite painting had left her and she thought that Anthony might have reappeared.

She met him about five minutes later, coming towards her down a dark, narrow little street across which a mangy cat was slinking. He stopped a few feet away from her, obviously astonished to see her in such an unappealing area of Venice.

'Were you looking for me?' he asked, almost defensively.

'Yes. I came to the hospital earlier to find you and thought I'd try again,' said Julia.

'But why? Are you ill?'

'No,' said Julia. 'Shall we get out of this dingy alley?'

'All right,' said Anthony, wheeling around to walk beside her. They retreated to a small square into which a faint, fugitive sunlight managed to reach and perched on a broken wall. 'Well?'

'I've realised that I have to go home,' she said after taking a moment to collect herself. 'I can't work here any more and there's nothing for me to do. I can't help you in the hospital. I can't spend any more time sightseeing. Hanging about just makes me depressed. And there's work waiting for me in London.'

'I think that's quite a good idea, Julia,' said Anthony quietly. 'You've not exactly been happy here, have you?'

'Not exactly,' she repeated with her familiar lopsided smile. 'I don't think either of us has. Will you mind if I go home sooner than you?'

He looked a little surprised at that and she remembered that he had never actually made any reference to going home at all.

'No, of course not, my dear,' he said very kindly. 'Your work and your health are very important to me. I'll miss you, of course. When do you want to go?'

'There's a seat available on a flight in three days' time,' she said. 'I thought I might take that. Anthony, what are your plans? Long term, I mean?'

'To train up my Italian successor,' he said at once. 'It ought not to be too long now. He's straining at the leash already and in a year or so we foreigners are going to be merely in the way over here.'

A whole year, thought Julia. Well, it would give her a chance to get back some kind of sense into her life before she tried yet again to mend her marriage.

'Now, can you find your own way back or would you like an escort?' Anthony asked.

'You're probably too busy for that,' she said, anxious as always to be accommodating, even as she battled with the curdled emotions that were making her feel so ill.

'Well, I am on my way to a patient.'

'I'll be perfectly all right,' said Julia. 'Shall I see you at dinner?'

'If possible,' said Anthony, helping her up off the wall and brushing down her dusty behind for her.

Julia set off back to the Venice in which she felt more comfortable, struggling with herself and wondering whether she would ever feel whole and content again. Contentment she had once had and then it had seemed so little; now it seemed like a prize to be valued.

So buried was she in her own thoughts that it was some time before she became aware of the sound of footsteps behind her. They reminded her of her first few days in Venice, when she had been certain that she was being followed and had turned out to be wrong. She told herself to brace up.

What little sun there had been disappeared behind thick dark clouds and Julia walked on, trying to ignore the footsteps and the oppressing sensation of being followed. Looking back at one sharp turn in the narrow alleyway, she thought that she caught a glimpse of a thin, dark figure backing away from her, but she could not be sure.

She turned up her coat collar with one hand and stuffed the other deep into her coat pocket, gripping her keys. Just as she reached St Mark's Square, she felt the first heavy drops of rain.

With no mackintosh or umbrella, she did not much like the idea of getting drenched and stood for a few minutes in the portico of the basilica, hoping for some sign that the rain might stop. As she watched, peering out at the lowering sky every few minutes, the rain seemed to be getting heavier, and so she decided to get home as fast as she could.

Dirty water overflowed her shoes before she was more than halfway across and rain dripped off the brim of her felt hat and trickled down her neck. Even her thick overcoat could not cope with the storm and within minutes she could feel the wetness seeping through to her back.

A quick, harsh flash of lightning was followed almost instantly by a sharp, vicious-sounding crack of thunder, which ripped through the air. Julia was so startled that she did not look where she was going and fell awkwardly on the wet pavement as she caught her shoe on an uneven flagstone. Absurdly shaken, she picked herself up and set off again, not noticing that she was heading for the wrong exit from the square.

It was not until she was faced with a row of long-prowed black gondolas swinging on their ropes in a kind of pool at the angle of two canals that she realised her mistake and turned to go back. Hearing the footsteps again, she decided to let their owner get past her so that she could recross the square alone and walked quietly into a side street to wait. She pressed herself back into a shuttered doorway, trying to keep dry. Thunder crashed and boomed once more.

She heard footsteps echoing somewhere close to her. For a moment she thought that they were ahead of her and then behind and to the right of where she stood, pressed into the damp doorway. The sound seemed to be distorted both by the rain and by the hardness and narrowness of the little streets. Before Julia could work out where the sound of the steps was coming from, they stopped. There was no sound at all then except the rhythmic splashing of the rain on stone, punctuated by longer, sloppier sounds of drains and gutters inadequate to carry the immense quantity of water that was coursing through them.

Pulling herself together, Julia walked back out of her side street, recrossed St Mark's Square and walked out of her usual exit and down the wide street that led ultimately to the Campo San Maurizio. There was no one else about. Even the starveling cats had disappeared out of the rain. She tried to laugh at herself for her absurd fears.

By the time she crossed the little canal of Santa Maria Zobenigo, she had worked herself back into rationality. She could hear no footsteps at all, there was no one in the street behind her and no one ahead of her; she was almost in sight of the Campo San Maurizio. Speeding up, shaking the rainwater out of her eyes for about the twentieth time, she headed for the last canal before the square.

Just as she reached the bridge she heard footsteps behind her again, turned and saw a thin, dark figure stepping round the last corner of the street. Julia walked firmly forwards, determined to ignore the man behind her, reached her home and fumbled for her key. Before she could push it into the lock, the man caught up with her and astonishingly gripped her arm.

'*Dove Raffaella?*' he demanded hoarsely.

Really frightened at last, Julia said loudly in English:

'I don't understand you. Let me go.'

The man tightened his fingers on her forearm until they actually hurt.

'*Dove Raffaella?*' he demanded and then added what was obviously some gross insult, which Julia did not understand.

Julia turned her key and pushed open the door, trying to wrench her arm out of his grip without success. Before either of them could say any more a voice yelled in Italian:

'Paolo, let her go!'

Both of them turned to see David running from the corner of

the square, shouting at the man. He dropped Julia's arm at once and poured out a stream of furious Italian, pointing at Julia and gesticulating wildly. David said something sharply and turned to Julia:

'Are you all right? Has he hurt you?'

Julia shook her head, trying to control her breathing.

'Then go on in, my dear,' he said. 'I'll deal with this. You should never have been involved in it. I am most dreadfully sorry.'

Julia went inside, hardly able to bear what her mind was telling her, that she now had all the evidence she needed of a connection between David and Raffaella.

# Chapter Twenty-Two

Sitting strapped into the aeroplane seat, Julia stared out of the little porthole at her last sight of Venice. For once the city was bathed in sunlight that glittered off the tiny waves on the lagoon as brightly as off the glass and gilding of the palaces. It looked unreal and very lovely, the sort of place in which to be ecstatically happy, not cold and tired or ill and discouraged.

'Why didn't you tell me about Raffaella?' she had asked David when they were alone together just before she left for the airport with Anthony.

'How could I,' he asked in turn, 'without hurting you? I never wanted you to be hurt, Julia – and if you had to be, I so much wanted it not to be through me. I suppose it was cowardly, but it seemed very important.'

'Didn't you think that it might hurt more if I merely stumbled on the truth?' she asked, trying to control the hurt and the bitter anger that were tearing at her entrails.

'There are no excuses,' he said sadly, 'except that all I did was with the best intentions, and that's not much of one. Julia, please believe that I care more for you than –'

'Not now, David,' she said, sounding merely irritable in her attempts to prevent the tears her pride would not allow her to shed in front of him. 'I really can't take any more just now.'

'Very well,' he said, standing in front of her with his head bowed. 'Whatever you say. I promised that I wouldn't importune you.' Then he raised it and she thought saw again the hardness she had recognised on the train from Florence. 'But if ever you change your mind, if ever you need anything, or . . . please will you tell me?'

Remembering how his eyes had looked when he had told her he loved her and the feeling of his hands on her face, Julia took a handkerchief from her bag and blew her nose vigorously. She felt such a fool. Anthony had warned her about David and yet she had allowed her unlikely passion for him to overtake everything else.

She was honest enough to admit that a recognition of her folly was not what was making her so unhappy. Despite what she now knew about David, she had not managed to stop loving him. None of her carefully nurtured detachment or philosophy could ease the pain of knowing that she had probably seen him for the last time. Pride might forbid her to show it to anyone else, but that did not make it hurt less.

Anthony had understood that she was unhappy and she hoped that he did not know why. He had been angelically kind to her when he took her to the little airport to see her off, and had said:

'Take care of yourself, Julia. I know you'll feel better when you're working again, and I expect when I come to London you'll be your old self.' Then he had told her of the arrangements he had made for his lawyers to pay her an increased housekeeping allowance to tide her over until her practice picked up again. That piece of kindness set the seal on her humiliation, but she felt too tired to tell him that she had plenty of money of her own.

Trying to banish the humiliation from her mind as she sat in the uncomfortable aeroplane seat, she thought about her other two Venetian farewells. Giovanna had been acerbic as she complimented Julia on her good sense in returning to 'innocent England' and yet again Julia wondered how much Giovanna had really wanted the Allies to win the war.

Annunziata had been quite different as they said goodbye and she was the only person Julia was unequivocally sad to lose. When they had embraced and Julia had thanked her for all her care during the pneumonia, she had given Annunziata an envelope containing a hundred American dollars, saying:

'It is not a tip, Annunziata, but a present to help you when your son comes home. You will need it then.'

Julia was afraid that Annunziata's pride would not let her accept the money and was grateful when she did. She also pulled a creased letter from a pocket under her apron and handed it to Julia to read. With some difficulty Julia deciphered the unfamiliar handwriting and roughly translated the letter as she read it:

Dear Mama,

Hansl is dead, killed by the Russkies. I came here to the West and tried to get a job with the Amis but they won't have me. I am living in the cellar of a bombed house alone. You cannot imagine what it was like here when the Allies bombed us night after night or even last winter when it was meant to be all over but it was so cold and there was no food. I am afraid of another winter, Mama, may I come home?

Marcella.

Julia gave the letter back to Annunziata, saying:

'And so she is safe. Thank God.'

'Yes,' said Annunziata with a smile that cut right through Julia's own sadness. 'And so we can start again. Lucia is dead, but the other two are living. It begins.'

'I am so glad,' Julia said. 'Will you write to me sometimes, Annunziata? I shall miss you.'

Thinking of Annunziata and how much she had done for them all helped Julia to bear the long uncomfortable flight. But by the time the aeroplane was circling over the airport at Northolt she had a crunching headache to add to her depression. When the aeroplane landed she waited in her seat until the other passengers had disembarked and then put on her hat, gathered together her bag, gloves and newspaper and went out into the cool, damp air of the London suburbs.

Standing for a moment at the top of the steps and breathing in the mixed smells of rainy tarmac and petrol that filled her nostrils, Julia felt the first faint sense of hope renewed. London and her work between them might help her to refashion some kind of interior scaffolding that could hold her disintegrating self together.

Outwardly calm, determined and powerful, showing nothing of what she felt, Julia walked across the sticky, slippery tarmac and entered the low, flat building that housed the customs and passport-control men. There was the usual hubbub of anxious and excited travellers, but even from the doorway she could pick out the languid American drawl of Comfort and looked quickly away from the uniformed official who was examining her passport to search for her sister-in-law.

There, standing beside a short, stocky man dressed in grey-flannel trousers and a paint-stained sweater, was Comfort Gillingham. She looked as beautiful as ever and quite at ease, despite the dishevelment of the man at her side and the smear of raw umber paint that disfigured her right cheekbone. Julia felt herself smiling in relief. For some reason the familiarity of Comfort seemed to reinforce her own determination to submerge herself in the old life.

As soon as her passport had been returned to her, Julia went to collect her two modest bags from the customs official and walked as fast as she could to where Comfort was standing. She was so absorbed in her conversation with the untidy man who stood beside her that she did not seem to hear Julia's approach.

'Comfort,' she said when she was no more than five feet away. Her sister-in-law swung round and flung open her arms. Julia dumped both bags on the ground and allowed herself to be kissed.

'Darling, here you are back at last! If only you'd brought Anthony, too,' said Comfort. 'My God, you look terrible. Are you all right?'

'I soon will be,' said Julia. 'Anthony warned me that convalescence would take time.'

'When is he coming?' asked Comfort, ignoring the subject of Julia's health for the more important one.

'He'll be back presently,' said Julia, falling back easily into her role as soother and supporter. 'He's already training his successor. Now, Comfort, won't you introduce us?' she went on.

'Tibor Smith, Mrs Gillingham,' said the short man, holding out a surprisingly shapely (if rather painty) hand. 'I hope you do not mind that Comfort brought me with her today?'

'Not at all,' said Julia, liking his wide smile and his reliable-looking face. His deep voice was attractive, too, and he was obviously making Comfort happy. Julia smiled at him. 'But "Smith"?' she asked, managing to sound rather amused.

'Is much easier than my Hungarian name. When I was first in London I took so many hours to explain to the English how to pronounce or spell it that I thought Smith would be better. Good idea, no?'

'Very good,' said Julia. 'And it's very good of you both to come. I'd been expecting a dull drive on my own.'

'Let's go,' said Comfort, taking Julia's arm and wheeling her out of the building. Julia looked back over her shoulder to see the Hungarian painter obediently picking up her luggage.

When they got back to the big house in Brunswick Square, Julia had her first moment of genuine amusement. In order to appease convention, Comfort had installed Tibor Smith in Julia's rooms on the first floor, and had had to move him hurriedly up to the spare rooms when Julia's telegram arrived.

'But, Comfort,' said Julia when she had stopped laughing, 'you've never cared what anyone thought about you. You always said that rules did not apply to you and you despised middle-class convention. Do you really think that leaving a flight of stairs between you both makes any difference? Do stairs prevent impropriety?'

'It was Tibor,' said Comfort, clearly not as amused as Julia had been. 'He seemed to think that it was necessary to make some gesture to show people that I was not sleeping with him.'

'And you're not?' said Julia, trying not to sound surprised. Comfort's letters had suggested that she was falling much more in love with the Hungarian than with any other man she had ever known.

'Certainly not. He needed a home and somewhere to paint. I've told you all this already,' Comfort protested. 'I enjoy his company and admire his work. I'm not in love with him.'

'Well he certainly loves you,' said Julia, having noticed in Tibor's dark eyes the same light that David's had taken on whenever he had looked at her in the days before Florence. She must not think of David. 'Did Bob Storrington arrange a Paris exhibition of his stuff as well as yours?' She went on, trying to keep her mind on London matters.

'No. They showed mine all right, but were too stuffy to take a gamble on an unknown Hunk. But Marcus has agreed to a double show in his main gallery here. There's to be a huge party to launch it. You will come, won't you, Julia? It'll be just like old times,' said Comfort, tucking her painty hand into the crook of Julia's elbow.

'Well yes, if you want me,' she said, 'although I'm not sure my clothes won't disgrace you. I've nothing smart and Parisian like yours.'

Comfort laughed. 'No one expects lady lawyers to be fashionable,' she said. Julia was trying to think up a witty rejoinder when the sound of Tibor's rich, deep voice distracted her.

'You should rest, Mrs Gillingham. I have put your baggages in your room.'

'That was kind,' said Julia. 'And you're right. I am tired.'

She went up to her room alone and lay on the big bed, trying not to think of David, trying to make plans for the future and to feel excited about Comfort's exhibition.

The following morning she went to chambers, where Mark Heathwood gripped both her hands and stared down at her.

'Thank God, you're all right,' he said tensely. 'When I heard that you had pneumonia I could hardly ... Thank God,' he finished with a painful smile.

Julia, looking into his lined, familiar face, wondered how she could ever have thought that she loved him. The undoubted affection she felt for him was one part admiration, one part gratitude and two parts sympathy, and it must always have been so. Compared with the violence of emotion that David had aroused in her, her feeling for Mark had been almost nothing.

'Thank you,' she said, gently squeezing his hands before she pulled her own away. 'How have you been?'

He told her and they were soon joined by George Wilson, who had plenty to say until their clerk reproachfully interrupted them. Julia went with him to listen to his account of the work he had had to turn away because of her absence and the poor prospects with which she had left herself. Later in the day she met two new members of chambers, young men who had returned from the war after she left for Venice. They greeted her warily and just before she left for the day, she overheard one saying to the other:

'I thought the much vaunted Boadicea looked rather wan, didn't you, Wilkinson?'

'They do say she's been ill. Perhaps it's just that. But I rather agree that she didn't show many signs of being dangerous competition. Has she got any briefs lined up?'

'Only a couple of rather dull written opinions, I heard,' said the first speaker with a dismissive laugh. The two young men must have walked away then, because their voices became fainter and fainter. Julia, not surprised by their reaction to her, wondered whether they had meant her to hear them. She could not summon up much resentment or even irritation and shrugged off their contempt.

Nothing seemed to matter very much as she set about reestablishing her London routines. She did what work her clerk allowed her and dined in hall to show her fellow members of the Temple that she was back. She called on her tailor and established that she had enough coupons for either a new dress or a new coat and skirt but not both. Plumping for the suit because it would be more use to her, she sadly chose some good quality black barathea and ignored her memories of Comfort's glowing Parisian dress. She tried to find workmen to repair the remarkably slight bomb damage to the house and the less slight damage to the decorations wreaked by six years' wear and tear and was told over and over again that there was no chance of getting any such inessential work done in the foreseeable future.

She exchanged dutiful letters with her parents and with Anthony, who seemed far more affectionate to her on paper than he had ever been when they were actually together in Venice, and she resisted the temptation to write to David.

In the second week of May she read in the newspapers that the Kesselring trial had come to an end. The Judge Advocate General had summed up the evidence on both sides at considerable length, tackling the defence's position that the Hague Convention outlawed partisan warfare and permitted reprisals by pointing out that 335 men and boys had been killed in the Ardeatine Caves and that at the rate of ten Italians for every dead German that was five too many. Whether or not the remaining 330 could be judged to have been victims of legitimate reprisals or not, those five had been murdered.

The four colonels who were to judge Kesselring found him guilty and he was sentenced to death. It was announced that there was to be an appeal against the sentence and over the next few days *The Times* published several letters from people who were outraged at the sentence. Julia wished that she could have discussed it with David, who, unlike some of her London colleagues and friends who expressed their views with great force, would have known exactly what he was talking about.

It was three days after the last letter was published that Tibor asked Julia to sit for a portrait. She agreed listlessly, finding it odd that he should want to paint her but prepared to do what little she could to help his slowly burgeoning career. After the first two evening sessions she discovered that it was the best decision she had made since her return.

Comfort sometimes shared the studio with them, but more often they were alone and then Tibor would talk to her about himself, his work in the resistance and eventual escape from Hungary, his fears of what the Russians might do to his country and the rest of Eastern Europe, waking her curiosity and passion to know.

He answered every question she asked him, partly because he was homesick and loved talking about Hungary (which seemed to bore Comfort) and partly because Julia's face always lit up when she was interested and became far more paintable. Some evenings when she sat in the old beech-nut-coloured wing chair in which he was painting her, her face looked dragged and plain in its dazed weariness, but once she started talking and forgot herself, her wide lips curled, her eyes brightened and her face revealed both the essential strength of her character and a wistfulness that made it beautiful to Tibor.

There were evenings when she seemed so tired that she could

not even summon up the energy to ask him questions and then he would start to cross-examine her. It soon became clear to him that she did not want to talk at all about Venice or her husband and so instead he asked about her childhood.

Liking him, trusting him and wanting to repay him for all the things he had told her about his own past, Julia unbent far more than usual and told him a little about the lonely years she had spent as the only child of a brilliant, acerbic solicitor interested in nothing but his work and a self-absorbed, bored, beautiful woman who could not understand her clever daughter's lack of interest in clothes and parties and tried to goad her into behaving more conventionally by mockery.

Tibor, listening to Julia's matter-of-fact accounts, wondered whether her parents had understood the cruelty of what they had done or the extent to which they had driven their daughter into believing herself to be not only plain but also unlovable. Julia never said any such thing, but it seemed obvious to Tibor.

'I can see now how irritating I must have been to her,' said Julia one evening. 'Although at the time I was afraid of her and yet despised her too. All the things she thought were of paramount importance seemed horribly trivial to me and seeing all my life how much she resented my father and how much he disliked her I tried to persuade her to be interested in things that might have given them something to talk about.'

'She will have enjoyed this!' said Tibor with heavy sarcasm.

Julia smiled her lopsided smile.

'Exactly,' she said. 'How arrogant I must have been as a child! And yet it was all done with the best of intentions.'

As she said that, her face changed. Tibor watched the curly mouth straighten and her eyebrows draw together across the top of her nose. She looked almost as though she were in pain. Compassionate, and in any case wanting to be able to go on painting her, he changed the subject.

'Will you explain to me, please,' he said, 'about this India of yours and why you have ruled it for 250 years and why there is all this trouble now?' He was not in the least interested in India or the British attempts to limit the damage their withdrawal from it was bound to cause, or the Viceroy's friendship with Pandit Nehru or the reasons for Jinnah's determination to establish an independent Muslim state, but he listened to Julia's fluent explanations and had his reward as her face returned to normal.

When Comfort was in the studio with them, there was no talk of politics or Julia's family or the international situation for they all bored her. Instead the three of them discussed Comfort's work and success, the chances of Anthony's return, the possibilities of an end to rationing, and whether or not to retrieve the car which had been garaged with Julia's parents in the North since the beginning of petrol rationing.

Julia asked Comfort one evening after a particularly frustrating search for a pair of new shoes to wear with her suit whether she too found the shop assistants extraordinarily rude.

'Unspeakable!' said Comfort with energy. 'They have such power now and they positively delight in telling you that there are no nylons or whatever it is you want. And that's nonsense in any case. The spivs always have plenty. If they can get them, the shops could.'

'I must say I could do with some new stockings,' said Julia sadly. 'But a woman I overheard on the bus the other day said the only hope was to start queueing by half-past five in the morning and hope for a delivery. I just haven't the strength for that sort of thing yet.'

'It's all the fault of this damned government trying to punish anyone who has more than the absolute minimum,' said Comfort. 'How I hate them, interfering, punishing, steamrollering people with their wretched "planning"! I'll get you your stockings: don't worry.'

'But not from a black marketeer,' said Julia. 'I won't do that.'

'Oh, don't be so prissy,' said Comfort. 'You've spent too much time listening to that infuriating protégé of Anthony's. Buying stockings from a spiv is hardly going to damage the health or wealth of the nation.'

'Nevertheless I won't do it,' said Julia.

'But. . .' Comfort was beginning when Tibor laid a hand over hers and stopped her protest.

'Let Julia do as she wishes. She has enough to worry about without that,' he said and Julia smiled gratefully at him. 'What about some coffee, Comfort? Isn't there some left from your mother's last parcel?'

Comfort obediently brewed them some American coffee and Tibor picked up his brushes again.

'Turn your face a little to the left and down, please, before you rest it on your hand,' he said to Julia, who had lost the position while they talked. 'And shake your hair forward a bit. Good.'

Julia obeyed and tried to blank every thought out of her mind, but that was as hard as usual. Whenever Tibor did not distract her during these sessions of enforced idleness, memories of David came flooding into her mind: memories of his gentleness, his idealism, his wittiness, his complete lovableness. She made herself remember Raffaella, too, and her dark-haired, blue-eyed baby, and then her face would harden and Tibor would patiently lay down his brushes until he had talked her back into serenity.

'Here you are,' said Comfort, bringing Julia's coffee to the wing chair. 'I've put the sugar in. It's the last of the ration until next week. Would you like some brandy? You look faint again.'

'I'm just tired,' said Julia, accepting the coffee. 'I'm sorry, Tibor, my face must change each time you try to paint it. Perhaps you ought to use Comfort instead.'

'He's done me,' said Comfort, with a sparkling smile.

'You look as though you approve of it,' said Julia, pleased to see Comfort so happy.

'I do,' answered Comfort, 'and so will you. You'll see it at the opening tomorrow. Don't forget, will you? Five-thirty sharp.'

# Chapter Twenty-Three

Julia did not forget the exhibition, even though her clerk presented her with the first important brief of her return just as she was leaving chambers. She did not make the mistake of sounding too grateful for it, but she was surprised that it had come so soon.

'Mr Norgrove asked for you especially when he heard you were back,' her clerk told her. 'He wants to talk to you tomorrow afternoon. He won't be in court.'

'All right,' said Julia coolly. 'I'll read all this tonight. Thank you, Tomkins.'

Feeling slightly cheered, although the usual evening's lassitude was dragging at her body, Julia went to the washroom to do her face and hair. Then she put on an elegant new hat, the result of her one successful shopping expedition, and sallied forth to the big Bond Street gallery where Comfort's dealer was greeting the usual crowd of critics, customers, and members of the smart set. Remembering some of the glittering pre-war parties there, Julia felt sad as she noticed the inevitable changes.

The two huge chandeliers in the main room were the same as ever and the parquet floor as glossy, but the shifting crowd looked different. Gone was the old atmosphere of utterly certain wealth and success. That evening many of the people looked as tired and tense as Julia felt. The men's clothes were indistinguishable from the old days, if a little shabbier, but most of the women's frocks and hats showed signs of what the magazines called 'inventive little touches' to disguise their origins. More than one, Julia saw, wore streakily applied leg make-up instead of stockings.

She caught sight of Comfort, looking magnificent in her

blue-and-green Dior dress, and thought of going to talk to her, but she seemed occupied by eager and probably important guests. Depressed, Julia walked over to the bravely arranged buffet table to get herself a drink.

At pre-war parties it always used to carry great silver dishes of smoked salmon and foie gras, ice buckets of champagne, and trays and trays of canapes, bottles of whisky, cocktails and every conceivable drink that Marcus's patrons might demand. Now, the silver dishes were artfully sprinkled with inadequate numbers of cheese straws and sausage rolls, made to look as lavish as possible with bunches of unrationed greenery. In place of the champagne and cocktails was a single anonymous concoction served in long glasses from a series of huge punchbowls.

Julia, sipping it in a gingerly fashion, thought that there was a little gin in it, quite a lot of cider, and probably well-diluted orange squash. Chopped mint leaves cut the sickliness of the orange and made it look prettier but tended to get stuck against the roof of her mouth.

'Isn't it Mrs Gillingham? Do you remember us?' A cheerful American voice made Julia stop her gloomy diagnosis of the drink in her hand. She looked up to see two men dressed in impeccably cut suits smiling at her.

'You look puzzled,' said one. 'Bob Storrington and John Tonsley. We first met at Cumnor all those years ago.'

'Yes, of course,' said Julia, holding out her hand. 'How are you? Are you based in London now?'

'No, we're back in Paris these days,' said Bob. 'But we couldn't let one of Comfort's shows pass without showing up. We're very proud of her.'

'So am I,' said Julia, smiling widely. 'And I haven't even had a chance to see any of the paintings. Will you take me round?' she went on, remembering that the Americans were both knowledgeable about modern painting and admirers of Comfort herself.

'Sure,' said John, offering her his arm. The two men walked her slowly round the big room, pausing before paintings that they particularly liked. Of them all Julia liked best the series of ink and wash drawings of the London ruins that Comfort had been working on before she went to Venice, but she dutifully admired many of the bigger oils.

'And Tibor Smith's paintings?' she said, when they reached the end of the main rooms. 'Aren't they here too?'

'Upstairs. Shall we go? They're very exciting,' said Bob. 'Much more interesting than Comfort's in a way, though not as saleable.'

The first painting they saw at the top of the stairs was the portrait of Comfort herself. Julia saw at once why Comfort had smiled so happily at the thought of it. It was an unusual pose that Tibor had arranged, with Comfort apparently lying flat on her back on a plank floor with her luxuriant blonde hair spread out all round her head. Her eccentric beauty was unadorned by any jewels or props or brocade hangings and Tibor had painted her with ruthless, almost photographic, accuracy. Comfort looked magnificent, and Julia's first thought was that she must buy the portrait at once.

'Clever, isn't it?' said Bob. 'He's caught the glamour and a considerable part of the serpent-like character of the matchless Comfort.'

'What do you mean by serpent-like?' said Julia, suddenly angry.

'Oh come on, Mrs Gillingham,' said Bob. 'You know what a monster she can be.'

'I thought you were her friends,' said Julia, adding with a courtesy that showed none of her outrage at what he had said, 'Thank you for taking me round.'

She left them standing by Comfort's portrait to walk slowly down the wide, gracious staircase. Halfway down she stopped to look at her sister-in-law, still surrounded by an admiring crowd. Almost as though she could feel Julia's attention, Comfort looked up and waved. Julia waved back. She hated to think that Comfort's so-called friends were criticising her in such terms, but she also wondered what it was that Comfort had done to provoke them.

Julia's back ached and so did her head and she wondered how soon she could leave without upsetting either of the painters or their dealer. She glanced down at the glass in her hand.

'May I get you another of those?' said a soft, gentle Virginian voice. She looked round and recognised Jackson French, the young man from UNRRA. For a moment she could not think what he was doing there and then remembered Comfort's making him promise to visit her in London.

'Thank you, Mr French,' said Julia. 'I didn't know you were back.'

'I've been here nearly a month, although I had to go back to Italy last week to help sort out a nasty little mess. Comfort's been very good to me since I've been here in London,' he said. 'I'd have been lost without her. Would you like a drink?'

'Yes, I'd love one,' said Julia, glad to be with someone who seemed to appreciate Comfort, 'if there's any left that is.'

When he had brought her another drink, Jack French urged her to one of the few empty corners of the great room. They chatted for a while about Venice and Julia asked about the mess he had had to clear up.

'Rather a tricky business,' said Jack French, wrinkling his nose. 'A woman who's done a lot of good with refugees in the city was found to be dealing in the black market. We'd thought she was merely a minor customer and let her alone, but she was too deeply implicated. It had to be done.'

'I'm sure it had,' said Julia in a tight, cold voice. Before she could ask any questions, Jackson French started to talk again.

'Mrs Gillingham,' he said, having taken a deep breath, 'may I say something rather cheeky?'

'If you must,' said Julia, taken aback and wondering whether he was about to ask her questions about the Venetian black markets and what she knew of Giovanna and her protégées.

'I'm worried about Comfort,' he said, surprising her. 'Like I said, I owe her a lot and I'd like to do something to help her.'

'Yes?' said Julia, when he said no more.

'She needs her brother back in London,' he said.

Julia's cold stare had quelled argumentative lawyers and recalcitrant witnesses, but it seemed to have no effect on Jackson French. Without waiting for her to say anything, he hurried on:

'She's afraid you're very angry with him. And I just wanted to say that we all did things in the war that we regret, and . . . life was tough up there with the partisans. There was always a pretty good chance that none of us would get out alive. Ordinary life, wives and families, seemed a hell of a long way off. And your husband was in the thick of it. Ah, hell, all I really want to say is: don't be too hard on the guy. It was a mistake anyone could have made.'

'I thought you didn't know my husband,' said Julia, her voice sounding inside her head as though it came from a long way off. Americans were really too extraordinary, she thought as though fending off the knowledge he was offering her; they plunged without warning into intimacies an Englishman would take years to attempt.

'I didn't,' said French, 'but it was a small world and it got smaller once most of the guys went home. We all heard things about each other,' he said. 'It's not surprising I got to know about her, and Venice is pretty small, you know. Besides . . .'

Julia tried to concentrate through the waves of heat that were washing over her. The sound of French's voice dwindled into the background. Jagged arcs of light began to fizzle in her eyes. She put out a hand to stop herself overbalancing and was overtaken by the nauseating sensation of falling into nothingness.

When she came round it was to hear Jack French apologising, Comfort explaining that Julia had recently suffered from pneumonia and Tibor sensibly sending someone to fetch a taxi. When it came he insisted on accompanying her back to Brunswick Square, despite Comfort's furiously whispered reminder about all the important critics and collectors whom he ought to have stayed to impress.

He did not talk at all on the journey home, not even to ask how Julia had come to faint, for which she was profoundly grateful. She felt not only ill and bruised from her heavy fall on the hard parquet floor, but also badly shaken by the information Jack French had delivered. It might have been elliptical, but Julia was beginning to understand it and could not imagine how she had misread all the signals she had been given in Venice. Looking back, she saw that there had been a great many of them.

Raffaella had disappeared almost immediately after Anthony had taken Julia's message to her while David was in Florence. Anthony had always refused to talk about what had happened while he was with the partisans, while David had spoken far more readily about everything except the action that had brought him his MC and the details of his instructions from Peter Suvarov.

Looking even further back, to the Christmas when Anthony had come home to London, Julia remembered that he had reacted very oddly to Comfort's questions about Rome and what it had been like when he went there after the war. Since he must have recently left Raffaella there to have her baby, throwing a handful of money at her as a sop to whatever conscience he felt, it was not surprising that he felt peculiar about it. Perhaps that episode also explained both his devotion to Flavia and his refusal to have a child with Julia, and even his obvious reluctance to have her living with him in Italy.

Julia found it hard to believe that the fastidious Anthony could really want to spend the rest of his life with a girl like Raffaella, undeniably pretty though she was, and yet it seemed clear that he had removed her from Giovanna's as soon as he had discovered her there and installed her on the opposite side of Venice, conveniently close to the hospital where he spent his days.

'Why didn't he tell me?' she asked herself, furious, humiliated and disheartened as she thought of the efforts she had made to try to understand him and make him happy. She recognised bitterly that her efforts must have irritated him. It seemed unnecessarily cruel of him to have allowed her to go on doing it instead of explaining himself. She told herself that the conditions in which he had lived with the partisans and the things he had had to do then could have explained almost any behaviour, but she could not make herself believe that they excused the lies he had let her believe once the war was over.

If Julia had only known what it was Anthony really felt and wanted, she would never have gone to Venice and never have got herself in such a muddle over David. The memory of her own coldness to him as she left Venice hurt almost more than anything else, but she could hardly write to David, explain that she had suspected him of fathering Raffaella's child and now knew that he had not, that she had enough evidence of adultery to divorce Anthony and therefore wanted to resume her love affair with David. Knowing that he must have misunderstood her accusatory questions about Raffaella just as she had misunderstood his answers, Julia covered her face with her hands.

Tibor watched her as he leaned back against the corner of the taxi. He did not want to add to her burdens by making her tell him about them, but he wanted to help or somehow to comfort her. When the cabbie drew up outside the big house, Tibor paid and tipped him and then helped Julia into the house and upstairs to her room.

'Lie down,' he said, 'and I will fetch you some tisane.'

'I'd rather have a drink,' she said with a hint of a smile. She had only once drunk the herbal brew he had concocted in the studio and had thought it disgusting.

'You ought not to drink too much now,' he said severely and went out, shutting the door carefully behind her.

Julia lay down on her bed, trying to ease her aching back and for once letting herself think of David. Through her physical weakness and her shame at having assumed – on so little real evidence – that he had been responsible for Raffaella's plight, she felt an unexpected happiness. Whatever Jack French's revelation told her about Anthony and her marriage, it had also told her that David had not lied to her. He was the man she had thought when she fell in love with him. She was no closer to him than she had ever been, she would probably never see him again except by chance meeting, but she was glad to know and to be able to look back on their few ecstatic days together without bitterness.

The sound of the door's opening stopped her meandering thoughts. Tibor gave her a large cup of steaming hot water vaguely flavoured with dried herbs and flowers and she tried to look properly grateful.

Waking late the next morning, Julia tried to get up in good time to do all the work she needed for her meeting with the KC, but she was overtaken by nausea and had to rush to the bathroom, where she was disgustingly sick. When the spasms had passed and she had carefully rinsed her mouth and wiped the sweat off her face with a cool flannel, she peered at her face in the mirror. Her skin was pale, and there were huge dark semicircles under her brown eyes, but otherwise she looked perfectly normal. Her tongue, when she stuck it out, looked healthy enough. But she felt ghastly.

'It must have been that peculiar drink last night,' she said aloud, going down to the big basement kitchen to make herself some breakfast, 'or perhaps Tibor's disgusting tisane.'

She boiled a kettleful of water for tea and toasted her usual two pieces of grey, austerity bread. When she had spread them with her share of the marmalade ration, she found that the very thought of eating them made her feel sick again. Almost in tears at the thought of wasting so much food, she tried to choke down the sweet, soft toast, but was sick again.

Drinking her tea with a spoonful of sugar but no milk seemed to control the nausea, and after two cups she managed to clear up the kitchen and get herself out of the house without being sick again. Taking a taxi to chambers instead of walking, she was afraid that she might disgrace herself by being sick all over the silk who had insisted on having her as his junior and losing her most important chance of re-establishing her practice. But as the morning wore on she began to feel better and during the meeting the effort of concentrating on what he and their instructing solicitor were saying banished her malaise.

She spent the rest of the afternoon working on the papers they left with her and it was not until well after five that she remembered it was her turn to buy and cook some food for supper. Putting away her papers and collecting her hat, she thought with regret of the servants who had worked in Brunswick Square before the war, and of all the empty hours she had had to fill in Venice while the efficient Annunziata did the marketing and all the cooking.

All that was left for Julia to buy that evening was either snoek or whale steaks. The one had a flavour she hated and the other tasted of nothing so much as cod-liver oil. Deciding that it would have to do she bought enough for three and hoped that there might be some tins of tomatoes left from Comfort's last American parcel to help it down.

When she got back to Brunswick Square, she felt so tired that she thought she might lie down for a few minutes. Putting the whale on a dish in the larder, she dragged herself up to bed and lay down on her unmade bed.

She must have fallen asleep almost at once, for she woke with a tremendous shock. The room was still light and she grabbed blindly for her illuminated alarm clock, forgetting the gold watch she wore on her wrist. Seeing that it was half-past seven, Julia wondered what could have woken her so sharply. Then came a knock at her bedroom door.

'Come in,' she called quickly and was not surprised to see Tibor peering round the door.

'I know,' she said. 'My turn to make dinner. I've got some whale. I'm sorry.'

'Don't be silly, Julia,' he said, coming to sit in a friendly way on the edge of her bed. 'I will cook it and bring you some here if you feel too tired to get up.'

'Of course I'm not,' said Julia, holding her head, which seemed to be aching fiercely again. 'And I'm coming up to sit for you, afterwards.'

'You don't have to,' he said, laying one of his short-fingered hands across her forehead. 'It is bad, yes?'

'Quite bad, just for the moment,' said Julia, 'but never mind; I'm sure it will go off quite soon.'

'You have been sick too, I think,' he said, still holding her head.

Finding his hand enormously comforting, Julia rubbed her forehead first one way and then another against his cool palm.

'Yes,' she said at last. 'Did you hear me this morning? How horrible for you. I am sorry. I think it must have been that peculiar drink at the opening last night.'

The Hungarian laughed.

'You do not really think that, do you?' he said. 'Comfort, yes. She would never imagine anything else, but you? You are a married woman.'

'What is the matter with me?' said Julia, rubbing both hands over her forehead. Yet again she had ignored something so obvious that an illiterate peasant could have understood it. Tibor, misunderstanding her despairing rhetorical question, said gently:

'But you have known that you are to have a child, surely?'

For a moment Julia could not answer. Her mind seemed to have stopped working altogether. 'I can't think why it never even occurred to me,' she said at last. 'I suppose that was why I fainted yesterday too. You haven't said anything to Comfort, have you?' she added urgently. He shook his head.

'Don't tell her then, please, Tibor,' Julia begged. 'She must not know. Will you promise to say nothing?'

'If you wish it,' he answered, the amused smile on his face fading into incomprehension. 'But why?'

'Because . . . because it may not be true. I have to see my doctor first. Don't tell her, Tibor.'

He took both her hands in his and patted them.

'It's all right, Julia. I won't tell until you wish. But she will be happy and that will be . . . nice for you,' he said. 'She has talked so often about wanting your children.'

# Chapter Twenty-Four

By the end of that week Julia had her doctor's confirmation that she was pregnant. He congratulated her, mentioned how pleased Anthony would be and asked her what arrangements she would like to make for the birth.

'I'm not absolutely sure,' said Julia, playing for time. 'Must I really decide now?'

'The sooner the better,' said the doctor, who was an old friend of all three Gillinghams. 'It's no joke having a first child at your age and you'll need the best care. Besides, there's rather a shortage of maternity beds just now: you're not the only wife who's woken up to the importance of having children. Why do you want to wait?'

'Oh, to get used to the idea and to tell Anthony, who is still in Venice, you know,' said Julia with a smile of deceptive sweetness. 'But I do want to know a couple of things. How soon will this wretched sickness stop and how soon will it start to show that I'm pregnant?'

'Well,' said the doctor, looking at a calendar on his desk, 'you say that conception must have been in the first week of April. You should stop feeling sick at about twelve weeks, say by the end of the month. And I think you could probably disguise your pregnancy for perhaps two months after that. But you'll surely stop working now.'

'I haven't decided anything,' said Julia firmly. 'Thank you. I'll be in touch when I want to make arrangements.'

'All right, but don't leave it too long. This isn't a time to take risks, and it most emphatically is a time to put your family responsibilities ahead of your job,' he said, making it quite clear that he severely disapproved of professional women who subordinated the needs of their unborn children to their work.

Julia left the expensive consulting rooms and walked slowly through the streets back to Bloomsbury. She let herself quietly into the house, because she did not want to have to talk even to Tibor just then, and went up to her dark-green study. There she sat, looking out of the dusty window on to the back of the house opposite, trying to decide what to do.

Whenever she thought of all the implications of her condition panic threatened to overwhelm her and so she did her best to concentrate on her instinctive, unthinking happiness that the splendidly fulfilling night she had spent with David should have resulted in the conception of a child. There were occasions when that happiness banished all her anxieties, but only for a few moments. For most of the time the appalling practical problems that would be caused by the child's existence took up all her mental energy.

Julia tried to think of only a few at a time: what Anthony would do when she told him, as inevitably she must; what would happen to David's promising political career if the scandal ever leaked out into the press; what prospects she could possibly have of continuing at the Bar if that happened; what would happen to the child if she were to die and it survive the birth; what the knowledge of its paternity would do to her friendship with Comfort; what David would do if he knew that she was pregnant.

There was no doubt in her mind about the last. If Anthony were to divorce her and David knew why, he would insist on marrying her, whatever he actually wanted and whatever the marriage did to his career. Julia knew that she could not let that happen. David was the kindest and most unselfish person she knew and she loved him. She was not prepared to risk damaging him by involving him in her predicament.

There was of course one way out of all the problems, but Julia did not think she could take it. She had come across one or two women during the war who had conceived children while their husbands were abroad and had found doctors to rid themselves of the partly grown foetuses. She had even prosecuted a retired midwife who had gone about the task with a crochet-hook, severely damaging several of her patients as well as destroying the children.

Thinking about them, Julia felt suddenly cold, despite the easy warmth of the June morning. She wanted the child too much to do anything so desperate. She wanted David, too, but had to face the fact that she could not have him. He had made it abundantly clear that he could not marry her and she had nevertheless asked him to make love to her. The child was therefore her responsibility. She could not run to David and lay the burden of it on him, even though she knew that he would take it up instantly.

There were three courses she could take, she decided at last, trying to treat her dilemma as dispassionately as though it had nothing to do with her personally. She could disappear into the country to have the child and pay someone else to bring it up, perhaps acting the part of a distant relation; she could leave Anthony and live independently and publicly alone with her child; or she could do as countless other faithless wives had done during and after the war and send the child to an orphanage.

The last option she discounted immediately. The cruelty of allowing her own child to be brought up in an institution, however reputable, was more than she could bear. Before she went to Venice, Julia had met a woman whose returning husband had insisted that she send her illegitimate child to an orphanage, although by then the boy was three years old. Thinking of what that child must have felt always made Julia sick with rage.

The second option was the one that seemed most sensible, although Julia knew that it would be a drastic step to take. She was not certain that she could carry it off successfully enough to ensure that the child was not penalised, but thought that if she could do it, he or she would have a better chance of a happy life.

During the war Julia had bought her Kensington house and accumulated what seemed like a small fortune, but it was too small to support her and the child for the rest of her life if she had to stop working. Without her career, she would not be able to keep the child. Keeping the child might destroy the career.

The telephone on Julia's mahogany desk gleamed seductively, promising advice and help and friendship, and yet she could not think of anyone in whom she could confide, until she remembered Felicity Suvarov. Felicity was pregnant; she had seemed intelligent and full of common sense; even more important, she had said enough about her own unconventional life for Julia to be sure that Felicity would neither criticise nor betray her.

Julia rustled through the pages of the telephone directory until she found the number for Peter Suvarov and dialled it. After three rings the telephone was answered:

'Suvarov.'

'Hello; this is Julia Gillingham. You may not remember . . .'

'Venice,' he said. 'How could I forget? I did not realise you were back. How long have been in London?'

'Oh, since about the middle of April,' said Julia, feeling limp in contrast to the energy implicit in his vigorous voice. 'I . . . I was wondering whether I could come and see your wife some time soon.'

'How splendid!' said Suvarov down the telephone. Julia thought from the sound of his voice that he must be smiling, but she could not quite imagine why. 'This morning?' he suggested.

'Well, that would be lovely. Would about twelve suit her, d'you think?' Julia asked, looking at her watch. Suvarov thought that would be perfectly all right and told her he would see her then.

Julia took a taxi to the Suvarovs' small Chelsea house and rang the bell only a few minutes after midday. The door was opened by Peter Suvarov himself, looking extraordinarily relaxed. He shook her hand briskly and then took her upstairs, saying:

'Come on up. Flixe was delighted when I told her you'd be dropping in. Darling,' he said, raising his voice as he pushed open a door on the first floor, 'here she is.' He held open the door for Julia and she walked past him into a white room filled with flowers and sunlight.

The first thing she saw was the broad, competent figure of a nurse dressed in a grey uniform with terrifyingly starched white collar, cuffs and apron. A steel watch hung on one massive breast, and her formidable front was bisected by a straining elasticated belt, buckled in what looked like antique silver.

Impressed as well as taken aback by the sight of the nurse, Julia allowed herself to look round the rest of the pretty room. As she took in the significance of the massed pink, white and green flowers, the child's cradle in the window and Peter Suvarov's obvious delight, Julia could have kicked herself for being so obtuse.

'Julia,' said Felicity from the banked up pillows of her enormous bed. 'How sweet of you to come and see us. Wonderful as it all is, the hours spent in bed do get a bit dull and they say I have to stay here for another two weeks!'

She looked even more ravishing than Julia had remembered her. In Venice Felicity had looked gloriously – and happily – pregnant, but tired too, and suffering from swollen ankles and a bad back. Now, lying at ease, her golden hair loose about her face, her deep blue eyes sparkling under her lashes, and a creamy lace bedjacket covering her shoulders, she looked superb. As a bizarre touch of eccentricity, which only seemed to underline the happy normality of the picture she presented, pinned in the lace at her throat was the most enormous diamond and sapphire brooch that Julia had ever seen.

'How are you?' asked Julia, approaching the bed and trying not to stare at the jewel. She shook the hand Felicity held out to her and then went on: 'I hadn't realised that it was so recent. I'd never have imposed myself on you this soon.'

Flixe shook her golden head and smiled.

'It's lovely. Really. Peter has to go out any minute now and Nurse won't allow me to disturb the infant when he's supposed to be asleep and so – as I said – I get very bored. Ah, this seems to be authorised cuddling time,' said Flixe as the nurse bent over the white-painted, wickerwork cradle that stood in the sunny bay at the front of the room. 'Would you like to hold him, Julia?'

'I?' she said, surprised. 'Oh, well . . . if you're sure. I'd love to.' Julia felt her arms arranging themselves in a cradle even before she had thought about it. With an expression of disapproving obedience on her strong face, the nurse lowered the child on to

Julia's lap. The baby was tightly wrapped in a Shetland lace shawl, and Julia could see very little except for a crumpled red face and a little straight black hair; but she recognised the warm weight from the dreams that had tormented her in Venice. She looked up from her examination of the dark eyes, minute nose and peaceful mouth to see Flixe smiling with a slightly quizzical expression in her large eyes.

Julia smiled back, unaware that her eyelashes were damp.

'Thank you, Nurse,' said Flixe suddenly. 'We'll be all right now. Why don't you go and get yourself a cup of tea?'

'Very well, Mrs Suvarov,' she said after a moment, during which Julia felt that she might well protest. 'I'll be back in twenty minutes to . . .'

'Put him down again. Yes, Nurse, I know,' said Flixe. As soon as the white-panelled door had been shut behind the stout woman, Flixe let out the breath she had been holding.

'She's said to be wonderful with first-time mothers, but golly she does cluck,' said Flixe, laughing.

'I can see that it must be tiresome,' said Julia. The child kicked suddenly and the carefully arranged shawl was dislodged. Julia saw that it was dressed in a cream-coloured flannel nightgown. Its heels drummed into her thigh and its fists clenched as its mouth opened and its face reddened. It was clear that there was about to be a bellow of rage or hunger. Without even thinking about it, Julia took one of the angry fists in her hand. The small fingers unclenched and the baby's eyes opened again. Julia smiled down and felt the child's hand cling to one of her fingers.

'Lovely,' she said, looking up at Flixe. 'Have you decided on a name yet?'

'Andrew,' said Flixe. 'Andrew Peter Felix in all, but I think we'll call him Andrew. Apparently it was Peter's father's name; they didn't get on, I gather, but the arrival of this Andrew seems to have made Peter feel some nostalgia for his family.' She touched the enormous brooch at her throat and smiled: 'This belonged to his mother and was brought out of Russia after the Revolution by one of his sisters. Peter went specially over to Paris to ask if he could have it for me. Embarrassing, isn't it?'

'Touching, too,' said Julia, no longer surprised that Felicity should be wearing jewellery in bed. 'But I expect you want Andrew now,' she went on, standing up and walking carefully across the strip of moss-green carpet between her chair and the bed to deposit the child in his mother's arms.

Flixe took him, rearranged the shawl and stroked her son's face with a gentle finger.

'I must say I quite like him,' she said, looking back at Julia. 'But you didn't come here to admire my effort, did you? Tell me what's up.'

'To tell you the truth,' said Julia, smiling her lopsided smile. 'I had completely forgotten the fact that your baby was due to arrive about now. I really came for some advice.'

'From me?' said Flixe, looking and sounding startled. 'What could a professional woman like you possibly need to ask me?'

'A great many things, I suspect,' said Julia, actually laughing at that, despite her troubles. 'But my specific problem is that I've discovered that I am pregnant.'

Felicity looked so fulfilled and happy as she lay against the linen-covered pillows with her child in her arms that Julia found herself unable to go on with any of the details of her predicament. Instead, she said:

'You look like some painting of motherhood.' The words were said in admiration rather than bitterness, but the tone gave Julia away. Flixe's eyes narrowed.

'And there's some difficulty? Does your husband not want children? Or is it you? I can see that they would make your work very difficult.'

'Neither – or rather both. But neither of those is what makes the situation so peculiarly difficult.' Julia stopped there, partly to order her thoughts, but partly because she could not bear the thought that the child she and David had conceived could be thought of as the result of some shabby affair that she wanted to conceal. Reminding herself that there was no point in saying anything to Flixe if she did not tell her the whole truth, she gritted her teeth and then went on.

'I want the child very much indeed. My husband does not want children and therefore made quite certain that we could never have one. This child,' she said, laying a hand protectively just below her breasts, 'is not my husband's. There is no possibility that it could be – which I suppose protects me from one particular dilemma.'

'Ah,' said Flixe on a long breath. 'David Wallington?' Julia nodded. 'And does he know?'

'No,' said Julia. 'And he mustn't. He'd rush to my support if he knew and that would ruin his career.' She laid both her hands palm upwards in her lap and stared at them. For one moment she uncharacteristically wondered whether the lines on her faintly glistening hands meant anything, whether her predicament could have been foretold from the pattern of creases, triangles, stars and diamonds marked there. There was a faint, wholly illegitimate comfort in the thought.

'Felicity, what on earth should I do now?' she asked.

'You must tell David,' she said simply. 'After all, the child is his too.'

'I know,' said Julia. 'But he made it clear in Venice that what was happening to us – what we did – was not for ever. He has plans for his future that do not include marrying a woman five years older than himself who would already have a child. If I tell him now it would look as though I were trying to blackmail him into changing his mind and marrying me.'

'From what I saw of you both in Venice, I cannot imagine that David Wallington would want to pursue his career at the cost of your happiness,' said Flixe seriously. 'Besides, he must have inherited that place in Scotland. He could live up there and run it all.'

'Do you mean that you knew – even then . . .' Julia began, not listening to what Felicity was saying, and then broke off.

Flixe, thinking that clever women could be unbelievably stupid about ordinary things, smiled.

'It was the most obvious thing I've ever seen,' she said. 'The two of you showed what you felt about each other by almost everything you said and did.'

'But we hadn't even . . . I mean, neither of us had said anything at that stage,' said Julia, faced for the first time with the possibility that if her feelings for David had been so obvious then Anthony, too, might have noticed them. Perhaps that was why he had changed so much in Venice and become colder and colder towards her. Only when she was leaving both Venice and David had Anthony turned kind again.

There was a knock at the door and the formidable nurse came bustling in.

'I'll take little Andrew now, Mrs Suvarov,' she said officiously. Flixe handed her child over without protest, but she did say:

'Mrs Gillingham and I have some things to discuss. Could you take Andrew to your room for a while, please?'

Looking outraged, the nurse scooped the wicker basket off its stand and carried it out of the door, which she shut behind her with a distinct snap.

'I'm sorry, Julia,' said Flixe. 'She can't understand that one can be wholly and completely besotted by one's son and yet occasionally want to be in only adult company sometimes. Never mind. They're out of the way now and we won't be disturbed until lunch.' She looked at Julia through her blonde eyelashes. 'You must tell David,' she said again.

'But I can hardly write to him with this news while he's living in the same house as my husband,' said Julia.

'But surely he isn't still there?' said Flixe. 'The Kesselring trial is long over. I thought David was to be demobbed as soon as it finished. Unless he's been waiting for the appeal and even that's been settled now.'

Julia put a hand to her forehead.

'I can't think what's happened to my brain,' she said. 'It seems to have gone all mushy. Of course you're right. I read about it last week: the sentence has been commuted to life imprisonment.'

Julia got up from the deep-cushioned chair in which she had been sitting and walked quickly across to the bay window. She noticed irrelevantly that it was curtained in ivory chintz printed with coral-pink roses and moss-green ribbons. She stood with her back to the room, staring out at the narrow sunlit street below. Watching her tense back, Felicity said softly:

'It would be absurdly quixotic to ruin your own life and live in miserable loneliness just to protect a political career that might never happen anyway.'

Turning back at last, Julia leaned against the wall.

'You may be right, but I don't think I could bear it if David hated us both for ruining him,' she said with transparent honesty.

Felicity was silenced by that. Both of them were too adult and too experienced not to know that of all things in the world someone else's feelings were the most difficult to assess or predict accurately.

'Come and sit down again, Julia,' said Flixe eventually. 'I remember so well how ghastly it feels in the early stages. I'm not surprised that everything seems so tragic. Take the weight off your feet. I think you have to take that risk. There is no alternative.'

'Except not telling him,' said Julia drearily. 'I suppose I'd arrived at that myself. I'm sorry to have come and laid it all on to you when I've really decided what to do anyway.'

'Don't be sorry. I'm glad you came,' said Flixe, smiling and holding out a hand. Julia took it in both of hers.

'You have been very kind – and very rational,' she said. To Julia those were the two most important characteristics in anyone. 'Thank you.'

'Well I'm not sure that I've been all that helpful,' said Flixe, squeezing Julia's hands affectionately. 'But I do believe that secrets are bad, dangerous and wickedly destructive things.'

'I'll let you rest now,' said Julia, whose professional life necessarily contained innumerable secrets. Unlike Felicity, she positively valued the ability to keep them. She released Flixe's hands.

'Can I rely on you not to tell anyone?' Julia asked urgently enough to make Flixe blush.

'Of course you can,' said Flixe. 'Come again soon, and tell me if you need any practical help – a place to stay in the country perhaps until the child is born. One of Peter's cousins lives near where I was brought up and last time I saw her she told me that she was thinking of having a paying guest or two to help with the expenses of keeping the place up. I know that she would have you if you needed sanctuary.'

'Thank you, Felicity. I'll let you know. Goodbye,' said Julia and left the pretty house with the first faint stirrings of an idea for smashing through the impasse that faced her. It would be violent, but it might be the only way.

When Peter Suvarov got home later that afternoon, having scoured the local greengrocers for grapes to take his wife and paid exorbitantly for them, he found her unusually introspective. Assuming at first that it was just an effect of the immense physical upheaval that she had endured, he said nothing, but sat on her bed and stroked her lovely head. She leaned into his hand, responding as generously as she always did every time he touched her.

'Peter,' she said after a while.

'What can I do for you, my dearest heart?' he said.

'Julia Gillingham is pregnant,' she said and told him the whole story, knowing that he would never betray the confidence.

'You needn't worry about her, Flixe,' he said when he had heard it all. 'She's the most competent woman I've ever met – and that includes your elder sister – and she's got tremendous guts, too. She'll be all right.'

Flixe was silent for a while, thinking that over.

'I suppose,' she said at last, 'that it wasn't really her I was worrying about.' She twisted her head against the pillows so that she could look at her husband. 'Julia said that being pregnant she was afraid that David Wallington would think she was trying to blackmail him into marrying her,' she added so fast that the words tumbled over each other.

Suvarov took her face between both hands and kissed her.

'Flixe, darling,' he said. 'The only reason you and I did not get married on VE Day was because I was still married to Diana. You may remember that I asked you to marry me then.'

'Yes, I do remember,' she said in a small voice, 'but you only asked me because she had told you to, and you might well have changed your mind before she died.'

Her purplish-blue eyes looked enormous in her pale face and her mouth was pinched. Suvarov decided to tackle the root of her fears.

'Darling,' he said firmly, 'I know that I had a terrible reputation as a rake; I know that I had a short and stupid affair with your sister; I know that your father told you you would never be safe with a foreigner of such dubious reputation as me, but do you really think that if I had fallen out of love with you I would have done anything so silly as to allow us to conceive a child?'

Flixe looked at him, searching his face for clues as to what he really thought. He was a master of concealment and had successfully hidden the fact that he loved her at all for the entire war. She longed to believe him and yet it was hard.

'Come on, Flixe,' he said, spreading his hands with their palms upwards. 'A man of my experience?'

She laughed then, recognising the sense of it.

'I love you so much, you see,' she said after a while, 'that I . . . Oh, never mind saying it. You know, don't you?'

'Yes,' he answered. 'I know and because you are you, it's the greatest compliment that you could pay me.'

'Good,' she said, sitting up and looking much healthier than when he had returned. 'Let's have some of those grapes and decide how we can help poor Julia Gillingham deal with this catastrophe.'

'Poor Julia Gillingham is quite capable of helping herself,' Suvarov said, breaking off a small bunch of grapes and handing them to his wife. 'This "catastrophe" as you called it will be the making of her if it rescues her from that marriage.'

'But do you know anything about the marriage?' Flixe asked, eating a grape and closing her eyes in delight as her tastebuds recognised the smooth sweetness of the juice trickling into her mouth when she broke the grapeskin with her tongue.

'Not a lot,' answered Peter as he watched her in amusement. One of the things he loved about his wife was her capacity to enjoy every kind of sensuous pleasure to the full. 'But I know quite a lot about her husband and so, having met her, I can imagine it.'

'What's he like?' asked Flixe. 'Or rather what was he like with the partisans? I presume that's why you know about him?'

'Yes; David reported fully. He had to, after all. We sent him to join up with the partisans so that we could find out who was doing what out there and how powerful the Communists were likely to be once the war was won. And then when I went to Rome at the end of the war I had to interview Gillingham myself. That may well be why he refused to dine with us. We didn't get on.'

'And?' said Flixe. 'Come on, Peter. The war's over. You don't need to conceal it all any longer.'

'You'd be surprised,' he said, absent-mindedly eating one of her grapes. 'I can't tell you much except perhaps that he's said to be a brilliant doctor, he's undoubtedly very arrogant like so many of them, he was physically brave and quite prepared to make sacrifices for the good of the war.'

'That all sounds admirable,' said Flixe. 'There must be more.'

'There is and I'd say it boils down to the fact that, unlike David Wallington, Gillingham is a man who uses other people whenever he needs them and is not able to give anything back when his need for them is over,' said Suvarov at last. 'And I don't think that he has much natural warmth, unlike her; I'd have said he was not at all . . . sensual. I feel sorry for her. She'd do far better with David.'

'Poor Julia,' said Flixe when she had digested that.

Julia would have been surprised if she had heard Peter Suvarov's strictures on her husband. At the time he made them, she was sitting at her desk in the dark-green study writing to Anthony.

> I can only appeal to your generosity [she wrote towards the end of a long, frank letter] and you have always shown me so much of that before. This child exists and I cannot take steps to change that: it must be born. I want to bring it up myself, which I can do provided there is no scandal that might prevent my continuing to work. What I should like to do,

therefore, is to remain married to you in name for as long as you continue in Italy and then try to arrange a quiet divorce. That way the child would bear your name, but of course I would not want you to have to take any financial responsibility for either of us.

I don't want David to know about the child, because he would rush to our support and that could ruin us all.

She thought for a while and then added:

I don't know what you plan to do about your future and whether you intend to come back here at all. I am sorry that our years together should have ended like this. I have never wanted to hurt you and I know how badly it can hurt to discover that your spouse has a child conceived with someone else.

Julia.

That oblique reference to Raffaella's child was the only one in the letter and Julia was sure that it would be enough. She was sure, too, that most men of her acquaintance would consider Anthony's illegitimate child to be of infinitely less significance than his wife's, but she had a high enough opinion of his intelligence and his basic decency to believe that he might think differently.

# Chapter Twenty-Five

A week later Julia shared a perfectly cooked omelette with Comfort and Tibor. The eggs, a lavish half dozen, had been given to Comfort by an admirer who kept chickens, and she had decided to blow them all on one delicious meal instead of eking them out for weeks to augment the mean ration of one each a week. The butter had been contributed by Julia from her weekly six ounces. Tibor had done the cooking and provided a bottle of claret, which he had bought on the strength of the proceeds of his first sale of the exhibition.

Comfort had got out the Waterford glasses and the best china in celebration of the extravagant omelette and enjoyed the contrast of the rough deal table with her smooth white bone china, which was was decorated in dark-blue and real gold leaf. She began to toy with the idea of a still life, a watercolour perhaps, that would point up the contrasts and provide a pleasantly witty commentary on post-war life. She leaned slightly to her left so that her bare forearm just brushed Tibor's arm and turned to smile at him. He looked at her from under his drooping eyelids and she wondered again whether he really loved her as he said he did or whether it was her house and her china and her money that he wanted.

Julia, almost at peace since sending her letter to Anthony, watched them across the wide, scrubbed table and thought that she had never seen Comfort so easy or so ordinary. She was working well and apparently happy, still looking beautiful, but far less eccentric or intense than in the old days. Tibor seemed to have found a key to her that had eluded every other man who had tried to love her. He stood no nonsense from her, Julia had noticed with amusement, and when she tried to manipulate him into abasing himself so that she could despise him, he simply went away.

He was in a difficult situation, having lost everything in the war and having to live on Comfort's charity, and yet he managed it with great dignity, contributing to the housekeeping budget whenever he could and unobtrusively taking over more than his share of household chores when he could not, and taking immense care not to compromise her. Julia hoped that the two of them would make a success of life together and marry, but she suspected that Tibor would not even consider it until he had made enough money to salve his pride and allow him something to offer Comfort.

Rather bleakly Julia realised that even if they did marry she would be unlikely to know much about it. David's child would come between her and Comfort more surely than almost anything else. There were going to be very few more evenings when Julia could sit and watch Comfort smiling at her with all the old open affection in her slate-grey eyes.

David's child, Julia thought and recognised that she was bracketing them together in her mind. She knew that she had to stop that. My child, she corrected herself.

'Isn't it time for the news?' said Comfort. 'Come on, Julia, what's the matter with you? You're usually itching to hear the latest slice of BBC gloom.'

Julia smiled a little sadly.

'I was dreaming,' she said.

'Of what?' asked Comfort, swivelling in her chair and reaching to the big, cream-painted dresser behind her to switch on the wireless.

'Oh, a time in the future,' she said and then flogged her mind to produce some optimistic hopes. 'When a six-egg omelette will seem no more than a matter of course and when the country isn't on the brink of ruin and when everyone has come home and the Middle East is at peace and Cyprus is sorted out and India is not being torn in pieces by its own people,' she said.

'Some hope,' said Comfort as the wireless crackled and the sound of Big Ben's chimes boomed through the basement kitchen. The three of them listened in growing surprise to the first item of news: an account of a speech to be delivered the following day at Harvard by General Marshall, in which he explained that America would have to provide financial assistance if the ruined countries of Europe were ever to be rebuilt.

'The truth of the matter is [went the speech] that Europe's requirements for the next three or four years of foreign food and other essential products – principally from America – are so much greater than her present ability to pay that she must have substantial additional help or face economic, social, and political deterioration of a very grave character.'

'You see,' said Comfort, her face glowing, when the news ended, 'America is going to save the world after all.'

'Thank God,' said Julia quietly, remembering the bitter arguments she and Comfort had had in the summer of 1945. 'There's hope after all.'

'There is always hope,' said Tibor, who, alone of the three of them, had known at first hand what it was to be occupied by an enemy like the Nazis. Compared with the bleakness of his future then, Julia knew that her difficulties were small.

She got up from the table suddenly and ran for the sink. Reaching it just in time, she vomited up all the omelette and the vegetables and the wine. While she was being sick, Tibor followed her and held her head until she had finished.

'What a waste,' she gasped when it was over at last. 'I'm sorry.'

'Never mind,' he said, pouring her a glass of water. She rinsed her mouth and started to clean the sink.

'Go and sit down,' said Tibor. 'I can do that.'

'But it's so horrible . . . Julia began.

'Go and sit down,' he said more firmly and gratefully she obeyed.

'Are you all right, Julia?' said Comfort when Julia sat back in her hard chair and leaned her head in her hands.

'Of course she's not all right,' said Tibor. 'She's just been sick. Make some tea, Comfort.'

'It's all right. I'm fine,' said Julia, waiting for Comfort to draw the obvious conclusion, which she did soon enough.

'Yes,' said Julia to the inevitable question.

'But that's wonderful, darling,' said Comfort, coming to embrace her. 'It's what I've always wanted for the three of us. You and me and Anthony and a child. He'll have to come back now.' Her face was radiant as she laid her head on Julia's shoulder. Julia felt cold all through her bones.

'We'll see,' she said. 'I've written to him, but I haven't heard yet.'

'I'll write too,' said Comfort, lifting her head to smile at Julia again. 'He'll have to come back now. Well done, Julia. Now we can all be happy again.'

Julia could not answer. She felt sick and afraid and, for the first time, guilty. Whatever Anthony had done had been done in the war. It was Julia who had threatened the life they might have regained in peacetime.

'I never thought it would happen,' said Comfort.

'Nor I,' answered Julia truthfully, removing herself from Comfort's embrace as gently as she could. 'I must go to bed.'

'I'll take you up,' Comfort said, but Tibor gripped her wrist and stopped her following Julia.

'She's too tired, Comfort,' he said firmly. 'Let her go.'

Julia pulled herself up the stone stairs alone.

She woke the next morning to one of the most horrible sounds in the world: bitter voices arguing furiously but very quietly. It was obvious that Comfort and Tibor were fighting a battle and trying to keep it from waking Julia. She lay against her pillows with her eyes closed, hoping that it was just a skirmish rather than all-out war.

Up in Comfort's studio it was clear that it was war. She was standing with her back to the green-and-blue tapestry screen, staring at Tibor as though she had never seen him properly. His short legs and his exceptionally broad shoulders looked almost grotesque and she wondered why she had never noticed before that his hair was pathetically thin over his scalp.

'I do not have to give you reasons,' she said coldly, 'I have no obligations to you. The boot is firmly on the other foot. I have housed you and fed you, given you canvasses and paints, introduced you to critics and European dealers and made sure you could have a major exhibition. That is enough. I have put up with your sponging for long enough.'

'I do not understand,' said Tibor quietly.

'What don't you understand?' asked Comfort. 'It all seems quite clear to me.'

'I do not understand the word "sponging". What does it mean?' he asked with a dangerous note in his voice

Comfort laughed, but quietly, because she did not want to wake Julia, who needed all the sleep she could get.

'Taking,' said Comfort. 'Take, take, take. You're like a sponge soaking up water – but it isn't water, it's money and food and canvasses and –'

'You said that you loved me,' said Tibor blankly, interrupting the flow of accusation.

Comfort wished that he had lost his temper so that she could lose hers, but he sounded merely puzzled.

'For a time I thought that perhaps I did,' she whispered, turning away and filling her kettle. With it held in her wet right hand she looked round the screen again: 'But now I know that I do not, and I am fed up with having you hanging around sponging on me and Julia.'

'I see,' he whispered back, 'I am sponging on her, too, am I? What has made you so protective of her? A few months ago, you told me that she had ruined your brother's life and that you would never forgive her.'

Comfort put the kettle down on the gas ring and washed her hands. She hated him for reminding her of the things she had said about Julia in the unhappy past and could hardly bear to look at him any more. But she had to say something to prevent him going straight to Julia and spoiling things again.

'I thought so at the time, but I was wrong,' she said. 'I'll make it up to her. But it's none of your business. I want you out of here. There isn't room in the house any more and I don't have to explain myself to you. You've had plenty out of me; you can hardly complain.'

'Stop,' said Tibor loudly. He stamped on the bare polished floorboards.

'Shhh,' said Comfort. 'You'll wake her.'

'That is enough,' said Tibor. 'I am going. I will send for my things.'

Julia heard that, although she could not hear what Comfort said in reply. Then there was the sound of a door opening and Tibor's heavy tread coming down the stairs. Julia flung back her blankets and got out of bed, thrusting her arms into her grey dressing gown before she opened the door. She was just in time to see him pass Anthony's dressing-room door.

'Tibor,' she said urgently.

He looked back for a moment and then shrugged.

'I am sorry,' he said and went on down the stairs.

Julia shuffled her feet into a pair of bedroom slippers and followed him. She caught him up in the high, cold hall.

'Don't go,' she said. 'At least not without telling me why. Please, Tibor.'

He shrugged again, but he also turned back to face her.

'There is not much to tell,' he said.

'Never mind. Let's have some breakfast and you can tell me what there is,' said Julia. She looked at her watch. 'It's only half-past six. You must have something to eat before you go. Come on.'

Together they went back to the kitchen, where Tibor made Julia sit down while he brewed a pot of coffee and put two slices of bread under the grill. When they were toasted he brought them to her with the marmalade jar and the coffee pot. When Julia had poured them each a cup, without even noticing that she no longer felt sick, she said:

'What's happened?'

'I don't know,' said Tibor. He drank a little coffee and then put the cup down. 'I don't understand what she wants. She has been so good to me since we met in the winter and even when we have had misunderstandings they have not lasted. And last night she was so happy – it was good that, because she is often not happy.'

'I know,' said Julia, 'and I have been very impressed with the way you have understood her and not allowed her moods to make you angry and hurt her. She has been badly hurt, you see.'

'Why should I be angry?' asked Tibor, genuinely surprised, and Julia thought again that he would have made a wonderful husband for Comfort.

'Most people find themselves angry with Comfort's moods at times,' said Julia with a smile. 'What changed?'

'This morning early I heard her moving in the studio and knew she was awake,' he said, 'and I went to make a cup of tea. She likes this in the morning. And she told me very quietly that I must go . . . like a servant dismissed. I thought she was joking and I reminded her that I loved her.' He broke off and just before he hid his face by drinking some more coffee Julia thought that she saw an expression of anguish in his eyes. When he put the cup down the expression he revealed was serious and unhappy, but nothing more. Julia waited.

'She said that did not matter,' said Tibor at last. 'That I was a sponger. I did not know this word until today,' he added bitterly.

'But, Tibor,' Julia protested, 'she can't have been serious. You've made her so happy.'

'I thought so. Oh yes. But I am wrong. It seems I am a sponger, a third-rate amateur painter who is using her influence to get attention I do not deserve, a man who thinks . . . Oh, what is the use? Even if she does not mean any of it tomorrow, she meant it today and that is enough for me. I must go. I shall miss you, Julia. I hope all goes well with you and the child.'

'And I you, Tibor,' answered Julia. 'But if you love her, isn't it worth trying to –'

'To "sponge" a little longer?' he said with extreme if understandable bitterness. 'No.' He got up and stood for a moment with both fists on the table, looking at Julia.

'Comfort often does things,' she began carefully, 'that make people very angry. I don't always understand, but I think it may be that

326

she cannot believe that people really care for her and so she tests them, doing worse and worse things until they prove . . .'

'That they don't care enough,' said Tibor, draining the big flowered breakfast cup. 'I must go before she comes down.'

'I suppose that is the inevitable end,' said Julia. 'Will you be all right?' He nodded and his full lips were twisted into a self-mocking smile. 'Where will you go?' Julia asked.

'I have friends,' he answered. 'Hungarians. And there is Marcus, who does not think I am a third-rate Sunday painter. I will be all right, but will you?'

'I?' said Julia, surprised. 'Why yes.'

'You are too . . . fair to her. I think she is not wounded, but treacherous,' said Tibor. 'And selfish, and not able to share for very long. I did not let myself believe the people who said it, but it is true.'

'Ah no,' said Julia. 'Don't say that, Tibor. She is terribly generous, but she finds it difficult . . .'

'She is generous for her own ends only,' he said, 'not for other people. I worry for you.'

'You need not,' said Julia, propping her head up on her clasped hands. 'I've known her since I was nineteen. But I can't bear it if you think so harshly of her. I thought you loved her.'

'I thought so too,' he said. When Julia looked up she saw that he was smiling again, but his teeth were clenched. 'I think you have forgiven her too many times.' He turned then and left the house without another word.

Julia sat with her head in her hands, ignoring the toughening toast and the cooling coffee, wondering whether it was possible for human beings to be happy with each other for more than a day or two at a stretch. It ought to be so easy. Everyone wanted it. With a modicum of decency, kindness, unselfishness and tact, it ought to be possible for any number of people to live together and be happy, and yet she could not think of anyone among her friends and relations who had managed it for long.

There were the Heathwoods, unable to give each other anything they wanted and looking to other people for it. There were herself and Anthony; his parents, who had given up the struggle to live together and so made both their children too aware of the fallibility of love too young; and her parents, who had decided that it was better to live in a state of irritable misery rather than to give in and try to learn to please each other. Of everyone she had ever met, only Allegra Wallington seemed to have had a truly happy marriage, and that had been smashed.

'Oh David,' she said into her hands, just for one illicit moment, letting herself remember Fiesole and think of what it would be like if he were to come back to her.

The front-door bell shrilled and Julia lifted her head, pushing the uncombed hair away from her face.

'I'll get it,' called Comfort from halfway down the stairs and Julia got up to wash her face at the stone sink and comb her fingers through her hair to try to reduce it to some kind of order before she faced Comfort.

'Telegram, Julia,' she said from the top of the basement stairs.

'Anthony,' said Julia before she could stop herself. She stayed with her back to the sink as Comfort ran down the stairs and handed her the envelope.

Her fingers felt as clumsy as they had when she had wasted the week's egg trying to reproduce Annunziata's delectable pasta and ended with a mess of sticky, inedible paste that had to be thrown away.

'Here, let me do that,' said Comfort, putting out a hand to take the crackling envelope back. Julia held it to herself.

'It's all right. I'll do it,' she said, thrusting a shaking finger under the glued flap and ripping it open. She looked down and, as she read the first words, they flashed in front of her eyes and moved, jogging up and down so that she needed all her concentration to read them.

We must talk stop Do nothing until I come stop Arriving London July 10 stop Anthony.

'He's coming home,' she said dully to Comfort, who stood in front of her.

Light broke over Comfort's anxious face and made it beautiful again.

'I knew he would,' she said. 'Didn't I tell you last night that everything was all right now? We can be happy again, Julia my darling. At last. The war and his disappearance and your illness and that wretched peasant girl – it's all over.'

'You mean you knew about Raffaella?' said Julia, who forgot what she had meant to say about Tibor in her astonishment.

Comfort smiled at Julia's naivety.

'Of course I knew,' she said. 'Anthony told me while I was in Venice, and I thought it was sweet of you to try to protect me from knowing, although . . .'

'Yes?' said Julia, beginning to understand the odder parts of Jack French's elliptical announcement at the exhibition.

'For a while I thought you were being unnecessarily critical of poor Anthony,' said Comfort. 'You see, I thought you'd come home alone and told him that he couldn't come back because of her. I hadn't realised it was for your health – yours and the baby's.'

'I must get dressed,' said Julia, thinking that she could not talk to Comfort properly until she knew exactly what it was that Anthony was coming home to say. She could not even make the necessary practical arrangements for actually having the baby.

When she had dealt with the immediate tasks awaiting her in chambers, she telephoned the agents who had let the house she had bought in Kensington, to tell them that she would need it herself as soon as the tenants could be moved. Whatever Anthony was going to say, she could not go on living with Comfort in Brunswick Square.

It became more and more difficult as they waited in mutual dissatisfaction for Anthony's return. One morning at breakfast Comfort asked for about the tenth time who were to be the child's godparents and Julia snapped at her.

'I've already told you that nothing can be decided until Anthony's back,' she said. 'I must go or I'll be late for my meeting.'

She left Comfort bemused and sore that Julia seemed incapable of understanding the importance of the child she was carrying. That she should worry about her work instead of concentrating on the child seemed perverse and positively dangerous. Comfort had almost given up hope of Anthony having children and in the excitement of discovering that there was still hope had looked forward to being involved in every aspect of Julia's pregnancy and plans for the baby. It seemed oddly cruel of Julia to keep it all to herself.

Julia, meanwhile, was walking briskly to chambers, delighted to be relieved of the almost permanent nausea that had affected her and determined not to allow herself to quarrel with Comfort whatever she said. Once at her desk, surrounded by urgent work, Julia managed to put most thoughts of the child out of her mind and worked with virtually unbroken concentration until she was interrupted soon after twelve.

There was a knock at the door and her clerk popped his head round to ask whether she would see a Mr Wallington. Julia felt the blood rushing to her face. She pulled herself together and nodded to Tomkins. A few moments later he ushered David into her room.

Julia got up and walked round her desk to shake his hand, trying not to allow herself to feel the intense pleasure that flooded her at the sight of him. He looked so exactly like her memories of him that it was hard to believe he was not some image conjured up by her fantasies.

'How are you, David?' she asked formally.

'Well,' he said in the same tones. He did not smile. 'And you?'

'I'm fine now. Won't you sit down?' It was all she could do not to reach out and touch him and she thought that if they were sitting on the opposite sides of her wide desk it might be easier to keep herself as distant as she knew she must.

'Thank you. You said "now",' David said, much less distantly. 'Have you been ill again?'

'No, just convalescent,' said Julia with a slight laugh in her voice. Then she added abruptly: 'David, why have you come?'

He looked down at his long hands in silence and then raised his head to look straight at her. His blue eyes were duller than she remembered and there was no hint in them of the warm light that had first told her that he cared for her. She tightened her grip on her own emotions.

'Because I'm starting in Michael Farewell's chambers next month and we're bound to meet,' he said in a rather abrupt voice. 'I thought we ought to talk in private before that happens. I'm not –'

'About what?' asked Julia, suddenly afraid that Anthony or Felicity Suvarov had told him about the baby.

'About us,' said David, sounding surprised. 'I know that I promised you once that I wouldn't importune you.' He stopped there and went back to studying his hands.

'Yes,' said Julia gently.

'Julia, it's so impossibly difficult,' he said, leaning both elbows on her desk and resting his head in his hands. His voice sounded angry.

'I know,' she answered, almost certain then that someone had told him about the child. As calmly as she could, she added: 'But I'm afraid I can't change it.'

'I know,' he said. 'I also know that I should never have allowed myself to tell you that I had fallen in love with you. I just . . .' He dropped his hands and looked at her again and smiled wryly. 'It's just the kind of thing that gets said in those circumstances.'

'Yes,' said Julia rather stiffly. 'I rather thought so. David, what is it that you have come to say?'

'That I want to marry you,' he said in a despairing voice that told her how much it had cost him to come.

'I can't,' she said, gritting her teeth against the pain. Her resolution slipped a little and she added: 'I wish that I could, but it isn't possible.' She loved him far too much to take advantage of him.

David said nothing and she waited for him to tell her that he knew about the child, wondering whether she could bring herself to lie and say that it was Anthony's if he did. But he did not. Instead he picked up his hat and stood up.

'I'm sorry,' he said, sounding almost bitter. 'I ought never to have come. I'll try not to embarrass you when we meet in court – or anywhere else.'

'You mustn't apologise,' said Julia, keeping control of herself with difficulty. 'No one was ever paid a greater compliment.'

David's face lightened then and one of his hands reached out towards her as though he could not help himself. As soon as he noticed what he was doing he withdrew it.

'I hope we can be friends,' said Julia, her resolution slipping a little more. 'I would value that so much.'

'Would you?' David asked a little wistfully. 'Then of course we shall. I hope that if you change your mind, you'll tell me.'

'Yes I will,' she said, holding out her right hand. 'Thank you for coming, David.'

He just looked at her and then, with an effort, he smiled.

'My mother asked to be remembered to you,' he said.

'How kind. Will you send her my regards?'

David nodded and on that absurdly formal note they parted. Julia sat back at her desk, feeling as though she had lived through the Blitz all over again. It seemed impossible to believe that only just over three months ago she had slept in his arms. Felicity's voice echoed in her mind: 'It would be absurdly quixotic to ruin your own life for a political career that may never happen.'

The temptation to run after David out into the Temple was almost overmastering.

Her office door opened again and Tomkins stood there with a pile of papers in his hands. He brought them to Julia and reminded her that James Norgrove wanted her report on them by the end of the day. She dismissed him gratefully and buried herself in her work.

# Chapter Twenty-Six

Anthony came back to London on the day when all the English newspapers were delightedly reporting the engagement of Princess Elizabeth to Lieutenant Philip Mountbatten. The crowd waiting for a glimpse of the couple on the red-draped balcony at Buckingham Palace seemed to be trying to reproduce the euphoria and hope of VE Day, and all over the country people welcomed the chance to revel in spectacle and romance as an antidote to the dreariness of austerity.

Julia hardly noticed the fuss, although she was amused to see a pair of bedraggled children obviously playing 'Royal Marriages' on a bombsite amid a group of cheering, flag-waving friends on her way to chambers. She tried to spend the day as she usually did, concentrating on her work, chatting to colleagues and parrying the efforts of her clerk to dump all the most boring work on her desk, but thoughts of Anthony and what he had come home to say kept intruding. She would be distracted from whatever she was reading by imaginary scenes with him and often found herself drafting replies to what he might say.

Eventually, soon after four o'clock, she gave up the unequal struggle to pretend that it was an ordinary day and took a taxi back to Brunswick Square. Anthony's familiar, battered brown suitcase stood on the chequered floor of the cool hall, but there was no sign of him in any of the ground-floor rooms. Shrugging, Julia went up to her bedroom to take off her hat and change her shoes, and from there she heard the sound of voices coming from the studio.

When she had changed Julia went into her study to unpack the briefcase she had brought back from chambers, knowing that Anthony and Comfort must have heard her arrival. Within ten minutes he was at the door, saying:

'May I come in, Julia?'

Feeling as nervous as she had ever done facing a hostile judge in court, Julia put down the opinion that she had been drafting, screwed the lid on her fountain pen and turned in her chair to smile at her husband. Only the knowledge that he had not been faithful to their marriage either helped her to keep her voice and eyes steady.

'Yes, come in, Anthony. How are you? You don't look well at all,' she said, sounding quite calm.

'I'm all right,' he answered, dropping into the wing chair beside her desk. 'As far as possible in the circumstances. You? How is it going?'

'Not too bad. I've stopped feeling sick,' said Julia, assuming that he meant her to introduce the subject of her pregnancy with his vague question.

Anthony looked down at his hands, those beautifully kept surgeon's hands with their pristine nails that were almost more familiar to Julia than her own, and said slowly:

'Your letter shocked me.'

Julia raised her eyebrows involuntarily, surprised out of her careful composure by his uncharacteristic lack of finesse.

'I'm sorry about that,' she said inadequately. 'Knowing what it felt like when I learned about Raffaella, I can understand that, but truth seemed more important then than diplomacy. I didn't want there to be any more fudging between us.'

'Oh I quite agree,' said Anthony, looking up with a faint smile. He put his hands in his trouser pockets and leaned against the chair back as though he were relaxing, but Julia could see that all his muscles were tense.

'You're angry,' she said, suddenly recognising what he was feeling without any of her usual difficulty. It was as though in letting herself stop the battle to believe herself in love with him, she had become able to see him properly for almost the first time.

'Are you surprised?' he said in a voice of detached inquiry. 'You are my wife, after all.'

'Anthony,' she said, looking at him with what he irritably recognised as pity, 'don't let's play games with each other. I am your wife, but hardly the wife you want. It's taken me a long time to admit that, but I have recognised it at last. You didn't want to come back here to live with me after the war and I realised too late that you didn't want me to come to Venice either. Now I know why. You were determined that we shouldn't have children and did everything you could to separate us from each other. Isn't it a bit undignified to play dog-in-the-manger now?'

'You have grown hard, haven't you?' he said, watching her through narrowed eyes. 'Comfort's right.'

Julia winced, but she said nothing. After a moment, Anthony visibly pulled himself together and said:

'I was angry enough to discover you had seduced David, but it was your suggestion that you should bring up a child without a father that was so shocking. You really can't do that, Julia.'

'I don't see why not,' she said, furious at his assumption that she had inveigled a reluctant David into her bed. She looked sideways at the pile of work on her desk and tried not to let herself sound either angry or defensive. She decided to treat Anthony's objection as a practical rather than an emotional one. 'My fee income has risen dramatically since you were last at home; I can afford a very good nanny –'

'As a matter of interest,' he said, interrupting with a sharper voice than before, 'do you think a very good nanny would agree to live in such a household and look after a bastard child?'

Julia felt suddenly desperately tired. She had not expected the confrontation to be easy, but she had banked on Anthony being reasonable and wanting to be free of their unsatisfactory marriage as much as she did.

'I can't see why she should have any objection,' Julia said carefully, 'if she did not know of its illegitimacy. If you are prepared to help me avoid a scandal, there should be no problem. I know that I have landed us in this situation, but avoiding a scandal seems to be in the best interests of every one of us. . . . It's not just selfishness.'

Anthony took his hands out of his pockets and started to fiddle with a big bunch of keys, turning each one over and examining it before dropping it with a clatter against the next. Julia felt increasingly puzzled. She had never seen him so restless or – she realised with surprise – so uncertain of himself, despite the anger that showed so clearly.

'Anthony, this feels like cat-and-mouse teasing,' she said. 'What is it that you've come all this way to say to me?'

He got out of the chair then, still jiggling his keys in his left hand, and walked about the small square room, picking things up at random, squinting at the titles of the books in the mahogany shelves on either side of the fireplace, straightening the carriage clock on the mantelpiece and stopping at last in front of a framed drawing of his sister that Julia had hung over it. Julia could see his reflection in the glass, lying over Comfort's face. Their eyes matched and so did their impressive noses, but in the drawing Comfort smiled. Anthony's delicately modelled lips were taut and straight. He turned back to face his wife.

'I agree that we need to avoid scandal over your child,' he said coldly, 'but that can't be achieved with a divorce, however quiet. I am not prepared to divorce you or let you divorce me.'

'But Anthony –' Julia began. Before she could finish her protest he went on:

'And I can make an appalling scandal if you try. I can't agree to your living alone with the child – even with the best nanny in the world. It is simply not fair to bring up a child in such circumstances. I have decided that we should continue as we are, with the child living here with us all, knowing that it has both father and mother,' he said, looking over Julia's head.

For a moment Julia could neither speak nor distinguish among the violent emotions that were making her mind reel.

'But you don't want a child,' she said at last, seizing one distinguishable feeling from the mass. 'In Venice you were adamant that we could not have one. What on earth has made you change your mind to the extent that you are prepared to pretend to be the father of someone else's? Have you gone mad?'

'Certainly not,' he said, sounding far more sure of himself than before. 'The idea of a child in the abstract is entirely different from the reality of one you are already carrying, a child who is nearly halfway to term. Whatever it is that you want to do, you must admit that the child's interests should come before your own.'

Never in all her married life had Julia felt so angry with her husband. Even when she had understood the truth about his dealings with Raffaella, what she had felt had been complicated by her determination to see the best in him and to make allowances for the circumstances that had caused him to do what he had done. Always in the past, any irritation or resentment she had felt towards him had left her feeling tired and inadequate, but she had lost that feeling for ever. He had set her free.

Julia suddenly felt stronger than she had done for months and more determined. For the first time since they had met at Oxford, she managed to look at Anthony as though he were a client or a witness, to try to discern the weaknesses behind his actions and the hidden motives for his words.

As though he recognised some change in her, Anthony shrugged slightly, put away the keys that he had been rattling so maddeningly and went back to his chair.

'What is it,' Julia asked carefully, 'that makes you think a child would be so badly off being brought up as I propose? Most of the people you and I know were brought up by nannies, seeing their mothers only once or twice a day and their fathers far less than that. What is so different?'

'Most of the people we know were aware that they had both mother and father,' said Anthony.

Julia noticed that he looked pleased that she had asked that particular question and added it to the facts and inferences in her mind.

'But I did not,' Anthony went on in a voice of frigid disdain. 'My mother deserted us when I was six and I know what it is like to live without a mother – and Comfort without a father. Neither of us would wish that on any other living soul. We know, you see, and we are determined that it shan't happen to your child.'

That moving declaration ought to have convinced Julia of his sincerity, but something in it did not ring true. Her brown eyes narrowing, she concentrated on all the things Anthony might be thinking and not saying, on his tension, the way his eyes kept sliding away from her so that he could look at the drawing of Comfort.

'Does Comfort know about David?' she asked at last. 'I haven't told her, but have you?'

'Absolutely not,' said Anthony, looking at her again. Julia believed that. 'She mustn't,' he went on with an extraordinary pleading note mixed with the coldness in his voice. 'She is so happy about the child.'

'I know,' said Julia slowly, 'but what has that got to do with your refusing to let me leave?' Even as she put the question an intimation of the truth occurred to her. For a while she could not bring herself to put it into words or to believe it, but it made sense of everything else. They both sat silent, absorbed in their own thoughts.

'I feel such a fool,' said Julia at last. Anthony raised his head and looked at her with eyes that seemed at last to be filled with regret. 'You're in love with her, aren't you? That's what all this has been about ever since Oxford: you and Comfort.'

Anthony's face as much as the hopeless set of his shoulders told Julia that she was right. For nearly five minutes her mind was wiped clear of every feeling, but then they flooded back with the force and violence of the water that thundered over the Niagara Falls. She felt as though she must always have known and yet refused to know.

'How stupid I've been,' she said, trying to control the deluge. 'I've thought I wasn't sophisticated enough for you, that I was too fat or too thin to attract you, that I bored you, or worried you by loving you so much more than you did me. I've been afraid that you were in love with Sister Caroline or with Raffaella; that what happened in the war had frightened you out of being able to show any kind of love. I've thought of almost every reason for our difficulties except that you were in love with your own sister.'

Anthony said nothing, but stared at the drawing. His face was white and his dark-grey eyes looked huge.

'I take it that you don't actually sleep together?' Julia remarked in a light, sarcastic voice that was designed to rouse him into answering her.

'Certainly not,' he said, looking and sounding shocked by the enormity of what she had said.

'No,' agreed Julia, coldly angry, humiliated and bitterly hurt. 'You would hardly have needed me if you had.'

Something of what she felt reached him and he dropped his face into his hands.

'It's never been as cold-blooded as that,' he said at last, when he was sure he could control himself. 'She loves you: you know that. We both love you.'

'Do you?' asked Julia, still cold.

Anthony looked at her and the frank misery in his slate-grey eyes brought back some of her self-control.

'Perhaps you do in a way,' she said more gently. 'Or perhaps not. I sometimes wonder if any of us knows what that so misused word really means. We all think we've found it, but it turns out to be a reflection of what we want or a shadow or a mirage. What a ridiculous, bloody awful mess!'

'Yes, but we're deep in it,' said Anthony, sounding a little more like himself, 'and –'

'Where does Raffaella fit into all this?' Julia asked, interrupting him without scruple. 'I gather you told Comfort all about her, although not me. I ought to have understood when I discovered that, instead of wondering what it was that Raffaella could give you that I could not.'

Once again Anthony shrugged and pulled a face.

'She doesn't really fit anywhere. It was one of those unimportant wartime things that made a hideously unpleasant life a little more bearable for both of us,' he said with a casualness that shocked Julia all over again.

'And the child? Doesn't Comfort want that child too?' Julia could hear the bitterness in her voice, but had no intention of apologising for it. She felt that she had every right to bitterness. But Anthony's face changed and the pain in it reminded Julia of how much she had loved him once and how hard she had worked to make him happy. A little of her anger and her bitterness died.

'I'm sorry,' she said simply.

Anthony heard the sympathy in her voice and saw the old unfailing warmth dawning in her eyes and almost broke down. He felt as though he had been pulled apart on a rack. He had learned that his attempt to save himself and Comfort by staying in Italy had failed when she told him that she had sacked Tibor Smith from her life. He knew that he had failed Julia when he had not been able to give her the kind of love she deserved when she married him. Belatedly he let his anger at what she had done slip enough to accept that he had damaged her, too, and he thought that perhaps what Raffaella had done to him, the fool she had made of him, was a suitable punishment.

'She has gone back to Rome, where she intends to further her career as a tart,' he said with a bitterness that excelled even Julia's. 'It seems that the child was probably not mine after all and that her unspeakable brother was more accurate than any of us knew. She was not picked up for interrogation at all, but had a regular rendezvous with the German at which she exchanged sexual favours and information for food and a guarantee of protection.' As he spoke, he could see Raffaella's cold, green eyes and hear her mocking voice:

'Yours or the German's? What does it matter, *dottore?* I needed you both then; and I needed you again while Paolo was back in Venice. I don't need either of you now that they have caught him. I'm free of you all.'

At least, he thought, her announcement had freed him of the guilt he had felt whenever he thought of her child, wondering always whether it might have been his and what its future could possibly be.

'Anthony, I'm sorry,' said Julia again and he suspected that she was apologising more for what she had thought about him than for what she had actually said. 'I think we ought to stop talking now. None of us can decide anything while we're so . . . so raw. Let's leave it for a bit. How long are you staying?'

'I have to go back on the fourteenth,' he said. To Julia it sounded like an ultimatum.

'Four days to make the most important decision of our lives,' she said slowly.

Anthony looked at his fingernails again.

'There's no decision to make. Legally, the child is mine,' he said.

'I am well aware of that,' Julia began and then caught his real meaning. In a voice of complete disbelief she said: 'Are you telling me that you would invoke your legal rights to keep a child who is no . . .? Anthony, I do not believe you. I may not have understood your relations with your sister, but you cannot be so different from the man I married.'

'Comfort wants it,' he said as though that explained everything.

Perhaps, thought Julia, it did.

She got up. The study that had been her refuge from the war, from depression and loneliness, offered no bulwark against the feelings that were battering her. She knew suddenly that she had to get out of the house, but before she left there was something more to say.

'Anthony, there is one thing that I have to ask you now. Will you answer realistically this time?'

'How do I know until you've asked?' he said, assuming that she was going to ask him something about Comfort.

'What was it that David did to make you so angry just before I came to Venice?' Julia asked for the third time.

Anthony looked at her, surprised that she should care so much.

'He insisted on giving evidence on behalf of that lout, Paolo, when he was on trial for murder in Rome,' he said with a cynical laugh. 'He even wanted me to do it, too: after what Paolo had done to Raffaella in the war!'

'That was it?' said Julia blankly. 'All those warnings about David's destructiveness just because he gave evidence?'

'Think of the ramifications before you so firmly take his part,' said Anthony in a cool voice. 'David knew as well as I that Paolo had sworn to kill Raffaella and her child once the war was over. That trial gave an opportunity to have him put away and because of what David did, Paolo was left at large.'

'David would not have lied,' said Julia. 'At a trial like that, he would have told no more than the truth. You can't blame him.'

'Oh, yes I can,' said Anthony. 'And think what happened because of him: if he had not insisted on telling the court how wonderfully brave Paolo had been in the war, what a hero he had been, he would probably have been safely in prison before he had been able to frighten Raffaella out of Rome; you would never have been troubled with her story; I would never have been led up the garden path for a second time; you would never have been terrified by Paolo chasing you through Venice; and your friend Giovanna Whatsit would not now be in prison for black marketeering.'

'What?' said Julia, surprised out of her preoccupations.

'Oh yes. The reason Paolo discovered his sister in Venice was because he had come to report on his activities to the woman who had set him up in his black-market business – your Giovanna. I have told David so damned often that his ideals will always cause trouble, but this time he excelled himself.'

'Did he know? About Giovanna, I mean,' said Julia, trying to grapple with the shock of what Anthony had said. He shook his head.

'No: as usual too ready to believe the best about people. Though, to be fair, no one else knew either. She successfully disguised her hatred of the Allies from everyone and persuaded everyone who knew her that her only concern was healing the wounds left by the war by housing her refugees. It was bad luck for her, too, that Raffaella should have fled to Venice.'

'You mean, I take it, that Raffaella told the authorities?' said Julia.

'Oh yes. Once she had seen Paolo in the house, she knew the sort of thing that must be going on and saw a way to protect herself and take a little revenge of her own at the same time,' said

Anthony sounding more bitter than before. 'I don't know whether she informed on Giovanna as well as on Paolo, or whether it was merely her bad luck that the police uncovered her activities too.'

He had never loved the girl, but they had made love with each other and consoled each other for nearly two years. Thinking of that time, knowing what he did of her real self, he felt as though he had waded through a cess pit.

'I see what Flixe Suvarov meant when she said that secrets were dangerous,' said Julia after a long silence. 'If you had told me about Paolo and the trial, and about yourself and Raffaella; if you and Comfort had told me what part I really played in your lives; if I had told you that I'd fallen in love with David ... none of us would be in this mess.'

She crossed her arms protectively across her womb and added silently to herself that if none of that had happened she would not be carrying the child either. Because of that, that one saving grace, the horror of everything she had heard was diminished.

'I have to go out,' she said.

Half an hour later Julia's taxi stopped outside the Suvarovs' small white house in Chelsea. She paid the driver and walked up the four shallow steps, wishing that she had thought to telephone first. But she had not, and she needed them. She rang the bell.

Suvarov himself answered the door, with a white damask table napkin dangling from his hand. Its significance occurred to Julia and she looked at her watch.

'I am so sorry,' she said. 'I hadn't realised the time. I'll go.'

'Don't be silly,' he said, reaching across the threshold to draw her into the house. 'It's only Flixe and me. Come in.'

He did not ask her why she had come, only taking her coat while Felicity fetched plates, glasses and cutlery and more food.

'Sit down, Julia,' she said, ladling a helping of rabbit stew on to her plate. Peter poured wine into her glass. Having felt sick and certain that she could not eat anything, Julia shook her head, but they paid no attention, merely finishing their own food. Almost absent-mindedly she picked up her knife and fork and then found that she was hungry. When she had finished the stew and drunk the wine, Peter at last said:

'What's happened?'

'Anthony's back,' said Julia. 'I don't terribly want to talk about it, so I'm not sure why I came.' She looked from one to the other and then smiled helplessly, looking lost and years younger than they had seen her before.

'It doesn't matter,' said Flixe, putting a hand on Julia's arm. 'You needed help. We're here. Do you want to stay the night?'

'Oh could I?' said Julia, realising how badly she had needed help and how difficult it was for her to ask.

'Of course,' said Suvarov. 'I'll go and telephone your husband. Presumably he doesn't know where you are?'

'No, he doesn't,' she said. 'But what will you say?'

'Don't worry,' answered Suvarov. 'I've made lots of difficult telephone calls in my time. This won't be hard. You look exhausted. Why don't you let Flixe take you up to the spare room?'

'All right,' Julia said, unused to having anyone giving her orders and taking all responsibility from her. She was too tired to be anything but grateful for it and did as she was told.

When she was lying in bed in the pretty spare room, Julia knew with complete certainty that whatever else happened she could never allow David's child to be brought up in Brunswick Square, believing Anthony to be his father and having Comfort pretending to be his mother. That decision made, she pushed everything else out of her mind and let sleep overwhelm her.

Downstairs Felicity was washing up in the kitchen and trying to persuade her husband to telephone David Wallington. Inexpertly but willingly drying up, Peter refused.

'She has to sort it out herself,' he said. 'No one can impose a solution on her. We can only offer her sanctuary – and advice if she asks for it.'

'Such as?' asked Flixe curiously.

'To tell David, of course. She has to do that, and she'll come to it herself in the end. She is too accustomed to carrying all the responsibility for her life and she has to realise that in this case at least she can't do that. Protecting David from the knowledge of his own child is a bad mistake.'

'Then why won't you help her to put it right?' asked Flixe, as nearly cross with him as she ever became.

'I love you, you know,' he said, tweaking her chin. 'You'd go charging in to help, wouldn't you? But, darling Flixe, that would be hellishly dangerous. Unless Julia does it herself and sees how David receives the news, she will never believe in the genuineness of anything he says to her. If he cares for her . . .'

'I'm sure he does,' said Flixe, remembering the condition he had been in when he thought that Julia was dying in Venice.

'Probably, but we don't know. No, my darling, this is something we cannot interfere with.'

Flixe was silent then, apparently accepting his prohibition, but that night she lay beside him as he slept and knew that he was wrong. Without some intervention, Julia's determined self-reliance could be a disaster for herself, for the baby, and for David. Flixe hated waste, and wasted love most of all, and she was determined to prevent it.

As soon as Peter had left the house the following morning, she made certain that Julia would keep out of the way by taking her a tray of breakfast in bed and then telephoned Allegra Wallington, whom she hardly knew.

Upstairs, Julia had finished breakfast and woken up properly. She felt deeply ashamed of her melodramatic flight from Brunswick Square and was thankful that she had at least not poured the whole story out to the Suvarovs. She got up and dressed quickly, before stripping the bed and remaking it with sheets she found in a vast lavender-scented linen cupboard on the landing. The dirty ones she left neatly folded on a stool at the foot of her bed.

Then she went downstairs to find Flixe so that she could thank her and go. Pushing open the door of what was obviously the drawing room, she was confronted by a large, airy room, decorated in pale, elegant colours that made the most of a wonderful if faded Aubusson rug. There seemed to be no one there, but just as she was wondering where to try next, she heard voices from the other side of the hall.

A door opened and Flixe emerged.

'There you are,' she said. 'Do you feel better this morning?'

'Much better,' said Julia politely and then in a rush of frankness added: 'and idiotic for appearing on your doorstep like an orphan of the storm.'

'Don't worry. Come on in. We're having a cup of coffee,' said Flixe.

Julia had no time to protest that she did not want to disturb Flixe and whatever guest was waiting for her. Flixe almost pushed her into the room, went out and shut the door behind her. Julia, surprised, looked back. When she saw that Flixe had disappeared, she turned round and recognised David's mother, standing in front of an empty fireplace.

They stood, looking at each other in silence until Allegra nodded her dark head.

'Now I understand,' she said. 'Come and sit down, Julia.'

'I don't understand what you mean,' Julia said, once more doing as she was told. 'What is going on?'

Allegra smiled.

'I understand why Mrs Suvarov summoned me here this morning and would not say why, and I understand at last why you told David that you did not love him.'

'Do you?' said Julia quietly. Allegra nodded again.

'You are pregnant. So of course you can't leave your husband,' she said. Then her voice turned almost cold. 'But why didn't you tell David? Wouldn't it have been more fair to tell him instead of leaving him to think that you did not care?'

'So Felicity didn't tell you,' said Julia slowly. She pulled herself up out of the deep armchair, which was upholstered in thick, russet-coloured corduroy. 'I wish she hadn't troubled you with this,' she added, looking down at Allegra's tired, beautiful face.

'I was troubled anyway,' Allegra said. 'I have been staying in London with David while we decide what we're going to do about the estate and where I am going to live, and I have never seen

David so unhappy before. I knew that I could not leave him here alone in that state; and I could not understand it. It was so clear that you loved him when you were both with me in Fiesole, and so clear that he loves you. I made him go to see you: did he tell you?'

Julia shook her head silently.

'I thought that perhaps you did not believe how much he needed you,' said Allegra simply. 'When he came back, he told me that we had both made a terrible mistake. Now I am not sure. I think you do love him.'

'Yes, I love him,' said Julia, staring at a small bronze of a rearing horse that stood on the mantelpiece. 'But I don't think he loves me. He asked me to marry him because he would never shirk what he thought was duty. I understand that.'

'Oh Julia, my dear child, of course he loves you. Was that why you sent him away that day? Did you think he only asked you to be his wife because of the baby?'

Julia had not been called 'my dear child' for years and the warmth and kindness of Allegra's voice as she said it reached down into some essential loneliness that only David had touched before. Julia turned her back to the little statue and told the truth.

'The child is David's,' she said. 'And I can't bear to cause a scandal that might ruin his life.' She felt Allegra's arms around her shoulders.

'No scandal could be worse than the two of you making yourselves and each other as unhappy as you have,' said Allegra gently. 'Come and sit down again. We are two intelligent women. Between us we can sort it all out.'

At that, Julia managed to smile and let herself be led to a large sofa. They talked for a long time and in the end Allegra said:

'I'm staying in David's house here for a few days. Will you come back there with me now and tell him?'

'I can't,' said Julia instinctively. Then she thought of an acceptable reason. 'I have to go to chambers. I'm going to be appallingly late as it is.'

'Then come this evening and stay with us until your plans are

347

settled,' said Allegra, laying a hand on Julia's knee as they sat side by side. 'Please, Julia. You owe it to him.'

There was a long silence as Julia struggled with her needs and desires and her determined, solitary stoicism.

'All right,' she said at last.

# Chapter Twenty-Seven

That evening David was walking from the tube station to Kensington Square, depressed and wondering whether he was ever going to be able to forget Julia. There were twin images of her in his mind: the dauntingly serious woman he had collected from the airport at Venice and met again in her London chambers, and the warm, touchingly unsure lover he had found in Fiesole. She had unlocked in him feelings he had never believed he could have and was quite sure that he would never have again. Reaching the dusty lilacs that guarded the path up to his house, he felt in his pocket for his keys.

'David!' A breathless voice and the sound of running footsteps stopped him and he wheeled round. Coming towards him through the stuffy London dusk was Julia, impeccably dressed in black and white, with her hair pinned back in its austere bun but with her eyes alight and her smile whole. David began to breathe faster.

'Julia,' he said, dropping his briefcase on the grubby pavement and holding out both hands to her.

With her doubts about his feelings disappearing fast, Julia took his hands.

'Why have you come?' David asked, bracing himself for the ultimate denial of his hopes.

'Because I need you and I can't pretend any more,' she said.

A smile broke the mask of careful detachment over David's thin face and revealed the lively eagerness that she loved so much. He stared at her for a long time and then suddenly became aware that they were still standing in the street.

'Come on in. We can't talk here,' he said, releasing one of his hands to pull out his keys.

Julia picked up his briefcase and followed him into the house. He took her into a small book-lined room at the back of the house. There was a desk in one corner, a glazed cabinet holding some old glass in the other, a small squashy sofa in front of the fire and four superb oils on the terracotta walls. The deep rusty-pink carpet that had been spread over the polished parquet floor was badly worn, but even to Julia's inexpert eye it was identifiable as an antique Bokhara.

The room presented her with a side of David that she had never considered since the earliest days in Venice when he had taken her sightseeing and told her a little about his family. Since she had fallen in love with him, she had thought of him only as a young lawyer with political aspirations, whose integrity and good name she would have gone to almost any lengths to protect. His house reminded her that there was far more to him than that, that he had resources and probably power that she had underestimated.

As she turned to tell him how much she liked the room, she saw him looking at her and thought that perhaps she had underestimated him altogether.

'Well, Julia?' he said with a smile that looked a lot more confident than the one with which he had greeted her in the street.

'I've come to tell you that I am pregnant with your child,' she said.

David said nothing as he absorbed the news that ought not to have surprised him as much as it did.

'I never thought of that,' he said eventually. 'How long have you known?'

'Since the end of May,' she said. David watched her face, trying to understand her.

'Why didn't you tell me?' he asked, at last realising that he could not understand.

'Because I couldn't bear you to think that I was trying to blackmail you into –'

'Come and sit down,' he said abruptly. 'What do you mean, blackmail? Didn't you believe me when I told you I loved you?'

Julia shook her head.

'In Florence I knew that you cared,' she said moderately, 'but I also knew that you did not want to marry, and when you asked me I thought that someone – Anthony – had told you about the child. I thought that you asked me because you felt you had to,' she said.

David put his arms around her and leaned his cheek on her soft hair for a moment.

'For a woman as clever as everyone tells me you are, you are a clot. Couldn't you tell? Couldn't you feel that I loved you?' he asked, sounding worried.

Julia withdrew a little and leaned back against the soft cream-coloured sofa cushions. There were a lot of things she could have told him, all of which were true: that Anthony's warning had left her afraid that there were aspects of David she had not discovered, that in Venice she had become so muddled by her efforts to make sense of Anthony's emotions and her own that she had misread almost every piece of evidence and trusted people whom she ought not to have trusted and vice versa, but all those explanations would come later.

'I wanted to believe it so much,' she said quietly, telling the most fundamental truth, 'that I suppose I couldn't let myself in case it turned out not to be true.'

She looked at David, at the fine lines at the corners of his blue eyes, at his straight nose and firm chin, and smiled at him.

'Even so, I knew all along that I loved you. I just muddled the rest,' she said.

They talked then about everything that had happened, stripping away the layers of concealment they had assumed to protect each other and learning at last what the weeks in Venice had meant to each other, and what they might mean in the future. Julia looked progressively happier until she had to tell David what Anthony had said to her as he heaped revelation on revelation during their painful talk. Then David watched her face tighten up and her eyes darken.

'What is it?' he asked gently.

'I'd been letting myself forget that he still stands in the way,' she said in a tight voice. 'I'd begun to feel so safe.' She looked down at the huge, diamond-encircled emerald on her left hand and suddenly gripped David's hand. 'David, we can't lose each other again. Not now.'

'We won't,' he said with a firm confidence that delighted her. 'Will you let me talk to him?'

'You? Why?'

'Because you've been hurt enough,' he said gently. 'This is something that I can do for you – if you will let me.'

Julia leaned forward again until her head was resting on his shoulder. Many people had helped her during her life, but until that moment she had always felt that in disaster she would be alone. The strength people had divined in her had been partly the rigidity of her defences against that fear. Now, at last, the defences crumbled and she looked at David with all her real vulnerability exposed.

David, who knew her better than anyone, understood and was profoundly touched.

'We'll be stronger as two than either of us could ever have been alone,' he told her. 'Whatever happens.'

'I think you're right,' she said as seriously as he had spoken. But then her face changed again, her brown eyes took on a mischievous gleam and she said more lightly than he had ever heard her speak: 'I hope you are, because between us we've a lot to do.'

A little later David said:

'I think I ought to go and see Anthony at once.'

'Will you take him these?' asked Julia, pulling off the emerald and her wedding ring as well. She handed them to David, who nodded. As he went to the door, Julia could not help saying:

'Don't let him . . .' David turned and she could see the confidence in his eyes and in the carriage of his head and the set of his shoulders.

'I'll be all right,' he said.

He was, but he held on to his temper with difficulty and he never told Julia what had been said during the painful interview he had with her husband. Nor did he tell her that as he was leaving the house he was confronted with Comfort, who had obviously been listening to them. She had stood in his way to the front door and said:

'So you've won. I knew that you would make trouble when I first saw you, but what makes you think that a woman who has betrayed one man won't betray another? You'll never be sure of her and you'll never be happy.'

He had looked at her beautiful, hateful eyes and knew that she was wrong. He thought of answering her, but decided that there was no point.

When he got back to Kensington Square Julia and his mother had long since finished dinner and were both in bed. He went to see his mother first and then knocked on the door of the spare bedroom. When Julia asked if he was all right, he simply said:

'It's all arranged. Anthony will give you evidence and you'll have your divorce. It won't be pleasant, but you will be free.'

Julia sat up in bed, brushing the long hair away from her face.

'I'm sorry it was so bad, David,' she said and when she saw his face change, she added quickly: 'It's all right; I won't ask any questions.'

He nodded and felt in his pocket.

'I don't suppose it is proper to give you this yet, but nothing we have done has been quite proper has it?' He held out his hand and in the palm she saw a square-cut ruby ring.

'When did you get it?' Julia asked, looking at the glowing jewel and thinking that he could not possibly have had time to buy it since she had handed him her other rings.

David smiled ruefully.

'As soon as I got back to London,' he said. 'I suppose it was an act of faith. I hope you like it; Flixe Suvarov helped me to choose it.'

'We owe those two a lot,' said Julia, staring past the ring to the unhappiness that would have been her lot without David. 'We'd never even have met if you hadn't worked for him, and she helped me to see . . . to understand.'

'Did she?' said David softly. 'I'm glad. But the ring, Julia: do you think that you could bear to wear it?'

'It's lovely,' said Julia, putting out her hand at last. David looked down at her as she sat in bed with her hair falling about her face. He pushed the ring on to her finger.

'Do you believe me now?' he asked.

'Believe you?' she repeated, puzzled.

'Believe that I love you?' said David, looking at her seriously.

Julia felt the old fear stirring somewhere in her mind. David was holding both her hands and she looked into his eyes, trying to find some certainty.

'Well?' he said very gently.

Julia took a deep breath, straightened her shoulders, and gave up the last of her defences.

'Yes, I do believe you.' As she spoke she felt really safe for the first time in her life, as though her private victory had just begun.